Earth Legacy
AWAKENING

LAURIE RYAN

www.laurieryanauthor.com

EARTH LEGACY SERIES

Survival
Enlightenment
Birthright

Earth Legacy
AWAKENING

LAURIE RYAN

DEDICATION

To Michal, for reminding me that
it's okay to have an opinion
and to stand up for what I believe in.

TRANSFORMATION

EARTH

I'm dying, and those who rely on me for sustenance are the very ones orchestrating my demise. They make changes, but not quickly enough to end my misery. Do they not see what they are doing? They are killing me with every piece of garbage that finds its way to my waters. They dump toxins that poison me, and they do not consider the lasting effects of pollution.

They cut down trees faster than the ones planted to replace them can grow. Do they not know from whence comes the air they breathe?

My pain is too great. Each needle they thrust through my surface, each field plowed to make way for those tall, concrete, unnatural things where they spend all their time. It all adds up. They used to stay outside. They used to play with me, enjoy the bounties I provided.

Now, they huddle in structures and stare at screens. They think I do not see. They think I do not care.

I do not want to die. Each time I plead for help, they turn away. Only a scant handful, by global terms, follow the old ways, trying to protect what resources are left to them. Even these select few people fight a losing battle. The power has tipped toward annihilation: mine and theirs, because they do not see that there are ramifications to what they do.

If they will not help me, I must help myself. So be it. This will be my last, and greatest, act. To save myself, and, by extension, those who seek to destroy me. Maybe, this time, they will understand that we cannot stand in opposite corners. We must work together for all to survive.

Or we will all die.

News Alert: Some much-needed rain is heading California's way. The drought is over.

CHAPTER ONE

Damian Royan stood on the promontory and stared out over the lake, enjoying a warmer than usual day for mid-September. Nearby, the organized chaos of visitors arriving to see the carved faces of Mt. Rushmore would soon begin. Here, though, serene water reflected majestic evergreens reaching for the scattered clouds in an otherwise cerulean sky, a stark contrast to Damian's mood. If what he'd heard held any truth, this peaceful place would soon be disturbed. No, not disturbed. Removed. All of this sacred beauty—gone. Sold to the highest bidder. The idea was unconscionable. How could anyone destroy this?

A warm breeze lifted his shoulder-length hair with gentle abandon. For now, birds still sang their songs. A fish leaped from the water, daring a branch-sitting hawk to catch him. Accepting the challenge, the hawk dove with reckless speed, braking at the last moment to dip talons beneath the glassy surface, coming up with the arrogant fish in its claws. Wings back-stroked, grasping air as the hawk rose higher and higher with his breakfast.

Even the tufts of grass beneath Damian's feet spoke of rejuvenation and renewal, though spring lay several months behind them. This was a special place. A sacred place. With closed eyes, Damian prayed to the world around him. This new peril was beyond anything he'd ever dealt with. He needed guidance. Advice on how to placate this threat to everything he held dear. Everything that all of humanity should consider important.

The sound of pebbles trickling down the twenty-foot rock wall he'd climbed to get there caused Damian to turn and grin as the dark-haired, blue-eyed beauty—the reason for his existence—pulled herself up to join him.

"I knew I'd find you here," Valena said, wrapping her arms around his waist.

Everything felt better when his wife stood with him. Damian hugged her close. Valena Royan was the balm to his disquiet. He loved her more than life itself.

She gazed out over the water and, for a while, they enjoyed the moment, the harmonious connection with each other, and everything that surrounded them. A moment of tranquility.

Damian sighed. How long would they have this?

"You seem troubled."

Damian leaned down to place a kiss on Valena's dark hair, a thick, glossy band that fell to her waist. He loved these mornings, before her hair was confined in the braid that made living outdoors tolerable. His wife only stood as tall as his shoulders, but her diminutive stature ended there. In all other aspects, she was a force to be reckoned with. A strong partner and a loving wife who shared his beliefs.

They followed the druid way. Harmony with Earth and awe for the living world that surrounded and nourished them.

Damian frowned. How long could Earth withstand the over-exploitation that reduced it to a commodity?

"What worries you?" Valena asked.

Everything. Damian took a deep breath, letting nature's perfume calm him. To put voice to his concerns lent them credence. Made the possibilities real. Yet this was not a burden he should carry alone.

"Does this have anything to do with the letter Wyeth brought in with the supplies yesterday?" Wyeth, the thinker, the quiet one in their group, had made the run into town the day before.

"Yes. It seems this land has been leased out."

Valena stared at him, her hand clutched over her heart. "That can't be. This is government land, a national forest."

"Nevertheless, it has been. Somehow."

"To whom?"

"A man named Gordon Darcy." Damian gestured to the computer atop a canvas bag on the grass beside him. "It didn't take much research for me to become concerned about this news."

"Why? Who is he?"

"A man who buys and sells based on his whims. He's into everything. Stocks, real estate, gold, oil, minerals." The last two worried Damian the most.

"Even if Gordon Darcy has somehow convinced the government to lease him this land, they would never release mineral rights to him," Valena said.

Damian reached down and picked up the letter from an attorney friend living in Washington, D.C. Valena took the letter and scanned it, her fingers tightening on the paper as she read. When finished, she looked up at him with tears in her blue eyes. "How did this happen? How can they do this?"

"I don't know, but we have to fight it."

"Agreed. We need to talk with everyone, make the decision together."

Damian nodded, placing his things in the bag and slinging it over his shoulder while he slipped his sandals on. He climbed down first, then reached up to help Valena, who batted his arm away.

"How many times have I made this climb to find you deep in thought, or working on that druid-lore book of yours?"

"A thousand, maybe more," Damian said with a laugh.

"Yes." She jumped the last few inches to land on both feet. "We even planted one of your favorite oak trees on that plateau just so you'd have one to lean against. I think I can manage to get up and down a small rock wall I've navigated many times before."

"I know you can." Damian kissed her. "You are precious to me, my love, so if I get overly protective, you must forgive me."

Valena tugged at his shoulder-length blond hair, pulling him down for a kiss. "There's nothing to forgive."

Arm in arm, they walked the path back to the tent sites they shared with their friends. As a group, they provided duties as campground hosts. They took turns manning the trailer that sat at the entrance to the park. The truck, their only motorized transportation, sat beside it, unused except for runs into Rapid City to stock up on supplies. Though other campers came with RV's and modern conveniences, Damian, Valena, and their friends preferred a simpler way of life.

Their homes, canvas tents, sat in the more rustic, walk-in sites near the lake. They lived with few amenities, although they'd made arrangements with a local hotel, trading landscaping and maintenance for the barest necessities. All in all, they had everything they needed.

Granted long-term rental of their sites, they acted as caretakers of the campground and surrounding land, a coexistent life that had worked well for several years. Now, it seemed, they were about to lose it all.

It didn't take Damian and Valena long to get back to their communal home. At the moment, seven of them lived in five sites that circled their community area.

Bhren, his bound white hair a stark contrast to his dark skin and eyes, stood in their outdoor kitchen stirring a pot of something smelling very much like apples and cinnamon. He'd drawn breakfast duty this morning. That meant oatmeal, about all the man knew how to cook. Damian laughed.

"I'm a scholar, not a cook," Bhren grumbled.

"Then why do you always get breakfast duty?" Damian clapped him on the back, then plugged in the laptop to charge at the site's lone power source. "Seems like a scholar could figure his way out of this predicament."

"I've been set up." Bhren's glare held more smoke than fire. For the most part, everyone got along and everyone did their part.

Damian left Bhren to his oatmeal-stirring and sat down at the table, watching Valena and Gwen put the finishing touches on a plate of fruit. Wyeth, Gwen's husband, brushed wavy blond hair out of his face as he set out dishes, bowls, and silverware. Off to the side, waiting for her usual dish-washing duty, the seemingly happy Taegar sat weaving daisies into a crown of flowers for her head, smiling as she worked. Tall and rail-thin, her blonde hair, blue eyes, and all-encompassing smile made her happy mood infectious. When she'd shown up a year earlier, a young woman in emotional pain, she'd wholeheartedly adopted their simple lifestyle. She'd refused to talk about her life before she joined them, though they'd each tried to help her let go. There were moments when the sadness in her eyes tore at them, Valena most of all, who'd become a pseudo-mother to Taegar. She and Damian had spoken many times about how they might bring Taegar out of her shell. Nothing they'd tried had worked. Whenever Taegar caught them watching her, she tucked her sadness quietly away. Even after all this time, she did not want their relationship tainted by her past. So they allowed her to bury what she must, though it wasn't healthy.

Luther had been the last to join their group. Close shaven, dark haired, with a personality to match, he was the pessimist of the group, even though he swore their simple life was all he wanted in the world. He'd become a bit of a camp sheriff. When an injustice occurred, he dealt with it, though sometimes with less tact than Damian would prefer.

Bhren brought the oatmeal over and dished up bowls as they all sat. As a group, they thanked Mother Earth for their bounty and dug in.

Damian passed the letter around as they ate, hoping it wouldn't sour their food like it did his.

"This is ridiculous," Luther said. He waved the letter in the air. "They can't do this."

Wyeth tugged the piece of paper from his hand, taking only seconds to scan it before handing it to his wife. "No one should be able to use this land like that. This is part of the Black Hills National Forest. It's protected."

"We thought it was," Valena said.

"Are you sure this information is reliable?" Gwen, quiet and analytical like her husband, tucked the crazy curls of her red-tinted blonde hair into a rainbow-colored ball cap, then swallowed a spoonful of oatmeal.

Taegar ate with abandon as if nothing in the world mattered except what she did at that moment. The girl focused on one thing at a time and gave it her all. Damian wondered if she even listened to the conversation, and what thoughts rambled around in that head of hers. When she did join their discussions, her comments were sometimes profound and sometimes ridiculous. They never knew which way her wisdom would skew.

"I trust the man who sent it," Damian said. "We went to college together and have a lot of the same beliefs about preserving our resources. He chose to further that cause by working as a lawyer in Washington while I took a simpler path. So yes, I believe this information is accurate."

Luther pounded the table, getting even Taegar's attention. "This is insane. It shouldn't be happening."

"Whether or not this can happen is no longer the point," Damian said. "Apparently, it's a done deal. The issue now is what to do about it."

"Who is this Gordon Darcy?" Wyeth asked.

"I did some research this morning. Seems like a corporate type, in it for the money."

"You don't think we'll be able to persuade him of the importance of this place?"

They all grew quiet. Everyone knew what was at stake here. Damian and Valena had come to this area several years before and immediately felt the difference. Life was fresher here, more abundant. The trees sang, the breezes whistled sweet lullabies, food and vegetation grew better than any other place they'd visited. There was almost a sentience, a oneness with the earth, the sky, the universe.

"I think we have to try," Valena said.

Wyeth nodded. "Reason tends to be the best way to convince someone to change their minds."

Damian sighed. "I guess that means I'm going to Los Angeles."

Valena entwined her arm with his and leaned against him.

Her long, dark hair tickled his arms, its sunshine and citrus scent calming him. Almost. With her head on his shoulder, nothing else should matter. Normally, nothing else would, except now the adversarial life they'd left behind had been tossed back into their laps with a resounding plop.

"I'll go with you," Valena said quietly.

That suggestion cost his wife a lot. Since there was no time to drive, they'd have to fly. He and Valena had met when he'd guided a rescue team deep into the Congo to recover what they'd expected to be bodies from a small plane crash. It had shocked them all that two of the ten people had survived the two weeks it took them to get to the wreck: the pilot, and Valena. They'd had to medicate her to get her back to the states, and she hadn't set foot on a plane since.

Smitten from the first moment, Damian couldn't have left her if he'd wanted to. So he'd stayed, and he'd held her. Eventually, the nightmares she'd suffered since her ordeal diminished until they were only a rare occurrence during times of high stress.

"You love me so much, you'd get on a plane," he said.

Valena turned to look at him, touching his face. "Of course. I love you that much."

Damian held her hand to his cheek, soaking up all the tender reverence in her eyes until she snuggled deeper in his embrace, thereby gifting him the time to think. Something she always knew he needed, just one of the ways Valena saved him even more than he'd saved her. He'd tried so hard for so long to change things. Fighting aquacultures that would further taint the oceans, standing strong on the tracks to stop coal trains, even a sit-down to keep a proposed pipeline from crossing sacred ground. Each time, shot down. Each time, he got angrier. He'd been arrested so many times, he could say without blinking an eye that he had an extensive rap sheet.

Everything he'd tried, whether drastic or diplomatic, had failed. He'd been in a tough place, mentally exhausted and completely demoralized, when he'd moved to Africa. Those months had proved to be the best thing for him. He'd met Valena, his voice of reason, the one who reminded him that everything mattered, and that small changes could add up to bigger things.

This, though, the pillaging of this sacred land, would be the biggest fight of his life. Damian was certain of it.

"I always want you beside me, my love," he whispered into her hair. "But I think it's better if I make this trip alone."

When her shoulders relaxed, Damian knew his decision had been right. He couldn't put her through that. Not unless there was no other choice.

"I'll go as soon as possible," he said with more vehemence to the group who sat quietly waiting. "Let's see if I can get a meeting with this Gordon Darcy. I'll fly down to Los Angeles and try to convince him how important this land is."

"And I'll load you up with some facts to showcase the importance of leaving this land untainted," Bhren said as he got up to grab the laptop.

Damian smiled as everyone nodded their approval. While Damian had been designated the unofficial leader of their druid circle, all bigger decisions were generally discussed and decided by the entire group.

"It should be you," Wyeth said. "As long as you can hold down that rabid temper of yours."

A chuckle rumbled around the table, verifying the hard-won patience Damian had worked to attain. He didn't suffer fools easily, but Valena had helped him restrain his emotions and channel them into more positive actions.

"It's settled, then." Damian stood. "I'll call Darcy's office and make arrangements."

His wife stood with him. "I'll pile the dishes for Taegar and check the gardens," she said, giving him a lingering kiss before walking off.

"I've got to check the trailer's generator. It's been acting up," Luther said, heading off with a disgruntled wave.

"Financials and world news for me," Wyeth said, setting his laptop on the table.

Damian loved the cohesive camaraderie of their circle. Everyone knew what must be done. Everyone had their strengths.

He glanced at Taegar, who'd gone back to weaving flowers into the headdress she'd designed.

And their weaknesses.

~~~

"I don't give a hoot who's at lunch. Get me that information now. Or find yourself another company to work for. If you can." Gordon Darcy set the phone in its cradle with considerably less ire than his words indicated. Being forceful got the job done. He turned his chair away from his desk to look outside at a landscape he rarely noticed.

Force was the way businessmen grew their power, and Gordon lived for power. He spread his fingers then clenched them together, taking a deep, heady breath of the authority he commanded. There was no such thing as enough.

He wanted it all.

The door to his inner sanctum opened and his secretary walked in. Most of the others wanted to be called administrative assistants. If Rose ever mentioned that
~~~

phrase to him, she'd be gone, and she knew that. She would play his game to keep her very lucrative job. Gordon didn't need her respect. He needed her silence and her ability to get things done.

"What?" he asked, adding a touch of harshness to his tone. It wouldn't do to give anyone the idea they had even one bit of control. That was his. All his.

"Your three o'clock is here," she said with mild distaste.

"Send him in." Gordon sat back, a framed photograph catching his eye. Decorum required that he have a picture on his desk of his wife of almost thirty years, a hag more interested in what new body sculpting procedures were available than she was in him. They disliked each other and that worked just fine for him. The picture included his daughter, Cait. Not a bad sort, though rather plain with that nondescript auburn hair. Not a child he wanted anything to do with. A weak female. The one thing he'd needed from his wife, she hadn't been able to produce. Gordon scowled. He'd rather not have either woman adorning his desk. That he had no son to inherit his empire was a deep wound.

The man who strode in looked nothing like the kind Gordon would know. His clean-shaven head, beady, dark eyes, and body bulked up by what had to be steroids were a far cry from the people Gordon normally associated with. But he served a very important role in Gordon's plans. The man didn't sit, instead standing in front of Gordon's desk, damn near at attention as he stared out the window behind Gordon.

"The evictions have been posted and everyone notified," the man said with no preamble.

"Do you think they'll leave?"

"Doubtful."

Gordon drummed his fingers on his chair arm. "We

may have to escalate."

The man shrugged. "Whenever you want. We're ready."

Gordon reached into his drawer and pulled out an envelope, handing it over. "Another installment."

The man fanned the notes in the envelope and nodded.

"I want you in the field."

"I'm on a plane this evening."

"Good."

The man of few words walked out of Gordon's office as quietly as he'd entered. Gordon had never learned the man's name, though he didn't need it. All he needed was his loyalty and unfailing ability to do whatever task Gordon set for him.

Still, meeting with him left a bad taste in Gordon's mouth. He rose, loosening his tie, and headed for his in-office bathroom.

Later, after he'd showered and dressed in a suit from his office closet, he stood and stared over the evening landscape. Los Angeles during the day looked like New York's sun-baked, dingy second cousin. At night, though, it came alive with lights and activity. He had a dinner meeting in half an hour. This one would be particularly tiresome. The man wanted to convince him not to change anything on the land that would soon be the focus of his biggest deal yet.

National forest land. An unheard of transaction unless you knew the right people to get the job done. That had been quite the coup. It had cost him dearly, and his government man had bartered for upfront payments as well as a hefty percentage of the profits.

But his man on the inside knew a good bet. Of particular interest regarding this land were the mineral resources that lay beneath. Thanks to a report he got a look at before it went public, he knew just how profitable this venture would be. The site was just large enough for the oil derrick he intended to place there. Drilling for oil right next to Mt. Rushmore. Who'd have thought that would ever be possible?

Thinking of tonight's meeting, Gordon sniffed with distaste. He'd initially refused to meet with the man. However, this Damian Royan's insistence that he had good reason for asking Gordon to change his plans had piqued his curiosity. Was there more to this place than the reports he had? More to profit from?

He'd agreed to dinner, if only to satisfy his curiosity.

Gordon picked up his phone. "Have my car brought around. Then you're free to go for the night." Slipping into his coat, he strode from the office toward his private elevator.

Outside, he pulled up the collar of his coat as the wind whipped up, promising more rain. This was god-damned Los Angeles. It wasn't supposed to rain here. Rain was for those northern idiots, like the greenies in Seattle.

Disgusted, he settled in the limo's back seat for the short ride to one of the most exclusive restaurants in town. A curious choice, picking a place this expensive. One that got Gordon's attention. He liked expensive. It generally meant more power for him.

A short while later, the maître d' led him to a table off to the side, where quiet conversation could be had with few prying ears. The man he was supposed to meet stood up, and Gordon almost laughed out loud. Good God, the man wore a tunic. Gordon leaned to the side for a better look. Loose-fitting pants, the putrid color identifying the material as most likely hand-dyed, little-processed cotton. And sandals? The man actually wore sandals. Of course, they went well with the ponytail. In one of L.A.'s ritziest restaurants. Gordon couldn't help but wonder if he'd be pulling out his magic lantern to pay for this shindig.

The man held out his hand. "Mr. Darcy. It's nice to finally meet you. I'm Damian Royan."

Gordon nodded and grasped the hand with his typical "in charge" handshake, surprised at the strength in the man's return grip. Royan also matched Gordon's stare without blinking. He'd need to watch his step with this one.

They sat down and Gordon waved the waiter over. "My usual," he said.

"Just water for me," Royan said.

Gordon rolled his eyes. If a man couldn't do business over drinks, he had no right to do business at all.

"What's this all about, Royan?" Get right to the point. That was his motto.

Damian Royan smiled as Gordon took a sip of his drink.

"I'd like to talk to you about the acreage you've leased in South Dakota."

"There's nothing to talk about."

"It was a surprise that you managed to get access to federal parks land."

Gordon shrugged. "Anything is possible if you work hard enough for it."

"That shouldn't have been able to happen, though. The laws state—"

"For every law that protects something, there's a law of acquisition that allows it to be used for the gain of all Americans."

"That's why you leased this land? To help the American people?"

Gordon laughed. "Hardly. But oil is at a premium, so if we can mine it or frack it locally, there's a benefit to the country.”

Royan's eyes widened, telling Gordon he hadn't known the purpose for the purchase. Good. Things had been kept well under wraps, an important need until they'd tied up the mineral-resource rights, finalized last week. Now, it didn't matter who knew.

When the man's nostrils flared as he took a deep breath, Gordon knew he had him. This was not a discussion this Royan hippie would win, but it amused Gordon that he intended to try.

"There's also a benefit, and financial gain to be had, in keeping the area open for recreation."

Gordon shook his head. "That's peanuts, and nowhere near enough to sway my plans."

"Well, how about research. The area—"

"Again, doesn't help me one bit."

"Please," he said. "I beg you, don't drill in that area. It's precious."

Gordon smiled. "I'm very aware of that."

"It's not the oil beneath it that's special. The land is sacred."

Gordon laughed out loud. "Nothing is sacred, especially not land."

"This land is. I've lived there for several years. There's something special there. A...bond with the earth. A oneness. Earth is stronger there, and that area helps feed an ever-enlarging ecosystem that is necessary to the continuation of Earth and mankind."

"Hmmm." Gordon frowned, playing along with the man's delusional ideas for the moment. "Do you have any proof of that? Have you found, say, remnants of gold or other precious metal mines?" He knew that those had been tapped out in the 1880's.

Royan tightened his lips. "If you'd come visit, see and

feel the land for yourself, you'd understand."

"I think not. Honestly, there's nothing you can say that will stop my plans. Nothing anyone can do. This is a done deal." Growing tired of this chatter, he emphasized the last words.

Royan clutched a piece of paper in his hands. He opened it, glanced at some sort of list, then shook his head and closed it, his fist crumpling the paper. "You can't do this," he ground out. "This will make matters worse for Americans. For the world. You will be killing the Earth if you pursue this madness."

"I can, and will, kill whatever I want, and I will do it simply because I have the right."

"We'll fight you. To the highest court."

"You can try. For the record, there was nothing illegal about this. It's above board and you'll lose every single battle." Gordon swished his drink around and looked Damian Royan in the eye. "Save your money. And get the hell off my land."

Royan stood, red in the face and with fisted hands on the table. He leaned forward. "This isn't over."

"Yes. It is. You have ten days to vacate *my* land."

The hippie whipped out a wallet and threw a couple of bills on the table, then strode out without another word.

Gordon Darcy swished the amber liquid in his glass, watching Damian Royan walk out. The man had more backbone than Gordon had expected. He might actually be able to cause some trouble. Waving the nearby waiter away, Gordon pulled out his phone and dialed a number few people had.

"We might have a problem," he said to the man on the other end. He described the meeting in succinct words.

"There's no problem," the man said. "There can't be. Everything was done within legal loopholes. There's no evidence of any wrongdoing. I'm telling you, this is locked up tight. Even if they try for an injunction to stop us, they won't succeed. Everyone's been paid. We're rock solid."

"We'd better be," Gordon said, hanging up. He grabbed the glass, downed the rest of his drink and set it down, the table shaking with the force of his effort. No longer in the mood for food, Gordon left the restaurant and stepped outside, then back under the awning as the rain poured down. He texted his driver to pick him up. Huffing in air while he tried to let go of the niggling worry that he'd missed something, he glanced down the street. Los Angeles' night lights were dazzling even in the rain, brilliant with the promise of exciting things to fill the evening. A couple walked by, their arms wrapped around each other so tightly under their umbrella that he didn't know how they managed to walk. They laughed, barely noticing the people moving aside to let them through. Totally immersed in their own world. Little did they know how easily that world could be shattered.

Theirs was a world Gordon did not indulge in because he'd learned the hard way how fragile it could be. Gordon never played. Never went to clubs. Never did anything not directly tied to increasing his portfolio. Leasing this land was the biggest coup he'd ever pulled off, and he'd poured much more money into making it happen than he was comfortable with, not that anyone else knew that. This South Dakota property had to pay off, and pay off big, or he'd be in serious trouble. Maybe it was time to send a message to that hippie and his fellow idealists.

His car pulled up to the curb and his driver got out, coming around and opening the back door for Gordon with a nod. "I hope you had a good meeting, Mr. Darcy."

Darcy ignored him. As he stepped toward the car, a breeze caught him unawares, rain hitting his face sideways,

a chill omen that made the hairs on the back of his neck
pay attention. He glanced back, seeing no one, but sensing
that something or someone had just sent him a warning.

News Alert: Two weeks of rain in California is proving too much for the overtaxed system to handle. Flooding is widespread.

CHAPTER TWO

A week after his meeting with Gordon Darcy, Damian sank into the not-so-comfortable chair in his motel room. A chair as hard as the brick wall he'd just hit with a Mac truck at ninety miles per hour. At least, that's what his efforts to save the land felt like. Loosening the tie he hardly ever wore and yanking the band out of his bound hair, Damian leaned back and raked his hands through the untamable mane, restless with worry and desperate for any plan that would work. He turned on the TV, searching until he found a twenty-four-hour news network, letting it drone on in the background as he tried to reason things out.

Gordon Darcy was as cutthroat as they came. As soon as Damian had walked out on that soulless man, he'd booked a flight to D.C. Now, after days of meetings, the only thing he had to show for his efforts was a king-sized headache and a lot of frustration. He'd visited each of his congressional representatives, and each plea for assistance had been summarily dismissed. He'd gone to the EPA, explaining that Darcy would be drilling for oil in what had been until recently a national forest. With no environmental impact studies completed, the aftermath could be disastrous. He'd spent the day at the EPA, working his way up the chain of command. When he finally got in to see one of the directors, the man gave him a once over and, from his closed-off expression, had apparently decided to dismiss what he had to say without even hearing him.

"No one can lease national-park property. Ever." The man had said this even after Damian set a copy of the proof in front of him. He'd eventually managed to get the man to promise he would check into Damian's claims, but the possibility of that actually happening was remote, if the denial in the director's face gave any indication.

Every person he'd gone to had shut him down. It was as if Gordon Darcy owned D.C. Damian thrummed his fingers on the chair. Could Darcy have bribed that many officials? It wasn't unheard of, and if the reports just coming to light were any indication, oil was plentiful beneath the park. Most likely, this would be a very lucrative venture and that gave Darcy a lot of clout.

"...the worst hurricane season in the history of the Caribbean, with Humberto moving faster than any prior storm, gaining strength as it speeds along," the male newscaster intoned.

Worst season ever. How many times in the past few years had Damian heard that phrase? Too many times to count. Increased hurricanes, tornadoes, heat-enhanced wildfires. Climate change was real, yet few believed Earth was sending humanity a message. A tipping point was coming, and soon. Damian could feel it in every cell of his body.

He needed to center himself and get rid of all this negative energy. He settled on the floor, legs crossed, arms relaxed in a meditation pose. Tuning out the television, he focused on his breathing. In. Out. Slow down. Relax with each breath. In. Out.

The motel room's phone jangled, breaking Damian's concentration. Maybe that EPA guy had taken him seriously.

"Hello?"

"Damian. Something's happened!"

"Taegar?"

"Yes. You've got to come home. Now." She spoke with the stutter of someone certain they only had seconds to say something before tears made it impossible. Damian had to take precious seconds to interpret her jumbled words.

"Home? Why? What's happened?"

"It's Valena!"

The acid rock entrenched in Damian's stomach launched itself, ping-ponging around his body until it settled against the rapidly beating heart lodged in his throat.

"Valena?" He barely croaked out the words, his throat was so dry. "Is she all right?"

"That's what I'm trying to tell you. There's been an accident. Valena's been hurt."

~~~

Damian raced off the plane, uncharacteristically jostling people as he flew up the Jetway and into the airport. He raced outside baggage claim, thankful he hadn't needed to check a bag.

"She's going to be all right," Gwen had told him on the phone before he boarded the flight, in that quiet, calming way of hers. Except the news hadn't calmed Damian one bit. Reassurances weren't working for him. He needed to see Valena. To touch her. If anything happened to her...

Although he'd been more than grateful for the optimistic report on his wife's recovery the doctor had
~~~

given him by phone, Damian had barely tamped down his anxious need to be at Valena's side long enough to endure the airport wait and flight home. All that patience flew out the window now that he was in Rapid City. He needed to be there. At the hospital.

Damian looked around, frantic. Wyeth had said he'd pick him up.

"Here, old man." Wyeth, standing right in front of him, pulled Damian into a bear hug. For one long microsecond, Damian returned the fierce hug. He needed that energy.

"I have to get to the hospital," he said.

"Climb in. We'll talk on the road."

"Maybe I should drive." Wyeth, the methodical one, didn't drive often, and he always thought three times about his route and how to handle the other cars on the road. He also believed in going the speed limit and not a single mile over.

Wyeth chuckled. "No way. You're too emotional."

Rather than argue with him and delay them another second, Damian tossed his backpack behind the truck seat and climbed in.

Wyeth got behind the wheel, put his seatbelt on, and put the key in the ignition. Then he turned to stare at Damian's lap, waiting.

"Oh, man, you've got to be kidding me," Damian mumbled, reaching for his seat belt and snapping it into place. "There. Happy?"

Wyeth nodded, checked his mirrors, and pulled away from the curb like a plodding mule. Slow but steady. Too slow.

"I should have driven," Damian mumbled under his breath.

"With me behind the wheel, at least we'll get there.

Valena is stable and doing well. It won't help her if you get in an accident en route to her bedside."

"I can't believe she fell, Wyeth. It's not that far up and she's climbed that rock wall hundreds of times, both with me and alone. She's as sure-footed as any of us. How could this happen?"

"That's a good question, and one we've been trying to answer." Wyeth did something Damian had never seen before, taking one hand off the wheel. He reached with slow caution for an envelope that sat on the dash.

Damian opened it and several pictures spilled out, all depicting the precipice wall he and Valena regularly climbed to get to their special place. He looked at Wyeth, who did not take his eyes off the road. "Look closer at the rocks, especially toward the top."

Damian scanned the picture again. The rocks looked darker at the top, but that could be the picture. Except the rest of the precipice had normal coloration. Damian pulled the picture closer. Those few rocks toward the top were darker. Plus, there almost looked to be some sort of sheen where they were darkened.

"I think it's motor oil."

Damian whipped his head up, wrinkling the pictures as his hands tightened on them. "Motor oil?"

"I've sent a sample to a friend of mine at a lab to see if we can pin down where it came from, but it's definitely oil of some sort."

Damian blanched as the fruit and vegetables he'd eaten on the plane threatened to make a comeback. "But that means..." God. He couldn't even say the words. A deliberate act?

"It means we don't think this was accidental."

Who would want to harm Valena? She was sweet, caring, empathic, and had latent healing properties. She had a way with animals and humans alike and had never met either without finding something to like about them. Her deep sea-blue eyes and gentle demeanor could calm any ire. How could anyone want to hurt someone like her? It was unfathomable. It was sick. That's what it was. Some sick bastard... Damian froze, staring at the pictures again. Whoever did this must have known his wife climbed up there often.

"Someone knew we regularly went to this place."

Wyeth nodded. "We thought the same thing."

"So either someone's been doing reconnaissance, or it's a local."

"We don't have a solid lead yet, but that's my assumption. I think we will need to be very, very careful until we figure this out."

"Agreed. We should stay in pairs and someone should always be in camp. Who's there now?"

"Bhren and Luther. Gwen and Taegar are with Valena."

"Good." They pulled into the parking lot of the hospital and all thought of sabotage disappeared from Damian's mind. There was only Valena. He needed to see her more than anything.

"I'll drop you off, then go park."

"Thanks."

Wyeth pulled up to the entrance. "Fourth floor, room 419."

Damian waved his acknowledgment and ran inside, heading for the stairs and taking them two at a time. Barely out of breath, he burst onto the fourth floor, turning his head until he figured out whether he should go left or right to reach room 419.

Just outside Valena's room, Damian paused. It would not do to upset his wife, and she would see his emotional upheaval if he couldn't control it. He leaned against the wall next to the door, closing his eyes and taking deep breaths. Calming breaths. Centering himself.

After another minute or so, he'd calmed, so he pushed quietly into the darkened room. It took long moments for his eyes to adjust. Taegar sat on the far side of the bed holding Valena's hand, with Gwen in a chair in the corner. He couldn't see Valena's shadowed face. Damian stepped closer.

"She's sleeping," Taegar whispered. "First nap she's been allowed due to concussion protocols."

Damian nodded, sinking to the chair on his side of the bed, getting his first look at her bruised and battered face. God, but he was glad she slept and didn't see how badly it shook him. He picked up her hand, his own shaking so hard he almost dropped hers. Even her arms were bruised. The doctor had told him she had a concussion, but no skull fracture, thank goodness. A broken leg, but the ribs were only bruised. She had to be in a lot of pain.

Someone had done this unconscionable act. Someone had hurt this precious woman. Fury threatened to consume him and he worked hard to stifle his negative emotions. He needed to focus on Valena, on her healing. He willed himself to stop shaking and bent his head over their entwined hands, praying for her recovery.

"Damian," Valena croaked from the bed. "You're here."

"I'm here, sweetheart. I'm here. I've got you now."

He barely noticed Wyeth come in, or Gwen and Taegar picking up their bags as they left the room with Wyeth. His total focus was on the woman he'd never be able to live without. Ever.

"I'm all right."

She was reassuring him? He should be making sure she

was calm, not vice versa. "I know you are. I spoke to the doctor this morning."

She reached for his face, but the tubes coming from her free hand impeded her.

Damian smoothed her hair back. "I bet you have one hell of a headache."

Valena turned her head and winced. "A bit."

"And you're exhausted."

"Completely."

"Then sleep." He smoothed her hair again. He noted the pain wrinkles easing, so he kept it up while speaking to her in the calming voice she used with others. "I'm here, baby. I'm not leaving. Sleep."

Valena drifted off quickly, probably because of the pain meds. Damian sat back in the chair, still holding her hand, and pinched his nose to keep the tears at bay.

If anything happened to Valena, he didn't know what he'd do. She was his life, his everything. Sitting there, rubbing his hands over the soft skin of her frail hand, Damian sorted through the people in his life. Friends, associates, and yes, maybe an enemy or two. But none who would stoop to this level.

Except one.

Gordon Darcy.

Could he actually do something this malevolent? Damian had nothing to go on besides a growing gut feeling. The man seemed driven to attain more wealth, more power, more everything. He'd certainly been ruthless when they'd spoken, and in the aftermath. He'd proved it by serving papers the day after their meeting, informing the occupants of the camp group they had to vacate. Plus, Damian truly believed Darcy had locked Washington, D.C., down tight, closing every door of opportunity to save the Black Hills National Forest.

But attempted murder?

Things had gotten way more serious than even Damian thought they could.

Valena stirred in her bed. Empathic as always, even in a drug-induced sleep, she sensed her husband's unease. Now was not the time to reason out a plan. Damian cleared his mind and focused on Valena, on her healing, on getting her home.

What to do about preserving that home would just have to wait for another day. Hopefully, there was still time.

Watching Valena sleep, Damian smiled. She was his life and, for now, that was where his thoughts needed to be.

News Alert: Corporate profits are up, yet satisfaction rates amongst employees have plummeted.

CHAPTER THREE

"As you can see, Mr. Darcy," the slender, red-headed woman said, "we've outperformed any other department with this new style of operation."

Gordon watched her with a dispassionate eye as she stood in front of his desk. If she were anyone else, he wouldn't even be listening to this drivel. He glanced at the obligatory photo on the edge of his desk—his wife and daughter. She'd grown since that picture had been taken. Not in form, since she remained stick-thin like her mother. Her face had changed the most. Gone was the sparkle in her eyes, the guileless joy of a child. Her hair color might indicate her hot-blooded nature, but those dark green eyes were shrewd and cunning. Just like his, and that was the reason he required her to address him formally. All his employees did, to remind them who called the shots.

If only she'd been born a son so he could pass on his empire. Someone he could trust with every aspect of the Darcy Corporation. A man, who wouldn't disappear as soon as he got what he wanted. Someone who would stick around, carry things further, and grow what Gordon had created.

Not some gold-digging female. Certainly not someone the spitting image of his wife. How could his chromosomes have betrayed him like this?

"Here's the proof." She shoved a report at him.

Gordon glanced at the first couple pages, then tossed it to the side of his desk. Her department *had* out-performed all the others, but it wouldn't do to let Cait Darcy know that. "The government relaxation of rules could easily account for the increased outflow."

"It's not the damn government." Cait leaned in, one hand gripping the edge of his desk as her eyes flashed. "It's how I treat my people, allowing for flexible scheduling, time off, daycare." She pounded her finger into his desk with each point she made. "Making people happier in the workplace gives them a reason to want to come to work. They want to produce more because they're more content." With one final pound of her finger, Cait stood and crossed her arms over her chest, daring him to disagree.

She had fire in her. Gordon had to give her that. But that's all she would ever have. She was a woman, driven by hormones and greed like all the rest. He waved at the report. "There's nothing in this that validates the extra costs associated with those *programs* of yours." Daycare? He almost shuddered. "Kill the programs. Immediately."

He could see her chewing her jaw, trying to maintain control. God, but he loved being able to subdue people, to force them to do his bidding. He could feel the rush of power.

"No," Cait said. "I won't. I'm doing something good here and it's working. You need to acknowledge that, and we need to expand these programs. It's time to bring this archaic company into the twenty-first century." Her nostrils flared as she raised her chin higher.

She had guts. Got that from him. Still, it wouldn't do to let her know that. "Then I'll have someone else kill your babies for you. You're fired."

"You can't do that," she said, her voice surging with anger.

"I can and I have."

Several moments passed, her mouth opening then closing with tossed thoughts. Gordon almost smiled.

"You're firing your own daughter?" she finally asked, though the words sounded dragged from her.

"Yes."

"I'll sue."

"Go ahead. Just do it from outside this building." He picked up his phone. "Send security in."

Then, Gordon turned to his computer as if she wasn't even there while Cait stood in front of him, her mouth slack and her face almost as red as her hair.

Thirty seconds later, a burly man entered the office.

"Please take Cait Darcy to her desk, where she will clean it of personal items. Then escort her off the premises. She no longer works here."

Cait's eyes flashed with barely suppressed anger. "I'll need to stop by the in-house daycare to pick up your granddaughters."

Gordon nearly grimaced. She'd had twins, what, a year ago? No, must be two years by now. Both girls. It figured. The only thing he'd hoped his blood relation would do was provide him with a grandson. Cait couldn't even do that right.

"Get them. And while you're there, you can let them know we'll be shutting that program down by the end of the week."

Cait stood stock still, the glare in her eyes fueled by his own unwavering stare. Finally, when the security guard took a step forward, she moved. Before she left, Cait glanced back. "I hate you, and I hope you burn in hell."

After the guard closed the door behind them, Gordon sat back and closed his eyes. God, he lived for these moments. Power was everything. His smile widened as he reached for his phone. "Have the vice president from Cait Darcy's section in my office in half an hour."

Later, he sat thinking about the afternoon. Cait's boss would quickly dismantle all the damage she'd done. There was no need to think about that anymore. It would be done or the man would follow Gordon's daughter straight out the door. Gordon could now get back to more pressing matters, like this Black Hills deal. He liked that name. The place would soon be raining black oil. That would be the name of his new venture there. Black Hills Drilling.

Everything had been expedited faster than even he thought was possible. Poised to begin what promised to be the most prosperous venture he'd ever coerced into existence, only one thing still stood in his way.

Gordon frowned. Damian Royan and his motley crew of hippies refused to move from the campground. Everyone else had vacated. The signs were gone. Nothing remained but water, power, and bathrooms. He'd had to leave them intact. The construction crews would need them.

Yet they stood their ground. Gordon grudgingly respected their willingness to fight. Any other time, he would love that fight, but not now. On Monday, crews would arrive to begin clearing the land. The Darcy Corporation would lose money each day after Sunday that these greeners kept the workers at bay.

Someone from their group had even contacted the major news media outlets. Thankfully, he'd thought of that. He'd made certain any editors not already in his pocket knew the folly of giving this piece too much attention.

Still, he needed them gone. Drumming his fingers on the desk, Gordon stared at the work schedule on his computer. He reached for his phone and punched in a number.

When the person answered, Gordon said simply, "I have another job for you."

~~~

Walking toward the glass doors on the ground floor of the Darcy Corporation, Cait hiked an overfull bag back onto her shoulder, then regrasped the hand of two-year-old Fallon, always the mischievous one of the twins. She asked Willow to hold on tight to her sister's hand. Cait couldn't get out of this building soon enough. She pushed through the door using her back and tugged her daughters along. Just as freedom lay within her grasp, the bag slipped off Cait's shoulder, jerked her arm, and caught in the closing door. That yanked her backward, which pulled on Fallon's hands. Both girls started crying.

Cait barely held onto the scream bubbling up inside her. She let go of the bag and set each child against the wall. "Stay," she admonished with a finger.

She stepped the two feet to the door, opened it while watching the girls, grabbed her bag, and stepped back. God, but she wished she could slam the softly closing door. It would be a nice final epitaph for her time here if the glass shattered as she left.

Normally, she would have the valet bring her car around, but word had gotten out, thanks to dear old Daddy. The valet handed her keys over without saying a word. No one from the Darcy Corporation could lift a finger to help her without putting their own job in jeopardy. Cait wanted to hit something. Needed to hit something, pacifist tendencies be damned.
~~~

She wanted to rail against the corporate giant, but her children needed her, so Cait dropped to her knees, gathered both girls in her arms and soothed them, talking in low tones as the city moved around them. When their cries turned to sniffles, she pulled back a bit.

"What say we go get some ice cream?"

"Yeeessshhhhh!" They screamed, all smiles now.

After wrestling kids and bags to the car she had to search for, then driving through midday L.A. traffic, Cait sat in a slightly sticky booth at a fast-food restaurant watching the girls slurp their drippy cones and trying to wrap her head around the turn her day had taken.

Her father had just fired her, and he'd done it with a gleam in his eye. Everything she'd spent the last year working on had been for naught. She'd been doing a good thing, too. Flex hours, in-house daycare...it all made for better productivity, and the report she'd agonized over had proven her results. Not that he cared. All that mattered to Gordon Darcy was money and power, even though, according to him, he had no one to inherit his legacy. Cait had worked her ass off to get through college summa cum laude with a business degree, then law school with the same accolades. She'd gained an entry-level position at the Darcy Corporation without her father's help and worked her way up to a director's position. Now, he planned to destroy it all simply because he could. She should sue. At any other company, firing her would require months of warnings and documentation.

The thing was, if she'd been a boy, she'd be working beside him. Gordon Darcy was the most chauvinistic pig she'd ever met.

Cait knew she was better off with no ties to that place. Or to her father. It was toxic and there was too much to be joyful about, like the ice cream smiles in front of her. Fallon and Willow giggled between bites. The looks between them spoke a language only twins knew. They were what was important. They were the best part of her life.

Harrison didn't know what he was missing, dodging parenthood. What was it with the men in her life? No one wanted to stick around. They were engaged to be married, but when she'd announced that his condom had failed, he'd gone white as a sheet. Two months later, when she'd brought home the double-bubble ultrasound picture, he'd packed up and left within an hour, leaving her with one parting sentence.

"They're all yours. Kids aren't my thing."

Cait hadn't seen or heard from him since. She hadn't even tried to find him to claim child support. She could raise her children, and had proven that over the last two years. It hadn't been easy. Her mother's involvement had been limited to having pricey gifts sent, two by two, each birthday and Christmas. Her father, initially showing some interest, had dropped all pretense when the twins were both girls.

She was better off without these poisonous relationships. She and the girls were all better off. Cait mentally ticked off the pluses and minuses. Minuses: she was out of a job, had just lost her only daycare option, and had no parents she could rely on. Pluses: her house was paid off and she had money enough in savings and investments to live for a while, thanks to a grandmother who'd left Cait everything she had. Cait sent silent thanks toward heaven. Because of Grandma Lila, she would be okay until she found something else.

It was time to organize that to-do list. Feeling better now that she had a starting point, Cait dug through her bag for wet-wipes and cleaned the kids' faces.

Fallon squirmed the whole time.

"Stop. Sit still while I clean your hands."

Willow slipped under the table and was well on her way to escaping by the time Cait finished with Fallon. She moved her cleaned-up daughter behind her, then grabbed Willow. Cait made quick work of cleaning Willow's face and hands, swiped the table clean, then pulled both girls into her arms and shouldered her way out to the car.

On the way home, both fell asleep. They'd wake up as soon as she pulled into the garage and she'd never get them down for a nap. She smiled. That was okay. Used to doing her own work after she'd wrangled them into bed, Cait knew the rest of the afternoon would be spent playing games and watching a fish movie with the two most precious things she'd ever been gifted.

News Alert: Rumors indicate the Black Hills National Forest may have been leased to a private investor. Investigation continues.

CHAPTER FOUR

Everyone had come into town to celebrate Valena's release from the hospital and her journey home. Damian could see how the joy in their faces lifted his wife's spirits. Still, their exuberance was a bit overwhelming.

"Valena's coming ho-ome. Valena's coming ho-ome," Taegar's sing-song voice intoned as the nurse wheeled her patient down the hall, Valena's ragtag gang leading the way like a pack of minstrels. The flower headband Taegar had ceremoniously placed on Valena's head tipped, and Valena pushed it back into place, blowing an errant strand of hair out of her face. She leaned on the arm of the chair, head canted into her hand. They hadn't even made it out to the truck and the exhaustion was evident on her face. Damian reached for her hand, trying to infuse a bit of his energy into her through the power of touch.

Valena's grateful smile warmed his heart. She was still pale, though. Too pale for his liking. He'd quizzed the doctor at length about the wisdom of sending her home only two days after her fall. He'd been reassured the concussion protocols showed no further danger and now it was a matter of healing the head, the ribs, and her casted leg.

The medical staff had armed him with antibiotics and pain pills but Damian would have felt better if they'd kept her in the hospital another day or two.

Before he knew it, they were out the front door and at the truck. They snuggled Valena into the truck's back seat with pillows behind her. Damian climbed in with her, settling her injured leg over his lap with tender care, though even that made her squint. The sooner they got home and she could rest, the better.

Bhren and Gwen climbed in front, with Wyeth driving. For once, Damian wanted slow and steady. Precious cargo lay with him in the back seat. Luther hopped in the back of the truck, helping Taegar up to join him.

The nurse waved goodbye with a laugh and they waved back without missing a beat of their song, a ballad about going home, then Wyeth pulled away from the curb with great care.

Damian covered Valena with a light blanket. She reached for his hand, squeezing gently with a timid smile on her face. That smile disappeared much too soon, replaced by a pain-induced frown. She leaned against the pillows and closed her eyes. "I'm all right," she told him softly. "Just tired."

"And in pain."

"A bit. I just want to get home and rest."

Back at the campground, Wyeth got them over the speed bumps and they pulled into the camp host's parking spot. They'd decided, against Valena's wishes, to ensconce her in the trailer until she felt a little better.

"I want to hear the birds. The water. Feel the breeze on my face."

"And you will," Damian said as he climbed out and

turned to her. "As soon as you get better."

"Nature helps me feel better." She scooted toward Damian and grimaced.

"I'll open a couple windows then. Humor me," he said as he helped her out of the truck. "Rest here for today and we'll decide about tomorrow when it gets here."

Valena leaned heavily on him. "Maybe you're right."

Damian lifted her into his arms. Even with the casted leg, she didn't weigh enough for him to break a sweat.

At the trailer, it took all of them to maneuver the tight spaces and help Valena to the bed. She sat on the mattress edge, out of breath. "Just give me a moment."

"I'll get you a pain pill." Damian turned to get a glass, finding Gwen already holding one out to him. He shook out a pill and held both out to Valena.

"I don't like taking these. They make my head rummy."

"I know. My wife, always the clear-headed one. This has been a tough day for you, though. It's up to you, but I suggest you take the pill to help you rest, and heal."

"I'm better than I look, you know."

Her eyes were clouded with pain. Everyone could see it, yet still she tried to minimize it.

"You look pretty rough, so I'm betting you don't feel as good as you'd like us to believe."

Valena wrapped her arms around ribs that seemed to be causing the worst of her pain. After a few moments, she reached for the pill. Damian helped her slide back onto the bed and lay down, placing a pillow under her cast and handing her another one. "To hug, when the ribs bother you."

"Which is constantly," she whispered, her eyes already closed.

Damian leaned over and kissed her cheek. "Sleep, my

love. You're home now. You can heal."

Her answer was unintelligible as she drifted off almost immediately. Damian wanted nothing more than to slip into bed beside her and hold her in his arms, keeping her safe from everything and anything. God, but she looked so fragile. She needed sleep more than anything and his concern would keep her from that.

So he stepped back, scrubbing his face with his hands. He felt like he'd aged a few years in the last couple of days. His travel bag sat on the table, reminding him that he'd brought home gifts. He dug out the small paper sack and joined the others, who'd left the trailer and waited for him at the nearby picnic table.

"Is she settled?" Gwen asked.

Damian nodded. "She's already asleep. The trip home took a lot out of her. Even with your tender driving, Wyeth." He placed a hand on his friend's shoulder.

Wyeth patted his hand. "She's going to be all right, you know."

"I know. But I don't feel right leaving her. I'll stay here tonight."

"We had pretty much figured that out," Bhren said.

"I brought you all something. Picked up various sizes so I hope there's one to fit everyone." He held out the brown paper sack.

Gwen peeked inside, smiled, then pulled out one of the silver rings inscribed with an oak tree.

"I thought it was a fitting tribute to our circle," Damian said.

"It's lovely." Gwen placed the ring on her finger. A perfect fit, the silver shimmered in the early October sunlight as she turned her hand this way and that. The engraved tree sparkled, as if happy to have found a kindred spirit to rest upon.

Passing the bag around, they each picked out an appropriate size as they thanked Damian. He set the bag with the last few rings on the table. A sixth sense had urged him to buy more than he needed. He would keep them until others came along who recognized Earth's importance. He tucked two into his jeans pocket for later. He and Valena would don their rings together, paying homage to both their bond with each other and their love of all things earthly.

Gwen gave Damian a much-needed hug. "We'll bring you some dinner."

"Thanks." He watched them walk away, grateful beyond explanation for their love and friendship. The best of the best surrounded him. Surrounded them, he amended. He glanced at the trailer. Not wanting to risk disturbing her, he left the door open so he'd hear if she needed him and settled in one of the camp chairs, snugging his jacket against the cool air. Breathing deeply, Damian watched the treetops swaying in the slight breeze. His wife was home, and she would heal. He could relax, probably for the first time since he'd heard Valena had been hurt. He turned his hands upward on his knees and said those words over and over again.

She's home. She'll heal.

He gave thanks to the restorative powers of Earth, centered himself, and prayed for wellness and healing for several minutes. Finally, the adrenaline of worry left his body, and he slumped in the chair, his own eyes closing for the first time since he'd gotten that call from Taegar.

~~~

Bhren contemplated Luther as they walked toward their camp. Right after Valena had been injured, they'd had a group discussion about whether her fall was accidental. Ever since, Luther, especially, had gone quiet. Too quiet.
~~~

He'd mumbled something about needing to run off some energy, disappeared for over twenty-four hours, and returned with no explanation, still exuding anger in every movement and glance. Even now, he clenched and unclenched his hands as he led the way. Unaware of exactly what Luther's life had been like before he came there, Bhren did have an inkling that he'd had some rough teen years and did some time in juvenile detention. For what, Luther had never told them. Still, he'd adapted to this lifestyle. Bhren and Damian had thought he'd adjusted to a peace-filled life and let his anger go.

Now, Bhren wasn't so sure.

"I still don't get it," Luther said.

"What?" Bhren stepped closer to him.

"Who would do something like this? To Valena, of all people. She's the nicest, kindest person I know. We've done nothing to incur anyone's wrath. We're just trying to live a quiet existence. Why did this happen?"

Bhren worked hard to keep his eyes from widening at the discourse. This was the most he'd heard from Luther in quite a while.

"I don't know," he answered. "I wish I did."

"Hell, we don't even know if this was some chance thing or planned to scare us off. If it was random, the world is in dire straits, with people going around just deciding to hurt someone like this. And if it isn't random..."

"We've got a whole lot of trouble on our hands."

Luther froze, causing Bhren to hurriedly side step to keep from running into him. Gwen didn't fare so well and lurched right into Luther. Wyeth caught her before Luther could. They all righted themselves in time to hear Taegar, who'd come up from the rear of their little troupe, gasp.

Their home lay in ruins. The biggest tent, Damian and Valena's, looked as if a bear had sharpened its claws over and over again on the canvas. In places, you could see clear through to the lake. Bhren's tent, the smallest, was nowhere to be found. It had just disappeared. Bhren leaned down and picked up a book, the one he'd been reading last night and left on the little table by his bed. The table was gone, and all that remained of his sleeping bag were tufts of cotton batting strewn around like a pillow fight gone bad.

They should never have gone into town en masse to bring Valena home. Someone should have stayed behind. Bhren would forever regret that decision.

"What the hell happened here?" Luther ground out.

Gwen and Taegar stood holding each other, their mouths agape. The shock on their faces mirrored his own.

Taegar sank to the ground, her eyes full of tears. "Who would do this to us?"

"I don't know," Luther growled. "But we're damn sure going to find out." He picked up one of Taegar's woven hats, now trampled and broken, and tried to brush the dirt from it without success. "I'm sorry, Taegar."

She took the hat from him, running her hands over the woven strands, now all but shredded. Taegar sniffed, raiser her head, and tossed the hat into a fire pit that looked as suspiciously dark as the rocks Valena had slipped on.

Oil. It had to be, which meant they couldn't burn anything there without spewing pollutants into the air. Bhren looked around at the thoroughness of the damage. This was all so frustrating. Pages were torn out of the book he held. He wouldn't be finishing this one now.

"I can't deal with this," Luther mumbled, then stomped off into the brush.

Bhren watched him walk off, worried. Should he follow him? Let him walk it out?

Wyeth settled a hand on his shoulder. "He'll work through this in his own way."

"And if he doesn't?"

"We'll deal with it. We've got enough to worry about right now without adding to the pile."

Gwen and Taegar were picking up their things, trying to find something usable in the mess. Both of them wiped tears from their cheeks as they walked through their now-destroyed home.

Bhren nodded to Wyeth. "You're right. I guess we'd better help clean this up before we lose daylight." He pushed his sleeves up on his arms and headed for the tent Damian and Valena shared. The shell still stood, though the canvas was in tatters. But inside...

Gagging, Bhren backed away, a hand over his mouth to keep from losing whatever was left in his stomach. Urine and feces permeated everything. It looked like a pack of bison had camped inside for a month. The stench was horrible. Gwen and Wyeth joined him.

"Oh, my God," Gwen said, turning into Wyeth's arms. "They targeted Damian and Valena worse than any of us. Who would do this?"

When Taegar started to walk their way, Bhren stopped her. "You don't want to see this, little one."

"I can tell from the smell that it's bad." Tears welled anew in her eyes and Bhren hugged her while she echoed Gwen's question. "Who would do this to us? Why? We're nice people."

"I don't know. I wish I did." Though Bhren wasn't certain he meant that. The anger and malevolence behind this showed in every tattered piece of their lives, a powerful message that he did not feel prepared to face. Not at the moment, at least. Maybe later, after he'd had time to process it all, he'd get angry. For the moment, pain held him for ransom.

Bhren turned Taegar toward Wyeth, indicating with a

nod of his head that Wyeth should take Gwen and Taegar elsewhere. "I'll deal with this tent myself." Once they'd backed away, Bhren pulled a kerchief out of his pocket and tied it over his nose and mouth, then pulled on rubber gloves. He reached for the large, non-compostable garbage bags. They were rarely used but this job was too big for anything else. Taking a deep breath, he stepped inside and started shoveling everything into a bag.

He could hear the others talking from the other side of camp as he slogged through the putrid debris. Both Gwen and Taegar were crying again.

"I can't b-breathe," Gwen said, taking deep gulping breaths.

Through the shredded tent wall, Bhren saw Wyeth wrap his arms around her. "Shh, shh. You're safe. We'll be alright."

"No," she cried, pounding his chest. "We won't be. First Valena and now this? And the land threatened? Everything seems so terrible."

"We've survived worse, sweetheart."

"But this... Oh, God. How could this happen?"

She clung to him, listening to whispered words Bhren couldn't hear. Taegar sat beside them, silent and awash in her own misery. None of them deserved this.

Over the next couple of hours, they managed to calm themselves and clear most of the destruction off to one side. Since garbage pickup had been discontinued, they'd need to make a trip to the dump. But not today, Bhren decided. Gwen's shoulders were sunken, despite regular hugs from her husband, the trail of silent tears had not yet dried on Taegar's cheeks, and he and Wyeth were exhausted from doing most of the heavy work.

Everything salvageable was stacked on or around their tables, so they walked over to the next campsite and sat there to rest.

Bhren suspected he looked as grim and grimy as Wyeth. Gwen clutched her stomach and Taegar gripped a cap she'd been knitting just this morning. The thing was trampled and muddy now, and so far, no one had found her needles.

Luther hadn't returned. Probably just as well. Bhren didn't feel like diffusing Luther's anger at the moment. He wanted to crawl into his tent and sleep. Except he no longer had a tent.

Gwen turned to Bhren and Wyeth, a haunted resentment beginning to replace the tears. "How are we going to find out who did this?"

"I don't know," Bhren said. "That can't be our focus right now. We need to figure out how to survive tonight. Then tomorrow and the next day. And we need to let Damian know what's happened."

"Oh, God, he doesn't need this. Not on top of what happened to Valena." Gwen pulled back to look up at her husband, grabbing his shirt. "You've been suspicious about how Valena got hurt. Could the two events be connected?"

Wyeth took a deep breath. Bhren knew that sign. It meant the logical side of his brain was taking over, sorting things out, determining the facts. They all relied on his ability to see things from an overall perspective.

"We don't have any idea who did this, or who caused Valena's fall. Could they be connected? Maybe. But that's a conversation for another day. Right now, I think Bhren's right. We need to tell Damian. Then work on food and more shelter than just the trailer. It's a good thing all the other campers have cleared out, although if they hadn't, there might be a witness to this crime."

Gwen nodded.

Wyeth cupped her face. "Better?"

Gwen nodded again.

"Good." He kissed her with gentle care.

"Taegar, you all right?" Bhren asked.

She met his gaze and nodded, her eyes clear and resolute.

"All right." Bhren stood and held out a hand to her. "How about we walk over as a group to see if Damian's up."

They walked quietly, each overwhelmed by their own thoughts. The magnitude of what had happened this day encroached on what little joy they'd found in unearthing items still usable. Looking at Wyeth, at the bow in his shoulders, Bhren knew they were all deeply affected. He'd need to be a rock of calmness. For them, and for himself.

News Alert: A small group of self-proclaimed druids fights an uphill battle against the corporate takeover of Black Hills National Forest.

CHAPTER FIVE

In stunned silence, Damian sat in the chair where he'd been sleeping until they woke him with the news that camp had been destroyed. He didn't even know what to say. "Everything?" he asked again.

"Pretty much," Bhren said.

Damian stood and raked his hands through his hair, glancing at the trailer where Valena still slept, judging by the lack of noise. Why was all this ruin raining down upon them? They were a ragtag little group trying to keep one of Earth's last sacred places from being exploited for profit.

"First Valena, and now this. I don't get it."

"None of us do."

"I sure as hell don't," Luther said, walking in from the woods to join them. "Not one bit. We've done nothing to hurt anyone."

That wasn't true, though. Damian knew that. There was one person they'd pissed off. "Gordon Darcy."

"Do you really think he'd stoop this low?" Gwen asked, hugging herself.

"This all started after Damian went to visit him," Luther ground out. "It's got to be him. I'm going to find him—"

"Let's not go off half-cocked," Wyeth said. "We don't have any proof."

"We don't *need* proof," Luther said, his voice raised.

"Shhh," Damian said. "You'll wake Valena. And Wyeth's right. Now's not the time for revenge. We have to find a way to survive, first and foremost." And take care of Valena. That was Damian's priority. "I need to see the damage."

He glanced at the quiet trailer.

"I'll stay here and listen for Valena," Bhren said. "I wouldn't mind a moment to meditate."

Damian nodded. He hadn't seen the destruction, but he understood the need to get an emotional handle. "Don't tell her anything. Not yet."

He could see the relief on Bhren's face. He loved Valena. They all did, and none of them wanted to be the bearer of ill news any more than he did.

A few minutes later, standing in front of the large pile of debris they'd cleared away, Damian was once again at a loss for words. His mouth went dry as he bent down and picked up a pink baby sweater, remarkably clean, the only physical reminder left from Valena's miscarriage the year before. Tears stung his eyes as the pungent stench from the garbage filled his nose. Turning away with the scrap of pink still in his hand, Damian prayed to God this would all stop. They couldn't take much more. He allowed himself a few more moments of sorrow, for himself, for them all, then he slipped the pink cloth into his tunic pocket, tucking his grief inside with it.

He looked around at the faces of his friends. Gwen, with her arm through Wyeth's. Luther, standing rigid, a deep scowl on his face. Taegar, tears drying on cheeks that drooped with misery. They needed guidance, and he was their leader. He needed to lead.

"All right. We can't turn back time, so we have to move forward."

Everyone nodded.

"At the moment, survival is the first order of business. No one else camps here anymore, so let's set up elsewhere and let this stench die off. He waved at the items stacked on their two picnic tables. "Did any tents survive?"

Gwen shook her head.

"Food?"

"A little."

"We'll move everything to the campsite next to the trailer site and pull together whatever we can for dinner. The rest, we'll sort out later."

No one spoke. They just picked things up and headed down the trail, heads bowed, but with resolute steps. Damian watched them for a long moment, pride filling him at their ability to set aside their worry and fear and get to work. He needed to do the same. He picked up a pile of clothing and headed for the other site.

"She's still sleeping," Bhren told him in a quiet voice after Damian dropped an armload at the site next door to the trailer and checked in.

"Good. Will you stay here? We're going to bring the rest of what survived the attack over." He reached for one of the walkies on the table. "Call me if she wakes up before I get back."

Bhren's quick smile didn't reach his eyes, though he looked calmer. "I will."

An hour later, what belongings had survived lay on two tables next to the trailer. So much waste. So much loss. He couldn't fathom how someone could destroy so completely.

They stood in the new campsites around the pitiful

remnants of their possessions. Damian's grimace was mirrored in everyone's faces.

"All right. We need water, food, and new tents. Why don't a couple of you go into Rapid City." He reached in his pocket and handed Gwen the credit card they used for necessities and food they couldn't grow. "Four of us can sleep in the trailer, so see if you can find one large tent. And some food for dinner and breakfast. Containers to hold water, too, and fill them before coming back. Maybe a few pots and pans and something to eat on. We'll figure the rest out later."

"I'll make the new site more habitable," Luther said, walking off.

"Damian?" Valena's voice seemed small and timid as it reached him.

"I'll help Luther." Bhren quickly followed the man to the other site as Damian entered the trailer.

Valena sat up. "I need to use..."

She scooted to the edge of the bed, her forehead deeply lined. Damian helped her stand and walk the two paces to the bathroom door. Waiting for her to finish, he sank into a chair. How was he going to tell her what had happened?

When she'd finished and splashed some water on her face, he tried to help her back to the bed.

"Please, no. I'm so sick of laying down. I want to feel the fresh air. Can we go outside?"

"If you think you're up to it."

"I can't lie in bed forever. I think it will do me good to move around a bit."

"All right then. Whatever your heart desires, dearest." He set her crutches outside and helped her to the door, where she scooted down enough steps for Damian to help her stand.

He could see she wasn't yet used to the crutches, but she managed a circle around the trailer before sitting down in a chair. Her face remained pale. Too pale for his liking.

"I'm all right," she said, knowing him well enough to realize he'd be worried.

"I'll get you a pain pill."

"Not one of the hospital pills. Just an ibuprofen."

"I think you should take a stronger pill."

"They make me too sleepy."

"Sleep is the best thing for you."

Valena reached for his hand. "You are the best thing for me. You and the outdoors. Air, space. Just to breathe for a moment. To be at peace."

Damian opened his mouth to tell her what had happened, then closed it. This wouldn't be easy. So instead, he bought some time and went for the ibuprofen. After she'd taken her pills, he pulled a chair up next to her and sat down.

Valena reached for his hand, running her other hand across his forehead. "Something has you bothered."

He tried to chuckle, but it stuck in his throat. "You know me well."

"What's happened?"

There was no easy way to say it. "Camp has been destroyed."

He told her everything, leaving nothing out. She'd know if he had.

Tears fell silently from Valena's eyes as he spoke, but she remained quiet until he'd explained that he'd sent Wyeth, Gwen, and Taegar into town for supplies.

"So," she said. "Everything salvageable is sitting in the next campsite over?"

"Yes."

Valena pushed up from the chair. "Hand me my

crutches."

"I don't think that's wise."

"I'm not going all the way to our home. I get that I'm not strong enough for that yet. But I will see what's been salvaged."

"Stubborn woman," Damian said as he reached for them.

"And don't you forget it." She tucked the crutches into her armpits, took a step, then faltered.

Damian caught her before she fell and opened his mouth to say I told you so until he saw her glower. So instead, he raised his hands in surrender and took a step back. Only one, though. She'd have to tolerate him shadowing her, at least for now.

She steadied herself and, within a few steps, had found a rhythm that relieved Damian. Too soon, she stood in front of the small pile of dishes and other camp items. Bhren and Luther watched from where they'd been raking the ground flat for the new tent.

"This is all?"

Bhren nodded. "They made certain very little was usable. The tents were shredded into strips not even big enough to be bandages."

"Our tent?" she whispered to Damian.

"They took particular care to destroy everything inside and around our tent. I'm sorry."

Damian reached into his pocket, pulling out the little pink strip of cloth. "This is all we found."

Valena nearly fell when she saw it. Damian rushed to catch her, helping her to sit on the bench of the picnic table, letting the crutches fall where they chose. Luther quietly picked them up.

Covering the scrap of cloth as Damian held it with her own shaking hands, Valena closed her eyes. He knew the deep sorrow in her soul over the loss of their baby girl. He knew it because that same grief coursed through his heart, infused his blood.

He knelt in front of her, resting his head on their intertwined hands. Valena brushed her free hand through his hair. Time passed as they stared out into the woods. Bhren and Luther had moved off to give them this moment. How long they sat there, neither remembered. Finally, Valena stirred, folded the cloth with reverent care, and tucked it in her pocket.

"This will get us nowhere. How can I help?"

By going back to bed and healing yourself. But Damian wisely kept his thought to himself. "There's not much we can do until the others return with supplies."

His stomach growled and they both chuckled.

"And food," Valena said.

"Yes. There's some soup in the trailer, and a few other things to eat, but not enough to sustain us."

"Then I'll rest until they come back." Valena stood and waited until he'd retrieved her crutches. "But don't even think of letting me sleep past then, husband. We have plans to make and I want to be involved in those choices."

Once again, Damian held his hands up in surrender. "As you wish, dearest." He was grateful that she was willing to rest for a while. And she had every right to be involved in this evening's discussion.

Tucking her back into bed, Damian settled next to her. He needed her near him, needed her aura of peace to calm the chaos in his mind and heart, for Damian had no idea whatsoever how to fix what had happened. They might have to leave this sacred place, find another homestead from which to fight for Earth's survival.

For the moment, he tried to clear his mind and just be. Here. With his wife. Safe.

He woke to the smell of food cooking outside.

"I was wondering when you'd wake up," Valena teased.

He smiled up into his wife's eyes, tugging at her hair until she lowered for his kiss. Searching her face, he was happy to see some color in her cheeks. "You feel better."

"Sleeping with you. That's the best healing power I know."

Her stomach grumbled as Wyeth entered the trailer, chuckling. "I heard that. And just in time. Dinner, such as it is, is ready."

They both helped Valena down from the trailer, but she relied on her iron will to power herself to the picnic table. That was his wife. Nothing kept her down for long. She had to be in a lot of pain from those ribs, but she didn't let that stop her.

Everyone clapped. They all needed some joy after the last few days. Even Luther smiled, who'd done nothing but scowl since they returned from the hospital.

Gwen passed out wine, a rare indulgence. "I figured we earned this tonight."

Everyone nodded as they sat down at the table. They bowed their heads in silent tribute to Earth and the sustenance it provided.

Dinner consisted of produce from the nearby farmer's market and an eggplant casserole cooked at a local co-op then reheated over the campfire. The day's trials slid away, and they each took this moment to remember the good in their lives.

"You're tired again," Gwen said to Valena.

She was right. The circles beneath his wife's eyes had deepened. "Maybe it's time—"

"I'll go to bed when I'm good and ready, husband." Her gentle smile, full of love, took the sting out of her words. "This evening has been better than any of us expected, given the events of the past few hours. Still, I think we have some decisions to make."

"Yes," Damian said. "We need to figure out how to recover from this."

"We *will* recover," Valena said.

Murmurs of assent moved around the table like dominoes falling.

"I think that answers the first question. Do we find a way to keep going or cut our losses and move on?"

Taegar had been quiet and pensive all afternoon—not even knitting since they'd never found her needles—but now she spoke up. "We can't leave here. This place is special." There were tears in her eyes. "This is where we have to make our stand. I feel it in every cell of my body. In every whisper of the wind. This is where the battle rages."

Everyone's eyes widened. Taegar had never made such a passionate speech.

She grabbed Wyeth's arm. "We have to."

Slowly, the nods around the table backed her up.

"All right," Damian said. "That answers question number two." He looked at each face, saw their belief in what they were doing. "So we make our stand. Here. The place each of us was drawn to by a force beyond our control. I'm—" He stopped for a moment to get his emotions under control. "I'm glad," he said simply. "It's what I want, too."

"And I," Valena said, taking Damian's hand on one side and Taegar's on the other. One by one, they joined hands, one circle of druids, all ready to do what they must to save that sacred land.

After some silent prayer, Damian asked the question of the hour. "What's next?"

"I think," Taegar said, "we need to ask Earth for

help."

Wow. When this girl decided to finally speak up, she made a universe worth of sense. Damian stepped behind her and placed his hands on her shoulders. She barely flinched, which was progress. Taegar never talked about her past and what had brought her here to them, and no one asked. It was her story to tell when she was ready. For now, he took pride in how her comfort had grown within their circle.

"Taegar is right. I suggest we all sleep, and spend tomorrow's daylight securing our ability to feed and house ourselves. At sunset, we'll meet in the glade and pray for Earth's help.

Everyone nodded. Damian glanced down at his wife's stooped shoulders and moved his hands there. "You need some sleep."

Valena nodded, leaning her head against his hand. "I need some sleep."

She stood and turned into arms that were ready to carry her. Damian glanced at Wyeth. "You, Gwen, and Taegar can sleep in the trailer with me and Valena. I'll get Val settled, then your beds set up."

"We picked up a second-hand tent," Wyeth said. "It's large enough for Bhren and Luther. We bought sleeping bags, too. We'll help set up out here, then join you in the trailer."

Damian made quick work of covering the distance to the trailer. His side step into the trailer with Valena in his arms was awkward but effective.

"I need a few moments." Valena glanced at the bathroom.

"Figured. I'll set up the other beds."

Minutes later, Damian gave Valena a pain pill. She didn't argue, a sign that she was deeply tired and in a lot of pain. Damian sat on the bed beside her. "Comfortable?" he asked.

"For the moment. I'm afraid to move."

"Then don't." Damian turned on his side and settled next to her, adding his warmth to her own. He leaned in and kissed her, gazing into her blue eyes. Eyes he wanted to stare into for eternity. "I don't know what I'd do if I lost you."

Valena reached up and touched his cheek. "We have more mountains to climb, Damian."

"Right now, sleep is the only mountain we need to tackle." But his words fell on deaf ears. Valena's eyes were closed and her breathing had already deepened.

Damian lay there long into the night, awake, listening to his wife's even breaths. And trying to find a solution to an impossible situation.

News Alert: The unemployment rate is rising. Whether due to summer weather giving way to fall, or the advent of new and less expensive automated processes, continues to be debated.

CHAPTER SIX

Cait woke to her alarm clock, groggy from too little sleep. She rose and headed for the bathroom, automatically working on her to-do list for the day.

Twins up, fed, ready for daycare.

Review notes for meeting with accounting.

Pick up the new daycare brochures at the printers before work.

Everything flooded back, and she stopped short. There was no work. Nothing to hurry off to accomplish. No meeting to prepare for. No need to pick up the brochures, because she was out of a job.

She wilted against the bathroom door jamb.

What do I do now?

She'd worked so hard to make a difference at the Darcy Corporation. To be the antithesis of her father and show that a department could be profitable and happy at the same time. Now, everything she'd done would be dismantled, tossed aside and replaced by the harsh environment of a dictator. She hadn't even had the chance to talk to her people, to warn them.

What would they think? What would happen to them? Many of the women were single parents. And George and Paula, ostracized by other departments because of their gay and transgender statuses... Would they be shoved out the door like she'd been?

Her father was the worst sort of human being. There'd been too many times in her life when she'd longed for a different father, a more cherished relationship. Now, after years of disappointment and tears, she felt more numb than anything else. The time had come to break ties with Gordon Darcy, mentally and emotionally. Cait straightened. From this day forward, he was no longer her father. She would keep the Darcy name because her children carried it. She refused to claim the heritage that went along with it. What was it with men choosing to have nothing to do with their progeny? First her father, then the twin's bio-dad. The two most important men in her life had deserted her family. Didn't they understand how wonderful children were? Did they not recognize that the future of the world lay in the hearts of children?

Shaking her head, Cait pulled off her bathrobe and grabbed her casual clothes. She came up with a new to-do list.

Call the daycare. Make sure they know I won't be back. Warn them.

Get the twins up, dressed, and fed.

Start looking for a new job, this time a place with some ethics, somewhere that shares my ideology.

She could hear Fallon and Willow stirring. Cait smiled, envisioning them waking up, seeing each other, showing their joy at a new day to explore. She'd watched them on the camera many times. Their happiness began when they caught sight of each other. That bond was the most precious thing in the world to them. To her, too.

She would adopt that same cheerful attitude.

Today was going to be a good day.

She would make it so.

~~~

"Are they gone?" Gordon Darcy drummed his fingers on the desk.

"Not yet," the voice on the other end of the phone said. "But they no longer have any reason to stay. We destroyed everything, ruined their food and shelter. They can't survive out there that way."

Gordon pursed his lips. This wasn't happening fast enough. "I told you to get them out of there now, not give them a reason to consider leaving. They need to be gone."

"Trust me. They have to leave. A day, maybe two and they'll be gone."

"If they're not, deal with it. Do whatever is necessary. Those bulldozers are moving in three days."

"It'll be done."

"Make certain." Gordon hung up the phone with more force than usual. He didn't like delays. They cost money. And those hippies should have been gone days ago. This was too important, not to mention the fact that Ramsey was breathing down his neck to get a move on.

With a sneer, Gordon took a moment to relish what he would do to the vice president when he no longer needed him. The man's self-importance grated on him. Ramsey had no right to issue orders to him, Gordon Darcy, one of the richest men in the world. Orders. The man would pay for that mistake. Hopefully soon.

Those hippies would be out of his oil field or there would be hell to pay all around. And Gordon would gladly dish that hell out personally, one strip of skin at a time.

Needing something else to focus on, Gordon picked up the reports he'd never really looked at when his
~~~

daughter brought them to his attention. He glanced through them now. She'd been right, though he found that hard to believe. Still, the reports showed that productivity had increased.

Tough. Gordon threw the pages in the mini-incinerator he kept in his office. Her figures didn't matter. Gordon did not run, and had no intention of ever running, a daycare.

Did it bother him that he'd fired his own daughter? Gordon cocked his head as he ran the thought through his head.

No. Didn't matter at all. She was nothing but a disappointment to him. Females did not belong in the corporate world. Now that Cait was gone, every executive who worked for Gordon was male and subservient, exactly how he liked them. Women thought too much. Argued too much. There was no place for them, working for him.

Ever.

~~~

Cait swirled her wine, oblivious to the deep, red color and the hint of cherry. It was an expensive wine, one she'd been gifted when promoted to director of her department. Probably something a secretary sent.

What she really wanted to do was throw the wine at the computer. Every avenue she'd tried today, even just to get an interview or meet for drinks to chat about the job market, had been summarily shut down.

Cait didn't have to think hard to figure out why. Her father—no. She refused to use that word in conjunction with him. Gordon Darcy had influence, and she was certain she'd been blackballed. She wouldn't work in L.A. again, not in any type of business even closely associated with finance. So Cait had some decisions to make. She could stay here and find a different line of work, or she could move,
~~~

though Gordon's reach was extensive.

She would not crumble under his maliciousness, even if the fact that he wanted nothing to do with her or her daughters rankled. Was that the right word? Cait rested a hand over a heart still aching for something she would never have.

Her eyes fixed on the ceiling, Cait thought about her girls. They would adapt no matter where she lived. So the question was, what did she really want to do? Did she want to work for corporate America? The allure that had gotten her through school had worn off. Maybe she'd been trying to get her father to notice her. Maybe not. She had to admit she'd been more interested in the programs she'd instituted to make workers happier and more productive than the actual mechanics of buying and selling. She'd stifled her employee programs to please Gordon. That was no longer an issue.

Cait straightened, setting her wine glass down with a crack and reaching for her phone. Why hadn't she thought of this before?

Ten minutes later, she had an interview for the next day at her alma mater, the University of Southern California.

It was time to move on.

News Alert: Earthquakes have increased along the Ring of Fire, as well as in less typical places, including India and Antarctica.

CHAPTER SEVEN

Damian surveyed their day's work. After deciding as a group that they wanted to fight to keep this area, to mount a last defense, they'd all risen at sunup, anxious to get to work. After eating a quick breakfast, they'd begun the exhausting job of removing the carnage from the sites by the lake.

The trash and excrement got loaded in the truck for a trip to the dump since nothing was fit even to recycle. The ground was scraped clean and prepped for the additional tents they planned to purchase. A makeshift kitchen of three picnic tables in a "U" shape with the seats detached gave them a place to prepare food. Wooden boxes were repurposed to hold dishware and kitchen supplies.

Their fire pit had been cleaned and sported a warming fire where they all now gathered, grimy but content with the day's work.

"We got a lot done," Gwen said.

"We sure did," Taegar agreed. She'd worked harder than anyone, a scowl on her face Damian had never seen before. A scowl that had softened as their cleaned-up camp had taken shape. Now, she stood with dirt smudges on her face and arms, sweat stains on the back of her t-shirt, and a broad smile on her face.

Valena stood with them, her crutches steadying her. "Yes, we did. Although none of you let me do much."

Everyone immediately had answers to that.

"You can't lift or shovel," Bhren said.

"You're still recovering from a concussion. And those ribs," Gwen exclaimed, patting Valena's hand.

"You were our watchdog." Luther chimed in.

Taegar hugged her. "And you sang for us, Valena."

"I would not have let you lift a finger if you'd tried," Damian finished.

Valena nodded, laughing. "Still, I think we're well past the quitting hour. I did manage to prepare a simple dinner over at the trailer."

Damian frowned. She shouldn't be doing anything. Her pale cheeks and drooping shoulders showed that the pain still bothered her.

Valena smiled at him. "It's nothing that took much to make and it will bolster your energy for the evening. I suggest, since they haven't turned the water off, that we all take an hour to clean up, then meet for dinner."

"I get first dibs on cleaning up," Luther called, already heading for the bathroom where the sinks still worked. Gwen and Wyeth said they'd take the last load in the truck to the dump and pick up more linens and a change of clothes for everyone, as well as a few more groceries. The money they made from odd jobs here and there wouldn't get them far, but they didn't need much, and had some put away for a rainy day. That drenching didn't need to be in liquid form, apparently.

~~~

After dinner, Damian walked out of camp alone,
~~~

crossing the street to the glade where they held most of their prayer groups. Somehow, whoever had vandalized their home had missed this place. This sacred spot, the place they'd each been inexplicably drawn to, was the reason they all fought for the land's survival.

He placed a hand on one of the trees, bowing his head. It was as if he could feel the life thrumming inside. Here, they were closer to communing with Earth than anywhere he'd ever been.

The evergreen trembled, yet no breeze stirred the limbs. A sadness emanated from it, a whisper of dire need. A glance at the tree's needles confirmed Damian's fears. Even with adequate rain, they were changing color from a vibrant green to rust, something that shouldn't happen. A blight, one he'd not noticed before, had taken hold. Needles covered the ground. Damian picked up a handful. They were dry and weightless as he let them sift through his fingers and fall away. He didn't have enough knowledge to understand why this tree failed to thrive, but he knew death when he saw it. This tree was well on its way.

Having always had an affinity with nature, Damian wandered around the edge of the glade, reaching out with his mind, searching for answers in the rough bark, the dry needles, the roots. All remained silent, leaving only the inference that decay grew in their midst.

He sat down in the center of the glade, wanting these few moments to clear his mind before the others came. As leader, it fell to him to initiate the group connection with Earth. He would search for that first tendril of unity that bound them all together.

Sitting cross-legged, he glanced around, the cool evening air adding a crispness that made him smile. Damian closed his eyes and began his meditative chants, getting lost in the movement of air, time, his breathing.

Peace filled him, as it always did when he meditated. Yet something else floated at the edge of his consciousness. A beckoning, a pulling on his attention, which had never happened to him before. Damian slowed his breathing further as he followed the thread. For the first time in Damian's years of doing this, everything around him melted away, replaced by some sort of vision.

An oak tree stood in front of him, wise and venerable in its ancientness. Its branches dipped in weariness when it sighed. It spoke no words, but one branch waived like a pointing arm and Damian followed its direction. Earth lay before them. A vibrant, green land with startling blue seas, free of the spoils of humankind. This was Earth before his time. Slowly, the green dimmed, replaced by the modern conveniences of people. The waters turned dark, then gray, the skies paled and filled with sickness.

Then, amid all this decay, a ray of hope. Light erupted from Earth in three different places, cauterizing the decay and pouring nutrients into the soil.

Earth had healed itself.

But how?

The vision faded and Damian reached for it, not ready for it to end. He wanted more, craved this ethereal contact with the land they sought to protect. He hung his head, left with nothing except a lingering sense of oneness and a puzzle. What did the vision mean? Unaware of how long he'd been sitting there with his eyes closed, he felt Valena settle beside him and take one of his hands. Then Taegar on the other side. One by one, the others joined him, chanting, feeling his wonder, his confusion.

Now was not the time to sort out this happenstance. Now, it was time to pray. To be one with Earth and ask for guidance. Damian settled his breathing, found the cadence of the others, and joined in. Once their rhythm had merged into one breath, one sigh, he began the prayer.

"Mother Earth, we treasure your leaves, your roots, the ground we sit upon. We thank you for clouds, which bring the waters that sustain us. We thank you for the animals, for you. For the sunshine that infuses all life with energy. For the oxygen we breathe and the fruits we eat. We are one with you. We are of the same accord."

He repeated the words over and over, slipping deeper into the moment until the air around them unified with their breath. For the first time, true sadness filled that sound. Fear flooded his mind, desperation slipping through the pores of his skin. Their skin. Damian felt the same chill from his earlier vision surround them all, a deep shudder of cold. Beneath them, surrounding them. Making them shiver along with the trees.

Had the tipping point been reached? Was this the end, with Earth so bespoiled it could no longer sustain life?

One last gift.

The words were a whisper of thought, foreign yet familiar.

Earth? Damian asked.

Dying. This. Only way. Use. Wisely.

What did it mean? Damian swayed with worry. Without opening his eyes, he knew everyone moved with him, their breaths quickening, heartbeats racing.

The ground beneath them shook, lightly at first, then harder. Damian broke the connection with his friends to steady himself. The earthquake grew beneath them, yet no tree tumbled.

The soil inside their circle cracked and split. Everyone scrambled back, watching as the hole grew to about the size of a circle Damian could make with his arms.

Everything around them grew still, an utter silence rang in the air. Before they could question the changes, white light erupted from the hole. Brilliant white light. It flowed up and up in a thick stream, wavering and wafting like a flag in the breeze.

Damian knew he should still be afraid. For his life. For Valena's. For everyone's. Yet the surge of fear he'd felt had subsided and he sensed nothing sinister from this light. The gentle undulations calmed him as the light flared skyward. Plus, he had knowledge to which the others weren't yet privy. He knew from whence this light had come and for what purpose.

Joy overwhelmed him. Tears of happiness streamed down his cheeks. When the ground stopped shaking, he stood and helped Valena up. She touched his cheek, his happiness wetting her fingers. "This is good?"

"This is good," he said. "Did you hear? Earth... She spoke to us."

Understanding dawned in their eyes, a euphoric glow filled them with awe. One by one, the pure essence of Earth's goodness infused them with joy.

Damian drew a deep breath, energy coursing through him. Vitality, strength, love. Everything good in the world filled him to overflowing.

For you. For some. To help. Save me.

He heard Earth clearly now. Felt the gift he'd been given.

Valena reached for his arm. She stood without crutches. On one leg, her injured one. "I'm healed." Wonder suffused her quiet voice.

Wyeth stared at the trees. "Everything seems so clear. And look." He walked over to the edge of the clearing and pointed to the light green tips of the tree Damian had considered to be dying a short while ago. "New growth. In a dead-looking tree. In October."

Gwen joined him, reaching for the tender needles. When she touched them, her eyes widened. "They grew."

She turned to Wyeth. "I saw them grow when I touched them."

Wyeth touched the tree, his smile as bright as his tear-misted eyes. Nothing happened that they could see, yet his grin widened. "I can't make things grow like Gwen, but there's a new clarity for me. I know how Earth is feeling. Gwen's emotions. Everyone's."

"You can read our minds?" Damian asked.

"Nothing so intrusive," Wyeth said, his voice reverent. "I get a sense of things, a feeling."

Gwen moved from tree to tree. Wherever she touched, growth accelerated. She raced around the glade, laughing and hugging trees, watching them sigh with happiness.

Luther straightened, flexing his muscles. "I feel like I could lift a building!" He walked over to a downed tree, bent and picked it up like it was a toothpick. He tossed it and they all watched it soar over the trees.

Damian tried Luther's trick. Strength flowed through him as he lifted another tree with ease. Bhren mimicked their actions, with the same result.

"Taegar?" Damian looked around and found her sitting beside the magical light. He crouched down beside her as she stared into the light with awe. "It's so beautiful," Taegar said. "I've never seen anything so beautiful."

"It is the *awen*," he said. "Earth's essence, gifted to heal us all."

When she reached out to touch the light, Damian stopped her hand. "We should probably understand a bit more about this before we start touching it."

Taegar blinked, then smiled at Damian. "The *awen* won't hurt us," she said. She settled her hand on the ground beside the light and a flower sprung to life. "It's here to help. It's here so I can weave more flowers. So more can grow from the soil. So we can all be happy again."

"Still, let's think this through before taking a step that might be irreversible, all right?"

"All right. For now." Taegar returned to staring at the light, her eyes shining with love.

Everyone wandered around the glade, testing their newfound abilities.

Damian sat next to Taegar, stunned by all that had happened. He could feel the *awen* thrumming through him. And Earth. She'd spoken to him. To them. How could that be?

He combed grass he'd never seen so lush and green. Dug through to the loam dark with nutrients. He picked some up in his hand and the glade transformed as he was carried into another vision.

Damian floated above the glade. Above the trees, soaring like an eagle. He could see the magic light streaming straight up. And there, in the distance. Another one. And a third. All three columns of brilliant, white light, twining together high in the sky. Earth's light, gifted to them to help Earth and, by default, humankind. Animals, sea life, plants, everyone and everything would benefit from this miracle.

Use the awen, Earth said to him. Make things grow. Heal. Make all understand. Last chance.

Damian opened his eyes. He was back in the glade, sitting next to Taegar with dirt in his hand as if he'd never left. He nodded. He knew what to do now. "Thank you, Earth," he whispered.

Brushing the dirt from his hand, Damian patted Taegar on the back and stood, calling everyone to join him near the light. Valena hugged him tight, staying inside his arms as he spoke.

"I've had a vision. I don't know if it's because of this— " he waved at the light behind them. "Or a coincidence. I've never had them before tonight."

"What did you see?"

"I saw two other streams of light and all three intertwined high in the sky. I— " He paused. This would be the part that others might have trouble believing. "I heard words. Earth's words."

He waited for their reactions. No one flinched, squinted, or otherwise indicated disbelief. Valena hugged him tight again. "What did Earth say?"

Damian let his love for Valena shine as he gazed at her, then back at the group. "That this was our last chance. We should use these powers to heal, to help things grow, to help humankind understand that changes are needed."

"Wow," Gwen said, staring at her hands.

"Wyeth?"

He stared off into space, which generally meant he was considering the options.

"I get a sense of wonder much bigger than us," he said, still looking off. "We're not the only ones who've been given this power. There are others."

"Good. Hopefully, we can gather them and work together to change attitudes."

"No," Wyeth said. "You don't understand. There are many others. Not just here, or surrounding the magical streams. They're spread throughout the world." He cocked his head. "If I had to guess, I'd say maybe a tenth of the world's population has been touched by the *awen*."

They all paused to consider what this meant.

"That's a lot of people," Luther said slowly.

"A lot of people we have to trust to do the right thing," Wyeth said.

"And, if they decide the opposite, that's a lot of people with the power to do some damage."

Perhaps seeking to reassure them, Valena spoke up.

"Some aspects of this gift can't be used to harm." She reached for Luther's hands. He'd done the bulk of the heavy work the day before and had cuts on his hands and arms to prove it. Valena held one hand between her two, then the other. After a few moments, she pulled her hands away. They all looked in awe at Luther's hands. They were completely healed.

"Wow," Taegar said, grabbing Luther's hands. She turned them over and over. There were no scars at all.

"How did you feel after doing that, Valena?" Bhren asked.

Good question. Damian searched his wife's face for any signs of stress and found none.

Valena laughed. "I feel fine. Great, even! I can't see how this could be used for ill."

Damian could. He looked at Luther, at the raw power the man oozed. He, himself, thrummed with that same energy. If someone with no moral compass got hold of this kind of power...

His blood froze. If Gordon Darcy was one of the select few...

"What's wrong?" Valena asked him quietly.

Damian took a deep breath and tried to still his racing heart. "I need to think something through before I talk about it."

She looked long and hard into his eyes before she nodded.

"For now," he said so everyone could hear. "How about we gather around and say a prayer of thanks to Earth, to the trees that give us oxygen, to the skies that rain water for us to drink, and all other things of nature that provide and nurture us, including this new blessing."

DESCENT

EARTH

Finally. The last of my energy is released into the world. Now, those who live upon my surface will understand. We must work together. That is the only way to survive.

I selected well. The humans I chose will work hard to change attitudes.

I am not certain it will be enough. Only time will tell.

If it is not, the consequences will be dire for all.

This is our last chance. If humanity cannot change, only the final doom will be left to them.

I am hopeful.

News Alert: People the world over are displaying talents never before seen. They've been coined "Mods," a shortened form of "Modifieds."

CHAPTER EIGHT

"Mods?" Luther growled. "They had to lump us all into one term like a bunch of lab rats? And what kind of name is that? Mods."

Taegar laughed. "I like it. Makes me feel trendy." She went over and kissed Luther on the cheek. That was the only thing making him smile this morning.

Damian agreed with Luther, though he kept that thought to himself. So much had changed since the revelation two nights ago that keeping up with the momentum wasn't easy. Within hours, people had begun arriving at the glade, drawn by the contemporary need to be the first one to document a new phenomenon, or by simple curiosity. Selfie-sticks abounded, along with cameras flashing and phones taking videos. One man had gotten in Luther's face over the lack of any wifi signal or hot spot.

"This is a closed campground, not a hotel," Luther had answered with more cordiality than Damian expected. He wasn't clear what had stopped Luther from doing bodily harm to the man, but he'd kept himself in check, stomping off and muttering something about doing the dishes.

Luther hated dish duty.

Wyeth, through his new perception, got the distinct impression that the same curiosity-seekers had arrived at the other two light streams, both emitting from inside caves. At least here, Damian and his friends could try to guide awareness, to show the importance of the *awen*.

Damian, Bhren, and Valena had tried to talk to these first visitors, to explain how monumental this was. None listened. It was all about the experience, not the meaning behind it.

Then even more curious people arrived, and Damian hoped they would have better luck convincing these folks that change was mandatory in the wake of this event. He stood on the outskirts, searching for the right person with whom to start a conversation.

A large group of people had gathered in the glade, staring at the light with varied expressions on their faces. Two men in hard hats looked disgusted. An older man in the back leaned against a tree, a wide smile on his face. Even further back, Damian could see a bald man with black eyes watching, his face devoid of emotion. He took note of the man, his dark looks, his "ready for a fight" stance. Whoever he was, he had a mission, and Damian strongly suspected it was not a mission that would mesh with their own. The man would bear watching.

Closer to where Damian stood, a young couple, hikers by their attire, sat with smiles on their faces, staring not at the light but each other, holding hands, showing their love. The grass around them blossomed with flowers. These two had been gifted.

"We should talk to them," Valena said, joining her husband and motioning to the couple.

"Definitely."

"I'll go."

Valena settled on the ground next to them. Soon, they were a triangle of joy and awe, speaking quietly.

Damian smiled. His wife had such a peaceful way about her. Now, that presence was even more profound. She would be better than him at conversing with people. She had infinite patience. Damian knew another trip to Washington lay before him, though he didn't envy himself the task. People needed convincing that this was a good thing, but also a wake-up call. He'd need his wife's patience, her perception, and most importantly, her diplomatic abilities. That meant a bus and train trip. Maybe it would allow them to spread the message in a grassroots kind of way.

For now, the more people who came to see the light stream, the better, though he found it hard to have their home so crowded. For now, no other choice presented itself. This was a gift to the world. Telling everyone to go away because the quiet beauty of this place had been disturbed would not be conducive to the acceptance of their message.

A dark-haired, clean-cut man walked down the path and into the clearing. He wore faded jeans and a t-shirt with a *Dark Side of the Moon* logo on it. When he caught sight of the light stream, his jaw dropped. His gaze followed it up until it met the sky. Several times he scanned the phenomenon. He closed his mouth, but his eyes were open wide.

He pulled a pack off his back and set it down, digging inside. What he pulled out surprised Damian. A Geiger counter. Valena had convinced him nothing harmful would emanate from the light, but others would take more convincing.

This man was a scientist. The first he'd seen show up. Damian drew a deep breath and pushed off the tree he'd leaned against. This was where it should start. With a man of reason. A man of science. If he could convince him, he could convince anyone. Right?

He walked over to him.

"Pretty amazing, isn't it?"

"Definitely," the man said, smiling.

"A miracle."

"I'm not sure I'd go that far."

"Ah, a skeptic."

The man shrugged. "A scientist. I'm paid to be skeptical."

"It's kind of hard to refute this kind of proof."

"You sound like a believer."

"I am. I was here when it happened."

"Exactly who I was hoping to meet, then," he said, holding out his hand. "Tom Gallows, from the local United States Geological Laboratory."

"Damian Royan. Resident druid."

It was a good sign that the man didn't blink at the druid reference. Not many knew, or wanted to know, anything about their beliefs.

Tom glanced at the light, then back at Damian. "I'd love to talk to you about how this occurred."

"I'd be happy to tell you everything I know about the *awen*. Have you had breakfast?"

Tom nodded.

"Then how about some tea back at our campsite."

With only a touch of hesitation, he followed Damian away from the light, the pull to learn winning out over any reluctance to leave the glade.

Back in camp, Damian made tea, then they settled on opposite sides of the picnic table.

"Nice setup you have here."

"Thanks," Damian said, glancing around, trying to see

things with a stranger's eyes. "It's...gone through some changes recently."

"Still, looks comfortable."

"It is. Do you like to camp?"

"I work in a lab with no windows, so I try to get outdoors as much as possible."

Definitely someone Damian could like. "What questions can I answer for you?"

Tom's eyes brightened. "You might be sorry you asked that. How did this happen? What precipitated it? Did the light just burst out? How did it feel?"

Tom fired questions back-to-back, hardly pausing for breath. Damian laughed, holding up his hands. "How about if I just tell you what happened?"

Tom nodded, digging out a notepad and pen.

Old school. Another reason to like the man. Taking a deep breath, Damian began, leaving nothing out. It still filled him with awe that this had even occurred. The retelling made his heart swell again over the gift Earth had given them.

"You say you got these new powers from this light?"

"Not powers. Well, not exactly. More like enhancements of our natural abilities."

Tom shook his head. "I don't understand."

"Well, Valena, my wife, has always been an empath and had good instincts for healing. Now, those traits are stronger. She can touch someone and aid their healing. Another person in our group is a botanist. Her affinity with nature has increased tenfold. When she touches things, they grow. Visibly."

"What about you?"

Damian grinned, walked to the end of the cement and wood picnic table, and lifted it like it was a toothpick.

Eyes wide, Tom grabbed a hold of the table to keep

from slipping off. Damian set it down in time to catch the cups sliding toward the edge.

"Okay," Tom said, clearing his voice. "That's pretty impressive. But...people do that. Every day. They work out and improve their strength through natural methods."

"For me, this isn't the biggest change. I can see things others can't. If I connect with the earth, the soil, I have a prescience I've never known before. I can see, not really the future, but tendencies. Ways things could go."

"That's a little hard to believe."

"I've done it. I haven't left this area since the *awen* arrived, yet I can describe in detail what the other two points of release look like. I can see them in my mind. Wyeth, one of the people who live at camp here, has always been the pragmatist of our group. He's the voice of reason, the one who can look at all sides of a situation. Now, he can actually reach out and sense people's emotions, how they're reacting to, well, anything."

Tom took a moment to process, his mouth hanging open. "I'd love to talk to him."

"He's struggling right now with the influx of people. New talent plus more people have given him a whopper of a headache. He and Gwen, his wife, have gone hiking in the hills to give him some relief."

"If what you're saying is true, I can see how hard this could be for him."

"We're all dealing with these new....modifications." Damian frowned.

"I've heard that term. Mods. Doesn't feel right."

"No, but we don't get a say in it. Here's the thing. It's not just me, Wyeth, and the others in our group. Wyeth thinks at least ten percent of the world's population will be stronger, healthier, more able to help. All because of light emitted by Earth in three places less than one hundred miles from each other. It's pretty phenomenal when you think of it."

Tom nodded, picking up the half-spilled tea they'd both forgotten.

Damian climbed on his metaphorical soapbox. "That's how Earth wants us to spread the healing. By touch, by helping, by convincing others to change their ways. That's also why I'm telling you. No one else knows as much as I've told you. And for now, I'd appreciate it remaining that way." He didn't want to think about the panic and ensuing witch hunt if folks knew just how many people now had enhanced capabilities because of the *awen*.

Tom took a deep breath. "I can't keep my findings and interpretation of this light from my superiors. That's my job. But I can, and will, keep the rest to myself. Although, I highly doubt everyone who's been touched by this will keep it secret."

"Agreed. Still, I'd like to downplay it for now. At least for myself. We need to get the government involved in changing people's minds and I'd like to talk to them without bias."

"Oh, they're already involved," Tom said. "I'm here at the request of the powers-that-be, and more will be coming."

"We knew that would happen." Damian looked around. "Somehow, I don't think our home will remain the sanctuary it's been for much longer."

Tom nodded.

"Still, I hope people can recognize the sacredness of this site. It's special, and it deserves to be treated as such."

"I'm not a religious person, but I recognize special when I see it," Tom said as he stood, "and I agree. This place needs to be preserved as such. Want to help me take some readings and gather facts? Maybe we can come up with enough proof to convince Washington."

"Sure. By the way, what did that Geiger counter show?"

"Nothing. Not one bit of radiation."

"I thought so," Damian said.

They walked back to the clearing together, both deep in thought about how best to help humanity come to terms with the momentous change that had just occurred in all their lives.

~~~

"They did what?" Gordon didn't yell often. It was easier to get your point across with cold steel than with hot pokers, but this was absurd.

"They yanked the lease-rights to the Black Hills property."

Gordon clutched the phone. Vice president or not, Ramsey was getting on his last nerve.

"They can't do that. The deal is closed. That land is mine!"

"Well, they did."

"Gah!" Gordon felt the anger building within him. He needed something to hit, to assuage his rage. "Do we have any recourse?"

"Not since those light streams showed up. Zealots have set up shop all around the site—scientists, priests, truth-seekers. And whatever those things are, Washington is very interested."

Damn it. He'd been so close to the biggest cash-in of his life, and now it lay all but destroyed by a bunch of do-gooders. How the hell had this happened?

He hung up on Ramsey. The man had nothing else to tell him. In fact, Ramsey was no longer of any use to him at all. Probably best to deal with that now. Gordon pulled a burner flip phone from his drawer and spoke briefly, then
~~~

snapped the phone in two and tossed it in the garbage.

Even that didn't settle him. Those streams of lights. If they hadn't shown up, he'd be in like Flynn, flying high, and would never have to think about the next score. He'd be set.

A week had passed since the skies of South Dakota and Wyoming had lit up with what folks were calling magical light. Why had it happened right over the largest oil reserve in the world? In the exact spot Gordon planned to drill.

The conversation he'd had with that hippie came back to him. The man, Damian Royan, had called the land sacred.

Hmpf. Nothing was sacred, including land.

Some people had enhanced abilities because of that light or whatever it was. Magical. Hah! Gordon had noticed no difference in his own body. No increased strength or cunning. Well, he didn't need more of that last one. He had enough to get him through whatever roadblock stood in his way.

This light was a roadblock, that's all. It was time to check it out first hand, so he could formulate a plan to get rid of it and get his Black Hills project back on track.

Yes, he needed to see this anomaly in person. Gordon picked up his phone. "Call for my car and my jet. I'm going to South Dakota."

~~~

Cait found the university office building with little trouble. Students milled around. At least, if all the strategic holes in their jeans were any indication, they were students. She smoothed her pencil skirt, thinking about all the suits hanging in her closet. It might be time to rethink her wardrobe. After all, she was venturing out in a whole new vein, planning to leave the corporate world behind. At least
~~~

for a while.

She pushed through the door and on to the next iteration of her life, smiling but nervous.

An hour later, she exited, her smile wider than before, her shoulders more relaxed and the nerves pretty much gone. She'd done it. She'd interviewed for a teaching position in business/human resources. Cait wanted to help shape ideals before college students started their careers, help them see how effective a good working environment could be.

She reached her car and climbed in, sinking into the leather seats, happier than she'd been in a long time.

"Thanks, Dad," she said, capping the last word with sarcasm. "You've given me the first and last gift I'll ever need from you. My freedom."

After a stop at the grocery store, she drove home to the only family she needed. After seeing the babysitter off, Cait changed into sweats—clothing built to handle whatever two-year-olds could throw at her—and went into the playroom to see what her girls were up to.

She froze. The entire couch floated about six inches in the air as if held by strings. Yet no one stood at each end, holding it.

Willow lay beneath it, only her feet showing.

"No!" Cait leaped toward her daughter, fear cutting off her scream. She grabbed Willow by the legs and yanked her out from under the couch. The child clutched a yellow ball like it was a lifeline. Cait hugged her tight, then set Willow back from her to check for any injuries, only to see the girl's lips quiver as she let loose with a wail. Fallon quickly joined her, the couch dropping with a loud thunk behind them.

Cait sank to the floor and pulled both daughters into a hug. She tried to calm them as she willed her own racing heart to slow down. What had just happened? Had she actually seen a couch levitate?

She smoothed Willow's curly auburn hair with her hand, patting Fallon's back as their cries turned to whimpers, then disappeared completely. The girls crawled off her lap and began to toss the found ball back and forth. Willow still threw the ball wide, as she always had. But Fallon's accuracy was dead on now. She got the ball to her sister every single time. It was uncanny.

Cait couldn't believe what she was about to ask. She'd been watching the news about that strange phenomenon occurring in South Dakota and Wyoming, but that was so far away. Still, she'd seen what she'd seen. She gulped and caught her eldest twin's attention. "Did you—did you lift that couch?"

"Yes." Her two-year-old enthusiasm almost made Cait smile. Almost.

"How could you do that?"

"Couch easy. I show you." Fallon stood.

"No!" Cait did not need a repeat of that. Panic edged its way into her throat, making it hard to breathe. Somehow, without Cait's permission or knowledge, her daughter had been granted an extraordinary talent, and that scared Cait more than anything had in a long time. What else had Fallon been given? A virus? Some mutation that would change her somehow? How had this happened? Why?

She needed time to think, figure this out. Until then— "Fallon, come here." When her daughter stood in front of Cait, she rubbed the girl's arms. "You can move things just by thinking about them?" she said, softening the question with a smile.

"I ver' strong." Fallon pumped her arms like they'd done in play so many times. "I want, it happens."

Cait tugged gently on a strand of Fallon's strawberry-blonde hair, its waves so different from her sister's tight curls. "For now, I need you to stop moving couches. Anything, really."

"But ball under couch."

"It's not anymore." Cait could see by the hands on hips that her stubborn daughter would not acquiesce. "I tell you what. When the ball, or anything else, is hiding under the couch, you come get me first, all right?"

Fallon scrunched her face, thinking hard.

"Please?"

Her daughter beamed. "Okay, Mommy. You aks'd nice." She ran back to play with her sister, leaving Cait sitting there, stunned. How had this happened? She tried to remember what she knew about the phenomenon taking over the world. Light streams, a burgeoning, growth-infused Earth? Rumors that some people have enhanced skills. Had Fallon been touched by this...magic? And, if so, how would it affect her life. Her growth? Her chances to be happy? Would she become some lab experiment, taken by the government to study?

God, no. Cait absolutely would not let that happen. Until she knew more, they would need to keep this very, very quiet.

She stood and went to the kitchen to prepare dinner. This day had ended up completely different from its hopeful start. She couldn't even begin to describe the emotions swirling through her, a million feelings run amok. Cait shook her head. One thing was certain. She had a lot of research to do after the twins went to bed tonight. And none of it had anything to do with class planning or teaching.

News Alert: There's still no explanation for the Mod-magic, as some call it. Interviewed mods are jubilant and already helping. Diseases cured, blights on the earth eliminated. Is this a miracle or the devil's work? Only time will answer that question.

CHAPTER NINE

Damian could see the changes occurring almost hourly. Their campground was overrun with people. The National Guard had been brought in to maintain some semblance of order and he'd heard the same was happening at the other two sites. Damian frowned, wondering who would be allowed into the caves that were the sources of both other lights. He'd been hard-pressed to convince Major Swanton, who led the Guard, that no one should be denied entry here. That this was a gift to the world. In the end, still unconvinced, the man chose a wait-and-see method.

"Just so you know," the major said, "if it gets any more out of control, I'll close this place down."

Their own camp looked nothing like it had, now overflowing with people and supplies. At least they had clean toilet facilities and showers again. Everyone wanted to see the light. Zealots, certain this was a message from God. Technicians, scientists, all trying to study the *awen*. The vital breath in druid terms. Earth magic. The vigor that had infused Damian when the light emerged had stuck with him, with all of them. It was an amazing and blessed feeling and attitudes were already changing. Not about the powers Earth had given them, but the need to change how they lived, worked, and used natural resources.

Damian's little group expanded, with more people opting to stay, to adopt a simpler, more focused lifestyle. They'd welcomed them all, inviting them to join the circle, to be part of the change. Some did. Others, those with doubts, stayed at the fringes, waiting for the next happening, proof to help them decide what they should believe or deny. And always, at the back of the pack, the man with the dark eyes. Ever watchful, ever wary. Who was he? Damian tried to be accepting of all, but something bothered him about the man.

At least Washington, D.C., finally took some notice. The senator who'd rebuffed Damian so completely only weeks earlier now requested his presence. And, according to Valena, that meant putting on the one suit he owned. Again. Damian rolled the material haphazardly and shoved the dratted thing into his backpack.

"That will make an excellent impression," Valena said. "A suit with more wrinkles in it than your forehead."

"I don't see why I have to put on airs. This isn't me."

Valena pulled the suit out of his pack. "If you want to make an impression, you need to play the game." She folded the suit, nicely this time, and put it in her case, which lay on the table next to Damian's pack. She turned and placed her hands on his chest. "I'm not asking you to be someone else, only to look the part for a little while. Do you remember those Comic-Cons we attended?

Damian nodded, pulling her into his arms. They'd had extravagant costumes, and had gotten a lot of appreciation for the intricacy of their elven designs.

"It's like that. You have to look the part so people will take you seriously."

"Nobody took us seriously in those costumes."

"Everyone took us seriously. Those costumes were awesome, and they put laughter back in our lives."

True words. Those had been early days in their relationship, when they'd needed joy to dispel the darkness. Now, the gloom encroached again. With such an amazing gift being offered to humanity, Damian found it hard to understand how some could want to manipulate it for their own agenda. Yet those rumors circulated. That was why he needed to be in Washington. To make sure they understood. This was a one-time gift. A last-gasp effort to save...everything. His wife was right. He needed to play the part so they'd listen.

"When did you get so smart?" he asked, capitulating as she no doubt knew he would.

"When I married you."

He kissed her. Touching her, being with her, never grew old and always renewed him. Still, he needed something more at the moment. Some sort of sign that D.C. was the right place to be.

"What say we take a walk down to the lake. We've got time before we have to leave for the bus."

"I'd like that."

Damian tucked her arm in his and they walked the path until they were lakeside. Small by most standards, the serene emerald waters were a sight that would never get old. Like Valena's calming demeanor, this view centered him. Now, though, it teemed with people. Scientists in boats, testing waters and fish. People gawking at the new growth that sprouted everywhere. He smiled as Taegar led a man to one of the pine trees, showing him the light green of new growth, something that shouldn't be happening in October. The young man held his hand with gentle care beneath new needles sprouting from the tree, as if afraid to touch them. Yet another man took samples of dirt at the base of the tree, focused more on the science than the wonder.

Taegar touched the crouching scientist on the shoulder and he looked up as she pointed to the tender needles. With a quick nod of his head, he bent back to his task. Taegar, undaunted, reached down and nudged him to stand. She touched the new growth and it doubled its length. This time, the man took notice. His jaw dropped and his hands fell slack at his side.

"How did you do that?" he asked.

"It's the light. Earth gave me this ability to save the world."

She wandered on to the next tree, both men now following her like acolytes as she showed them the magic of renewal.

Damian leaned down to whisper in Valena's ear. "I want to find a quiet place to meditate before we leave."

"Our spot?"

He nodded. They headed for the promontory and quickly climbed up. Sitting beneath the oak tree that always brought him peace, Damian closed his eyes, knowing Valena would watch for any intrusion.

He focused on Earth, brushed his hands through the grass beneath him. Touched the soil. The vision was immediate.

The man with dark eyes stood there. Right in Damian's spot. With a can of something. Grease? Oil? He poured it down the wall.

Struck by the nature of this sinister act, Damian's heart pounded. This was the past. The day Valena had fallen. This was the man who'd hurt his wife.

Damian raced to the man, his clenched fists ready to take their vengeance upon him. He slammed his fist into the man's jaw, meeting air instead of the satisfying connection with skin and bone he wanted.

He could not change the past. That's what this vision told him. But at least now he knew who had done this. The why... Well, that would come. He fully planned to seek out this man. Washington could wait.

Damian opened his eyes, his heart still not calmed.

"What's happened?" Valena asked, worry in her eyes. "What did you see?"

Should he tell her? No. He didn't want to worry her. Not until he got some answers. "Muddy waters," he said. "The way ahead is unclear to me."

She looked off into the distance. "I know you were seeking clarity."

He certainly got that, didn't he? Except, not the kind he wanted.

Valena continued to look beyond Damian.

"What's the matter?"

"I thought I saw movement, off in the trees."

Damian strode to where she pointed and saw nothing. No person, animal, nothing. Looking down, faint boot prints depressed the grass. Had someone seen him during the vision? Was this some new trouble brewing?

Luther poked his head over the top of the wall. "It's time to go."

Damian nodded, and with one last glance at their lake, he and Valena walked back to camp with Luther. Damian wanted more than anything to find the man from his vision. Pulling Wyeth aside, he told him what he'd seen.

"You have to go to D.C.," Wyeth said.

Damian shook his head. "I need to find this guy."

"That means telling Valena about the vision you just told me you held back from her."

Damian raked a hand through his hair. He really didn't want to worry his wife anymore. "You're right. I'll tell her after we're on our way."

"We'll keep an eye out," Wyeth said. "You go. Wow Washington. Knock 'em dead."

Leaving rankled when danger seemed to surround their circle. His head told him Wyeth was right. His heart was another story altogether. Heaving a deep sigh, he nodded.

"Be careful," Damian said, clapping Wyeth on the shoulder.

"You, too."

With nothing left to say, Damian grabbed his pack and Valena's suitcase and headed for the truck. Luther climbed in the driver's seat. "Wyeth and I figured you'd want to arrive in time for the bus, so I'm taking you."

Damian laughed.

Gwen stuck her head inside the truck, handing Valena a sack. "Some food for the trip."

Valena clasped her hand. "Thank you."

'Take care of...everything," Damian said.

"We'll try," Wyeth intoned from behind Gwen. "It's pretty crazy around here."

Was it ever. When Wyeth winced and touched his head, Damian wondered if he should go with them, get a break himself. Though, was it any less populated in Washington, D.C.?

Before he could say anything, Luther put the truck in gear and pulled away.

At the station, Luther made quick work of their goodbyes and went off to gather supplies while he was in town.

"Well, it's just you and me, husband," Valena said after they had their tickets and sat waiting for the bus to arrive.

"I like that idea, Mrs. Royan." He cuddled her into his

shoulder on the bench. "I like it very much. Though, I do need to tell you something."

"About the vision you had earlier that you didn't want to tell me about?"

Damian hugged her. "How do you know me so well?"

"Because you're the other half of my heart and soul."

"And you are mine." So he told her about the dark-eyed man.

Valena took it in stride and, when he'd finished, only said, "Next time, tell me right away. I can handled it."

That fact had just been reinforced. "I'm sorry. I know you're a strong woman."

"And even knowing that, you still try to protect me." She laughed, then they were called for boarding.

Once settled on the bus to Kansas City, where they'd connect with the train to D.C., they said goodbye to their home for who knew how long. If things went well in D.C., they'd stay as long as necessary to effect change. This was too important to let a little homesickness pull them away. The future of Earth and humanity hinged on whether or not Congress could be convinced that this was their last opportunity to make changes. Earth had given humankind the power to fix things. All they had to do now was pick up the mantle, spread the healing, and enjoy the bounty provided.

It seemed like an almost unclimbable mountain, but with Earth's gift, maybe they could glimpse the summit. If not now, then soon.

"It will be as it will be," Valena said, placing a hand on his arm.

Damian nodded, entwining their fingers together as he watched the land pass by out the window. Was it his imagination or did everything look...sharper. More colorful and vibrant. He smiled. The healing process had begun.

~~~

At three in the morning, they staggered off the bus and grabbed a taxi to the train station. Once there, they sat on hard benches like zombies until their train arrived. Late, of course.

"We should have flown," Valena said.

"I'm not going to ask that of you."

Her smile was tired. "It would be so much easier. You could just knock me out and we'd be there."

"Ah," Damian said, capturing her hand in his as he resettled his sore butt on the bench. "Then I wouldn't have you all to myself for two whole days."

"But we'd be rested and ready to take Washington by storm."

"We'll do that anyway, tired or rested, love. We have to."

Valena's nod faded as she slumped beside him. Damian put his arm around her, nudging her to lay with her head in his lap. "Try to sleep. I'll wake you when the train arrives."

"You need sleep, too."

"I'll sleep on the train."

With a gentle sigh, she followed his advice and her breathing soon evened out. Damian sat vigil, trying to work out in his head how he would convince one senator after another of the importance of his quest. And what to do about the vision he'd seen just before they left. That man must pay for his crime.

Valena stirred in her sleep, his disquiet filtering into her dreams. He eased his fisted hands, forced himself to relax, to be in the moment.

By 9 a.m. they were on the train trying to doze away an all but sleepless night, exhausted, heads together, minds filled with the fragile tranquility of the knowledge they
~~~

wouldn't have to transfer again. In twenty-eight hours, they'd be in D.C.

Another day or so, and they'd know what the political climate was and whether they had a chance to affect anything.

Damian hoped and prayed they could.

~~~

Gordon Darcy's private plane landed at the small airstrip outside of Rapid City. With little delay, he disembarked and was soon in a limo headed for his hotel. He'd spent the airtime reading everything he could about what had happened and about the ragtag bunch of hippies that lived at ground zero. His anger at Damian Royan and his group wasn't logical, but they'd been present at the inception of this wave of evolution and he had no one else to be angry with.

The rumors of humans who'd gained exceptional abilities since the appearance of the light streams intrigued him. Strength, healing, the ability to make things grow. Even, he'd heard, a sort of prescience. Oh, what he could do with that talent in his portfolio. He could rule the world.

To see if it was possible, he intended to visit this light. His cunning, his ability to calculate the odds and make things happen, that should be rewarded. He would have his piece of this so-called magic.

"You call this a hotel?" he asked his secretary as they pulled up.

"It's the best in the city," Rose answered.

God, but he hated backwoods towns, with their basic services and subpar amenities. Still, he'd sent himself on this cockamamie trip. He would see this light stream up close, then determine his next step.

Gordon exited the limo and walked past the bellboy as his secretary took care of the details. They shared the
~~~

elevator with their luggage, something he wasn't used to. And the suite, the best the hotel had to offer, looked no larger than a breadbox. Only one sitting room, one large bedroom with en suite, and one smaller bedroom, also with its own bathroom. Rose would be staying there. He needed her close. Eyeing her up and down, he wondered how far he could push their relationship.

When she glanced at him then immediately turned away, Gordon shut the door on that thought. This girl was the one person he'd kept at arm's length because she did her job well. He needed to keep it that way or he'd be looking for another secretary.

"Order me some dinner, then leave me alone for the rest of the night," he told her. "Arrange my ride for the morning. I want to go out to that property first thing."

"Yes, sir," she said, disappearing into her room.

~~~

The next morning, Gordon settled into his limo for the ride out to the Mt. Rushmore area. He'd been there once as a kid. He hadn't thought it was worth the parking cost to see dead presidents' images carved in stone. Apparently, the whole process had taken seventeen years. And nearby, the Crazy Horse monument was still being carved, mostly the old fashioned way. If he'd headed the project, lasers and targeted explosions would have finished the job ten times faster. Time was money.

The limo pulled over on the side of the road.

"What's the matter?" he asked the driver.

"I'm sorry, sir. Everyone wants to see this anomaly. There's a roadblock up ahead. They won't let me get any closer than this."

In a rare show of emotion, Gordon pounded the interior of the limo. "This is ridiculous." He reached for the door handle. "Wait here. I'll go talk to them."
~~~

Five minutes later and out of ideas, Gordon strode to the driver's door. "I'll be walking from here."

"Yes, sir. Here's my card. I've been told I must wait back a couple of miles. Call me when you're ready, or close to it, and I'll come back."

This day was going from bad to worse. "Fine," Gordon growled, already turning up the road. It was about a mile to the campground where he'd find all the action. The last time Gordon had walked this far, he'd been a kid. His exercise came from his home and office gyms. Walking wasn't his thing.

As the mile grew longer and his shoes got dirtier, Gordon's mood turned fouler and fouler. He'd left Rose back at the hotel, preferring to do this thing on his own, but it would be nice to have someone take his anger out on right now. He really needed to vent.

Finally, he reached the entrance to the campground and his man waiting for him exactly where he said he'd be.

"It's crazy here," Gordon said.

"And getting worse."

"Idiots. What do they think this is? Some sort of shrine?"

The man nodded. "Pretty much. The one in charge left yesterday."

"Royan? Where for?"

"Washington."

Gordon let out a harsh laugh. "That's no cause for concern. He won't get very far there."

"Saw something a little strange before he left."

More strange than what had been happening already? That piqued Gordon's interest.

"What?"

"That man, Royan? He went into some sort of trance. I think... "

"Spit it out, man."

"I think he was having a vision. Like he could see the future." The man with the dark eyes frowned. "Or the past."

"Visions? Bah."

The man shrugged. "I only report what I see and hear. And something he said afterward... Well, it was as if he'd seen what I did to cause his wife's accident."

Gordon knew all about Valena Royan's fall. He'd authorized the attempt to get those people off his property. Property now yanked out from under his feet because of whatever they did to bring on the light streams. His bad mood deepened.

"Let's go see this damned thing."

The man led him by the barrier meant to make people pause and turn around. Gordon barely noticed it. They strode along what he presumed was the path to the clearing, since more and more people came and went from that direction.

The world around him brightened as he neared. Everything looked more vivid, and, even though people were pretty much shoulder to shoulder, it was eerily quiet. Only the slight electric resonance of the light ahead of him and the occasional rustle of people intruded.

Gordon shivered. He didn't like this one bit. His man stayed back while he pushed through to get a closer look. No one even minded. It was like they were zombies standing in awe of some monolith. "These people are insane." His muttered words echoed off the wall of trees surrounding them. Still, no one paid him any heed. Frowning, Gordon made it past the final layer of walking dead and looked up at the light for the first time.

He looked up and up and up. It seemed to go on for infinity, just as described.

Realizing his mouth hung slack, he snapped it shut. Okay, so it was a good-looking light. He'd give it that. It was brilliant, yet it didn't hurt his eyes to stare at it. It was calming, even to him. He could feel the tension leaving him, feel the goodness starting to flow into—

Oh, hell no. Gordon shook himself and scrubbed at his eyes. He wasn't going to fall under some magical spell like these other saps. No. He was here for a purpose. If he could no longer own the Black Hills property, this magic was going to give him something in return for that loss. He wanted total control, and nothing less would satisfy him. He wanted more power than anyone else had. Those talents would be his. Reminding himself of that, he walked straight forward and thrust his hands into the light.

A collective gasp spread through the crowd. Gordon didn't hear it. He focused instead on the light. It was...talking to him. Whispering, really. Words he couldn't understand at first. He twisted his hands inside the stream, searching for some tendril he could grab hold of. "You will give me your power. You owe me."

This is not for you, Gordon Darcy.

Shock would have yanked his hands from the light if some force he couldn't see hadn't done it for him. The power threw him clear of the people—who stood with their mouths agape—all the way to the other side of the clearing. He landed against a tree, his head connecting with a thunk.

Gordon Darcy, rejected by the magic, slid to the ground and passed into unconsciousness.

~~~

Cait Darcy hadn't left the house in two days. She'd ordered in groceries and attacked the Internet in search of anything that would explain how her two-year-old could levitate furniture with just a thought. She watched the plastic jar of animal crackers on top of the fridge lift and
~~~

move through the air until it settled between the twins. Willow clapped her hands, laughing, as the lid twisted all on its own. Both twins dove in, their hands tangling as they tried to get too many cookies out of too small an opening.

How had this happened? She'd read about people all over the world gaining different powers. None of the stories mentioned any sort of levitation. Cait was beside herself with worry that this might have a detrimental effect on Fallon. She needed answers. It appeared that to get them, she'd have to go to the source. One of the light streams. Except she couldn't leave the girls with anyone. Not with Fallon testing these new powers of hers and Willow egging her on.

Cait walked over and picked up the container of cookies, screwed the lid back on. "No more until dinner."

"I want more," Fallon said, holding out her hand.

Cait could feel the jar trying to tug itself out of her hands. "No!" she said, too roughly. "Not until after dinner!"

The lips on both girls started to tremble. Before an all-out wail could begin, Cait shoved the cookies out of sight, then pulled her daughters into her arms. "I'm sorry, sweeties, that I yelled at you." She said the words over and over, soothing them until they quieted. Willow moved off to pick up a toy. Cait turned Fallon in her lap so she could see her face. She didn't look any different. No extra sparkle in her eyes, no growth spurt. She appeared the same as she had yesterday, and last week, and the week before that. "Sweetie, I need to ask you a favor." Again.

Cait's daughter stared back, her green eyes reflecting Cait's own.

"You can do special things." Cait added a smile to make certain Fallon knew she wasn't in trouble.

"I strong!" She lifted her arms to show muscle that

hadn't even formed yet.

"Yes," Cait said. "You're very strong. And you can make things move."

"Like cookies." Fallon looked around, ready for more treats.

"Yes, like cookies. But...you mustn't do that. Just like we talked. You have to stop doing that without asking."

"I hungie."

"I know you think you're hungry, but you must ask permission before eating. I'll get some cookies for you if it's time and you've been a good girl."

Fallon frowned, working her way up to a good pout.

Cait made her decision. "We're going on a trip, and I need you to act like any other little girl and not do these extra things. It's very important. Do you understand what I'm saying?"

Fallon scrunched up her face like she was trying really hard to process what her mommy had said. Any other time, Cait would have laughed at her antics. This situation was just too serious to find any humor. She was worried for her daughter. Scared to death that this would harm her in some way.

She needed answers. So they were going to South Dakota.

News Alert: "Forces are at work that we do not yet understand," the president said. "It feels like the chess pieces are moving, yet there is no clear indication of who's winning, or even who is playing the game."

CHAPTER TEN

After a couple of hours in various cramped positions, Damian gave up his attempts to sleep. He slipped past his slumbering wife and made his way to the dining car, surprised to find only a few people there midmorning. An older couple played cribbage at one table, the remnants of their breakfast sitting next to the pegging board. A family sat at another table. Father, mother, and three children, one looking like he wasn't much more than a year old, and quite energetic. The boy ran up and down the dining car, weary parents looking on.

Damian smiled at his antics, then grew pensive. He and Valena had talked many times about having children. She had such a nurturing way. She'd be a great mother, and he knew she wanted children. It hadn't happened for them yet, and after almost losing her during that miscarriage, he wasn't certain he wanted it to. Maybe they'd look at adoption.

Valena must not have been sleeping soundly because she joined him, scooting into the seat across the table, following his gaze. The hint of longing in her face tore at Damian's heart. He would give her the world if he could, yet this simple thing was beyond his ability to provide.

She clasped his hand. "It's not our time yet. Not for this."

"I don't know how you manage to keep such a positive attitude about everything." Damian stroked her hand as they watched the boy climb up onto a seat a few tables down.

"I don't always, as you well know. I get a sense, though. We'll have our moment to be parents. The time isn't right for us yet."

The little boy climbed onto the table. His parents had looked away to cut up food for the others.

"Is that an *awen*-gifted prescience?" he asked Valena as he kept an eye on the boy.

"I don't think so. It's more of a...mothering kind of thing. Children are in our future. I feel very strongly about that. Just not yet."

Damian looked at her. Her face was serene, her demeanor calm. She seemed okay waiting. He reached for her hand. "When it happens, you will be an amazing mother."

Valena smiled at him, the hint of tears brightening her eyes. "We will be great parents."

"Now probably isn't the best time, anyhow, with everything in such turmoil."

"Yes, I agree—"

A scream cut off her words. Damian turned to see the boy Superman off the table. He leaped out of his seat, but couldn't get to the child fast enough. Even Damian heard the crunch of bone as the boy hit the floor.

His parents jumped up as the boy's happy screech turned to wails of terror and pain. Damian got to him first, trying to keep him from getting up until they could check the extent of his injuries. The mother pushed Damian out of the way.

"Timmy, Timmy. Oh, my God." She picked up the boy, clutching him to her, which made him wail even harder. The father stood behind her, looking left, right, anyway that might offer some help.

The young man working in the kitchen joined them. With four adults and one wailing child in the tight train aisle, it was hard for anyone to move.

"Help," the mother cried.

"Please, we need a doctor," the father said to the worker.

"I'll call the conductor," he said.

"Wait."

Everyone's heads turned at Valena's quiet request. Damian stepped into a booth, giving his wife room to get to the boy. "I can help," she said.

Her voice was low, soothing, its effect calming everyone. The father focused on her, the mother looked at her with pleading eyes. "Are you a doctor?"

His wife remained focused on the boy as she answered, her voice quiet, calming, trying to gain their trust. "I'm a mod. I have healing powers."

The boy's wails trailed off to whimpers as he watched her with big, round, watery eyes.

"It hurts, doesn't it? I want to help. You're such a sweet, sweet boy. I can make the pain go away. Make you feel all better." Valena looked at the mother, waited until she nodded, then moved closer and closer to them as she spoke. When she reached out a hand toward the boy, the mother clutched him more tightly

Valena paused, holding the mother's gaze. Waiting.

"Can you really help him?" she asked in a timid voice.

Valena nodded.

And Damian worried. Since things had changed, since the magic had arrived, she'd done a few minor things to help people heal. But this was most likely a broken bone. She'd never attempted to heal anything this painful before. He had no idea what it would do to her. Fictional stories of healers who took on the injury themselves, then healed, roared through his mind. He touched Valena's shoulder.

She patted his hand. "It's all right. I can do this."

Focusing on the boy, Valena placed a hand on his pant leg. "What's your name, honey?"

"Timmy," his mother answered.

"Timmy, you were great, but only Superman can fly. Now, we need to figure out what got hurt."

Low and soothing, she kept talking, indicating everything she was doing as she rubbed the boy's legs, feet, torso. When she got to his arm, the crying started anew.

"See the odd twist to his arm?" Valena asked the parents, who both nodded.

"I'm going to lay my hands on it, Timmy," she said, smiling at the boy. "This isn't going to hurt. I'm not going to move you. I'm only going to rest my hand there."

When the parents gave their approval, Valena settled one hand on Timmy's head and the other over the obvious injury. Damian sat down to keep a close watch on them. Valena closed her eyes, a small frown marring her forehead as she concentrated.

"Warm," Timmy said.

"Yes. Warm." Valena spoke as if from a long way off. Not moving. Keeping her hands on Timmy. Damian could see sweat forming on her brow. This was hard work for her. His concern grew.

After what seemed like hours, Valena lifted her head and removed her hands from the boy. "I think it worked," she said to the parents. "How do you feel, Timmy?"

He lifted his arm. The telltale bulge of an obvious break was gone. No redness, nothing. He moved his arm around. "I good!" he said with a toothy smile. "I all good."

The older couple gasped. "How were you able to do that?" the woman asked.

Timmy's mother clutched him to her until he squirmed. Tears filled her eyes when she looked at Valena. "Thank you. Thank you so much."

The father's reaction was more reserved. "How—"

Damian assumed he didn't even know what to ask. This was new to all of them. Even he was in awe, and he'd had time to get used to the idea.

The food worker's reaction, though, was what worried Damian the most. Fear and horror shone in his round eyes, his mouth hung open and he looked around frantically as if searching for a weapon.

"Everything's all right," Damian said, trying to calm nerves long enough to take care of Valena. Helping his wife take a seat, he could see how tired she was. This had depleted her energy stores. He couldn't resist a quick check of her arm. No bulge. No reddening. Apparently, science fiction had its empathy and healing facts wrong.

"You really one of those people, aren't you?" the mother asked. "One of those mods. You've been touched by that magic."

Since Earth's magic had burst into the world, Damian and Valena had not strayed far from home. They had only word of mouth to ascertain how people were reacting to those with gifts. He stood close to Valena, ready to intercede if things turned ugly. Watching the faces of those who'd witnessed it.

The employee had backed off.

The father now stood ramrod stiff, a deep frown on

his face.

The mother's expression moved from confusion to awe as her eyes, still wide with tears, held Valena's. "It's a miracle." She reached for Valena's hand. "You fixed my boy. It's a miracle. Thank you, thank you, thank you." Over and over again she said the words, squeezing Valena's hand harder with each one.

The mother's gratitude broke the tension in the dining car. Both the worker and the father relaxed. The dad even smiled. When Timmy crawled out of his mother's arms and started racing up and down the railroad car again, everyone laughed.

"We're supposed to report all incidents," the young man—whose name was Peter, according to his employee tag—said gruffly. "I don't even know how to describe this."

"There's no reason to make a big deal out of it." Damian purposely kept his voice calm, though inside he was seething. His wife had just healed this boy's injury and two out of the three people who'd witnessed it had reacted with suspicion and fear.

"I suggest keeping it simple," Damian continued. "The boy fell, but there appeared to be no lasting injury."

Peter nodded, a more placid look on his face now that he stood behind the counter.

"I'm Marie," the mother said. "And this is my husband, Jeff."

"Damian and Valena Royan," Damian said.

"Oh," Marie said. "You're one of the first. I've been watching all the reports about those lights. They said it started with you."

"Not with us, but where we live, yes."

"Do you think it will turn dangerous?" the father asked, his eyes still guarded.

That was the question of the year. "The light, released

from Earth to heal itself, will not be a danger to anyone," Damian answered. It's a wonderful thing. Trees, plants, food, all will grow better because of it. And some of us will be able to help people heal, like my wife did with your son today."

"Well, I think it's a good thing," Marie said, nodding her head as if just making that decision.

Her husband nodded, too, but Damian could see the doubt in his face. Jeff would need some convincing. And if Damian couldn't help these people understand, how would he convince those who ran their country of the amazing benefit Earth had given them. "Would you like to hear more about it?"

"I would," Jeff said after a pause. "I need to understand."

Damian let go of his tension inside. The man's desire to know more seemed honest. They could, now, have a conversation. "Let me get my wife back to our seats to rest, then I'll come back and answer any questions you might have."

Valena's legs were visibly shaking when she stood. She leaned heavily on Damian as they moved back to their seats two cars up. People watched them as they moved through the aisle. Word had spread.

After she sat, he pulled a blanket over her.

"I'm all right, Damian."

It would take more than her words to convince him.

"I just need to rest. It sapped my energy, but it didn't cause me any pain. You go back and talk to Jeff and Marie. I'll sleep for a bit and be right back to fine before you know it."

While he still wasn't certain of that, Damian agreed rest would be good. He placed a kiss on her forehead as her eyes closed. "Sleep well, my love."

Then he headed back to the dining car for a real-life dry run of what he'd be up against in Washington, D.C. Peeking through the window into the dining car, he could see a large group waiting for him. This truly would be his first test.

Straightening an imaginary tie around his neck, Damian Royan took a deep breath and opened the car door.

~~~

"Are you insane?"

The one person Cait had opted to confide in—her friend Linda—looked at her now like she'd said she planned to climb Mt. Everest.

"Even if you could get close to one of those light streams, what do you possibly hope to accomplish?" The woman who'd been with Cait through good and bad, who'd been her coach during labor and delivery with the twins, sank onto the crib-turned-toddler-bed as Cait packed a small backpack with essentials for her girls.

"I *hope* to get answers."

"About some perceived power that your daughter has? This is nuts."

Cait stopped folding and stared at her friend. "Linda, you're my closest friend. Have been ever since high school. But you can't be skeptical about this. I need someone to know where I'm going. And I need you to water my plants." She grinned, hoping to diffuse her friend's worry.

"How can I not be skeptical? The news is full of all sorts of stories." Linda grabbed her phone and tapped away. "Here's one. Man lifts car off wife after accident."

Tap. Tap.

"And another. Man flies. Flies, for God's sake." Linda waved her phone in front of Cait's face— "How the hell am I supposed to believe any of this? It's ridiculous to think
~~~

things like this are actually happening."

Cait glanced at the twins, for once playing quietly with their toys in the corner. She looked at Linda, then at the jug of animal crackers she'd had to keep by her side ever since her life had tumbled into the rabbit hole. Linda needed convincing, so she picked up the plastic jug filled with little cookie animals. "Fallon, you and your sister can have a cookie now."

Fallon looked at her with wisdom beyond her years. "Really?"

"Really. Just this once." Cait wagged a finger.

The cookie jar lifted, moved through the air right in front of her gawking friend, and settled on the floor beside Fallon and Willow. The lid unscrewed without anyone touching it, at which point magic was no longer necessary as two hands dug for whatever they could grab in one dive.

"That's enough," Cait said. "Put it back now."

Dutifully, the cap screwed back on and the jug lifted, passing right by Linda again on its way to the dresser, where it settled peacefully down. Both her kids munched happily on their cookies as Cait turned to her friend.

With a finger, she raised her friend's chin, closing her mouth. "Get it now?"

Linda looked from the cookies to the twins and back again. "I— "

Cait stepped back and waited.

"I— "

"Pretty incredible, isn't it?"

Linda stopped swiveling her head and focused on Cait, waving her phone again. "All this. It's real?"

Cait shrugged. "Most of it, at least from what I can tell."

"I thought it was poppycock. Crazy talk."

"Now you know. And that's why I have to go to South

Dakota, to where it all started. I need to see if the people there have any answers." Cait dropped down in front of Linda, placing her hands on her friend's knees. "I need to know she's going to be all right. That this won't hurt her."

Linda glanced at Fallon. "I hadn't even thought of that. Oh, my God." Her eyes filled with tears.

"So you understand now, right?"

"Oh, honey. I totally understand." Linda dabbed under her eyes with her fingers, trying to quell the tears. Taking a deep breath, she looked at Cait. "How can I help?"

"Weeeelll, my plants *will* need watering." A smile played over her lips.

Linda punched her shoulder. "All right, all right. I'll water them."

The laughter that followed was both welcome and cathartic for Cait. She hugged her friend tight.

~~~

Gordon Darcy couldn't hear anything. Nothing at all. No car horns blaring, no stock reports ticking away on his television. Nothing. His bed felt different, too. Soft. Comfortable. He wanted to sink into its cushiness, lie there and let the day unfold without him.

Wait a minute. This wasn't him. This wasn't his penthouse, either. Where the hell was he? Gordon opened his eyes. Treetops and sky met his gaze.

What the hell?

He turned his head, then froze as the pain hit him.

"Try not to move too much."

Whoever's voice that was, she sounded like an angel. Melodic and lilting, it conjured up images of a golden Aphrodite sitting amongst the clouds with harps playing in the distance.

Oh, God. Had he died? Was this the afterlife?

Gordon struggled to get up, but the harps turned
~~~

discordant as the pain gripped him tighter than a noose. "Where am I?" he croaked.

"You're in our camp. In South Dakota."

He needed to see who spoke to him. Turning slowly this time, the pain remained tolerable. The girl who sat next to him almost looked like an angel, with eyes bluer than he'd ever seen and long, swirling, golden hair topped by a ring of flowers. A white peasant blouse added to the effect.

"South Dakota?"

"Yes. You...hit a tree."

Everything rushed back to him then. The light stream, touching it, being lifted. Then, nothing.

He'd touched the light. Gordon raised his hands, wondering if he'd thrown himself against that tree. Had the powers infused him with so much strength he hadn't been able to handle it at first?

Gordon pushed off the pad he lay on, his head pounding like bass cymbals.

"You should lay still and rest. Valena is not here to heal you."

He couldn't. He had to know. Brushing off the girl's arm, he made it to a sitting position, though his head exploded with every twitch and turn. Taking a deep breath to mark the occasion of his entry into this new way of life, Gordon reached out his hands, trying to uproot a tree with his mind.

Nothing happened.

Well, maybe something smaller. The leaf a few feet away.

Again, nothing.

If he hadn't been gifted with levitation, maybe strength. Or fireballs! He'd seen the movies. Gordon held out his hands again, wishing for a fireball.

Not even a wisp of smoke.

He pulled his hand back in disgust, hating anything that made him appear stupid, praying he hadn't been gifted one of those hippie powers, like healing people, or worse, growing plants and trees. Gordon laid his hand on the grass beside the pallet where he lay. Nothing changed. Then he cupped his pounding head. Nothing there either.

Gordon dropped his hands. He wasn't a mod. Well, that was a disappointment. That damn light had screwed him out of a fortune. If he couldn't share in the power, then he needed to find a way to turn this to his advantage and recoup the lost revenue.

He looked around. He wasn't in the glade anymore. He was in some sort of encampment, far enough away that he couldn't see the light that had ruined everything. Was there a way to destroy it? A way to get back to his original plan?

That would probably take something like a nuclear weapon, considering how far-reaching the outflow of magic from the light seemed to be. And destruction that big would negate his ability to drill here, so it wasn't an option.

"You really should lie down. You're pretty pale," the girl beside him said.

Gordon looked at her. Young, pretty in a simple sense. The ring of flowers around her head marked her as one of those greeners. "Do you have powers?"

"You mean, did Earth gift me with special abilities?"

Of course, that's what he meant. Idiot. But Gordon only nodded.

"Earth has found me worthy. I'm better than I was before." She cocked her head. "And you, somehow, are tied to all of this."

He leaned forward. "Do you have...visions?"

She laughed, a sound that almost made his insides go soft. Gordon held back a shudder, barely.

"Not quite, at least, not like you think. I get...feelings.

And I can do this."

Settling her hand on the grass beside them, she sat quietly for a moment. When she pulled her hand away, the grass beneath it had grown twice as long as the rest. She gazed around the area. The wonder shining on her face made Gordon want to puke.

Still, she wasn't bad to look at. And she might be useful.

Gordon settled back on the pallet. "Maybe you're right. Maybe I should rest."

"It will help you heal faster," she said, smiling.

"So, what's your name?"

News Alert: All the squirrels ain't in the trees, folks. If you could see all the rumblings going on in Washington, you'd think about a hamster on a wheel that isn't stopping and doesn't know where it's going.

CHAPTER ELEVEN

Damian and Valena were shown into an office he'd been in before. Comfortable, but a clear statement of power and station. The last time he'd been here, the man had looked down his nose at Damian. He'd explained in very clear terms that there was nothing he could or would do to keep the Black Hills land from going private.

Today, he came around the desk, reaching out to shake Damian's hand. "Hello, Mr. Royan. It's nice to see you again."

What a difference a few weeks made. Damian said a private prayer that this time, the man would listen. He shook his hand, then put an arm around Valena's waist. "This is my wife, Valena."

Senator Johns shook her hand as well, placing a second hand on top for a long moment. "Very nice to meet you, Mrs. Royan. Come, sit down," he said, indicating the chairs in front of his desk. "Can I get you something to drink?"

"No thank you," Damian said, taking his seat after Valena. "We'd like to talk to you about the changes that have occurred."

The man's eyes actually lit up. "Yes, yes. Crazy events, eh? I understand you were there when it happened? When the light showed up?"

Damian nodded.

"So," the man leaned forward, "is it true? Do you have special...powers? Like the other mods?"

Damian stiffened. Was this the only interest the man had?

Valena laid a hand on Damian's arm, reminding him that they were in this for the long haul. His quick temper would get them nowhere.

"We believe the light enhances the natural abilities of some people," Valena said. "And yes, we have both been given some of this...power, as you call it."

"What's it like?"

"I'm not sure that's pertinent to what we came here to discuss today," Damian said as deep furrows formed between his brows.

"It's all pertinent," the senator said, sitting back. "Everyone wants to know if this phenomenon will touch them and if it will be a positive thing, or negative."

Valena said, "It's been very positive."

The senator nodded. "So far. But things could turn."

"I don't see how," Damian answered.

When the senator's phone rang, he picked it up and listened for a moment. "All right," he said, then hung up and stood. "Looks like you're going to get a chance to explain this whole phenomenon. Come with me."

"Where?"

"This meeting has been escalated."

Damian opened his mouth to pursue the question. When Valena gave a brief shake of her head, he closed it.

"Follow me," the senator said, walking out without

waiting for an answer.

Soon, they were in a limousine sliding quickly along Constitution Avenue. Both Damian and Valena raised their eyebrows when they pulled into the side entrance of the White House. This was it. They were finally going to get the chance to plead Earth's case to the highest authority in their country. Were they up to this? Was he? This was exactly what he'd been wanting this whole time. To get the attention of the people who could initiate the changes necessary to help Earth survive.

Valena reached for his hand, clutching it tightly. She knew the importance of this meeting.

Damian placed a hand over hers and together, they prayed silently that they would make positive headway.

Because if it didn't start here, now, today, it probably never would.

~~~

Damian and Valena were ushered through security and into the West Wing to a conference room, where the senator left them. An hour passed before anyone even entered, and Damian's ire rose with each passing moment.

"If they don't arrive soon, we're leaving," he said.

Someone must have heard him because the door opened. An aid brought water and glasses and told them the vice president would be with them in a moment. A short time later, the senator rejoined them.

When Vice President Ramsey arrived, he stared at Damian until he became uncomfortable. When Ramsey finally spoke, he steepled his fingers, even more intense. "So you've got some of this...magic that came from those lights."

"Yes, but what we really need to talk about—"

"In due time. Our reports have indicated a wave of change."
~~~

"Yes, it's like a ripple of healing, spreading out further and further. It's Earth's—"

"And not all people are being bestowed with these extra abilities."

Damian clenched his hands in his lap then relaxed them slowly, trying to let the tension go. "Correct. By our reckoning, and based on reports, about ten percent of the population has had their natural tendencies enhanced."

"You were near this thing when it burst out of the ground?"

"Yes. If I could—"

"Did you touch it?"

"No. And this is not why I'm here, Mr. Vice President. We need to have a serious discussion about the ramifications of continuing on the downward environmental spiral that is causing climate change. Earth has—"

Ramsey held up his hand. "We will discuss what I say needs to be discussed. Did you touch the light? Is that how you got your powers?"

"Again, no." Damian ground the words out. "I did not touch the light. My abilities just...happened."

The vice president turned to the senator. "I'm not sure how we can utilize this. It doesn't sound like we can enforce who gets this power and who doesn't."

The senator shook his head. "That's what I'm hearing, too. We don't get to make that decision. What we must do is convince those who have extra abilities to work with us."

"Work with you? How? Doing what?" Damian clutched the arms of his chair.

When his wife's sharp gaze speared him, he looked down to see the wood arms working free from the seat, so fiercely had he grabbed them. He slowly released his grip, hoping the vice president and senator didn't catch what had almost happened.

"Doing the business of keeping our country strong. Seeing to the needs of hearth and home above everything else."

"Neither hearth nor home exists without Earth," Valena said. "If we don't make changes to protect our *world* now, there will soon be nothing to sustain us, much less to keep us strong."

"That is Earth's message to us, with the advent of this light," Damian said. He leaned forward. "If we don't pay attention, we'll die. Not just our *home*. Our entire world will be gone, and you— " He pointed to the senator. "And you, and us... None of us will survive the coming apocalypse."

That might have been overkill, but Damian knew he only had scant moments to drive his point home.

"Let me make this perfectly clear," Vice President Ramsey said, enunciating each word. "We do not care about your ideals or your thoughts. The world will not end. Not now, not ever. What we care about is how much of a patriot you are, Mr. Royan. Because, if you aren't a patriot, then there's nothing you can do for us."

The senator leaned forward as well, both men using their size and office to intimidate Damian.

Valena stiffened and the rock that had been sitting in Damian's stomach flipped, its sharp corners leaving painful divots. He clenched and unclenched his hands, trying to calm down before he spoke. After more seconds than were polite, he spoke with a calmness that belied the volcanic fury bubbling just beneath the surface.

"Is that what you think this meeting is about? Corralling power for you to use as you wish?"

Vice President Ramsey straightened in his chair. "It's your duty to your country."

Damian's hands clenched and unclenched faster and

faster. Out of the corner of his eye, he saw Valena watching him. He turned to her.

"I've got this," she mouthed to him, then faced the vice president and senator. "With all due respect, sirs, our *duty* is to Earth and the future of humanity. That is the only authority we answer to. We came here today to plead with you. There is no more time. We must make changes. Can you not recognize how close we are to dying? Not as a country, but as a world. Earth cannot sustain us for much longer and has given us this gift. We can use it for good and all will thrive, or we can use it to further agendas that will do nothing but speed our destruction. Which option do you choose?"

The senator, red-faced, stood. He towered over Valena. Damian stood, too. The chair arm he held came with him, ripped off by the simple motion of standing, reminding the politicians without him saying a word that Damian would protect his wife from anyone, no matter their station.

The senator blustered as he glared at Damian, then at Valena. "You cannot refuse your homeland's government. You will comply."

The vice president held out his hands, palms up. "There's no need for this. Come, sit." He took his chair. "There are others who won't try to stand on some pedestal that means nothing. We'd rather work with someone intelligent like yourselves. However, as you said yourself, probably ten percent of the population has been granted enhanced abilities by this...sentient Earth. If you aren't willing to work with us, I'm sure we'll find someone who is."

"Never," Damian said, tossing the wooden chair arm across the room. "I'll never be willing to work with you if it means that Earth's message is ignored."

"Then we're done." The vice president raised his hand, signaling to someone Damian couldn't see.

Within seconds, the door opened and two guards arrived, quickly escorting Damian and Valena out of the West Wing, through the White House side door, and off the grounds. They stood on the other side of the fence, staring at the building. Damian knew it was his mind playing tricks on him, but had that white paint just yellowed? Faint red streaks appeared every so often. The blood of those coerced to do the government's bidding? A shiver coursed through him at the thought.

"There's nothing more we can do here," Valena said, taking Damian's arm. "Let's go back to the hotel and figure out our next move."

Unable to think of a better idea, Damian hailed a cab.

By the time they returned to the hotel, the meeting had eaten a hole in Damian's gut. Anger had a tight grip on his heart and he couldn't think straight. Those buffoons had actually thought he would help them try to further the interests of the country at a time like this? This wasn't about the country. It never had been. This was about the world. Survival. Not dying.

"Gah! I don't understand the mentality of people like that."

"It astounds me that the people we elect can be such power-mongers."

"They need to understand that by not addressing climate change and the rampant use of our waning natural resources, they are killing Earth. Killing us. They are murderers if they don't change their ways." Damian hit the wall of their hotel room without thinking. Tapped it, really, yet he managed to put a hole straight through the sheetrock and into the next room.

"Oh, God." He leaned down and looked straight into

the large, round, frightened blue eyes of a woman, probably in her mid-forties. He'd never know for certain because at that moment, she screamed. Like a banshee. She backed up to her bed—thank God she was dressed—and picked up the house phone. He didn't need enhanced hearing to understand what she reported.

Scrubbing the beard he hadn't shaved in days, Damian turned to Valena. "Security will be here in moments."

His wife was already throwing their things into their bags. "We don't need an arrest right now. They'll blackmail us with it."

"You're completely right." They'd paid their bill upon arrival, so Damian slapped the room cards on the desk, along with enough money to fix the wall, cash he'd brought so the others back home would have the credit card in case something came up. Within moments, they had everything packed and were peering into the hall.

"It's empty."

They walked with casual speed to the stairs, opened the door, and entered the stairwell. Damian glanced back to see other doors opening at the same time. Elevator doors.

It didn't take them long to traverse the six floors and exit the hotel. They didn't stop until they'd reached the train station, at which point Valena grabbed his arm, slowing him down while she gasped for breath.

"A moment."

Damian was the worst kind of heel, making her run like a felon from a crime. He looked around, saw a bench, and helped Valena to it with more care and less hurry. "I'm such a jerk."

Valena sat down, pulling him with her. "You're not a jerk. Just an emotional man."

"I can't believe I did that. I lost control."

"That's not something you've ever done before."

"And I can *never* do it again. Ever." Damian clutched Valena's hands. "You have to know that, even though I've got this power, I would never hurt you." He watched her closely, looked for any sign of doubt.

There was none. Valena gazed back without wavering. She touched his cheek. "I know that, silly man."

Damian hugged her. "I love you so much."

"I love you, too. Let's find a park, have a seat, and try to figure out our next step."

~~~

Gordon Darcy watched Taegar weaving a basket as she sat cross-legged on the ground beside him. He'd been there four days now, recovering. Not that he needed it. Other than a continuing headache, he felt no ill effects from getting tossed like a hundred dollar bill at the whim of the wind.

He resettled on the mat where he'd spent most of his time. Foreign to him, this enforced relaxation did nothing to soothe his soul, as Taegar predicted would happen. She'd laid a hand on him and said his spirit was unhappy.

If she'd seen any further into his soul, she'd have probably run like the wind to get away from him.

He touched her leg to get her attention. Good, she barely flinched this time. He'd never seen a woman so skittish. "I think I'd like to go for a walk."

"That's excellent," she said, her smile brightening. Together, with her arm providing support he requested but didn't need, they strolled to the lake. After several minutes of boredom there, Gordon suggested they go to the clearing.

Taegar's eyes shone, then furrowed with worry. "I'm not sure you should return there."

Gordon patted her hand. "I promise. I won't do anything...stupid."
~~~

So they turned and walked through the campground, and Gordon reached for her hand. The smile on her face was damn near beatific. Maybe this would be easier than he'd originally thought.

At the clearing, the first thing he noticed was that the area surrounding the stream of light had been cordoned off and guards posted on all sides. Probably because of the foolish stunt he'd tried. Everything else looked the same. Oh, the faces had changed, but there were still scientists, believers, and gawkers. They stood further away now, but they were still there.

"Isn't it beautiful?" Taegar said.

Gordon watched her, saw the rapture in her eyes. Oh, boy, was this girl under the spell or what? "It sure is," he said, except he wasn't looking at the light.

Taegar turned to him, her wide, innocent eyes overfull with emotion.

Careful not to touch her beyond holding her hand, lest she freak out, Gordon leaned down and touched his lips to hers. A light testing of the waters. He withheld the shiver of disgust. Innocence repelled him. His wife had been innocent until her parents pushed her into marrying Gordon, dollar signs in their eyes. Now, she wanted nothing to do with him. Nor he with her. The witch.

Encouraged when the skittish girl didn't pull back, Gordon stayed close. Not moving.

"Why did you do that?" Taegar whispered, touching her lips.

He kept his voice low, even, seductive. "Because I wanted to." He looked at their intertwined hands. When was the last time he'd held a woman's hand? The games he must play... Gordon tucked her hand into the crook of his arm.

Those baby blues looked up at him with wonder and

awe and so much emotion, Gordon wanted to puke. He was prostituting himself for power, something he'd done before and would do again. But to rely on a woman grated on him. Women were weak and governed by emotion, unlike him. Still, for some reason this, right here, right now, put a bad taste in his mouth. He couldn't quite put his finger on why. He was missing something.

Gordon turned to stare at the light stream, hating the brightness, the purity of the white. Pure just like Taegar, who leaned her head on his shoulder as they stood side by side. For now, this seduction seemed his only way to get access to these new powers and control them. And control them he would. They were the ultimate clout, and his destiny, whether the magic thought so or not.

News Alert: Some are calling these mysterious light streams the harbingers of a clash between good and evil. Worldwide, despite many reports of changes for the good since the lights arrived, rumors abound of corruption, and of those who would harness the magic for profit.

CHAPTER TWELVE

Weary from two days of travel, Damian and Valena dragged themselves off the bus in Rapid City and stuck out their thumbs. They hadn't bothered to call for a ride home. Enough people migrated toward the lake nowadays that it was easy to find someone heading that way. Sure enough, within a few minutes, they were in the back of a truck headed for home, having struck out once again in Washington. Every door had been closed to them.

"I'm looking forward to laying on my own pillow tonight," Valena said, her head leaning against the truck's rear window. Her tiredness worried Damian. In fact, she looked more than tired. She looked beat down.

Exactly like him. So much had gone wrong already. And now he'd escalated his inability to effect change by angering D.C. and punching a hole in a hotel wall. He shook his head, watching the pine trees whizz by.

"I've screwed everything up," he said.

Valena reached for his hand and entwined their

fingers. "It's not your fault our government is so stubborn and so stuck on its agenda that it can't see how good this could be for everyone."

"Our government isn't of the people or for the people." Damian sighed. "It hasn't been for a very long time. Politicians work to further their own interests and line their pockets."

Valena nodded. "We elected them. Now we have to find a way to save our planet without their help. Maybe we need to play their game. Hire a marketing guru to spin the truth in such a way that people take notice and listen."

A marketing expert. Not a bad idea. Damian thought back to their train trip to D.C. After two hours with the parents of the boy Valena had healed, he'd been discouraged. He'd worked hard to convince the father and the others who'd gathered in the dining car that there wasn't some nefarious plan behind recent events. He'd answered all their questions honestly—about the light's arrival, his and Valena's enhanced powers, and what Earth had told him. How Earth had said it is dying and that this is a last gasp effort to sustain itself and the life that dwells upon it.

After Damian's explanations, the father's skepticism had not varied much at all. If he couldn't convince one man, how was he going to convince nations? The whole world waited for guidance, yet they seemed happier to accept untruths than to listen to the message.

The truck stopped. "Can't go any further," the man yelled out his window.

Damian and Valena grabbed their packs and jumped out of the truck bed. After shaking the man's hand and thanking him for the ride, they hiked the mile or so home to their lake. The closer they got to the glade, the better Damian felt.

Nothing had changed. The energy was as light and bright as before. He could feel it. Hundreds of people still milled around. Except...

Up ahead, Damian saw the ropes keeping people back. And guards. With guns. What the hell? This was not something to be cordoned off. This was a gift for everyone. He dropped his pack and strode forward.

"Hang on, Damian." Bhren arrived with Tom Gallows from the U.S. Geological Laboratory beside him. He grabbed Damian's arm and yanked him aside, away from the guards, giving him a quick welcome hug. "We need to talk before you do anything."

"Why are there guards here?" Damian asked.

Valena joined them, a pack in each hand. "What's changed?"

"Come with us," Bhren said as he took the packs from Valena. "Let's go rest and I'll explain everything."

Damian looked back, fury driving him to deal with this now. But anger hadn't helped them in D.C. He needed to be calm, to deal with this logically, not with his heart. That was the only way they'd be effective against what was happening.

He nodded, then, with head bowed, followed Bhren and Tom to their campsites. Gwen and Wyeth were already there and both rose to give Damian and Valena hugs.

"It's good to have you home," Gwen said, pulling Valena down to sit at the picnic table.

"It's good to be home."

"You look exhausted."

"We are."

"Where are Taegar and Luther?" Valena asked.

A lot of people were wandering through and around the campsite, but Damian didn't see their friends anywhere.

"Taegar's got some guy claiming her time right now."

Wyeth frowned. "I think all these people are giving Luther a bigger headache than mine. He went hiking in the hills. Said he needed to get as far away from here as he could for a bit."

Damian looked off into the distance. "He's not doing well with all this change, is he?"

Wyeth shook his head.

Sitting down with Luther for a heart-to-heart got bumped up on Damian's priority list.

"Things didn't go well in Washington?" Wyeth asked as they all settled around the table.

Damian raked his hands through his hair. "No. Senator Johns arranged a meeting with the vice president but they wouldn't listen. They want to use the light stream for their own ends, like it's some kind of weapon. After that, every door we tried to open was shut. I see things aren't much better here."

"They aren't," Tom said. "Things aren't going well at the other sites either, from what we've heard. The government is slowly but surely taking over."

"They can't do that," Damian said, pounding the sturdy table with his fists. "This is meant for everyone."

"Matters of national security." Tom held up his hands. "Their words, not mine. From what I can gather, other countries are decrying their lack of access to these sites. That, in the government's mind, gives them the right to try to protect it."

"Keep it for themselves, you mean."

"Most likely. Think about it. This is the equivalent of an extra-terrestrial contact, except it's coming from deep within the earth. Whoever controls it rules the world in its entirety. They can make all the choices, dictate the future. And all three light streams appeared on American soil."

Damian hung his head, the weight of everything

depressing him. How could these people not see what was happening?

"I think," Wyeth said, "that if the government won't listen, maybe the people will."

"What do you mean?"

Wyeth shrugged. "We've been focused on talking to the people who come here and the people in power. We've never taken it to the people of the world. Television. The Internet. I think we need to mount an advertising campaign."

"Valena just said the same thing to me."

Gwen hugged Valena. "I knew we were kindred spirits." She turned to the group. "I love this idea. I studied advertising in college before I realized plants fed my soul more. I could work up some copy."

Damian shook his head. "I'm not sure I could do some rehearsed thing."

"I've seen you read out loud, Damian. No insult intended, but you suck at it," Wyeth said with a chuckle.

"Yes, you kind of do," Gwen agreed. "And that's not what we need from you." Her growing enthusiasm showed in her rapid-fire words. "The copy will be for Facebook posts, Twitter feeds, and Instagram. You, you'll do the live stuff. You and Valena. You look good together and you work well together. You're the face of this effort. The in-person emotion. Everything else, well, it's just to back you up, to reiterate what you'll be saying."

"Me, in front of a camera?" Damian shook his head.

Valena touched his arm. "You took on Washington."

"And failed."

"But you tried."

Damian nodded and scanned the faces at the table. Hope had begun to supplant the despair in their eyes, though if this marketing stuff backfired, no one would listen to any of them ever again.

"We do need to get the word out," Damian said. "It's been more than two weeks since the light streams showed up and not much has happened for the better. If nothing else, we need to remind those with powers to use them for good. To help Earth regenerate and grow. To save those who need saving, feed those who are starving, to heal. This sounds like a good way to do that."

"And, at the same time," Gwen said, "we'll be subtly trying to convince everyone that this is a good, positive thing, meant to help them, not hurt them. That this is about humanity's survival."

"All right. Let's do it."

Gwen clapped her hands together and stood. "I'm going to the trailer to use the laptop. I'll work up a plan and we can kick this thing off tomorrow. Oh," she turned back to the table, "we'll need some footage of the light stream. And some video with Damian, and with both of you. We'll work on the live stuff after we get some basics done."

Wyeth stood. "I'll get the camera and shoot some video at the clearing."

Just like that, there were only four left at the table.

"That happened quick," Bhren said.

"I think we've created a monster," Damian mumbled.

"A very good, kind, loving monster," Valena said, laughing.

Only time would tell if this was a good idea or not.

"I think it's a great idea," Tom said, echoing Damian's thoughts. "I'm glad you got back before I have to head to the lab."

"How soon?"

"Tomorrow, most likely. I've been called back. Plus, I need to do an in-depth analysis. For that, I need my lab."

"We're going to miss you here," Valena said.

"I'm going to miss being here. You have a cell, right?"

Damian nodded.

"Give me the number. I'll try to keep you up to speed on what I hear from my end." Tom nodded in the direction of the clearing. "I'm still not sure what this is or what's happened, but I feel very strongly that this is a good thing. I don't want to see it destroyed by power-mongering or stupidity."

Damian clasped his hand as they all stood. "You've become a good friend, Tom. Valena's right. We'll certainly miss you."

"Oh, I'll be back. This place is special." He looked around, waving his arms at the forest. "I'll miss you all, but I'll miss this more."

Tom headed toward his tent and Bhren went to keep an eye on happenings in the grove, leaving Damian and Valena alone.

Valena turned the oak tree ring on her finger. "Got any more of these rings?"

"A few."

"I think we should give one to Tom."

Damian smiled. "I couldn't agree more."

"I'm exhausted," Valena said.

Damian put an arm around her. "How about a nap?"

"That sounds absolutely lovely," she answered, smiling up at him.

They walked to their site, where a new tent waited for them. They were grateful it was far enough away from the clearing to dull the ambient noise of humanity's crush. Damian gazed at the trees as they walked. This was home. He'd missed it.

His focus on nature almost caused him to overlook the couple walking toward them. Taegar. And...

Gordon Darcy?

"What the hell?" Damian froze in place.

Valena gasped and grabbed Damian's arm.

The two were hand-in-hand, damn near skipping, and Taegar's smile was bigger than ever before.

"What are you doing here, Darcy?" Damian growled. This man's presence tainted their home. Damian could almost feel the leaves curling.

Taegar's smile dipped. "This is my new friend, Gordon. Have you met?"

"Oh, yes," Damian said. "We've met. Taegar, do you know this man's last name?"

Taegar laughed. "We never got around to last names."

"It's Darcy. Gordon Darcy. The man who wanted to drill on this very land you stand on."

"Oh." Taegar's eyes widened as she pulled her hand from Gordon's and turned to look at him.

"You, more than anyone, know the change of heart I've had, my dear." He tucked a stray hair behind her ear. "I understand now. This land is sacred, and I've turned over a new leaf."

He cupped her face and she covered his hand with her own.

"I believe you." Taegar turned to Damian and Valena. "Gordon's different now. He doesn't want to hurt the land. He wants to protect it. To join our group."

"Over my dead body."

"How can you say that?"

Gordon Darcy kept his eyes trained on Damian as he smiled. Lifting Taegar's hand to his mouth, he kissed her knuckles. "Damian only knows me from before, in Los Angeles."

"You wanted to destroy this land by drilling for oil. I'm certain that now, you want to corral the light for your own selfish uses. We will never see eye-to-eye."

Taegar's mouth trembled.

"Don't worry, my pet," Gordon said, releasing her hand to put an arm around her shoulders. "He just needs time to get to know me, to understand and believe my sincerity." He leaned down, giving her a quick kiss.

Damian stepped forward, unwilling to let the man take advantage of Taegar's innocence. "You need to leave. Now. Taegar's too young for your machinations."

"I'm not too young," Taegar cried. "I love Gordon. And he loves me."

"He's not who you think he is. He's devious, and he doesn't care about anything but his own purse."

"That's not true. He's changed. That can happen, you know. The light has changed him."

"Taegar," Valena said, stepping forward.

Gordon tightened his hold on Taegar's hand and she took a step back, behind him.

"No," she said. "Don't try to convince me otherwise. We're in love and there's nothing you can do about it."

Damian watched Gordon's face while Taegar talked. A fiery look—supreme confidence mixed with the satisfaction of his plot coming to fruition—filled his eyes. He thought he'd won this battle. Again. Taegar was an innocent. They couldn't let her fall into this devil's clutches. What would he do to her? He'd destroy her.

"What's your end game, Darcy?" Damian asked.

"He doesn't play games, Damian." Taegar returned to Gordon's side and clutched his arm. "He's an open book."

Gordon stared back at Damian, grinning. He didn't need to speak because he had Taegar to do all his convincing for him. How had he managed to get her under his power so quickly? Did he have a latent ability? Had the light stream enhanced that? If it had, and he used that power, they were sunk.

"Why are you here?" Damian stared at the man.

"He's—"

Damian held up his hand. "I think Darcy can answer for himself, Taegar."

The pout on Taegar's face deepened.

"I came to see what this phenomenon was all about."

Truth. Damian's senses validated the temporary honesty in the man's words. Not that he liked it much.

"And what did you find?"

"Well, after my dear Taegar helped me recover from being tossed like a toothpick across that clearing..."

"Gordon touched the light," Taegar threw in quickly. "I saw it. The next thing we knew, his body went flying over all of us. He hit the tree, hard. Oh, Valena," Taegar turned to her, "I wish you'd been here to heal him. I was so worried."

Fat chance Damian would let Valena touch that man.

"Because of Taegar's excellent ministrations, and our long, long talks, I came to understand there's a greater good here." He smiled at Taegar, raising both her hands to his lips to kiss her knuckles again.

Damian could see the filthy lie as if it were a thick, muddied presence around them. He wanted to rip Gordon away from Taegar.

Valena touched him, reminding him they must be careful. Taegar's tender heart was at stake here. Hell, they didn't even really know how the magic had touched the girl. They'd seen bits and pieces of enhancements. For her to be under the spell of this man... It grated against every nerve Damian had.

Valena spoke up. "Taegar, maybe we should go start dinner and let these men hash out their differences."

"I won't be separated from him," Taegar said, thrusting her chin out. "We're soul mates."

"Nor I from her. She's exactly right. We are meant to be together."

"Besides," Taegar added. "Anything you have to say to him, or to me, can be said to both of us together."

Now was one hell of a time for Taegar to find her backbone. All this time, she'd gone along with what everyone wanted. She'd sat there, weaving flowers or knitting, happy in her little cocoon. What had changed?

"All right. So, Gordon, when you touched the light stream, did it grant you any powers?"

The fleeting hatred that crossed Gordon's face almost made Damian smile.

"No. I wasn't blessed with the ability to help Earth through touch or strength of muscle."

Truth.

"I'll have to be consoled by my ability to sway people's minds using my ordinary abilities."

Truth. Sort of. The man believed he could sway minds, but Damian knew he'd been given no additional power. Which was probably why he'd befriended Taegar.

"Is that why you're slithering up to one of our family?"

Again, the hatred flashed at the truth in what Damian had said.

"I'm no snake. I love Taegar."

Lie. Lie. Lie. Damian's body went taut. "No. You don't."

"Yes, he does."

"Taeger," Damian said, smoothing out his voice. "Do you remember the night the light arrived?"

"Yes. It was a blessed night, the best of my existence, next to meeting Gordon."

"Do you remember what I said my enhanced abilities were?" He didn't like explaining this in front of Darcy, but there was no other way.

"Yes. The light blessed you with strength and a sort of prescience."

Damian nodded. "We figured out when we were in D.C. that part of this prescience manifests itself as an ability to root out the truth."

From the corner of his eye, Damian saw Darcy straighten and squint in displeasure.

"I can tell when people are lying. Gordon is lying."

"No. I don't believe you."

"When you came here, you needed a place to heal, Taegar. We do not know why. You've never indicated a desire to speak of your days before you arrived here."

"You've become like a daughter to us," Valena said.

"And we don't want to see you hurt again. We don't want anything to destroy the happiness within you. You worked too hard to find it."

For the first time since they'd run into each other on the path, Taegar separated herself from Gordon. Hope blossomed in Damian's heart.

Taegar strode forward, taking both their hands and bringing them to her cheeks. "You are like a mother and father to me. You gave me a place to be, a place to find myself in the mess that had become my life. You gave me a chance to recover. To heal. And I have. Now, I'm ready to spread my wings again." She looked them both in the eye, one by one.

Damian didn't like the strength, the undeniable resolve he saw there. He knew then. They'd never convince Taegar otherwise. Darcy had dug his claws in too deeply.

"All children have to blossom into lives of their own. It's my turn for that. I love Gordon. And he loves me. We're together now."

Triumph widened Darcy's smile. Damn the man. How had he managed so much in so little time? They'd only been gone a few days.

Damian had only one card left to play.

"He cannot stay here. He cannot be part of our community."

Taegar backed up as if he'd slapped her. In a way, he had. He'd just torn the peace from her life. She didn't believe that he was saving her from a worse fate. He knew that. The pain bit deep because she truly had become like a daughter to them.

Tears filled Taegar's eyes. She stared at Damian, then Valena.

"I agree," Valena said. "This man does not want the same things we want. I sense nothing but evil from him. He cannot stay here." Valena's voice shook as she backed Damian up. She put her arm around his waist. He could feel her entire body trembling.

"If he's not welcome here, then I'm not welcome either," Taegar said with that same newfound resolve.

Damian felt his wife wince, a second blow because his own sorrow lanced his heart as well. He lowered his head for a moment, willing his emotions to stay in check. Then he raised his head to stare at Taegar, ignoring Darcy. "He. Cannot. Stay." The words came with sluggish finality from his mouth.

"Fine," Taegar said, tears falling unchecked now. "I'll pack my things and we'll be gone within the hour. Come on, Gordon. I thought this was my home, but apparently, it's just a way station in my life. It's time for us to leave."

Darcy tossed a triumphant gleam their way as he cuddled Taegar in his arms, consoling her with unheard words while they walked back to camp.

Valena's own eyes were filled with tears. "There was no other way," she said to Damian.

Bhren and Wyeth joined them, having heard the

conversation. "We agree," Bhren said. "That man radiates evil, but right now, there's no way to convince Taegar of that."

Damian nodded. "Follow them. Make sure he takes nothing that's not his."

Acknowledging Damian with a weak thumbs-up, Bhren and Wyeth headed back to camp.

"If you get a chance, pull Taegar aside," Damian said to his wife. "She might talk to you without Darcy around, better than she'll talk to me. Let her know that if things change, she has a home here. Always."

"Yes. If we're to have one final say, that's the right one," Valena said, hugging her husband. "I could never imagine not welcoming Taegar back into our circle."

Somehow, Damian knew Valena would never get that chance. Darcy would make certain of it.

~~~

Cait had never been so tired. One tiny thread of energy was all she could dredge up, and she still had more than a mile to walk.

With equally exhausted twins.

Having decided to hold off on family travel until the girls were older, Cait now completely understood the wisdom of that choice. Assuming that flying would be fastest, she'd learned the joys of changing diarrhea diapers in an airplane bathroom with all three of them tucked inside.

With hasty arrangements came surprises. When she arrived in Rapid City, there hadn't been a single rental car available. Even the chauffeured car service she'd checked into indicated she'd have to wait over an hour. Cait decided to get a hotel room and try to get to the Mt. Rushmore site the next day.

No luck. She wasn't the only one trying to get close to
~~~

this phenomenon. Stuck with two hyped-up two-year-olds and no other way to get to the people she'd come to see, Cait decided to wait for the car service. Two hours later, after chasing the twins around a park playground, she climbed into the SUV, grateful to contain the girls, if only for a little while.

Too little a while, as it turned out. Enough time passed for darkness to descend, though before her GPS said they were even close, the guy pulled over to the side of the road.

"This is as near as I can get you," he said.

Cait looked at the map on her phone, then up at the man. "But we're three miles from the campground."

"They're not letting anyone within two miles of the place. I hear there are cars parked everywhere, even blocking the streets. If I drive any closer, I'll never get out of there."

Her girls had finally dropped off to sleep about fifteen minutes before. They looked like such angels, and would do so right up until she woke them. Neither twin had angelic dispositions when they couldn't wake up to their own clock.

"That's an impossible hike with my twins." Something he said sunk in. "What do you mean, they aren't letting anyone near the place?"

"Exactly that. They are turning everyone around at the two-mile mark."

"You couldn't have told me this when you picked me up and knew where I was going?"

The man shrugged. Shrugged! Cait wanted to reach over the front seat and strangle him.

"I can take you back or you can get out of the car. Either way, I'm turning around here and heading back to Rapid City."

"I'll get another driver."

"No one's going to get you any closer, though some might be willing to try, for a price." He didn't even sound remorseful.

Apparently, capitalizing off this event had become the thing to do. Try as she might, Cait couldn't find a solution. Sleeping at the airport or trudging three or more miles through the woods. In the dark.

At least walking would get her there. The road was paved. How hard could the walk be? And, with all the people milling around and camping wherever they could plunk a tent, it had to be relatively safe, didn't it?

Five minutes later, the driver was gone. The girls woke up crying when she'd moved them, but once they were bundled in their blankets into the double stroller, they drifted back to sleep, thank goodness.

The stroller, one her car seats fit into that she used for jogging, had sturdy wheels. Still, she was grateful for the road, and there was enough light from all the people around to define the route. Cars dropped off and picked up more every minute. A ways ahead, even a limousine pulled away. Crazy.

Cait set off feeling more optimistic than she had in a couple of hours. She'd just have to deal with the roadblock when she got to it.

A mile later, that optimism tanked. A huge crowd milled around a true roadblock. Military trucks were parked lengthwise across the asphalt with orange and white striped sawhorses in front of them. Between the two, a line of military personnel, all armed with rifles, stood watch.

Cait moved off to the side and watched as two women tried to convince a guard to let them through.

"We've got people there. Family," whined a slender blonde.

"Yeah, we got family. We left to go get supplies." A

brunette held up a grocery sack. "They'll run outta food if we don't get back there."

"If they want to eat, they'll have to walk out. I'm not letting you through."

The guard set his legs apart in an at-ease stance, but the way he held his rifle broadcast that he meant business.

Both women pouted as they turned away.

There would be no going through the roadblock. Cait headed back away from the crowd and sat down, pulling out her paper map. Thank goodness she'd purchased one at the airport. She didn't have much battery left on her phone.

That jerk of a driver had been spot-on in his estimation. The campground was about two miles past the blockade. Two miles of winding road. Cait drew an imaginary line along the road to Horse Thief campground, then drew it back to where she was in a straight line. If she went off-road, it would cut the distance in half. And maybe, she'd circumnavigate the people trying to keep her out.

The park map indicated there were a lot of trails through here. One trailhead was even close to her spot. She followed the dotted line. It looked like it would get her pretty darn close to the campground. She might not have to all-terrain it after all.

Still, she had no GPS signal here and could get lost. And she had no guarantee the stroller could handle the terrain. What other option did she have, though?

None. She'd never before let fear of failure stop her. Cait wasn't going to let that become her mantra now. So, with a stroller full of little humans and a backpack on her shoulders, she walked along the edge of the road until she found the trailhead. Twenty feet in, very little light remained. Full darkness had settled and any ambient light from the road got swallowed up by the trees.

Cait had a flashlight and a penlight. She tested both,

and they were strong. Using the penlight first, she made her way along the trail, estimating it would get her to the campground in a little over a mile.

After what felt like twice that distance, her penlight dimmed. She shook it, trying to get as much life out of it as she could. The trail had gotten smaller, more closed in. There was very little moon tonight, so she couldn't see much beyond the light's beam.

Thunk.

Ugh. The stroller jerked to a stop without permission from Cait. She grunted as her stomach rammed into the handle. The jolt was enough to wake both girls up and their startled cries required her immediate attention.

"Shh, shh, shh," she said, letting go of the handle and coming around the stroller, which had started to cant to one side. "It's all right. Mommy's right here." She shined the penlight on her face.

Willow and Fallon calmed a bit when they saw her. "Where we?"

"We're on an adventure," Cait said, inspecting the four-legged stroller. A stick had lodged between the spokes of a back wheel and the entire wheel was bent. This wasn't good. No way could she continue on three wheels.

"I have to get you out of the stroller," she said, pulling Fallon out first, then Willow. "Stand right there and don't move." Cait watched them out of the corner of her eye as she turned the buggy on its side and leaned into the wheel, trying to straighten it. No such luck. The wheel was toast.

Crap. Now, what would she do? What the hell had made her think she could traipse through the woods like it was some urban adventure?

Both girls clung to her legs. Willow's grip was borderline too tight. Cait thought about the day she'd seen that couch floating in the air. Had that only been a few days ago? It seemed like weeks.

Maybe...

"Fallon, I need you to do something for me. Can you straighten this wheel?"

She showed her daughter the wheel. "See how it's bent? We need it round, like the wheels on your toy at home."

Fallon tried, she really did. It wasn't a strength issue that held her back. It was the concept of round and not bent-round that her two-year-old mind couldn't grasp. Finally, Cait gave up. They'd have to move on without the stroller.

An owl hooted, startling her, making her realize there could be more than owls in these woods. She was an idiot for bringing her daughters out here. Had she put them in danger?

With fear lodged in her throat, Cait tucked their water bottles into her hiking pack and shouldered it, grasping each girl's hand.

"I don' wanna walk," Willow wailed.

Fallon joined her in a cacophony of noise.

Would they alert some wild animal to their presence? Terrified at the thought, Cait tried her best to shush them, not an easy feat. "We have to walk. Just for a while. And we should be quiet as we go."

She calmed them down, then the penlight bit the dust. Using the flashlight, her last bit of power, they abandoned the stroller and headed along the trail.

Not much time passed before the complaints started again. Cait picked Willow up, telling Fallon she'd have to walk for a bit more. That set off another round of wails.

"Stop it," she said, her voice sterner than she'd ever used with the girls. Guilt filled her as Fallon's round eyes stared at her. "Please," Cait begged. "Just try to walk a little farther."

Before long, the trail in front of her widened. She stumbled over a root, barely managing to keep from tumbling and taking both girls down with her. Exhausted beyond anything she'd ever known, and still terrified, she put one foot in front of the other, moving toward the light she saw ahead.

Oh, please, let this be the campground.

She trudged ahead as fast as she could. Hoping. Praying...

News Alert: The frenzy around the light streams has not abated. Entry to the light-stream locations is being prevented by the National Guard, and protests are rumbling across the world.

CHAPTER THIRTEEN

After Taegar and Gordon left, a pall of silent worry settled over the druid camp. Those who had asked to join their circle after seeing the light stream wandered off to their own camps. Only seven people remained, and their late dinner was a quiet affair, with hung heads and murmured prayers that something would change the growing negativity.

Tom was the only bright spot. He'd joined them for dinner and had asked to become part of their circle, though he had no enhanced powers and explained he'd have to leave soon.

Damian sat next to him, handing him the ring he'd put in his pocket earlier for just this occasion. "You will always have a place in our circle."

Tom stared at the ring, turning it over in his palm. "I'm aware, from conversations with all of you, that you follow the druid way."

Each person nodded.

"I've never announced it to the world, and I know it

sounds like it's in direct opposition to my job as a scientist, but I follow a similar path. I believe the pursuit of science can coincide with the harmony of Earth."

"Then you are one of us in mind and spirit."

Nodding, Tom slipped the ring on his finger. "Thank you. I'm honored."

Damian reached for Tom's hand. Wyeth, across the table, took Tom's other hand, then Bhren's.

One by one, they held hands until the circle was complete. One circle, one mind. All silently devoting their lives to coexistence with Earth. To extending their knowledge and helping others to understand that Earth's plight was also theirs.

Silently, they bowed their heads and said their prayers.

When they raised their collective heads, hands still joined, Tom spoke first.

"So, does this druid circle have a name?"

Wyeth was the first one to laugh. "You know, we've never even thought of that."

"We've always been a family," Gwen said.

"One spirit," Valena chimed in.

"One mind," Bhren said.

Damian nodded. "Now we are tasked with guarding this precious gift Earth has given us. With making people understand we are at a turning point and their next moves will determine the fate of humanity and life as we know it."

"We are guardians, then," Bhren said.

"Yes. Guardians. Guardian druids," Damian said. As soon as he said the words, the pressure on his heart eased. This felt right. His face lit up with the first true smile he'd had all day.

"I like that," Tom said.

"It's a strong name," Luther added.

"Now and forevermore. Protectors of Mother Earth,

of the planet that provides us sustenance and life."

One by one, they nodded in agreement, then everyone raised their joined hands and intoned, with one voice:

"Guardian druids."

They sat like that, hands raised, the emotion of the moment washing over them, until Damian looked behind him, alerted by a sound.

"Help."

A woman stood there, a young child asleep on one shoulder, another walking beside her, though just barely. A hiker's backpack sat askew and the woman's red hair looked as though it had been a long time since she'd tugged that ponytail into place. She drooped with her own brand of exhaustion.

"Are you the people the light first appeared to? I...I need help," she said as she sank to her knees.

~~~

Damian raced to help but Valena was the first to reach the family's side. She caught the slumping woman as Damian took the sleeping child from her shoulder. Where had they come from? And why was a woman with two small children out in the woods after dark? Damian's head was full of questions. Answers would have to wait, though.

Gwen dropped to her haunches near the other child, who grasped her mother's legs like they were her only lifeline. "It's all right, sweetie. I can help." Soothingness emanated from her voice, the same tone she used when coaxing growth from the trees and plants. It worked, because the little girl's grip lessened. In another few seconds, she was in Gwen's arms. "Sleepy," she said, laying her head on Gwen's shoulder. Just like that, she was out.

Slipping the pack off the woman's shoulders, Luther carried it while he and Wyeth helped her to the table.

"What's your name?" Valena asked the woman.
~~~

"Cait. My girls—"

I'm just going to make sure they're okay." Valena laid her hand on each child's head, one at a time. "They're all right. Just tired."

"We had to walk a long way," the woman said. "I—I didn't think we'd make it."

"Shhh," Valena said. "Rest. I'm going to touch you. Is that all right? I have healing powers."

The woman's eyes widened, but she nodded.

Valena sat beside her and placed her hands on the woman's clothed shoulders, running them down her arms until she reached her hands. Grasping both, she bent her head and focused. She'd need to rest when this was done. Each act of helping another took a toll on her energy for a while.

"You're all right. Just exhausted," she told Cait. For a moment, they stared at each other, then Valena pulled her hands away. She staggered a bit when she stood and Damian rushed to keep her balanced.

"I'm all right. I just gave her a touch of energy. Enough to help her get settled for the night and be at peace."

Cait straightened. "I feel it. I don't know how, but thank you," she said to Valena. "I can't sleep, though. If you are the ones, the first ones the magic appeared to, I need to talk to you. I need your help. My two-year-old, she's one of you. She has abilities."

As much as Damian wanted to know more now, Valena's look told him it wasn't the time. "We're happy to give you any assistance we can," Valena said. "I think the morning is soon enough for that, and for introductions. It's late and your daughters are sound asleep in my friends' arms. We have a tent you can sleep in tonight. We'll help you bed down and tomorrow we'll talk."

"But—"

"My wife is right," Damian said. "Healing tires her out, and you've been through an ordeal. Your children are safe. So are you. Isn't that enough until morning?"

The woman looked at her sleeping babies, then at Valena, and nodded slowly. "I guess. I've come a long way, though. I hate to wait."

"We'll still be here tomorrow. And we'll all be better prepared to assist you."

She nodded and stood. Within minutes, all three were bundled into Damian and Valena's tent. Soon, a gentle snore validated that the woman had given in to her body's need for sleep.

Together, Damian and Valena walked to the trailer.

"A two-year-old mod? I wonder what her power is."

Damian shook his head. "We'll find out in morning. For tonight, I'm looking forward to a familiar bed."

News Alert: The appearance of the light streams has not led to a consensus among the populace. Many people wonder who they should believe, those who stand on street corners and shout that the end of the world is nigh, or skeptics who scoff at all belief in climate change and light streams sent to heal. People seem to be doing their own research and coming to their own conclusions.

CHAPTER FOURTEEN

Cait opened her eyes to light filtered through canvas, except the filter didn't work too well. Her surroundings were bright, and colder than normal. After a moment of confusion, the events of the previous night flooded back. She was a long way from her bedroom. Having found the people she'd been searching for, she'd pretty much collapsed in their laps unable to utter a single coherent word.

She lay in the tent where they'd let her sleep. The girls were on one side, curled into each other, their hair barely showing above the blankets.

Relief coursed through her and she relaxed. They'd made it. They were safe. The foolish choice she'd made hadn't meant their demise. She sent a heartfelt prayer skyward for whoever had watched over them and helped them find this camp.

Cait didn't believe in God. Her father didn't believe in anything he hadn't created himself, and her mother had gone in the opposite direction, dragging Cait to this church and that throughout her childhood, all in search of something more, something better.

Once Cait had been old enough to have her own opinion, she'd refused to go. It wasn't that she didn't like God, or people's idea of God. She just hadn't wanted it forced down her throat. Ever since then, she'd placed low importance on determining her faith.

She'd need to rethink that, because someone or something had helped her through those woods. She believed that with everything she had inside her.

Edging her way out from under the blankets—still in her clothes from last night—she unzipped the tent flap, careful not to wake the girls. She needed a few moments to assess the situation before dealing with their morning energy. And their questions. Because, as she poked her head outside, she knew they'd have a lot of them.

There were three other tents in the circle. A makeshift table held cooking supplies, and the fire pit showed the remains of a fire. Two people sat at the picnic table. They looked like two from last night, but Cait's brain had been so muddled, she couldn't be certain. She smoothed her hair and her clothes and walked over to the couple.

The woman smiled. "You're awake. Excellent." She indicated Cait should sit next to her on the bench. The man sat across from them. "Let me get you some tea to ward off this morning chill."

When she returned, Cait cupped the mug gratefully. She hadn't prepared well enough for a chilly morning.

"How are you feeling?" Concern filled the woman's eyes.

"Fine. A little cold. And a bit overwhelmed."

The man left, returning in a moment with a blanket that he placed around Cait's shoulders.

She smiled in gratitude, letting go of the mug to clutch the blanket closer.

"Do you have any injuries? Pain?"

"No." Thank goodness. "I don't think I'm hurt at all. I was just tired. My stroller broke down on the path a ways back and the girls had to walk, and... " Cait reached for the woman's hand, surprised when a peaceful warmth filled her. "Thank you." She looked at the man. "Thank you both. I don't know— " her voice caught, " —if we'd be alive if it weren't for you."

"We're just glad we were here to help." The woman cocked her head toward the tent. "Are the twins your daughters?"

Cait nodded.

"And you had them out in the woods, in the dark?" the man asked.

"Shh, husband," the woman said. "There's time for that later." Turning back to Cait, she patted her hand. "We have questions and I know you do, too. Why don't you go freshen up? The camp bathrooms are just down the road a couple of campsites. We'll keep an eye out for your wee ones. And when you get back, we've got coffee and breakfast."

"And we'll have that talk," the man said.

Cait had no doubt they would, based on the perennial scowl on the man's face. But with her bladder pressing, the woman's welcoming smile offset those vibes and Cait grabbed the respite, hurrying off to the facilities. When she returned, a bowl of oatmeal, an apple, and the best-smelling cup of coffee ever waited for her, along with the scowling man and his gentle wife.

"Come, eat."

"The coffee smells heavenly. I learned back at the roadblock that supplies are hard to get in here. I don't want to take food you need."

"Don't worry. We're well-stocked for the moment. I'm Valena Royan, and the grouch on the other side of the table is my husband, Damian."

"You *are* them, then."

"We are who?" Damian asked.

"The people I was looking for. The face of this... " Cait waved toward the trees. "This phenomenon."

"Are you a reporter?"

"Do you really think I'd drag my daughters through the woods at night for a story? No, I'm not a reporter." She'd about had it with his high-handed attitude.

"Then why are you here?"

"I'm here because I need help."

Before she could explain further, the apple beside her bowl lifted, wafting its way like a trail of smoke across the camp to the tent where she'd slept with the girls. Fallon stood in front of the tent, her arm out, concentrating, grasping the apple when it reached her.

Cait turned back to the open-mouthed couple. "That is why I need your help."

~~~

Damian couldn't believe it. This was the first he'd seen or heard of anyone whose talents included telekinesis.

While Valena and Cait took the twins to the bathroom, Bhren joined Damian.

"Did you see that?" Damian asked.

Bhren nodded.

"Have you heard of that happening before?"

"No. Haven't tried it, either, though."

Damian and Bhren looked down at the table, quiet, introspective, focused.
~~~

"Nothing's moving," Bhren said.

"You tried it?"

"Yes. You?"

"Yep. Nothing."

Damian watched Bhren focus, his face scrunching up with intensity as he stared at a bowl. Not even a wobble. The absurdity hit Damian and he chuckled. "This, apparently, isn't one of our Earth-given talents."

A rare smile lit Bhren's face. "Guess not." They watched as the women walked back to camp with the twins between them. "This is a first."

Back at the table, Valena coaxed one of the children onto her lap. Gwen had made oatmeal for them and Cait and Valena helped the girls eat.

"When did this talent manifest?" Damian asked Cait.

"Talent?" Wyeth said, joining them. "Hi, I'm Wyeth. Gwen here's my wife."

"And I'm Luther."

"Tom," the last man to join them said, standing back.

Cait shook their hands in turn. "I'm sorry. I never fully introduced myself. I'm Cait Darcy."

All but one person around her stiffened at the introduction. "What did I say?"

"Darcy?" Damian asked, his voice flat and quiet.

"Yes. What does that have to do with anything?"

"Any relation to Gordon Darcy?"

It was Cait's turn to go ramrod straight. She never wanted to hear that name again. Ever. "I guess you could say he's the biological reason I'm here," she said with a grimace.

Damian stood. "You need to leave. Now."

"Patience, husband. Let's hear her out first."

"No." He paced away from the table, then back. "This is some sort of trick. A second layer of deviousness from that man's coffer of lies."

"You've met Gordon Darcy?"

"Met him? He just left here, with one of our family wrapped around his little finger. After unequivocally trying to kick us off of *his* property. The man is trying to destroy us for his own gain."

He watched Cait, who exhibited not one bit of surprise at his words. She was in cahoots with him. Had to be. And these poor, innocent girls were being used as pawns. Except, if Darcy had someone in the family with powers, why did he take Taegar with him?

"I am not my father."

Cait's gaze didn't waver from his and Damian saw the truth in her words.

"That doesn't mean you're innocent."

Cait took a deep breath and hugged her daughter close. When she spoke, it was with a different voice. A smaller one, a hurt one. "He's never even seen Fallon and Willow. I— " She raised her head, looking around at everyone before settling her gaze back on Damian. "I worked for him. Yes. I thought I was doing good things. Things to help make working environments better, happier, more productive. Apparently, I took that a little too far because last week, he fired me."

"Ass," Valena said under her breath, surprising Damian. His wife never swore.

"If I could disown my father, I would. I am not him. And I want nothing to do with him. Except, he was here? Why would he have come here? I know what I went through to get to you. Why would he— " She gazed off toward the clearing. "The light stream. He wants that power for himself."

"That's what we surmised."

Everyone nodded in agreement.

"Did he get it? Does he have powers?"

Damian applauded the edge of panic in her voice. Gordon Darcy, with more power than he already had, would be deadly. For Earth, for humanity, for the existence of everything they held dear.

"No. Apparently, he walked right up to the light stream and thrust his arm into it."

Cait's eyes grew wide.

"It tossed him across the clearing and into a tree." Damian chuckled. "Boy, would I have liked to see that."

"Me, too," Cait answered.

She did not share her father's evilness. Damian saw it in her eyes, heard it in the sureness of her voice, sensed it in the core of his being. He sat back down, running a hand over Willow's curly hair then clasping his wife's hand briefly before looking around the table.

"I believe you. We believe you, Cait."

Gwen put a hand on Cait's shoulder. "How can we help?"

Cait clutched Fallon to her. "I don't know what's happened to my daughter. I'm afraid of how it will affect her. That's why I came here. That's the only reason I went through everything I did to get here. Why I put them through," she waved towards the woods, "all that."

"When did this talent of hers manifest?" Damian asked again, though he knew the answer already. They all did.

"Shortly after those light streams showed up."

No one had been able to do what this two-year-old could do. At least, not that they knew. This was a new talent.

"Any other abilities?"

"Not that I've seen."

"And her sister?"

"Has exhibited no powers."

"We've been communicating more and more with others whose talents have grown," Valena said. "Strength, healing, plant growth... Those seem to be what most people received when the light stream showed up. But there's a smattering of other things. Fire-making, rain-calling, an innate ability to design and build things. No one has shown Fallon's abilities until now."

"Do you think these powers will harm her?"

The fear in Cait's eyes backed up her reason for coming. She wanted reassurances that her daughter would be all right.

"We don't have a lot of answers, Cait," Damian said. "What we do know is that Earth released this power to heal itself. We were given enhanced abilities so we could help that process, and, as a part of all this, help ourselves. If Earth's goal is that benevolent, I find it hard to believe that these powers will harm any of us."

Her shoulders slumping in relief, Cait hugged her daughter again, causing Fallon to squirm.

"Down, Mommy."

Cait set her down, watching as she explored camp, most likely looking for mischief. "I don't know how to handle all this," she said. "How do I keep a two-year-old from using a power that feels natural to her? How do I teach her to use those powers for good? To not use them around others?"

Luther chuckled. "She's the first youngster we've heard of. I don't think it will be easy to corral those abilities."

"Would it be all right if we stayed?" Cait asked Damian. "You all, with your powers, might be able to help. I can help, too. I'm not sure how, but I'm a hard worker."

They had so much to do. Taking on youngsters would be a significant time commitment, and time already slipped through their fingers too quickly. Yet they'd been tasked with helping Earth and humankind. How could they refuse?

Valena played patty-cake with Willow and the child's laughter rang like music through the trees. She glanced up at Damian, the plea in her eyes deciding what he already knew.

"Of course you can stay. We welcome you and your daughters to our humble community."

Tom cleared his throat. "I'd, umm, like you all to consider some additional testing. Like giving blood and DNA samples." He focused on Cait. "I'm a scientist."

"And he's our friend," Damian added.

"Thank you," Tom said. "Anyhow, the government sent me out here to make sense of all this. So far, I haven't been able to." He shrugged. "But I've come to believe that this is bigger than all of us. With your permission, I'd like to stay another day or two, draw some blood from Fallon for testing. From Willow, too, along with the rest of you."

Cait about shook her head off. "Absolutely not. No one is going to turn my daughter into some government science experiment."

"It wouldn't be like that."

"How do you know? You work for the government."

"Because I pretty much call the shots. I lead my department and I'm good at what I do." He spread his arms wide. "They gave me carte blanche. I'd keep it confidential so no one would ever learn where the samples came from."

Cait still shook her head, though not as emphatically.

Scratching a chin that needed a shave, Damian thought about Tom's request. Would blood and DNA tests be good things or turn ugly for them? With so many people across the world gaining talent, testing their circle would at least give them a decent control group. And they'd have a say in which tests were done. Damian looked at Valena, who gave a quick nod.

"We can't make a choice for you or your daughters, Cait. This is a personal decision each of us must make for ourselves. Valena and I, at least, agree to the testing. We trust you, Tom. You've been straight with us since the beginning. And we have to do whatever we can to convince the powers-that-be to recognize what Earth is trying to tell us. If we don't make changes now, there will be no tomorrow to rescue."

Cait's eyes widened. "It's that dire?"

When Valena nodded, Cait turned to watch her daughter, busy bouncing a ball without using her hands. Then she looked back at Tom. "If it will help, and if you can do it without any strife for the girls, then I'll agree."

"I'll make it as simple and pain-free as I can."

"Just one blood draw."

Tom smiled. "Just one. And a mouth swab."

With that, they all officially became guinea pigs. Tom wouldn't be ready for them until the evening at the earliest, so the others dispersed to their chores, leaving Valena, Cait, and the girls at loose ends. Damian pulled the laptop open to see if he could find news of any other telekinetic mods.

"I'd like to help," Cait said to Valena. "Do you have any work I can do?"

Valena laughed. "With those girls, especially Fallon, you've already got your hands full."

"I do." Cait smiled. "But I manage to get done what I need to. And I'd like to earn my keep here."

"Well, then, how about you and I cut up vegetables and get a nice stew going in the Crock-Pot for tonight's supper. Afterward, we can take the girls over to the playground, let them run off some of that energy."

Cait's grin widened. "That sounds perfect. Though their energy replenishes pretty quickly at this age."

Laughing, they walked over to the makeshift kitchen

area, talking about children like they were old friends. Damian smiled at the happiness in Valena's voice. She'd be a great mother. As for him being father material, that was another story. He wasn't sure he had the patience for children.

He watched the twins play. The ball rolled off into the grass and Fallon brought it back without lifting a hand. Yes, he was quite certain he didn't have the patience. Certainly not for this kind of issue.

What he did have was his own set of chores to do. He'd better get to it before Valena pointed that out to him.

Damian walked toward the entrance to camp, his mind full of problems that had no solutions.

~~~

Gordon's eye twitched as he sat watching Taegar from the bedroom window. He'd brought her to his hideaway, his private domain. A place he never brought anyone. It went against his ingrained need for privacy, but was necessary for her to trust him.

She sat now in the middle of the expansive lawn, twirling a long piece of grass for some damn cat. Why did he pay for all this expensive fencing if animals still found a way inside to defile his property? Gordon grimaced. Maybe he could have poison placed around the perimeter. A death or two might keep the damn things out.

He had to admit that his property had never looked so good, after five days of Taegar's ministrations. Everything she touched turned lush and green. His back yard had turned into a rain forest without the rain. Caretakers were complaining they couldn't keep the grass cut, it grew so fast. For him, it was too green. He needed less green. More gold.

That was the crux of his irritation at the moment. Taegar was his. He'd talked her into one bedroom instead
~~~

of two. Five days now, they'd slept together, something he never did. Ever. Adding insult to injury, they'd done nothing else but—he grimaced—cuddle and sleep. Gordon's patience was running short.

How could he utilize her skills to his benefit? He'd seen bits and pieces of what she could do. She was strong. He'd mentioned his armoire wasn't in the right spot and she'd moved it without sweat or even a grunt. And the things she touched grew faster.

That was the talent he needed. Could she make more than shrubbery grow? Like...money? Or minerals? Gordon smiled. He'd just figured out his next move.

She'd stopped twirling the grass and sat perfectly still, staring off into the distance like the spaced-out hippie she was. Except... Gordon peered through the window. Even from that spot, he could see that her eyes were unfocused. What had his man told him? That he'd seen Damian in some sort of trance, actually thought he'd visualized what had happened to his wife. Was that one of these mod powers? Could these people see into the past? And, if so...

Gordon tapped the newspaper he held against his free hand.

Could they see the future, as well? Could she?

His cell buzzed and he picked it up.

"Have you made any progress?"

"We've only been here a few days," Gordon said. "I'm good, but she's skittish and I'm not a miracle worker."

"We need to know how she can help us. How we can profit from those mod powers of hers."

"I'm aware of that. There's some finesse involved in bringing this one along."

"You don't do finesse."

"I don't have much of a choice. This one has a past. If I can't get her to trust me, she'll run." Or worse, use those powers of hers to thwart his plans.

"We need answers and we need them yesterday. You have to step it up."

Gordon had rethought the contract to make the vice president disappear. The man could still be useful, and Gordon liked knowing the government's plans before almost anyone else. He liked that he carried some influence in making those plans, or skewing them in the direction necessary to further their efforts.

For now, Ramsey was a necessary evil. He'd keep the man thinking he ran things when in reality, he was nothing more than a puppet.

"We *do* need answers quickly." Gordon thought again about minerals. Maybe it was time to test his theory. "I have an idea I'm going to run with. I'll call you in a couple of days and let you know how it went."

"You'd better. Feels like we're losing our grip on this. That's not good."

"Agreed." Gordon hung up without waiting for goodbyes. He tucked the business section of the paper under his arm and joined Taegar in the yard, the phone call forgotten. The stray cat, curled up in her lap and purring happily, raised his head. When he saw Gordon, he hissed, jumped down, and sped off into the trees.

Ungrateful bastard.

An uncharacteristic frown marred Taegar's face.

"Everything all right? You look upset," he said, planting a benign smile on his face.

Taegar's eyes slowly refocused on the present, on him, her lips quirking up into that innocent smile he'd grown used to seeing. "Hi, Gordon."

He reached down and pulled a strand of her hair through his fingers, uncharacteristically noticing how soft it was. "You looked sad. Anything wrong?"

"No," she said, sighing. "Just...thinking about the future."

Women and their futures. Gordon almost shuddered, the tender moment between them doomed by the merest idea of female machinations designed to trap men. Like his wife had done to him. And his mother to his father. Women were all the same and he would do well to remember that. *Focus on what's important.* He would concentrate on what fed his soul, not their cold, conniving, disappearing hearts.

Squatting down next to Taegar, Gordon opened the newspaper to the stock listing.

"If you were going to buy one of these stocks, which one do you think would grow the fastest?"

"I don't need any stocks."

"I know, but just as a game, if you were to want some, which would you buy? Which stock would make you money to buy pretty things?"

"I don't need pretty things, as long as I've got flowers and air and you."

He pasted a smile on his face. "Humor me for a moment and give this a try. Then I'll take you into town."

"I'd rather go see the ocean."

He'd promised to take her, but right now, there were more pressing matters. "We will. Just not today. Just this one little task, then I have a surprise for you in town."

Taegar jumped up and into his arms. "What?"

He waved the paper in front of her and waited.

Taegar's lips became thin lines, but not for long. The prospect of a surprise did the trick. She pointed to the paper. "That one."

A small yield stock that Gordon didn't think had any growth potential. "You sure?"

"Yep. That's the one. Now, what's my surprise?"

"You'll have to come to town with me to find out."

She kissed him, all smiles now. "I can be ready in ten minutes."

"Good, that gives me time for a quick call. Now, go. I'm anxious to be done and get back home."

He swatted her on the ass, eliciting a giggle that ran through him like a discordant note. As she ran into the house, he wiped her taste from his mouth.

Gordon went to his home office, called his broker, and ordered enough shares of that stock to use as a test subject. When he'd finished, he brought the car around and waited for Taegar, who perennially moved to the rate of some internal clock he'd never understand. She was late. Again.

When he got what he wanted, she'd learn the true destiny of someone who lived in Gordon's stable. She'd learn that he was the god she must worship.

Or she'd pay the final price.

News: With no explanation, climate change seems to be easing. While some refute the growing proof, severe weather events have dropped by twenty-one percent. Farmers are harvesting more foods naturally imbued with life-strengthening nutrients. And, wonder of all wonders, a natural compound has been found that regenerates a non-functioning pancreas. Diabetes may soon be a disease of the past, like polio and smallpox.

CHAPTER FIFTEEN

When Gordon walked Taegar into the jewelry store, she squealed with delight. Actually squealed, God help him. He pasted a smile on his face.

"I thought you deserved a treat," he said. "I want to spoil you with beautiful things."

After she hugged him for the third time, he got her off him by asking if anything in the store called to her. Taegar pulled him from showcase to showcase.

Gordon wanted her to hold things, try them on. He wanted to see how the metals and precious gems would react to her touch. Hopefully, with gusto. He grew increasingly frustrated when she adopted a "look, don't touch" attitude.

She stopped at a case containing sapphires and tapped the glass. "That's pretty, isn't it?"

"Yes. Let's have a closer look at that necklace."

"I'd rather keep looking."

"Whatever you want, sweetheart," he ground out. "Your will is my command."

Taegar giggled and continued to wander. She stopped at the last case in the store and Gordon heard a contented sigh. Maybe, finally, she'd found something.

Brushing her hands over the case with reverent care, she looked almost spellbound.

Gordon stepped beside her to see what she'd picked. Black opals. It figured. The most expensive gem in the place.

"Aren't they beautiful?" Taegar said.

"They are." Gordon motioned for the man, whose silence he'd paid for, to unlock the case. Now, finally, he would find out if Taegar's abilities included a Midas touch.

She pointed to a bracelet that had slivers of black opal throughout.

"Try this one instead," he said, pointing to the largest ring in the case, a gaudy square-set gem in a halo of gold.

"It's so beautiful," Taegar said, her hands twitching as the salesman picked up the selected ring and held it out to her. She turned to Gordon, questions filling her eyes.

He nodded. "Go ahead." He watched the ring closely as she took it from the man. Had it shimmered?

"What size is this?" he asked.

The man consulted the box. "Three carats."

Gordon almost whistled as Taegar slid the ring on her finger, looking at it this way and that. He kept a close eye on the ring, but nothing seemed to happen. "Do you have a black opal that hasn't been set yet?"

"We do. Some customers like to select a raw gem and dictate the shape."

"We'd like to see those."

"I'd be happy to get them." He took the ring back from Taegar and closed up the case. "Give me just a moment."

When he returned, he had a small locked box. He opened it, and inside were several pieces of opal. Some had already been polished, but a couple were in their cloudy, raw state. Gordon picked up one of those, pretending to look at it closely. He compared it to his thumb. It was about the size of the nail, only three-dimensional.

"Look at this one, sweetheart. You can see the color trying to burst free."

He opened her hand and placed the gem in her palm.

"It's beautiful," she said.

The gem, a milky dark blue with colors embedded beneath the cloudiness, shimmered just as he'd thought the ring's stone had. Only this time, the gem grew. Gordon quickly put up his hand to shield the stone from the salesman's eyes. It was quite a bit larger than his thumbnail now.

Yes! This was how he would recoup the staggering losses from the Black Hills fiasco. Except now, he needed raw material to work with. A gold mine. A diamond mine. Any mine he could manage to snag. *Oh, yes.* He almost rubbed his hands together. This was going to be better than drilling in a national forest. This would finally make him the richest man in the world.

"We'll take the bracelet, the ring, and this box of black opals."

The salesman's and Taegar's eyes widened.

"You're worth it, my dear," he said magnanimously. The only thing he needed to figure out now was how to get Taegar to cooperate. Over and over and over again. Well, if she wouldn't cooperate, he could fall back on the tools in his dungeon.

One way or another, he would get what he wanted. He always did.

~~~

Bang!

Valena screamed and Damian went from deep sleep to wide-awake, full-protective mode in zero point five seconds. He grabbed the knife he'd taken to carrying, flew out of bed, and searched the night-darkened trailer to find the danger. His breath heaved and his heart raced as he sought what he could not see.

"Not here," Valena whispered, whimpering as she clutched her stomach.

"What's the matter? What's happened?"

"Someone's been hurt. In the glade. I don't know how or why." She began pulling on clothes. "I need to get there. Someone's been hurt," she said again.

Damian yanked on pants and a shirt. "You're not going anywhere until I check out what happened."

"Then we'll go together." She touched his cheek to get his attention. "There's no time to do this the safe way. I'm needed."

He didn't like this. Not at all. The look on Valena's face said she wouldn't be taking no for an answer. Damian reached for her jacket and handed it to her. "Come on, then."

Outside, Damian caught sight of Luther disappearing at a run in the direction of the glade and the *awen* light. Wyeth and Gwen stood stock still, sleepy indecision evident on their faces.

"Was that a gunshot?" Bhren asked, joining them.

That was the sound Damian had heard. He was certain of it now. "I think so. Valena says someone's hurt and she needs to get there. Now."

Damian and Wyeth took the lead, with the women
~~~

close behind them and Bhren at the back. They hurried through the darkness, albeit at a slower, more careful pace than Luther had taken.

Then, another bang. Another shot.

"No," Valena cried.

They picked up their pace. Near the light, chaos had once again replaced order. Several people raced past them, leaving the glade, crying.

"What's happened?" Damian asked, stopping a young man.

"I don't know." The man was out of breath and clearly in full panic mode. "God, I don't know. There was such a crowd. They rushed the light. Then, a shot was fired and everyone ran." He looked everywhere at once, wildness in his eyes. "I've got to get out of here."

He yanked his sleeve from Damian's hand and took off running again.

Damian looked worriedly at Valena, who remained focused on what lay in front of them. As they came into the glade, the area surrounding the *awen* was devoid of anyone but the guard who stood on full alert, rifles at the ready. A small group of them stood around something that lay on the ground.

No. Not something. Someone. Two someones.

Valena pushed past Damian and straight for the people who lay unmoving on the ground.

"No!" Damian tried to catch her, but she got to the circle of armed men before him.

"Let me through," she said, her authoritative tone telling them she would brook no interference.

"No one gets through, Ma'am."

"Those people are hurt. I can help them."

"No one gets through." Major Swanton—who Damian knew to be the commander of the guard—strode up.

"I'm a healer," Valena said, taking a step forward.

A guard turned his rifle toward Valena and Damian erupted, reaching the man faster than humanly possible and ripping the rifle from his hands. In front of the guard's widened eyes, Damian ejected the bullets and bent the rifle into a "U" shape. He glared at the commander. "No one points a gun at my wife."

"All right, all right," the commander said, raising his hands. He peered intensely at Valena. "Medics are at least fifteen minutes away. You really think you can help them?"

"I've got to try. Please."

"Let her in."

The guards let her through and Damian, Wyeth, and Gwen pushed along behind her.

Valena bent over the first man. Damian stopped her before she touched him. The man didn't look good.

"Be mindful of your own energy, wife. You have limits."

She held Damian's eyes for a moment, then nodded. Without touching the man, she ran her hands over his head, his neck, his trunk. One of the guards pressed a scarlet-soaked cloth against his chest. The man's breath gurgled and Valena whimpered.

"I can't help him. The life force is leaving him. I can't help him."

She wanted to try. Damian could see that in the tears streaming down her face.

"Luther!" Gwen's exclamation behind them turned both their gazes toward the other injured man.

Their friend lay on the ground, shot, and the cloth Gwen held to his shoulder looked as soaked as the dying man's. How had he come to be in the middle of this fray so quickly? He'd run ahead scant seconds before them.

Valena looked back and forth between the two. She

reached blindly for Damian's hand. "I don't know what to do."

He took her hand, pulled her gaze to his. "You can't help this one. Help Luther."

"But he'll die."

"He's already dead."

As if those three words had signed his warrant, the man gave one last gurgling gasp and stopped breathing, his entire body going lax.

Valena hung her head over him for a moment, her tears dropping onto the hand she now placed on his chest. Then Luther's gasp of pain turned her. Recognizing the only need left, she quickly moved to Luther's side.

He grimaced. "Turns out, all this strength I've got doesn't stop bullets."

"Shh, shh, let me see." Valena removed Gwen's hand from the cloth and pulled it away. Fresh blood oozed from the wound in his shoulder. She held her hands over him, bowing her head.

Damian watched and worried above her.

"I don't think the bullet hit anything vital, but we need to remove it."

"Are you sure you can do this?" Damian asked.

"Yes."

"Without losing yourself?"

"I believe so."

Before Damian could react, she placed a hand on Luther's forehead, her other hand covering the wound, intermingling with the blood welling there. She bowed her head again.

Damian, fear rising in his throat like bitter bile, held his breath. In fact, it felt like the collective breath of everyone in the glade had paused. A faint golden light glowed around Valena, an aura of grace and healing. It grew brighter as it extended down her arm, enveloping Luther's shoulder in its healing essence.

Valena started to shake and Damian put his hand on her shoulder to steady her. Then something else happened. Something more. Something he couldn't explain. He could feel his energy transferring to her, shoring up her reserves.

He kept his hand there, gave her everything she could take, and let her concentrate. Finally, after what seemed like hours but in true time measured only minutes, Valena lifted her hand, turning it over and showing everyone the bullet now resting there.

"He'll be okay now," she said. The light around her dissipated and she sat heavily on the ground next to Luther, swaying. "He'll be all right."

Damian picked his wife up in his arms and searched for the commander. For the first time, he saw the shock and awe on everyone's faces. Bhren and Wyeth began clearing a path through the guards.

"I'm taking my wife back to our trailer," he told the commander. "Meet me there as soon as you can to discuss this incident."

The man paused, staring at Damian and Valena both, then nodded.

~~~

With Valena's assurances that all she needed was rest, Damian covered her with blankets. As her eyes closed, he stepped outside to sink into a chair. He felt like he'd just run a full marathon and he hadn't done a thing except place his hand on her shoulder.

"You look wrung out," Bhren said.

"I am wiped. And I have no idea why."

"When you touched Valena, there in the glade, her aura changed color, like your green mixed with her golden light."
~~~

"It felt like I was giving her some of my power, but how can that be?"

Bhren shook his head. "There's much we still don't know about the *awen* and how it acts. Maybe that's exactly what happened. Valena needed more than she could summon safely and your powers gave her what she needed."

Damian nodded. "She did the real work, yet I'm beat. I can only imagine how exhausted she feels."

"She'll sleep for hours, I suspect."

They both watched Major Swanton walk into their camp. Tom joined them from the tent area.

"I suspect that, after this conversation, you might want to catch your own nap," Bhren said under his breath.

Gwen and Wyeth joined them, too. "Where's Cait?" Gwen asked Tom. He'd taken to spending his time with them.

"She's trying to get the girls back to sleep. I gave her the abridged version."

"Lots of tired people around here," Wyeth said.

"We got Luther settled. He's sleeping now, and there's barely any scar," Gwen told them.

The commander swiped a hand over his face as he sank to the picnic bench. "If I hadn't seen it with my own eyes, I would never have believed it." He turned bleary eyes on Damian. "She pulled that bullet out of your friend's shoulder with nothing but thought."

"Trust me. A lot more than just thought went into that."

The commander nodded, glancing around at the group of friends. "I can see that."

"What happened? What led to the shooting?" Damian speared the man with a look.

"Got anything to drink? I could use some fortification

before we get into this."

Damian nodded to Wyeth, who snuck quietly into the trailer. He came out with paper cups and a bottle of whiskey. Pouring one for Damian, then the commander, he held the bottle and cups out to anyone else who might want a drink.

Most everyone there took him up on the offer.

"We've stopped allowing people into the site," the commander began.

"We know that."

"Things had become too unmanageable. We'd lost all control."

"This *awen* isn't meant to be controlled by the government. The *awen* is for all humankind to experience, to benefit from."

"Do you want to talk politics or find out what happened?"

Damian gestured for the major to continue.

"Apparently, several factions had formed outside the cordoned-off area. Two of these, the Russians and the Southerners, decided it was time for the U.S. Government to share this scientific bounty. Taking advantage of the darkness, they came in quietly, on a trail. We didn't know they were here. Didn't see them coming until they stormed the glade."

He took a stiff sip before continuing.

"I tell my men every day, guns are a last resort. They had no choice today. Three times their numbers were coming at them. Corporal Thomas shot into the air. That didn't stop the crowd, so his next shot went into the leader, though I wish he'd managed to wound him instead of hitting him square in the chest."

Swanton stared off into the distance, shaking his head. "Before we could even begin to process what had happened, your man barreled through everyone and yanked the rifle from Thomas' hands. One of the other guards managed to wound your man. After that, everyone took off running in all directions and we were left with one man dying and another wounded on the ground. It was a shit show, and it should never have happened."

"Agreed," Damian said.

"Reports indicate it's like this at the other two light-streams, as well. Little incidents are happening and the tension is building. Things are getting out of hand. I expect that, after tonight's event, you'll all be told to clear out."

Damian leaned forward in his chair. "I'll tell you this only one more time. This is not something the government can control. You'd be better off just letting those that want to see the *awen* in."

"Not my decision to make." The commander downed the rest of his whiskey and set his empty glass on the picnic table. "Thanks for the hospitality. I'd better get back to my men."

Damian stood and shook the man's hand. He bore him no ill will. The major was doing his job, caught between two very hard points of view. At least now, he'd seen firsthand what the *awen* could accomplish. After he left, most of the others wound their way back to their encampments, leaving the core group there.

Wyeth twirled the signet ring around his finger. "I think," he finally said, "if we're going to get the word out, now is probably a pretty good time to do it. It might be good to be away from here for a while."

"Things will probably get worse before they get better," Bhren agreed.

"If they get better at all," Damian said, tossing his drink back. He stood up, noting that none of his tiredness had abated. "Let's all try to get some sleep and we'll make plans tomorrow for the next phase."

He watched as everyone filtered away to their tents, then, feeling every bit of his age and then some, Damian dragged himself into the trailer and settled next to his wife, asleep almost before his head hit the pillow.

~~~

The next morning, Cait got the girls dressed inside their tent.

"Are you sure we aren't in any danger?" she asked Tom again.

Last night, he'd briefly caught her up on what happened, then repeated the story in more detail this morning, still leaving her dissatisfied. How dangerous would it get here? Should she stay or take the girls back to L.A.? They'd barely begun to work with Fallon's talent, so if she left now, everything she'd done this past week would be for naught.

"The glade, camp, and surrounding areas are calm at the moment. Major Swanton stopped by this morning to say more guards have been assigned to the perimeter and trails. There will be no more sneaking in like you and the twins did. I think that will help to keep us all safe."

"So you don't think I should leave?"

He sighed. "I'm not sure. If you do, you'll never get back here. Are you ready for that finality?"

It surprised Cait how unprepared she was for that. She'd grown to care about her new friends, including one Tom Gallows. Probably a bit too much.

He pulled needles, tubes, and wipes from the kit he'd brought into the tent with him.

"This won't hurt, will it?" Cait chewed her lower lip. Damian and Valena had given her their tent to use for as long as she wanted. It had seemed the perfect size until now. With two twins, herself, and Tom inside, any sense of
~~~

roominess had disappeared.

Here she was worried about the size of a tent when her daughter was about to be stuck with a needle. Cait shook herself and re-focused on Fallon. "Sweetie, Tom here is going to do a test with some of your blood."

"Like doctor?"

"Sort of."

"No. No. No." Loose items inside the tent started rising, right along with the level of tears in her daughter's eyes as she clung to her mother.

"She had a bad reaction to an immunization, so tests have been a struggle ever since."

"It's all right, honey," Tom said, setting down the syringe. "I won't do anything you don't want me to. Do you understand that?"

"No shot."

"If you don't want a shot, then we won't do it. Maybe instead, you'd like to hear a story?"

Everything floating in the air sifted slowly back to the ground. Cait could see her daughter's eyes. Still full of fear, still holding onto a few tears. Her lower lip trembled, but she nodded her head. Willow settled next to them.

"Well, once upon a time, there was a little...kitten."

"Kitty?" she asked.

"Yes. A very young one. And some bad men were being very mean to this kitten. They were trying to throw it up on top of a very tall house."

Fallon's eyes were wide and her focus was completely on Tom. Thankfully, the tears had almost dried up and she'd relaxed back into Cait's arms. Willow followed Tom's story with the same rapt attention.

"They would have succeeded, but for a lovely young lady with," he glanced up at Cait, "beautiful, long, reddish hair."

Heat crept up Cait's face. Had he just paid her a compliment?

Tom smiled at her before returning his attention to Fallon. "This lady took the kitten from them and ran them off."

"She strong. Like me."

"Yes. The lady was very strong. But that kitten wasn't. She was very, very scared. She trembled in the lady's arms, no matter how warm she made her."

"Poor kitty."

"Yes. Poor kitty," Tom said. He'd placed a hand on Fallon's tiny arm. "The lady felt the kitten's ears. Did you know you can tell if a kitten is sick by if its ears are hot?"

"Nuh-uh."

"Well, the kitten's ears were warmer than they should have been. The lady knew that meant she might be sick, so she took the kitten to the doctor."

Tom had begun to rub Fallon's arm with slow, methodical movements. Cait smiled. Her daughter was so into the story, she seemed to have completely forgotten that Tom was the needle man.

"The doctor was just as worried as the nice lady," Tom continued.

"I worry too."

He nodded. "They couldn't make the kitten better until they knew what was wrong with her. That meant they would have to get a little itsy bit of blood from the kitten, who hadn't stopped trembling."

"No. No. No shot, kitty."

"The lady didn't want the kitten hurt anymore, either. She cuddled it close to her and talked to it, just like we're doing now. The kitten calmed down. Then, she told the kitten what the doctor had to do and how important it was for them to do it. The kitten looked up at her with those big round eyes, but she didn't start shaking again. You see, she'd decided she could trust the nice lady and the doctor.

"The doctor took a strap and wrapped it around the kitten's paw. Just for a minute. Can I do that with you, Fallon, to show you how it felt for the kitten?"

"Umm, 'kay."

Cait and Willow both watched as Tom put a band around her daughter's tiny arm.

"There, little kitten, see? That doesn't hurt at all, does it?"

Fallon shook her head.

"Next, the doctor showed the kitten the needle." Tom picked up the syringe and showed it to Fallon, who cringed deeper into her mother's arms.

"'It's all right, little kitten. We can wait until you're ready,' the doctor said. He explained to the kitten that taking that itsy bitsy bit of blood would be just a little prick. Just a little bit of pain. Nothing big, or bad." He swabbed Fallon's inner elbow as he talked.

"Finally, the doctor asked the kitten if he could draw the blood. The kitten was very brave. It looked up at the lady, then at the doctor, and meowed that they could."

"Brave kitty," Fallon said.

"Are you brave, Fallon? Are you as brave as the kitten?"

She nodded.

"Will you let me take a little bit of your blood?" He held the syringe up.

Her lips trembled again as she stared at Tom. A long time passed before she slowly nodded. She looked up at Cait and the worry in her eyes about broke Cait's heart.

Tom patted her arm. "You are a very brave, brave kitten, Fallon."

"All done?" Fallon asked.

Tom grinned, holding up a small vial of blood. "Yep." He picked Fallon up from her mother's lap. "Did that hurt?"

"No!" Her exclamation was full of happiness.

"Good. Then I think you've earned a treat. If your mother will let me, we'll show your sister she's just as strong as you, then go to the playground to play, all right?"

"Can we, Mommy?" Fallon asked. "Please. I good kitten."

"Of course you can. We'll all go." Cait felt the tears welling in her eyes. No one had ever taken that kind of care with her daughters. Ever.

Willow, more willing to have her blood drawn after seeing her brave sister do it, held out her arm. Soon, they were done. Tom stowed the vials away and before long, they were at the playground, all thoughts of needles banished. Fallon and Willow truly believed they were kittens, though, if the meows coming from the sandbox gave any indication.

Cait smiled. "Thank you, Tom. You were extremely patient and gentle."

He sat next to her and the place where their hips touched grew warm. "My sister has kids, so I spend time with them whenever I can."

"It shows. You're amazing."

"Thank you." He reached for her hand. "You're pretty amazing yourself."

Cait enjoyed holding hands. Tom was considerate, caring, and seemed taken with the girls. So different from Harrison, who cared so little he'd given up all parental rights. And her father, with his complete lack of interest in either her or her children.

Together, they watched her babies run around the camp's playground. Fortunately, the equipment wasn't that high, because Fallon would be gone in an instant, climbing. And Willow would follow her sister anywhere.

Here, everything was low to the ground and there was even a short fence surrounding the play area. She could let her girls play and not have to chase after them all the time.

Thank goodness. She wouldn't trade motherhood for anything in the world, but being a solo parent was exhausting. Tom's help had been a godsend these past few days. She glanced at the backpack sitting next to him, not sure she wanted to know the reason for it being there.

"Tommm-cat. Meow." Both girls grinned at Tom, keeping the Tomcat reference up until he joined them in the sand, squatting down in front of Willow to help her reach a bar just above her head. They'd decided Tom was their friend and he didn't seem to mind at all. Cait's heart rose with Willow as Tom lifted her. Her little hands encircled the bar, then he let her hang there, laughing at the giggles that sounded more like hiccups because of her efforts to hold on.

When her small grip loosened and she let go, he caught her, exaggerating his fall, rolling onto the sand with her on top of him. Her giggles mounted. Fallon joined them, pouncing on top of Tom and causing him to grunt. Had she just kneed him in the groin? Cait got up to rescue him, but he waved her off.

"Just winded. I'm okay."

Tom Gallows was an intriguing man. A scientist and a believer both, he had an open mind and a good heart.

Don't fall for this guy.

Cait might remind herself of that, but it didn't mean her heart would follow the advice. Especially not when he was so good with her girls.

She glanced again at his backpack. It meant he needed to return to his lab. That shouldn't bother her since she'd only known him for a few days, but it did. Somewhere in the vicinity of her heart, a seam had been ripped open, and she wasn't quite certain she could sew it back together.

Tom sank next to her. "Those girls have a lot of energy."

"That they do."

"I'm going to miss them." His expression turned serious as he took Cait's hand. "I'm going to miss you, too."

Her hand felt good in his. His lips felt even better when they touched hers. Cait sighed. Yes, she was definitely going to miss this man.

"I have to go," he said.

"I know."

"I'll be back when I can, but honestly, I don't know how long that will be."

This was getting more depressing. Cait stared at their entwined hands. "I get it. There's too much at stake to let personal stuff get in the way. I know it's the right choice. Still, I wish we could stay like this for a while longer."

Tom put an arm around her shoulders as they sat there watching the twins. In too short a time, he stood, pulling her up with him. His kiss was sweet and gentle. "This is going to have to last us until we're together again. And that will happen. I'll make certain of it."

Cait hugged him tight, then leaned back to look up into his face, her arms resting on his chest. "You keep yourself safe, okay? I want you back."

"I'll give it my best shot. And you, take good care of yourself and Fallon and Willow. If I get anything substantial from my research, I'll let you know. Oh!" He stepped back, pulling his cell out of his pocket. "I need your phone number."

Cait laughed. "And I need yours."

They exchanged numbers and corralled the twins, then walked to the edge of the campground together.

"I'll have to hike out."

"It's a complete zoo out there, or was when I got here."

"I figured."

"You won't get back in once you leave. I barely made it, as you well know." She couldn't help the petulant tone of her voice. She was going to miss him terribly.

"I'll find a way."

He gave the girls one last hug each, kissed Cait, which set the girls to giggling, then walked off. Cait held her daughters' hands as they watched him walk out of their lives. When they could no longer see him, Cait took the girls back to camp and put them down for a nap, then started cutting vegetables for dinner. If a few stray tears streaked her cheeks, she chalked it up to the onions she diced.

News Alert: Countries around the world are up in arms over the heavy-handed tactics used by the United States government to keep them away from the light stream phenomena. A meeting of the United Nations devolved into a shouting match as tempers flared and demands for global access drowned out all other considerations.

CHAPTER SIXTEEN

One week after the shooting, at a dinner where everyone stayed quieter than usual, Damian broached the subject he and Valena had been discussing the last couple of days. "It may be time to spread our influence." The idea didn't sit right with him. He didn't want to let any member of his family out of his sight. Necessity might force him to it.

"Not that it will help," Luther growled, a pessimistic chip firmly lodged on that now-healed shoulder.

"We have to keep trying. To expand, reach out to more people."

"How?" Bhren asked.

"Well, our government, in all its infinite wisdom, has pretty much taken over this whole area."

Luther scowled while Gwen and Wyeth nodded.

"They've been trying to push us out of here. They want complete control."

"They sure as hell have been pushing," Luther ground out. "I'm tired of them ordering us around. I'm really close to pushing back. It makes me angry, how they analyze and look for ways to abuse this privilege. Access should not be restricted." He pounded the table.

"It's getting harder to be here," Valena agreed. "So much has changed. There's noise every hour of every day. Even the smells are different, with all the military machinery being brought in."

"Plus, we're no longer effective here," Damian continued. "Gwen, your online outreach is helping tremendously. Who'd have thought a simple blog would take off like that. The comments are encouraging."

"Well, the ones that aren't from kooks, at least," Gwen said.

"I'm not sure that's enough, though. Not anymore. The others—the people out there like us—aren't being vocal about how this gift can help the world. We need to find them, to make certain they understand the scope of their gift and how to use it. And we need to convince those without this gift that its nature is benign. That it's not meant to harm, but to help us all survive."

Heads nodded again.

"Cait," Damian turned to her. "You and the girls have become as much a part of our family as anyone here. If we moved on, spread out, what would you do?"

"I feel the same way you do. You've welcomed my family."

Damian could see the pride and love in Cait's face as she looked around, settling on Valena. She reached over and took her friend's hand. "The work you've done helping Fallon to understand this gift and how to use, and not use it, has been a godsend."

Like the time Fallon thought it was funny to lift

Damian high in the air. No harm had been done, and he'd been hard-pressed to keep from laughing as he explained the right and the wrong of doing something like that. Or when Fallon had seen a toy on the television and had tried to make it come to her. Damian smiled as he searched for a way to help her understand that a toy in a commercial wasn't something finite that she could bring to her. She'd understood far better than her years suggested, which was why Valena planned to get her said toy at the first opportunity.

"The girls are delightful," Valena said. "Fallon is headstrong, but even at her age, she knows right from wrong. She'll be fine now."

"Thank you for letting me interview you confidentially for the blog, too, Cait," Gwen said. "Stories like yours and Fallon's will go a long way to assuage the fears out there."

"I'm happy to help. This...feels right, being with you. And I want to help more. I'll do whatever I can. This change is a positive thing, not something to be feared." She smiled at Damian. "It's probably time for me to get back to my life. While this respite fed my soul, I had just interviewed for a position as a university professor before coming here. I got the job, and school starts in two weeks, so I need to get back. And to find someone who can babysit a couple of star two-year-olds, one with special powers."

"Cait, why don't we travel with you back to L.A.?" Valena said. "We can help you with Fallon and Willow, and we'd like to reach out to Taegar, make sure she's all right."

"That also gives us a chance to see if Hollywood would like our take on everything that's happened," Damian said.

"That would be awesome," Cait said. "My home is big enough that you're welcome there for as long as you wish."

Gwen locked eyes with her husband. Some unspoken communication between them led to a decision.

"You all know we're from Minnesota, and that I am estranged from my family because they did not approve of my life choices. Wyeth and I talked. We'd like to go home. If we can convince some of them that this is a good thing, well, then we can convince anyone."

Everyone chuckled, though it seemed muted by an underlying sadness.

"This I have to see," Luther said.

Everyone had heard tales of Gwen's patrician and autocratic family. The battles she'd had with her father had been verbal until that last night, years ago, when he'd hit her. Gwen had slugged him right back, smack in the jaw.

"My one and only moment of giving in to my anger," she said, shaking her head.

"Your actions that night probably saved your life." Wyeth hugged her tight as he turned to Luther. "You're welcome to come along with us."

"Wouldn't miss it. Besides, you may need my strength to get through this."

Bhren stood. "I volunteer to stay here. Keep an eye on the goings-on and help guide all of our new friends."

"And I'll stay here with Bhren," said Roulf, the newest addition to their circle. A little man with a bald head and large eyes, he'd appeared out of nowhere several days ago. Having the gift of subterfuge, he could disguise himself as a tree, a structure, even a bear. The man could hide in plain sight if he chose.

Bhren nodded and clapped Roulf on the shoulder. "You'll be a welcome companion."

"Gives us more time for you to instruct me in the druid ways," Roulf said.

"That I will do."

"Well," Damian continued, "I guess we all have our goals. If we can, Valena and I will try to spread out from southern California. I suggest, when we find people who've been gifted, we invite them into our circle and talk to them about our mission for humanity's survival. Let's plan to meet up, say, in six months, back here."

"Six months. Seems so...far away," Valena said. "And who knows if we can even *get* back here."

The pall of her words made the silence heavy.

"Yes. If we can get back here," Damian said. "Gwen, can you set up a closed group online so we can communicate?"

"Easily."

"Okay, then. Tomorrow, we'll talk to the other followers who've joined us and prepare to leave camp. Let's go into Rapid City and get cell phones for everyone who doesn't have them. Valena and I will keep the one we've all been using to date."

"I won't need the trailer," Bhren said.

Everyone chuckled. They all knew of Bhren's aversion to flimsy structures, ever since a shack collapsed on him during a tornado when he was a child.

"I'll be renting a car when we get out of here," Cait said.

"We'll go with Cait in the car," Damian said. He looked at Wyeth. "Do you three want to take the trailer.?"

"Sure," Luther said. "It'll be nice to have on a cross-country trip. And I can sleep in it while Gwen and Wyeth are being grilled by her parents." He looked like he planned to open a bag of popcorn, sit back, and enjoy the show.

"All right, then," Damian said. "We have a plan."

The finality of those words hit him like a gut-punch. The group was disbanding, at least for a while. A lump of emotion lodged in Damian's throat and he struggled to clear it. "We've been together a long time. Some have been here since the inception of our group, some came more recently, but we've always had a single focus: the betterment of our world and a kinder, gentler human race. That will remain our charge, to herald a new evolution and live in concert with the earth, not in opposition. We are the Guardian druids."

"Here, here," echoed through the group.

Standing behind his wife, Damian put his hands on her shoulders and gave a gentle squeeze. "We will miss this. Miss all of you."

No one minded that his voice broke when he said those words. Gwen's eyes filled with tears as everyone nodded.

"Let's meet up. Back here if possible," Wyeth said.

"Here, here," again resounded around the table.

Damian nodded. "Six months?"

"Done," they each said in one voice.

"And we'll stay in touch."

Again, nods around the table. Still, this was a change that made Damian's heart hurt. This was home, for all of them. This was the center of their existence, a sacred place.

As everyone moved off, sunk in their own thoughts, Valena rose and tugged her husband toward the lake. It didn't take much convincing. He helped her climb the short cliff to sit on the precipice overlooking the water. Arm in arm, they committed the view to memory. A hazy golden sun deepened to orange as it disappeared below the trees, twilight pulling the colors from around them, leaving everything in shades of black.

They sat in silent reverie.

"I will miss this place," Damian finally whispered.

With her hand, Valena turned his face to hers. Damian knew she felt the wetness on his cheeks.

"You are my home," she said.

"As you are mine."

"This is a new chapter in our lives, husband. We will survive it together."

Damian kissed her. "Your strength amazes me."

"I'm only strong because I'm with you. Now, what say we go get our things out of the trailer before Luther takes off with my favorite towels."

Damian laughed as he helped his wife down from the rocks. She was right. A new chapter lay before them, and it was time to embrace it. His mood was much lighter as they followed the campground lights along the trail.

After they'd all packed for the trip and contained their remaining belongings as best they could for Bhren and Roulf to watch over, they walked as a group to the glade where they'd prayed so many times, made life plans, and where the earth had first gifted them with light and magic.

The clearing was quiet at night. All that remained were guards who wouldn't let them very close and various pieces of equipment that did who knew what. Everyone else had been run off.

The light flowed strong and magical from the ground. Damian didn't see a bit of weakening, and that bolstered his belief that they could turn this tide. He held his hand up in front of him. The light shrouded his fingers in darkness, yet outlined them with slivers of white hope.

Hope they would need in the coming months. Damian squatted down and touched the trampled grass beneath his feet, searching for visions. Nothing came except a whisper of Earth's sentience.

We are setting off to convince the world what needs to be done.

Earth's reply was faint. *You must. I have done my part. Your time is now. If you do not succeed, all will perish.*

Then we will succeed.

One warning. Beware the golden one. She is capable of destroying everything we have wrought here.

The last words faded and Damian barely heard them.

Who is the golden one? he asked, waiting, listening, praying for an answer.

But none came.

He let go of the grass and stood, knowing that one more difficulty in an almost insurmountable task had been added to his load.

"You're tired," Valena said.

"Yes." He didn't want to burden her, or the others, with this new information that had no substance to it. Damian chose to wait and watch and hope that this golden one would show herself before things grew dire.

With his arm around his wife's waist, they headed to the R.V. for one last night's sleep on the lumpy mattress within.

~~~

Cait loaded the stroller into the trailer. Luther had been kind enough to repair it for her. Leaving the Black Hills would be much easier than coming in, at least physically. They'd all ride out in the truck and trailer. In Rapid City, Luther and the others would drop her, Damian, Valena, and the girls off at the car-rental office.

She'd packed up their meager belongings from camp earlier and left with the girls for the playground, giving everyone time to say their goodbyes. Now, minutes from departure, she choked up with her nostalgia. She and the twins had been welcomed here. This place had become home to them. Who knew she'd adapt to camping? She'd met Tom here, and now missed him more than she'd expected.

During their telephone conversation that morning, she'd told him the plan. Cait smiled. Tom had called her
~~~

every day since he'd left. The sense of no longer being alone in the world had been gifted to her through these friends, but Tom's caring and consideration had sealed the gaping holes in her heart.

Too short a while later, they all stood at the entrance to the campground.

"Time to go," Luther said, climbing into the driver's seat of the truck.

Cait and the twins would ride in the back seat because that's where the stroller system's two car seats were most easily secured. Valena and Gwen would ride in front with Luther, leaving Damian and Wyeth the bumpy trailer ride.

"I don't see why I can't drive," Wyeth said when Damian opened the trailer door.

"Because I'd like to make it to Rapid City before nightfall," Damian answered, giving everyone a chuckle.

They all hugged Bhren and Roulf.

"If things get any more dangerous around here, you two should get out," Damian said.

"We'll leave if we have to."

"Good. And keep an eye out for that man I described. We haven't seen him since before I went to D.C., but I have a feeling he's lurking here somewhere."

"We will. Don't worry. With Roulf's penchant for disguise, we'll know what's going on almost before it happens."

Too soon, the Guardian druids left Bhren, Roulf, and the Horse Thief Lake campground behind. Even the drive to Rapid City went far too quickly. Cait was grateful to find the car-rental company had brought in additional stock. She rented a van to get them home, then went outside to where everyone waited.

"They're bringing the van here."

After hugs all around and one last request from

Damian that they all keep in touch, the truck and trailer pulled away. Gwen stuck her head out the window and waved until they were out of sight.

Damian secured the car seats and twins in the middle row of the van, then, with Cait behind the wheel, they began their journey.

~~~

Taegar held her hand up to stare at the ring and bracelet again. So many beautiful colors. She liked the golden ones best. Even the gold of the band sparkled with brilliance.

"Thank you again, Gordon, for these," she said, kissing him. They sat together at the dining room table, having just finished a meal delivered by a local restaurant. She preferred to eat outside, but Gordon insisted they act civilized and eat at the table. Taegar took the last bite of her seafood fettuccine as Gordon pushed his plate away.

"You haven't finished your dinner," she said.

"I'm done."

"But it's a waste. A lot of resources went into making that dish."

"I told you, I don't want any more. Don't push me."

He'd never used that tone of voice with her before and it caught Taegar by surprise. "You hurt my feelings, Gordon."

"Tough."

Taegar could feel the moisture in her eyes. What was happening?

"Look, I need you to do something for me."

"Anything," she answered, still frowning. "You know I'd do anything for you." And she had. She'd pointed out things that her prescience indicated he'd like. He'd been happy each time he brought her the papers, so her choices must be helping him.
~~~

"Good. Gordon shoved their plates aside and set the raw stones down in front of her. "Make these grow."

"Why?"

He grabbed her arm and set her hand on the table next to the gems. "I'm not going to explain myself. Just touch them."

"Ouch," Taegar said, holding her arm to her chest. "You hurt me."

Gordon's nostrils flared. "Touch. The. Stones. And do it right. I want to see them grow."

He was angry. She could see it in his eyes, in the flushed skin of his face. But she'd done nothing wrong. There was no reason for him to be angry with her.

"I don't want to. You want to make money but that's not what my gifts are for. We're helping Earth so everyone can benefit."

Gordon grabbed her arm again, pulling her in close. "Look, I've put up with your shit, pampered you long enough. You're going to help me or else. Now. Grow the gems." He pushed her toward the table and her hip hit with a thunk; pain radiated straight through to her heart.

The tight hold of his hand on her arm left a red burn-like mark.

"You're hurting me, Gordon. Stop it."

He got in her face. "I'll stop when you do what I tell you to."

Fear raced through her. Familiar fear. He was behaving irrationally. He was acting...like her father. Taegar started to shake, unable to stop the cascade of memories she'd buried so deep she thought they'd never find her. She couldn't go through that again. Not ever.

So she touched one of the gems. It grew. Unexpectedly, it almost tripled in size.

Gordon picked it up, a wide, evil grin on his face,

petting it like something precious. "Oh, girlie, you and I are going to own the world."

"No. That's the only one. The others were right about you. You're only in it for the money."

The smile on Gordon's face grew wider, if that was even possible. "And you're going to help me get it. All of it. We'll corner the market on precious gems and minerals. No one will be able to touch us."

"Not without my help, you won't. And I'm leaving."

Smack! The backhand across her cheek sent Taegar spiraling backward until she landed on the floor, her head hitting with another loud thunk. This, and worse, was exactly what she'd endured from the earliest she could remember until she'd run away in her teens.

Taegar crawled away from Gordon and grabbed a chair to pull herself up. Trauma from her past bubbled up within her. All the pain and anguish and terror of being beaten and abused. All the memories of the times her father had come into her room and locked the door behind him. No one had come to rescue her. Not then. Not now.

All the rage she'd buried so deep that no one would ever know her shame boiled up and over, consuming her with the need for revenge. She stalked toward Gordon, who had picked up another stone. He turned to her. "Touch this one."

"No." Her voice reverberated off the walls. "I will not."

When he reached for her, the rage within her erupted and she shoved him. Hard. He flew into the wall then slumped to the ground, though he was still conscious. Behind him, the sheetrock had caved in where he'd hit.

"No one will ever hurt me like that again," Taegar said, her voice bouncing off the walls. She stomped out of the room and out the door to the garden. She needed its solace.

Once she was seated amid the greenery and colors of nature, she trembled. What had she done? She looked at her shaking hands. Where had that strength come from? Her only thought had been to get him away from her, to keep him from hurting her again. Yet that tap had… Well, she could have killed him. With her thoughts alone.

Taegar put her head in her hands and wept over the changes in her life. Would no one ever allow her to just be herself, quiet, communing with the only thing that made her happy? Where was Valena? Damian? Her friends. They'd tried to make her understand, back before she left. Now that she finally did, they were nowhere around. No word had come from any of them. It seemed even they had deserted her.

She cried for a long time now that the veil had been ripped away. Gordon Darcy was evil incarnate.

What was she going to do? Where could she go? Not back to her so-called friends. That bridge had been burned when they hadn't come after her. Hadn't protected her.

Taegar plucked flowers and greenery that Gordon would never let her cut, forming a bouquet of beauty to offset the ugliness of her life. She sat there until well after dark, making plans.

She would leave in the morning.

She needed to be anywhere but here.

News Alert: An international Earth coalition, newly formed after intense pressure from worldwide consortiums, will now study the light stream phenomena and share data. The coalition consists of scientists and military personnel. Not a single mod is included.

CHAPTER SEVENTEEN

Taegar went inside, carefully skirting the dining room, and crept up the stairs to the bedroom her clothes were in.

Tonight, she didn't expect to see him, but when she turned on the light, he was sitting by the little table on the far side.

"We need to talk, honey," Gordon said.

"I think you've said quite enough. Riches are more important to you than I am." She rubbed her arm. "You've made that painfully obvious.

He stood but stayed where he was when Taegar reached for the doorknob. "I'm sorry. I got excited. I didn't react well."

Taegar laughed harshly, her hand still on the doorknob. "No. You didn't react well at all."

He rubbed the back of his neck. "And you threw me into a wall."

"You deserved it."

Gordon's face turned red, but he didn't make a move toward her. Good thing, too, because he'd get the same treatment. No one would manhandle her ever again. Not now that she had Earth on her side.

"Yes," he said, his voice taking on a bit of gravel. "I deserved it. Come on. Sit with me." He pointed to the bottle and two glasses. His was already full. "I brought wine as a conciliatory gesture. Sit and drink with me and we'll talk this out. I'm sorry, honey. I was out of my mind with excitement. I shouldn't have treated you that way."

He sounded sincere, but Taegar didn't know if she could trust him anymore. Still, sitting down for a talk sounded reasonable. Besides, she had more strength than she knew. She could handle him if he tried to hurt her again. She could handle anything now.

Taegar stepped away from the door and crossed the room to sit in the chair across from Gordon.

He smiled. "Good, good. Now we can talk like civilized adults." He poured a glass of wine and handed it to her. "I really am quite sorry, my love. I don't know what got into me."

"Greed." She wanted him to know she was angry with him, but she softened the words as they clinked glasses. She took a sip of the bold red wine. It had a bit of an acidic taste. She'd grown to enjoy wine, something she'd never tasted until Gordon had convinced her to try.

"So, as I was saying, I'd like to find a way to make it up to you for our little fight today."

"How would you do that?" She took another sip of wine.

"I think we need to get out of here for a while. Maybe take a vacation."

The wine was good. Taegar took another sip. "I thought we were on vacation already."

"Well, true, and one of these days I do have to return to work. For now, though, we should enjoy each other, don't you think?" He watched her carefully.

"Shounds good." Had she just slurred her words?

Why was he staring at her? And smiling. It wasn't the smile she was used to. This one seemed...sinister?

"Whash goin' on, Gor— " Taegar's tongue thickened and speech became impossible. Movement became equally hard. Her body felt like rubber. She slumped, and Gordon picked her up and moved her to the bed.

"Just a little something to relax you, my dear."

What have you done to me?

Gordon pulled a syringe out of Taegar's bedside drawer and filled it with something from a small vial. "Don't worry. This will only sting for a minute. After that, you can rest. For tonight."

His voice had changed. Its tone was a harsher, more direct, all-business. Taegar didn't like it. Gordon slid the syringe beneath her skin. "Tomorrow, you and I have a lot of work to do."

He patted her cheek then left the room, turning the light off.

She was in complete darkness.

What was happening? What had he done to her? Why couldn't she move?

Somehow, she could think clearly. Knew where she was. But she couldn't move. Her body lay flaccid on the bed.

In the dark.

She was afraid of the dark. Had been ever since her father had thrown her into the coal room for hours at a time. Again and again and again, until he'd pulled all the light from her life.

Taegar screamed. Over and over again, she screamed

until her throat hurt from the effort.

Except no sound came from her lips. Even her vocal cords had been paralyzed by whatever he'd given her.

Valena! Damian! Help!

But Taegar knew no one could hear her. They hadn't come when she needed them. No one would come to her rescue now, either. She was trapped, much worse than she'd ever been with the no-account, abusive father she'd killed.

~~~

Cait pulled into her driveway exhausted, but glad to be home. They'd driven over thirteen hundred miles. Even though they'd split it over three days to give the twins a break, it had been a long journey. Damian and she had shared the driving, and Valena had been great at entertaining two girls much more used to an active lifestyle.

Autumn's early nights meant dark had fallen a while ago and the girls were fast asleep in their car seats. Cait was happy they'd been quiet for this last part of the drive. She didn't have a single thread of patience left. If traffic had been any heavier, she might have done bodily harm.

Damian opened the slider on the van and stepped out, helping Valena.

Guessing that meant it was time to move, Cait opened her door and put her feet on the ground. Standing took a lot of effort, but she did it, bending back to stretch under-utilized muscles.

"How about you give me your house key and you and Damian each take one of the girls?" Valena asked, coming around to the driver's side.

Cait nodded, too tired to even speak. She dug in her purse for her keys, handed them to Valena, then opened the van door ever so carefully to get Fallon out of her car seat. The poor girl was so tired that she never woke up. Her
~~~

head settled in the crook of Cait's neck and Cait breathed deeply, taking a moment to just be. She loved the smell of her kids. Was that weird?

Didn't matter. Damian had Willow in his arms, so she hit the button to close and lock the van doors and they followed Valena to the door.

"Alarm code?" Valena asked.

"Four, zero, seven, two, nine."

With the alarm off, Valena opened the door and Cait led the way to the girls' room. Before long, they had shoes off and covers pulled over them.

"That's good enough for tonight," Cait whispered as they all watched the girls sleep. "They'll be awake much too early for me to get a good night's sleep, but I'm glad we're home."

Backing out of the room, Cait closed the door and walked down the upstairs hall. "This is my room," she said, pointing to the door next to the twins' room. "This is the spare bedroom, which is yours for as long as you want it." She thanked herself for always having clean sheets on the bed. "You have your own bathroom, too. Everything's clean and stocked."

"This is so much more than we're used to," Valena said, smiling.

"Do you need anything else for tonight?" They'd eaten about three hours ago, an early dinner. Fallon and Willow had just about fallen asleep in their ice cream.

"No," Damian said, patting Cait's shoulder. "I think we all just need some sleep. Tomorrow, we can make plans."

Nodding, Cait said goodnight and opened her bedroom door. The room had always been her solace, filled with the colors of the sea and shore, with wispy curtains and plush, toe-sinking area rugs. Tonight, none of that mattered. She tossed off her shoes and jacket, pulled back the covers, and was asleep before she fully rolled over.

When she woke, daylight streamed in through windows whose shades she'd forgotten to pull down. Cait stretched her arms overhead, yawning. Her clock said eight, which woke Cait up the rest of the way. Her girls never slept this late, especially not when they had fallen asleep earlier than usual like last night. Cait tossed back her covers and ran for the twins' door, whipping it open. No one was there.

"No." Cait's heart hit overdrive as she searched the room, all her fears of them being taken, stolen, kidnapped, coalescing into one thought.

Find my girls.

Laughter drifted up the stairs. Valena's laughter, followed by the dual tones of joy she recognized as belonging to her daughters. Cait slumped against the door jamb in relief.

"You did most of the driving those last few hours," Damian said, coming up the stairs. "We thought you might need some extra sleep." He approached her. "Good Lord, you look like you've seen a ghost."

Cait rubbed her face and pushed her hair back. "Sorry. I'm not used to having anyone to share twin duties with. It gave me a moment of panic when they weren't here."

"Their father isn't in the picture?"

"No." Cait didn't like talking about the twins' bio-dad. He didn't deserve the attention. But Damian and Valena had extended their arms to help her. She owed them her honesty. "He wasn't thrilled when I got pregnant accidentally. When the ultrasound showed twins, he packed and left. Haven't seen or heard from him since."

Damian settled a hand on her shoulder. "His loss. I hope you don't mind. I borrowed the van and ran for groceries. Breakfast is about fifteen minutes from ready. Is that enough time for you to freshen up?"

"More than enough. I'm used to grabbing ten minutes while the twins are occupied. Thank you."

She rushed through a shower and showed up in the kitchen with a couple minutes to spare, her wet hair pulled back in a ponytail until she could do more with it.

"Hello, sweeties," she said to her girls, giving each a hug and smooch on the forehead. They were busy eating chocolate-chip pancakes. Whipped cream and syrup coated their faces, hands, and arms, more than was on their plates.

"I hope you don't mind that we went ahead and fed them," Valena said, coming around the island to give Cait a hug.

"Are you kidding? This is the ultimate pampering. I never get to sleep in."

"Eight is sleeping in?"

"With two-year-olds, it is."

Cait poured herself some coffee and indulged in her favorite hazelnut creamer. Leaning back against the counter, she took a sip and couldn't help the huge sigh that escaped.

"Oh, man," Damian said with a chuckle. "You were deprived, staying with us."

Cait laughed. "Honestly, I never missed this in South Dakota. And your camp coffee, while it took some getting used to, woke me up just as well."

"What?" Damian's face was awash in mock horror. "You didn't like my coffee?"

"Espresso in a tin can, with a few twigs for flavoring?" Cait said.

They all laughed, each knowing her description was pretty much spot on.

"Well, there's more pancakes, plus scrambled eggs."

"Wow. You really did make yourself at home in the kitchen. Thank you!"

When the girls began to squirm, Cait grabbed wipes and cleaned them up, then let them go play in the sunroom where she could see them from the table. She, Damian, and Valena cleared the mess and sat down to enjoy their own breakfast.

"What are your plans, now that we're here?" Cait asked.

"We're kind of winging it. We'd like to get on a news program or two. Meet with some other like-minded or like-talented folks. Contact with a few big names in Hollywood could also be advantageous."

Cait took a bite of really great pancake and thought for a moment. "My closest friend is a talent agent. She's not big, but she's not far off the A-list track. Gus Grandon is one of her clients. He's a huge eco-guy."

"*The* Gus Grandon? The actor? He's pretty big."

"That's the one."

"Sounds perfect," Valena said.

"I'll call her after breakfast and see if she can come over to chat."

By two that afternoon, the girls had been bathed and were down for their naps. Cait's call to Linda had been a huge success. The woman was so excited to meet Damian and Valena, she'd left right then. She was due any moment.

Cait managed to dig out some frozen cookies and bake them. She'd also baked a circle of Brie cheese in puff pastry, placing it out with some pita chips. And, since no one cared if it was five o'clock somewhere, she opened wine. Red and white. Plus a fresh carafe of coffee. Might as well be comfortable.

When her doorbell rang, Cait glanced at Damian and Valena. "Here we go."

Not only did Linda arrive right on time and uber-excited, she had company. Cait's jaw dropped when the drool-worthy Gus Grandon stepped inside.

"I hope you don't mind. I made a call and he dropped everything to be here. Gus was as excited as I was to meet your friends."

"You are both welcome in my home anytime," Cait said, finding her voice. She introduced them to Damian and Valena and everyone settled in the living room. Cait sent a prayer skyward that her girls would stay asleep for another hour or so. *Please!*

"I've been more than a little interested in what's been happening," Gus said. "I'd love to get your take on things."

His gray eyes were even more intense in person than on the big screen, especially with that dark hair. Cait couldn't help but geek out over this big of a movie star in her living room. Her life was changing so quickly whiplash was a serious possibility.

Damian started an animated conversation with Gus. Back and forth. Question and answer. Cait, Linda, and Valena sat off to the side, letting the men talk.

"Does Gus know about Fallon?" Cait kept her voice low, hoping to keep Fallon's talents a tightly held secret.

"No," Linda said. "I wanted to. Gus... Well, he and I don't have many secrets."

Cait noticed it then. The grin on Linda's face every time she glanced at Gus. The love. Her eyes widened. "Are you two?"

"An item? Maybe. Still feeling that out, but I think so."

"Oh!" Cait clapped a hand over her mouth when the men turned her way. "Nothing," she said glibly, waving them back to their conversation.

Linda blushed to the roots of her hair. "I don't know how it happened. One minute, we're talking about his next movie, then suddenly, we were on the couch making out. This is really new, though. And I don't know where it will go. I just want to follow it to its end, though I shouldn't. He's my client, for God's sake. If word got out we were dating, I'd be ruined."

"Your secret is as safe with us as your guarding of Fallon's privacy," Valena said. "We have become very attached to those girls and appreciate anyone who protects them."

Cait hugged her friend. "And I'm so happy for you."

"I'm happy for me, too. He's wonderful, Cait. So much more than the persona he projects. He truly cares. He's profound. It's almost scary. I...I haven't told him yet about, well, you know, the not-having-babies thing."

Doctors had told Linda she could never have children. It was one of her deepest sorrows.

"Is there a medical reason for that or a surgical one?" Valena asked.

"Medical."

Valena looked at Cait, asking the silent question. *Should I try to heal her?*

Cait placed her hand on Linda's arm. "Valena is a healer."

"A what?"

"A healer," Valena said. "I honestly don't know if I could help, but I'm willing to try."

Linda looked back and forth between them, confused.

"There's a chance—"

"A small one," Valena interjected.

"That she could help you."

"So you're a doctor?"

"No," Valena answered. "You know about Fallon and other mods. I'm one, too, having been given the gift of healing. It's possible I could help with your infertility. I don't know for sure, but I'm willing to try. I can't guarantee you children of your own. That's up to the cosmic powers. But maybe I can fix what's wrong inside you."

"Do you have to do something invasive?"

"I only have to lay my hands on you."

Cait saw the light of hope lift Linda up, the smile on her face slowly blossoming. "Honestly, If there's any chance, I'm in."

"All right, then." Valena settled her hand on Linda's stomach and focused, staying still for a few minutes. She looked into Linda's eyes for a long moment at the end before pulling her hand back. "Like I said, no guarantees, but I think that will help."

Linda placed her hands over her stomach. "I feel strange, energetic."

"Just a bit of energy added," Valena said.

"And you think I might be able to have kids now?"

"I think what's wrong has been fixed."

Cait looked at Valena, whose obvious fatigue reminded Cait that there was a toll for using this gift. Linda, however, was effervescent. Honestly, all of a sudden, her cheeks had more color. Her energy was up, too, if the arms she threw around Valena were any indication.

"Thank you," she said, with tears in her eyes. "I don't know what I can do to repay you, but I'll do anything."

"No payment needed. Just think kindly on us mods." Valena said, adding her own smile to their circle.

"Definitely," Linda said, glancing at the men. "Now I don't have to tell him anything."

Cait couldn't wipe the grin off her face. It was so nice to see her friend happy, vibrant, alive. She clearly adored Gus.

Thinking about Tom, missing him, Cait wondered if she'd ever have that kind of love. It seemed so far away.

For the first time in a while, loneliness crept back into her heart.

"You look like you're missing someone," Linda said.

Now, it was Cait's turn to blush. "I met him in South Dakota. He's a scientist. He's also a believer, like me. These people, and the messages they're spreading with the help of the light stream, are the real deal."

"I've been keeping up with the news. It's pretty amazing," Linda said, sipping her wine. "Gus is sure happy to be here."

"I am," Gus said, joining them and putting his arm around Linda's shoulders. She leaned into him and another pang of melancholy hit Cait. She *really* missed Tom. He'd been calling her every day, though. The thought made her feel better.

As the men sat back down, one of the cookies wafted off the plate.

Oh, no.

Thin air carried it in a wavy pattern past adults with their mouths gaping open. The cookie continued to the stairs, where Fallon grabbed a hold of it and handed it to Willow. Another cookie lifted and followed the first. Both girls giggled as they ate.

"Well, that cat's out of the bag," Cait said, getting up to help her twins down the stairs. "No more," she whispered furiously to them. "I'll get you some grapes if you just ask."

"Cookies!" they said in unison. The entire plate rose from the coffee table. "No," she said. "No more until after dinner." Both girls pouted and Fallon apparently let go of her mental hold on the plate by the way it wobbled. Thankfully, Damian grabbed it just as it began to tip in midair.

Willow ran for Valena's lap and Cait grabbed Fallon

before she could launch herself at Damian. "These are my girls, Gus. Willow there, and Fallon is the one with the cookie ideas."

Linda took a moment to coo over the girls, but Gus sat in stunned silence. Cait began to worry that he would out her and the twins. God, she didn't want her girls turned into science experiments.

"Are you all right?" she asked him.

He jolted as if coming out of a dream. "All right? I'm more than all right." He stood and closed the blinds behind him, then looked at each of them in turn. "This stays right here. You good with that?"

"Yes." No hesitation from any of them.

Suddenly, a third cookie lifted off the plate, only this time, it didn't go to one of the girls. It went straight to Gus Grandon. Cait looked at Fallon, who clapped her hands in glee. "Honey, you can't do that."

"Didn't, Mommy."

"She's right," Gus said. "She didn't. I did."

~~~

"You can do this," Wyeth told Gwen.

Clutching the door handle of the truck, she wasn't so sure. In fact, she was a lot less certain than she'd been last night and the night before that. She stared at the farmhouse as they drew closer. There were so many gaps in the dull white paint, it looked like the entire house had been scraped in preparation for a new coat of color. Except everything else seemed just as run down. The barn had gaping holes in its roof and one of the doors was unhinged.

They pulled into the yard and stopped. Shrubs her mother used to painstakingly trim were large and wild, the stairs leading up to the wrap-around porch looked off-kilter, and the railing was either missing or leaning at a sharp angle.
~~~

"What's happened to this place?" she said.

"It doesn't even look inhabited," Luther said from the back seat of the truck. They had decided not to bring the trailer in case they needed a quick exit. Gwen had tried to convince Luther to stay back, but he'd given her an unequivocal answer.

"No way. You're my family and they are, for now, an unknown enemy." He'd flexed his muscles. "I'm coming along to keep you both safe. If things are better than when you left, I'll beg off. But you're not going in there this first time without me."

Now, as they stared at the disheveled property, Gwen was glad he'd insisted. Her family home looked like something out of a horror movie. She'd left unable to tolerate the abuse that dwelled within these walls. It had about killed her to do that, but she was the youngest and the brunt of her father's ire had fallen on her shoulders.

"You had the strength to leave," Wyeth said beside her. "You have the strength to return."

Gwen nodded. Releasing a huge sigh of stress, she opened her door and stepped out. The men followed, Wyeth rounding the truck to stand beside her while Luther hung back.

"Don't come any closer." The voice came from inside the screen door. While they couldn't see who uttered the words, Gwen shivered as the memories assailed her. *You aren't worth the cost of water. Go bathe in the pigpen.* That and so many other phrases, other names her father had called her.

The screen door opened and her father came onto the porch, the barrel of his rifle leading the way. Wyeth tried to move in front of Gwen, but she stayed him with a hand on his arm. Luther remained where he was, though his fists were tight as they rested on the hood of the truck.

"I don't know what you want, but we don't need your

filth around here. You get, now. Go back to whatever commune you came from."

"It's good to see you, too, father," Gwen said, digging deep for enough voice to talk to the man.

"Get going, I said. I don't want to hear anything you have to say."

Nothing had changed at all, it seemed. Gwen shook her head, fighting to keep the mist from forming in her eyes. "I've been gone a long time, father. I'd hoped you'd want to see your only daughter."

"Well, I don't." He raised his chin.

"I'd like to talk to you about what's been happening in the world. About the wonderful new healing powers."

"Shut your mouth, little girl. I don't want to hear any of that devil talk."

That dried any moisture in her eyes. Gwen tried to relax her jaw, but it was next to impossible. The man would not listen to reason. "Fine. Then I'll just talk to mother for a bit and we'll be on our way."

"She's gone."

The surge of hope hit Gwen like a ray of sunshine. Finally, her mother had gotten away. She'd been stuck in this abusive relationship for so long, she didn't know another way to live.

"Do you know where she went?"

Her father barked a laugh. "Yep. To that cemetery over by Riverside."

Gwen gasped and faltered. If it weren't for Wyeth's arm around her shoulders, she probably would have sunk to the ground. "She's dead?"

"Yes."

"How long?" she whispered, leaning heavily on Wyeth.

"Been three years now."

Gwen gasped again. That long?

Luther came around the truck and the rifle turned to bear on him. "Stay put," her father said.

"Why didn't you tell me she'd died? Why didn't my brothers get in touch with me?"

"Didn't know where you were. Besides, you didn't have the right, running away like you did."

"How did she die?" Gwen gulped, certain she didn't want to hear this answer.

"Fell down the stairs. Darn fool woman."

"Fell? Or was she pushed?"

Her father squinted, staring at her for a long time before he spoke again. Gwen could feel the little girl inside her wanting to crawl to the closet and hide from his wrath.

"We're done here. You leave now, before I start using this rifle."

"Well, at least tell me where Jim and Chuck are."

"They lit out of here right after we buried your mother. Haven't heard from them since. No account boys, deserting their dad. Just like you." He waved the rifle at her and both Wyeth and Luther stepped forward, fists clenched.

The rifle cock sounded like a shotgun blast in the quiet yard. Gwen grabbed the arms of Wyeth and Luther and backed them up. "We're leaving. There's nothing I want to say to him anyhow." *Except that I hope he rots in hell.*

They each edged their way back into the truck. Gwen watched her father from the passenger seat. For a moment, just a fleeting look, he let the loneliness he must be feeling show. A sadness that he refused to acknowledge. She couldn't help him. He'd closed himself off from the world and now sat in a falling-down house, completely alone. His choice. He stood until they'd turned around and headed back down the driveway. Gwen craned her neck to see out the rear window, watching her father's shoulders hunch as he lowered the gun and headed back inside to his private hell.

"He's not worth crying over," Wyeth said quietly.

Gwen turned back around, hugging herself, surprised that her eyes were dry. "No, he's not." She would never again shed a tear for the man who'd provided the sperm that made her possible.

But her mother... Tears now slid down Gwen's cheeks and she swiped at them. "I can't believe my mother is gone."

From the back seat, Luther clasped her shoulder in support.

"Can we stop by the cemetery?" Her voice broke.

"Already on it," Wyeth said.

"Yep," Luther added. "Just pulled up the directions. Head into town and take the first right."

Gwen's heart overflowed with love for these two men. Her true family. One, a soul mate, the other, a big brother. God, but she loved them so much. She couldn't stop the tears now if she wanted to. So much love, so much sorrow, all intermingled into an emotional upheaval.

The cemetery was large enough to have an office. They stopped and got directions, then drove to the area where her mother was buried. It didn't take long to find the grave marker. Beautiful rose-colored granite adorned with inlaid flowers on a plaque that said "beloved mother."

Had one of her brothers done this? It had to be, but she'd never known either Jim or Chuck to have a heart. Maybe they'd come around?

"I need the truck for a bit," Luther said to Wyeth. Once he got the keys, he headed out, leaving them to their shared grief.

Gwen sank to the ground, brushing dried grass trimmings from the grave placard. "I just can't believe it."

Wyeth sat behind her and encircled her with his arms.

Gwen gratefully leaned back into her husband, drawing badly needed strength from him.

"I never got the chance to know her, except through your eyes. I think she was a special woman."

Gwen nodded through her tears. "She was."

"She had a lot of strength to tolerate what she did for all those years. A strength that you carry in you."

"But she never believed in herself enough to break free of him."

"No. She didn't. I'm glad you managed to, though. Really glad."

"Me, too." She hugged his arms tight.

"I wish I'd had a chance to meet her."

"She'd have liked you a lot, I think."

"You're biased, though."

"And you're as special as I think you are."

Gwen laid her hands on the grass surrounding her mother's grave. Flowers sprouted, first as seedlings, then stems and leaves, and finally, color burst forth. She continued all around her mother's marker until it was awash in the beauty of nature.

"Well, I guess we don't need these, then," Luther said, walking up to join them. His arms were full of flowers. He shrugged. "Saw them in front of a store as we drove here. Thought they might be a nice touch."

"They are perfect," Gwen said, standing up and hugging Luther. Together, the three of them arranged the flowers around the new growth, adding to the color and beauty. They stood there for a long moment, paying homage to a woman who'd led a hard life.

"She's at peace now," Gwen said. "I believe that in my heart."

"And she's smiling down on us."

That made Gwen smile. With a sigh, she turned away.

Arm in arm, the three of them walked to the truck.

"I guess we'd better head back to the trailer."

"Let's stock up on some groceries first."

Luther nodded. "And after all that, we can figure out where to go next."

News Alert: Some mods with healing abilities are charging exorbitant rates to help people. Farmers are hiring mods to work exclusively on their farms. People are protesting. People are marching. Anarchy has come to the streets.

CHAPTER EIGHTEEN

"Someone else has telekinetic capabilities?"

Cait heard the shock in Tom's voice. No less than her own, and she'd watched it happen. "Yes. Fallon isn't the only one."

"If that's the case, then there must be others. I've been working on an assessment of enhanced talents. I would have to say sixty percent are like Gwen's or Valena's—the ability to accelerate the growth of vegetation or to heal. Probably twenty percent of the gifted have strength, like Luther and Damian. The rest are a mishmash, though Fallon and the actor are the only two I've heard of who can move objects without touching them."

"This is so incredible."

"Yes. I've also been correlating my findings with my lab results."

Tom's prolonged breath worried Cait.

"Look," he said. "I don't want to stay on the phone too long. I was uncomfortable using my cell so I walked to a mall to call from a pay phone. Even here, I don't trust that this is a private conversation."

Had things gotten so dire that the government was spying on its own people? And, if they were spying on Tom, could they find her? And Fallon?

"I think I just hit scared."

"I know." He paused for a long moment. "Ask Damian and Valena to stick around, okay? Give me a few days. I'll get back to you."

"All right. Tom, be careful."

"Trying my best. I miss you."

"I miss you, too. I wish this were another time, another place, and we had time to get to know each other."

Tom chuckled. "Me, too. But if it were another time, we might not have met."

After a few more minutes of conversation solely meant to extend their tenuous contact, Cait ended the call but remained on the couch, weighed down by dissatisfaction and depression. And loneliness. She'd only known Tom a short while. How could she miss him so much?

Though, if she was being truthful, it wasn't just Tom's absence bringing her down. Keeping Fallon from using her talents had become increasingly difficult. Cait only left the house now when Damian and Valena could watch the girls. There were no more forays to the park after Cait had seen a little boy's toy moving through the air toward her daughter.

She'd been quick to grab it and give it back, glancing around to see if anyone had noticed. They hadn't, but that had ended their play days at the park for the foreseeable future. Thankfully, she had an excellent child's play area in her backyard, including a fort and sandbox. She didn't know what she would do if the word got out. It scared her more than anything to think of the government taking her daughter for...testing purposes. Was that movie paranoia or something that really happened? Cait didn't want to find out.

No one would get to Fallon or Willow. No one. That was why Cait had go-bags by the front door, in the twins' bedroom, and her car. She'd ordered additional strollers online and each go-bag had a double-stroller sitting next to it, ready to go. The strollers were stocked with extra water and food, too.

Cait had never been a survivalist, but she was learning how to become one.

"Everything all right with Tom?" Valena asked, walking in with two cups of coffee and handing one to Cait.

"I don't know. He was on a payphone at some mall and still said he couldn't talk openly. I think he's worried."

"I think he should be," Damian said, joining them with his coffee. "Look outside."

Cait and Valena set their cups down and went to the window.

"Carefully. Don't let them see you move the blinds."

"Them?"

Peeking through the slats wasn't easy. Even with reduced visibility, Cait pegged the black SUV across the street and two houses down, with two people sitting inside.

"Oh, God," she said, swamped with panic that pushed reasonable thought out of her head. "They've found us. Oh, my God. They're going to take Fallon. I just know it. I have to run. I have to get away." Her voice rose and she couldn't stop it.

"They haven't found you or the girls, Cait," Damian said as Valena nudged her back to the sofa. Cait wrapped her hands around the still-warm cup, staring at liquid as dark as her fear.

She looked up, knowing her bleak eyes would show them she thought the prospects for a decent future were dismal. "How do you know?"

"Because they've been here for two days."

"And you're just now telling me about it? I had a right to know about this, Damian."

"You did. You do," he said. "I needed to be sure about something before I mentioned it. They aren't here for you."

"They aren't?"

"I've been watching them watch us. You left to go to the store yesterday and they stayed here, eyes trained on this house. Yet, the two times that Valena and I have left, they've followed us."

"They're here for us?" Valena asked.

Damian nodded. "I believe so, yes."

"Are we in danger?"

"No. If we were, you and I would have left." He turned to Cait, reaching for her hand. "There's no way we would put you and the girls in any sort of danger. If I'd thought they would do more than just watch, we'd be gone."

Cait set her coffee down and clutched his hand and Valena's. "I know. I just... "

"Had a moment of panic," Valena said, smiling. "I did, too, and I'm not a mother."

"I can't let anything happen to Fallon and Willow."

"That's one of the reasons we're here, Cait," Damian said, taking his hand back then sipping his coffee. "We want to keep you safe. All of you." He glanced toward the window. "I don't know. Maybe it would be better if we left."

"You can't. Tom wants to talk to you."

"Is he coming here?"

"I don't think so, but he asked us all to give him a few days."

Damian glanced at Valena, who shrugged. "I guess that

means we stay. But if anything changes or begins to look dangerous, we won't wait to hear back from Tom."

"Thank you," Cait said. Hearing noises from upstairs that heralded the start to her day, she put down her coffee and went to get the girls, trying to quell her worry. She wondered how this would all unfold and if they could remain unscathed.

~~~

The day after they found out Gwen's mother had died, Wyeth sat with Luther and his wife at a local restaurant where the tinkling of forks and knives was the noisiest thing at the table. After dinner, they headed back to the trailer, still all deep in their own thoughts. Wyeth was worried about Gwen. She'd hardly spoken since the visit to her father. She'd pulled into herself.

The first time he'd ever seen her, she'd been curled up on a bench inside a bus station, counting change. That's what she'd been down to, quarters, dimes, nickels, and pennies. She looked like she hadn't eaten in days and had showered even less. He'd almost walked right by her until she'd looked up at him with those soulful brown eyes, full of pain and despair. He'd stopped, at which point those adult eyes had clouded over with defiance and one of the best "don't mess with me" looks he'd ever seen.

"You all right?" he'd asked.

Her chin lifted a couple degrees. "I'm fine, thank you."

I should keep walking, he'd thought to himself. *I should get on that bus leaving in ten minutes to take me home, back to the Black Hills and my friends. My new family.* But there was something about her that tugged at him and made him want to slip on his knight-in-shining-armor suit and save her, so he went to the terminal and traded in his ticket for one the next day. She still sat on the bench, staring at her money. Taking a chance, Wyeth bought a second ticket, then nuts and
~~~

bottled juice from the vending machine.

"Okay if I sit here?" He indicated the other end of the bench.

"Free world," she muttered.

He set the nuts and juice on the bench near her, then took a seat. Not close enough to intimidate her, but so they'd be able to talk.

"For you. Because you don't look like you're all right." He kept his voice carefully modulated. Frightening her wouldn't help either of them. And something about her feistiness said he wanted to know her better.

"I told you," she said, her eyes full of dark fire and attitude, though the fact that she kept looking at the snack and juice kind of deflated the attempt. "I'm fine." She didn't look away, didn't cow down. Not this girl, no. She matched his gaze, even raised him an attitude percentage. She had fire in her veins, that was for certain. And Wyeth wanted to learn more about that fire.

"Well, the way you look doesn't match that statement." Had he just told her she didn't look good? *Way to go, buddy.* "What I mean is, you look like you could use a good meal. Eat the cookie. I bought it from the machine right over there. The nuts and the juice are unopened. It's all safe."

She balled her hands into fists, as if wanting to reach out, but suspicious of his motives. Man, was this woman scared. What had she gone through that she suspected something as simple as a cookie and pop to have sinister intent behind it?

After a virtual war that he watched play out on her face, she grabbed the package, opened it, and ate the nuts in no time flat.

"You know, there's a diner across the street." He waved out the window behind him. "I'm buying, if you're able to take that chip off your shoulder long enough to let someone help you."

If it were possible, her glare deepened. "Thank you for this," she said, holding out the package with one cookie left, and the pop. Wyeth was drawn to her slender fingers. A pianist's hands. Dainty and tender beneath the grime.

"I don't need your help. And I'm not going to put out, either. So just get along, if that's what you're looking for."

"I can only imagine what you've been through, but please don't think I'm like that. I just want to help someone who looks like they could use it. My name's Wyeth. What's yours?"

Her jaw worked back and forth as she decided whether or not to answer him. "Rachel."

"I doubt that's your real name. I have good instincts and you don't look like a Rachel."

Again, her jaw noshed against itself. Rachel-whatever-her-name-is cocked her head and studied him for a long moment. "Gwen."

"Now that's more like it. That name fits you, like a fairy sitting next to a magical pond."

One corner of her mouth quirked up at that.

"So, Gwen, now that we've been introduced, I would love to buy you some dinner." He held his hands up again. "Absolutely no strings attached. When dinner is done, you can go your way and I'll go mine, if that's your choice."

He wanted to pump his fists in the air when fierce refusal turned to indecision on her face.

"Come on," he said. "What have you got to lose?"

Wyeth wasn't prepared for the stark fear that turned indecision back into denial. If he didn't backpedal, and quickly, he'd lose her. "I'm sorry. I think you're in terrible circumstances, for whatever reason. I don't want to hurt you. I don't want to do anything except help. No strings attached, I promise." He formed his hand into the Boy

Scout salute he hadn't used in years.

Gwen chewed her lower lip.

Wyeth sat quiet and unmoving, giving her the time and space she needed to decide.

When she nodded, he again wanted to pump fists. Instead, he stood and waited for her. She unpeeled long legs from the bench and stood. It surprised him that she was almost his height. He was six feet and a few centimeters. She had to be five feet ten or eleven.

He decided right then and there that he liked tall women.

She reached under the bench and pulled out a ratty backpack. Probably the only thing she had left in this world. Clutching the pack to her chest, she stood shifting from foot to foot.

Wyeth led the way, opening the door and holding it for her. He did the same thing at the diner, and soon, they were ensconced in a booth with a table between them. Gwen still looked like she would bolt at a moment's notice, but it felt good that she'd come this far.

Over dinner, he told her about the group he belonged to, stressing that they didn't live in a compound and they weren't some religious organization. They were simply a group of like-minded people who'd decided to live simply and try to help the earth.

Her eyes had lit up when he mentioned helping the earth. Turns out, that's all she'd wanted to do with her life. Everything else about her horrible life had come out in short spurts over the next several months. But that night, she'd let him get her a hotel room. The next morning, when she'd joined him again at the restaurant, he hadn't recognized her when she walked in until her eyes found his.

He'd asked Gwen to join them, had told her she'd have her own tent, her own space. That hadn't lasted long.

Within four months, they were married. He'd never looked back, except to thank whatever entity had led him to her that night. She hadn't eaten in three days and had been down to her last $2.76.

Now, five years later, the light was gone from her eyes again just like it had been when he'd first seen her. More than anything, he wanted to bring his Gwen back. To take away all the bad in her life and help her remember the happy stuff. Their time together highest on that list.

He sat down next to her at the trailer's cramped table and Gwen curled into him, holding on so tight he could feel her shaking, feel her pain. God, but he wanted to make it better for her.

"I can't stop thinking about how I'll never see her again."

"Except in your memories and your dreams."

"I don't know what I'll do. When I ran away, I at least had the possibility of her in my future. Now... "

"Now you can talk to her, just like you always have."

She nodded into his chest.

Luther joined them, setting down two bottles, one wine and one whiskey, and three glasses. "I say we get rip-roaring drunk and forget about everything for a while."

Gwen sat up, wiping the tears from her eyes. Her chuckle warmed Wyeth's heart. She heaved a big sigh, then reached for a glass. "Whiskey for me. Tall."

News Alert: The market may be experiencing a run on rare gems, minerals, and metals. Sources report that various entities around the world are buying up physical stores of diamonds, silver, and gold. Prices are artificially inflated due to a perceived shortage.

CHAPTER NINETEEN

"Hold out your hand."

Taegar lifted her arm. Someone put something cold and glittering in her palm.

"Now look at it. Make it grow."

Make it grow. She could do that. She knew how. But why? Everything was so foggy. She turned her head. She sat in a high-backed chair in a dark room with no windows, no pictures, nothing but a bed, a chair and a table. And an overhead light.

Where was she? Where were her friends?

A thick fog coated her thoughts. She'd been going to do something. What?

The slap came out of nowhere and almost threw her from the chair. Taegar didn't even have the energy to fight whoever had done that. She slumped down. "Make the damn rock grow, bitch."

She wasn't a bitch. Was she? Who tormented her like this? She tried to lift her head, but it was too heavy. She needed to figure this out, to get away. Yes, escape. That's what she wanted to do. But from what? To where?

It hurt too much to think, so Taegar stared at the sparkles in front of her, made a wish, and watched them grow.

~~~

Gordon stared at Taegar, already a shell of her former self. Once he'd gotten the drug in her system, she'd become compliant. He kept her sedated just enough to maintain it. She looked like hell. Her face was grimy with slobber, her hair was a mess of rat tangles, and her clothes hung on her. He'd brought in a doctor and nurse at great expense to insert a gastric feeding tube to keep her fed and hydrated. It had cost very little compared to the wealth he was amassing.

As he watched the raw diamond grow, Gordon almost rubbed his hands together in glee. His stockpile had grown exponentially, both from purchases of raw stock and from her talents. The skyrocketing price of precious gems had been a bonus. Everyone thought there was a shortage. Little did they know, the market could easily be glutted just from his coffers.

He'd have to be careful selling it all. Do it slowly to maintain the façade of a shortage and keep prices high. He'd also need someone whose discretion was assured. Gordon knew a couple guys, but not well.

He took the five-carat-plus diamond from Taegar's hand and thrust the newspaper in front of her, frustrated when she didn't even look at it.

"Pick a stock," he screamed.

Her head came up and she stared at the paper in front of her.

"Pick!"

A finger lifted, then fell, never near the paper. Her eyes, glassy and unfocused, rolled back in her head as she
~~~

slumped once again.

"Gah!" Gordon hit the paper against the arm of the chair. This was the one thing he'd lost, keeping her doped up. So be it. He filled the syringe and gave her the next injection, unwilling to trust anyone else to do this for him. He thought about how she'd thrown him with nothing but a thought. If there were a slipup, and the girl woke fully, he knew he'd be dead. Or worse.

With one last scathing look at the puppet she had become, Gordon left the basement room. It was time to do some vetting.

When his phone rang, he considered not answering it. He'd about had it with Ramsey's imperialistic attitude.

"What?" Gordon said.

"Not seeing any upflow from all that wealth you're amassing, Darcy. And I'd better see it soon or you'll pay a stiffer price than you want."

The conversation was over before it began. The vice president hung up without giving Gordon a single opportunity to respond. Not that he would have anyhow. It was definitely time to do something about Ramsey. He opened a desk drawer in his office and pulled out the burner phone he kept for special calls.

"It's time," he said when the person answered. Then he broke the phone in half and threw it into a special incinerator he kept in his home office.

Now he'd be able to focus on the next phase of his plan. Before long, he'd be the richest, most powerful man in the world. And soon, he'd take care of the only person who could stop him.

Yes, everything was going according to plan. Slower than he wanted, but patience was about the only virtue he possessed. Gordon Darcy could wait a bit longer for his payoff. But not too much longer.

News Alert: Vice President Ramsey was found dead this morning of an apparent suicide.

CHAPTER TWENTY

The doorbell rang. Cait, in the middle of corralling her girls to get them dressed, heard footsteps below so didn't worry about the door. Damian or Valena would get it.

"Willow, come here. You're naked as a jaybird. Let's get you dressed so we can go down to breakfast."

"Wheeeeee," naked girl said, racing around the room.

Fallon, with one arm in and one still out of her shirt, squirmed to get away. Cait had an arm around her waist as she tussled with the errant sleeve. Once the shirt was on, she held her on her lap and wrestled her pants on. She would have to worry about socks later.

"Willow, get over here," Cait said again, letting loose of Fallon.

"No. Want Thom."

"Tom's not here, sweetie." Cait pulled clothes out of a drawer for her other daughter.

"Is too."

She turned and her hand flew to her mouth. He was here. Tom. Squatting in the doorway, both girls in his arms, his face buried between them. "I've missed you girls." He looked through them at Cait. "I've missed you, too."

Tears blurred Cait's view and all she could do was nod.

Tom set the girls down. "Willow, let's get you dressed. Then you can go downstairs to Auntie Valena and Uncle Damian."

Willow nodded her head enthusiastically. Tom took the shirt and pants from Cait, lingering as their fingers touched after so long apart. When he turned to dress Willow, she stood quiet and let him help her without a single fight. Figured. Once both girls were dressed, he shooed them down the hall.

"Make sure they get down the— "

"Stairs all right," Tom finished. "I've got this."

He followed the girls out the door, tossing a look of regret over his shoulder. Cait knew how he felt. She wanted to hug him, kiss him, spend hours catching up, just the two of them. But the girls came first. Cait picked dirty clothes off the floor, light-headed with happiness. He was here. She couldn't believe it. She'd hoped, but he'd been so non-specific. And with so much going on, hope was difficult to hold onto.

Before she got to the hamper, he was back in the doorway. They stood there, feet away from each other, giddy smiles on both their faces. Then, he was across the room, slipping his arms around her waist.

Cait touched his cheek. "You're really here."

Tom's grin widened. "I couldn't stay away any longer."

When he lowered his head and kissed her, the last piece of Cait's unfinished jigsaw puzzle fell into place. This was where she belonged.

"God, I've missed you," she whispered.

"Not as much as I've missed you."

She wanted to stay here, in his arms, for eternity. Let the world and all its problems fade and just be. Here. With

Tom.

A scream from downstairs broke them apart. Tom looked ready to bolt in the direction the girls had gone.

Cait stopped him with a hand on his arm. "Happy scream. But we'd better go rescue Valena and Damian."

Tom nodded. Keeping his arm around her shoulder, they headed downstairs, where Damian chased after the girls with makeshift finger horns on his head. They chortled in happy laughter as he raced around and around the kitchen island. When he pretended to trip and fall, the girls turned and pounced on him and everyone laughed.

It took some time to get them simmered down and into their high chairs. Cait gave them Cheerios and their milk cups then went to the counter and reached for a banana.

"Here, let me peel that," Tom said, kissing her cheek. "You get a cup of coffee and sit."

"You just got here. You must be tired."

"I stopped for a couple of hours last night and got a great cat-nap, so I'm good. Now go. Coffee."

Valena and Damian grinned widely at Cait, and the heat of a deep blush filled her cheeks as she poured coffee and sat down next to the two high chairs.

Once the girls were happily munching on their breakfast, Tom poured coffee and settled next to her, knee touching knee. It felt so right, so normal, to have him here.

"How are things going for you," Tom asked Damian.

"Not bad. Not as good as I would like, but not bad. We've found some new friends here, but getting people to take a stand and help is slow going."

"New friends?" Tom tangled his fingers with Cait's under the table.

Damian nodded. "Turns out, a very popular actor has the same abilities as Fallon there."

Cait had already told Tom about Gus, but he didn't let on.

"Really? Wow, that's fascinating. I'd love to talk to him or her. Maybe get a blood sample."

"He's reticent to out himself," Damian said "so I doubt that will happen anytime soon."

"I can understand that," Cait said. "The business he's in can embrace or blackball someone on a whim. Careers are broken by a simple rumor."

"But," Valena said, "he's agreed to open some doors for us. We've got an appointment this afternoon with the biggest news agency in California."

"That's a good start."

"How is the testing going?" Valena asked.

Considering he was doodling on her palm, completely eroding her ability to concentrated, Cait was impressed by Tom's answer. "All the data collected about the light, and searches for its source, have been inconclusive. It's really strange. Based on air, soil, and other samples, it's like it's not even there."

Damian smiled. "It's a leap of faith."

"Basically. What's more interesting is the human side of things. I've been running blood and DNA tests. Some really interesting stuff has come from that."

Cait tightened her fingers around Tom's.

"Don't worry," he said. "I haven't found anything harmful, and my tests were extensive." Glancing around the table, he took a deep breath. "What I did find was an extra DNA marker in each sample from someone gifted. A marker that you have, Damian. And you, Valena. And Fallon, and Luther, and everyone else with these enhanced talents. Cait and I don't possess this marker. Nor does Willow. Valena, you and I have spoken already about your medical history. May I discuss that here?"

"I have no secrets from my friends."

Tom briefly put a hand over hers. "You had a miscarriage."

Oh, no! Cait looked at Valena, saw the sheen of tears in her eyes. The same sheen that now blurred her own vision. "I'm so sorry."

Damian put an arm around his wife's shoulders and she gazed at him for a long moment, an unspoken message of grief passing between them.

"It's all right," Valena said. "We've come to terms with it. Go ahead, Tom. You can finish your story."

"With your permission, I obtained the DNA sample they'd taken back then. They'd done tests, but not as extensive as I needed. I completed those tests a few days ago. Valena, you didn't have this marker then. It's new."

Quiet descended on the table, broken only by the skittering of Cheerio's on the girls' trays. According to what Tom had discovered, Fallon had been changed by this phenomenon. Cait's fear roared to the front of her brain then sank to settle in her heart with a dread previously unknown to her. What would happen to her little girl?

"What does this mean?" Damian asked.

"I don't completely understand it," Tom said. "But I believe, strongly, that this is not something harmful."

The dread in her heart eased a notch.

"We could have told you that," Valena said with a chuckle.

"I know. Well, now I have a bit of concrete evidence to back that up. Two things stand out. First, comparing your DNA samples, there's no change except for the marker. No degradation. No degeneration of anything in your body. The marker is there, and it's probably the reason for your enhanced abilities, but it's not harmful."

And another notch.

"Plus, it's been six weeks now, and no one, talented or not, has shown any sort of adverse effect from this phenomenon. As you know through your ability to heal people, Valena, it's just the opposite. I've been in contact with people all over the world. Those with this extra talent are healthier than ever. One mod had type 1 diabetes that disappeared after the light came and he gained his additional abilities. His pancreas began working again and his diabetes was cured!"

"That's pretty amazing."

"And there's more. The genes that determine how you age changed in a very specific way. I think those of you who are touched by this magic will have extended lives."

Silence ruled the room as everyone digested the information.

"You mean we'll live forever?" Damian said.

"I don't think I like that idea." Valena turned to Damian. "I've always envisioned growing old with you, husband."

"As I with you," Damian said with a poignant smile for his wife.

Cait stared at the twins. "Will Fallon not age like Willow? Will she be forever stuck in a two-year-old's body?" She didn't even know what to feel about that, if one twin aged and the other didn't. Cait had always considered herself someone who embraced differences and disabilities, yet this felt like her daughter's life would be stifled. The worry Cait had set aside about her daughter's well-being moved right back to center stage.

Tom squeezed her hand again. "That's another interesting part of this whole thing. That aging difference isn't there in Fallon. Not yet anyhow. Maybe it's because she's so young, or maybe not everyone will get this benefit. I don't know."

Cait's worry eased again.

"Earth has handed us a rare gift, giving us the time we need to effect change and to help us all survive," Damian mused.

"I agree. It's like everything's been slowed down for you, aging wise. I, umm, I haven't told anyone this. And I didn't want to mention it on the phone. Things are getting pretty strange around the lab. I think my phones are tapped, and I'm concerned I'm being watched."

"Are you in danger?" Cait asked, clutching his thigh.

"I don't think so. At least, not as long as I toe the line the powers that be have designated for me."

"Is... Were you followed here? There's an SUV outside that's been watching us."

Tom put an arm around her shoulder. "I took great pains to get here without being followed, just in case. It's possible, but I was pretty careful. Damian told me about that SUV. I doubt they'd have recognized me under my baseball cap from that distance. If they even knew who I was. I would never do anything to bring trouble to you or the girls."

She laid her head on Tom's shoulder. "I know that. I really do. It's just, well, it feels like the circle around us is tightening and we're all going to get squeezed out of our lives in the end."

Willow started banging her cup on the high-chair table. "Down, mama. Down."

Cait got a washcloth and cleaned up both girls, letting them go find their toys. Tom cleaned the high chairs and put the trays back on.

Damian put a hand on Cait's shoulder. "Things may get worse before they get better, but they will get better. I can't say when, but I have a certain prescience now. I see an abundance of blooms and growth and peace and happiness somewhere in the future. Have hope."

"The future. Not necessarily ours."

Damian cocked his head, acknowledging the truth in her statement. "For now, all we can do is fight for what is right, and for those two girls we've all come to love."

Valena joined him. "We'll do whatever we can to keep them safe. You've all become part of our family. I hope you know that."

Cait hugged them both. "I do know that, I really do. And I'm so grateful to you. To all of you," she said as Tom joined their circle. "It's all a bit overwhelming."

"It is. But we'll get through it together." Tom kissed Cait's forehead. Just that simple gesture soothed her ragged nerves. "Now what say we go see what those little devils are getting into?" He smiled.

"And we need to get ready for our interview this afternoon. We're going big time, thanks to our new friend. He got us a spotlight with L.A.'s biggest and brightest."

"We wish you every luck in the world," Cait said. "I'd like to help spread the word, but... "

"No word-spreading for you," Tom said. "Your job is to take care of what, to date, is the youngest person touched by this gift."

A sippy cup Cait had filled with water lifted off the counter and wafted through the air toward the girls' playroom.

"That is a full-time job," Cait said, following the cup, with Valena right behind her.

~~~

"Tom," Damian held his friend back. "How long can you stay?"

"Not long. Maybe three or four days. Why?"

"We have appointments set up over the next several days. After that, we're headed back to Washington.
~~~

Nothing will happen at any level if we can't convince more people to help."

"Agreed. Be careful, though. I get a sense that a battle is brewing on the hill."

Damian nodded. "Cait may be right. This is going to get dangerous."

"I think so, too."

"If we aren't careful, if we piss off the wrong people..."

"I'll take Cait and the girls and disappear," Tom said without hesitation. "That's why I was so careful about getting this information to you."

"Have you told the person you report to about all this yet?"

"No. I plan to hold off on that as long as possible." Tom took a deep breath. "There's something else. There's a whole wing of my lab that's been closed off. Lots of comings and goings. And gurneys. I think... "

"What?"

"I think they may be kidnapping mods."

Damian's eyes widened. If they were holding the gifted against their will, they would stop at nothing to harness their power. "This is not good."

"No. But I don't have anything concrete, just my own observations."

"You're an astute man, Tom. If you think something's happening, that's good enough for me."

Tom nodded.

"We need to be extra careful," Damian said.

"You do."

"You, too. Don't put yourself at risk."

Tom sighed. "I'm trying not to." He looked through the open door. "I think I have something I want to live for."

"I'm worried about their safety, now more than ever."

"Me, too. How are the others doing?"

"Bhren is pretty close-mouthed about happenings back home. I think he's worried about prying ears as well, though Roulf seems to think he can push a mute button on any of that, talent-wise."

"Roulf?"

"Funny little man. New friend, and a great asset. He arrived at camp after you left." Damian frowned. "I haven't talked to Wyeth, Gwen, or Luther since we parted. I think it's time to get in touch with them."

"Maybe they can come hang out here?"

Damian nodded. "Maybe. We'll get on the forum later today and see what's up."

"Good. We have a plan. Now you'd better go dig out that tie." Tom slapped Damian on the back.

"Oh, no. No ties for me. They can take me as I am. Though maybe I should have considered a haircut before this."

Tom laughed. "Yeah, maybe you should have."

News Alert: The Darcy Corporation has reported an unprecedented increase in assets. There's talk of a government investigation.

CHAPTER TWENTY-ONE

How much time had passed? Taegar didn't know. She floated in an ethereal world with no boundaries. Happiness, sadness, all had deserted her, leaving only nothingness. She wanted to climb her way out of the hole she'd fallen into. To get back to the light. Such a beautiful light.

Something hard was thrust into her hand. She stared at it, though it wavered and she could not focus completely. Still, it sparkled. Pretty sparkles.

"Make it grow," a man's voice said.

Unable to resist the summons, a familiar warmth filled Taegar. A soothing warmth. She liked this feeling. She felt safe, cocooned, loved. The shiny object grew to almost double in size. So pretty. She reached out with her other hand, wanting to play with the shiny ball.

But it was yanked away before she could. The warmth left her and that made her angry. She wanted the ball back. And the warmth. This wasn't right. Whoever was doing this was being mean to her.

Taegar searched the room around her, trying to focus on who was doing this. A man, there. In a suit. Someone familiar, but she couldn't quite put a name to the face.

"Stop doing this," she begged. "Please."

"Sorry, doll, but you're my ticket to paradise."

Paradise? How could she take him to paradise? Confusion filled her, coloring a growing anger an even deeper shade of red. A tube in her arm moved as the man stuck a needle in it. She pulled away until another familiar warmth washed through her and the room around her disappeared again. One name touched her mind before she gave herself to oblivion.

Gordon.

Who is Gordon?

Who cares?

~~~

"So what do we do now?" Luther asked.

Gwen had spent the last week improving the agriculture of this depressed area, and they'd been met with both gratitude and suspicion. Wyeth had needed to calm Luther down on several occasions. It didn't help that he'd grabbed a man's camera and thrown it as far as he could, which was a darn sight farther than could a normal human being. All the good they'd been doing disappeared behind everyone's fear of Luther's strength. Vegetation and the farm fields were thriving because of Gwen's magic, but it no longer seemed to matter. They'd probably done more harm than good.

"I'm not sure we should stay here any longer," Wyeth said.

"I said I'm sorry. What else can I do? The man was pissing me off." Luther had been grumbling ever since the event two days ago.

After helping one farmer with his crops, the word had gotten around that they offered free assistance. There'd been a line of requests until Luther's temper tantrum.
~~~

Wyeth had been just as ticked at the guy with the camera, but he'd managed to contain his anger. "There's too much at stake to let our emotions rule here, Luther. We lost more than we gained."

"Yeah, yeah."

"No, seriously. We've been given a sacred job to do and we can't screw it up."

"I know," Luther said, jumping up and hitting the sides of the trailer, denting one of the walls. "I get it. I screwed up. It won't happen again."

It's happening right now, Wyeth thought, thankful that only he and Gwen witnessed it.

"All right," he said. "No use crying over spilled milk. We're due to check in with Damian and Valena. Let's see if they have any suggestions on where we should go next."

Gwen handed Luther a beer with a pat on his back. That was his wife, always looking for ways to de-escalate a situation. She grabbed the laptop and settled next to Wyeth. Luther sat on the sofa behind the trailer table. He could see and be part of the discussion from there, and hopefully, Damian and Valena wouldn't catch wind of his foul mood.

Gwen texted Cait and five minutes later they could see their friends' faces through the online video chat.

"Tom," Gwen said, smiling. "It's good to see you again."

Tom slung an arm around Cait's shoulders. "It's good to be here. I've missed you all."

Wyeth and Gwen had noticed something between those two. Both their smiles widened at the message they'd just gotten loud and clear.

"Luther, that you in the background?" Valena asked.

"Yeah," he mumbled.

When Valena frowned, Wyeth gave a quick "later" shake of his head.

Valena shifted to look at Gwen. They already knew, through their email group, what had happened with Gwen's father. "We were so sorry to hear about your mother, Gwen. How are you doing?"

"Thank you. I won't lie. It hasn't been easy. But Wyeth and Luther won't let me get too depressed. I'll miss her. It's different now, knowing I'll never see her again. But I feel in my heart that she's at peace. And, well, I'm focusing on the family I have now. I'm grateful for every one of you."

"Still, I wish I were there to give you a hug."

Gwen placed a hand over her own heart. "I feel your presence, Valena. I truly do. How are things going on your end?"

"We're hoping to make some progress, starting today," Damian said, changing places with Valena so he could see and chat easier. "We've widened the circle by a few, and have a big news interview this afternoon."

"You look a little green around the gills, Damian," Wyeth said. Everyone knew public speaking was not their leader's strong point.

"Don't remind me."

"Just be clear, intelligent, and don't shove it down their throats. Lay out the facts and let folks make their own decision from there."

"If I don't, I'll have Valena kicking me under the table."

Everyone chuckled.

"Remember that," Wyeth said.

"It will help, but not enough," Damian said. "And there are...worries."

"What kind?"

"Not the kind I can discuss online. What are you all doing at the moment?"

Luther stiffened and Wyeth sighed. Would the man

never learn that Wyeth didn't throw his family under buses? "We're at loose ends at the moment. We've done about all we can do here."

"That's good," Damian said. "We could use some help."

"How soon?"

"How soon can you make it?"

Luther finally showed some interest in the conversation. "If I drive, two days. If we let Wyeth drive, two weeks."

Wyeth grimaced. "I'm not that bad."

The chorus of "oh, yes you are" that chimed in belied his statement.

Damian leaned forward. "The sooner, the better."

Wyeth looked at Gwen, who nodded, then craned his neck to check Luther's opinion.

"Hell, yes," Luther said.

"All right, then." Wyeth turned back to the screen. "We'll leave bright and early tomorrow morning. And yes, Luther will do *most* of the driving. So we should be there in, say, three days, give or take."

With that settled, they signed off.

"I'll get some dinner going," Gwen said.

"I'll help you," Luther said, jerking to a stand like a fidgety puppet.

Now, he was in a much better mood, but that didn't stop Wyeth from worrying about him. Luther seemed to bounce from high to low, then back to high. He'd never exhibited any bipolar tendencies back home, but something had changed for him now that they were out in the world. It was as if the cocoon had been stripped from him and he didn't know how to handle it.

Wyeth would keep an eye on him. Luther was family. He didn't want him to head down any dark tunnels. He wanted him healthy and happy.

Only time would tell how this would all turn out.

Only time.

~~~

"It was good to see their faces," Valena said after the screen went dark. "I miss them all."

"It definitely was," Cait said. She cocked her head. "I don't hear the twins." They'd left them in the playroom so she and Tom could take a moment to say hello to their friends. Cait got up and headed for the door.

Tom joined her. Standing in the doorway, they watched the girls quietly playing. Tom's arm rested around her waist, something that happened frequently now. It felt so good.

Fallon had built a tower from plastic blocks. It was almost to the ceiling, making it quite clear that it was a magic-enhanced tower. Willow sat beside it clapping her hands in glee. She clapped so hard and so wide that she whacked two of the blocks, sending them flying. The rest of the tower stayed put for several seconds, then fell to the floor all around the girls.

Fallon's face crumbled along with the tumbling blocks, her wail quickly becoming a chorus. Cait went for Fallon and Tom picked up Willow. It took some time to settle them down. Tom, who'd never had children, soothed the little girl he held with a seasoned demeanor. Cait's heart broke wide open. She'd only known this soul-encompassing feeling once in her life. Not from her parents, not from the girls' bio-dad. Only with the birth of her twins had she given her heart so fully. Her feelings for Tom exhilarated her. They also scared the crap out of her. With everything happening in the world, why had she chosen now to fall so deeply off the love-cliff?

Tom glanced at her, concern crossing his face, then—
~~~

blessing upon blessing—she saw her own emotions reflected there. He set a now-quiet Willow down and Cait let Fallon join her sister, both past their agony and ready to play again.

Cait and Tom met in the middle of the room. All she could do was stare at him. Tom reached up, cupped her face with both hands, and offered her the sweetest kiss she'd ever had.

"I think I'm hopelessly in love with you, Cait Darcy."

"I know I am over-the-top in love with you, Tom Gallows."

Cait leaned against him, reveling as his heart beat in concert with her own.

They turned in unison and watched a block float through the air to settle in place on the growing tower.

"We picked one hell of a time to do this," Tom said.

Cait chuckled. "We certainly did." She hugged him tight. "How long can you stay?"

"I'll stay until Wyeth and the others get here. If I'm gone any longer, someone will notice."

"I'm worried. For the girls, for us, for everything."

"Me, too," he said. "Me, too."

Together, they sat on the floor to play with the girls. Together, Cait thought. This was a first, having someone to share this with. As Fallon handed him a block and he mimicked trying to make it raise to the stack, Cait felt no jealousy. Only abounding love for the man with the weight of the world on his shoulders, who took time to play with her daughters.

News Alert: The public has had a mixed response to several recent broadcast interviews with Damian and Valena Royan, proclaimed by many as the leaders of this green revolution for change.

CHAPTER TWENTY-TWO

"That went well," Valena said as they walked out of yet another studio.

"It was fun to watch," Gwen said, tucking her arm into Valena's while Damian went to get the car. "I had no idea so much was involved in one little television news program."

"Not so little. They are nationally syndicated. I hope it helps get the message out."

"We need all the help we can get. It's a mixed bag out there. We talked with people everywhere we stopped en route to Cait's. I tried to help them with Earth's bounty in each place. It's not enough, though. People are still very suspicious. And scared." Gwen shook her head.

Damian pulled up. Valena got in front and Gwen hopped in the back.

"Scared? Of us?" Valena asked.

"Yes. Think about it. These people in the world with extra talents and powers probably leave the rest feeling like they've lost control. That must be frightening. And some who've been given this gift are exploiting their powers."

"True." Damian pulled out into traffic and headed for Cait's house. "Plus, tolerance for things they don't understand isn't humanity's strong point. Look at religion. If we could all understand that the belief in something bigger than us doesn't have to be the same thing for everyone, we'd all get along so much better."

"That's why these interviews are so important," Valena said. "We have to help them understand." She reached back and grasped Gwen's hand. "I'm so glad you're here. I've missed you."

"*We've* missed you," Damian added.

"It's good to have the core group back together again, except for Bhren. I do miss the lake."

"So do we," Valena said. "I can't believe you got up to do this interview with us after not getting into town until after two in the morning."

"I can nap when we get home. It's sure nice of Cait to squeeze us all in."

"Luther seemed disgruntled that we had to put him on the couch. I came downstairs this morning and he had his head under a pillow as the girls piled toys on top of him." Valena giggled. "He didn't seem to think it was as funny as they did."

Gwen's smile disappeared. "Something's happening with him. I'm not sure what, but he's more discontent with each passing day. It's like he's angry at the world for not accepting what we're saying. There was an incident in Minnesota. A newsman got in his face. Luther grabbed the man's camera and threw it with all the force of his new power, wiping away all the progress we'd made, all the good we'd been trying to do. Since then, he seems worse. We've been worried about him."

"I'll talk with him," Damian said.

"Thank you."

Damian inclined his head. "I think we need to gather. Maybe a prayer circle would be a good idea. We need to get in touch with our roots, with Earth. Everything we do drains the energy from us. We need Earthing, a physical connection with Earth's goodness, to reboot."

"That's a great idea," Valena said. "It's almost Thanksgiving. Maybe we could gather for that. And Cait has a nice backyard. We could do something there for our prayer circle."

"Should we consider a local park?" Gwen asked. "Show people there's nothing to fear? Invite them to join us?"

"I'm not sure the world is ready for that," Damian said.

"Plus, I think we need to be together, just us," Valena added. "To renew our bonds to each other and to Earth. I think Thanksgiving is the perfect night to do that. We have someone we'd like to invite to join our circle. You can meet him then."

"Who?"

Valena smiled. "I'd rather not say until you have the chance to meet him."

"Hmmm, intrigue," Gwen said as she leaned back in her seat. "I like it."

~~~

Three days later, Gus, in sunglasses and a ball cap, walked up to Cait's front door with Linda at his side. He hesitated.

"It'll be fine. I have a good feeling about these folks. They'll keep your secret," Linda said, shifting the sweet potatoes over to her other hand to squeeze his.

He was about to poke the bear, outing himself to more than just Damian, Valena, and Cait. If this little extra ability
~~~

of his got out, his career would be over. Yet, he'd had several conversations with Damian since they'd met, and his career no longer seemed as important. There was a bigger cause here, a bigger need than getting some movie contract.

Because of that, Gus, on the precipice of announcing that he was a mod, had chosen to start small, with Damian's core druid group. Sure, these were kindred spirits, so maybe it wasn't a fair test. But it was a start.

Never one to shy away from difficult movie parts, Gus took a deep breath and knocked on the door.

Damian answered almost immediately, inviting them inside. "Welcome."

"Thank you," Gus said.

Linda handed her dish to Damian. "We appreciate the invitation."

"Cait wanted you here. We all did." He shook Gus's hand. "So, you ready to expand your circle of confidants?"

Damian had urged him to tell the group tonight. "It makes me nervous, but you and Linda vouch for everyone, so yes, I'm ready."

"I do vouch for them. They're my family and we began this epic adventure together."

"Then let's get this done."

"Everyone's in the kitchen preparing dinner. Afterward, once Cait's twins are in bed, we thought we'd hold a circle gathering in the yard. A chance to commune with Earth. You up for that?"

"I'm interested in understanding all this better, so definitely."

"Great." Damian clapped him on the back, propelling him into the chaos of the kitchen.

And chaos it was. Cait, who Gus had met before, was at the stove with a man he hadn't met, heads together over a pot of... Gus sniffed. Gravy? A well-muscled man sulked in one of the kitchen chairs. Another, with sandy blond hair and a bounce in his step, set dishes on a tray. The way he and the woman next to him passed dishes so effortlessly, they had to be a couple.

Amongst all the chatter and work, Fallon and Willow ran in, out, and under everyone and everything, screaming happiness and faster on their feet than Gus thought two-year-olds could be.

The woman helping with the dishes turned around with a bunch of silverware in her hand. Her gaze whizzed past Gus, then stopped and swung back to him. Her eyes widened, her mouth turned into a perfect "o" and the silverware clattered toward the floor.

Letting instinct rule, Gus paused the silverware with nothing but thought before any of it hit the ground.

The room came to a standstill. Movement, noise, all of it stopped. Even the twins were glued in place. Only the occasional bubble of gravy gave away the passage of time as everyone stared at him. Gus gulped. Nothing like trial by fire.

He waved his hand and the forks, knives, and spoons all settled onto a nearby counter.

"Well, I believe that explains why Gus has joined us. Yep," Damian said, clapping him on the back again, "welcome to the ant farm." He moved past Gus and gathered up the errant silverware. "The nice lady here with her jaw on the floor is Gwen. That's her husband Wyeth behind her, and Luther's in time-out back in the corner. Tom, there," Damian pointed, "is the one burning the gravy."

Cait whirled back to the stove, casting a scowl over her shoulder as Damian laughed. He handed the errant flatware to Wyeth. "Everyone, this is Gus Grandon. But I'm guessing you already know that."

Wyeth nudged his wife, who came out of her star-induced trance.

"I'm sorry," Gwen said, moving to shake Gus's hand. "I was just so surprised."

"I gather he," Gus nodded toward Damian, "didn't tell you I was coming."

"Oh, he told us someone was coming. Just not who, or that he was one of us," Wyeth said, reaching out his hand. "Nice to meet you."

Cait grinned and waved at Gus. He'd noticed when he first met her how welcoming she was. It didn't seem to matter who she met, she made them all seem like friends. He understood why Linda considered Cait her closest friend. Gus returned her smile as he nodded in her direction.

Tom put his arm around Cait's waist and Gus got the message. His grin widened as he shook Tom's hand. "It's good to meet you, Tom. Have you met my girlfriend, Linda?"

Linda blushed, Tom immediately relaxed, and Cait's smile grew brighter.

Valena walked in the back door as Wyeth went out with the tray of dishes and flatware. "Gus. Linda. It's good to see you again."

Gus kissed her cheek.

"Help yourself to whatever you want to drink," Cait said. "Wine, beer, alcohol-free stuff; it's all in or beside the fridge." She turned back to the range, opening the door to check the turkey.

"Everything smells delicious," he said, helping himself to a beer and pouring a glass of the red wine Linda preferred.

"Won't be long before dinner," Cait said.

Gus and Linda headed outside. Cait's backyard was small, but lovely like a mystical garden. Trees had been trimmed into hedges along the fence line, giving her almost complete privacy, though there were neighbors on all three sides of her.

A long table sat on the small patio with a hodgepodge of chairs surrounding it. Back in one corner, a plastic climbing toy sat next to a small plastic pool. Something at the center of the yard drew Gus's attention. A round design lay embedded there, an intricate design of different colored stones, with grass around and in between. He squatted down for a closer look. There was no rhyme nor reason to the colors, yet it...made sense. He couldn't quite describe it, but everything in the circle felt...right.

"Cait designed and built this," Damian said.

"For tonight?"

Damian chuckled. "No. It took her an entire summer three years ago. She did it while she was pregnant with the twins. Said it was therapy and relaxing."

"Wow. That's quite a talent."

"I agree."

They gazed at the two-dimensional sculpture until the cacophony from inside broke through the door. Suddenly, it was a rush of bringing food, high chairs, drinks, and dishes outside. Gus joined in the chaos, suddenly missing the large family he'd left in Washington. None of them had supported his choice to become an actor, so he'd left them behind to follow his dreams. A couple of his brothers had sought him out later, once he'd gotten his first big movie role, but their needs had come first and the contact had been shallow. The only sibling he remained in touch with was his sister, Janice. Even that was few and far between, though. She was the most down-to-earth and accepting member of his family and had left their backward upbringing behind to find love in a small town over on the Olympic Peninsula. But she was embroiled in carpools and sporting events with her young boys, so they had little in common. He wondered how she would take the news of his new talents, and he made a mental note to call her before things went public. She deserved to know.

Dinner was a joyful, boisterous affair, with dishes passed from hand to hand, questions asked over other discussions, and laughter that came easily and often. It was as though, for this meal, they'd set all their worries aside. These were good people, and Gus felt privileged to be invited into their circle.

Until he'd come into this gift of his, he'd been skeptical that change could happen.

He wasn't so skeptical anymore.

After dinner, Cait and Tom put the girls to bed while everyone cleared the mess and cleaned up. Then, they settled on the ground around Cait's circle. One by one, they touched the stones, then clasped hands with the friends on either side. Linda grasped Cait's hand, then Gus's. A tingle, starting at the tips of his fingers, moved up his arm and through his body, infusing him with warmth and a sort of oneness. Like they were all connected somehow. It felt good. He stared at the entwined hands, knowing he'd just found his new family.

After a joint prayer for peace and growth, both for Earth and for humankind to open their minds and hearts to new ideas, Damian officially invited Gus and Linda to become part of their circle.

"But I don't have any powers," Linda said.

"You are a kindred spirit. That is the tie that binds you to us, as it does Cait and Tom."

Gus and Linda accepted, both smiling in awe of this very profound moment. Everyone hugged them as they left, and he missed his new friends as soon as the door shut behind them.

"Want to spend the night at my place?" Linda asked.

"You know I would, normally, but tonight, I need to go home. To think. To relive this evening."

"I get that."

He could hear the disappointment in her voice. Kissing her outside her apartment building, he almost changed his mind. Damian had called her a kindred spirit. Gus agreed. She was also his soul-mate.

Gus walked back to his car, still reeling from the intensity and privilege of his acceptance into the circle. These people were the real deal. They were trying to effect true change and keep Earth and its inhabitants from destroying each other. He understood that now more than ever. At the same time, he knew it was a monumental task and they were caught on a wave taking them farther out to sea, instead of closer to land and a positive result.

Would his going public help that or hurt it?

Gus couldn't decide. He started his car and, with one last regretful glance at Linda's apartment, he grabbed his phone. He called his sister's number before pulling out. It was time to ask someone he could trust.

News Alert: Public opinion polls show a growing distrust of mods, and increasing doubt that they are devoted to the Earth and society's well-being. Mods who seek to profit fromtheir newfound talents are especially unpopular. Previously, 56 percent trusted the mods to enrich their futures. Now, that number is down to 38 percent.

CHAPTER TWENTY-THREE

"I wish you didn't have to go."

Cait hung on to Tom. They'd said their goodbyes last night in private, and he'd fed the twins their breakfast, explaining that he had to leave. Both girls had gotten upset, and he'd been so patient with them. When Fallon's teddy bear wafted down the stairs from her bedroom into Tom's arms, Cait hadn't been able to help her tears.

Tom kissed Cait again and hugged the stuffed animal close. "I hate having to leave."

Unfortunately, he had little choice. His job had been a source of inside information, but even more important, he was closer than anyone to understanding what had happened to them. For that reason alone, he needed to return.

Cait melted into his kiss for a long moment, then broke it and stepped back. "Be safe, Tom. Be careful. It feels like things are starting to close in on everyone and you're right in the thick of it."

He tucked an errant lock of hair behind her ear. "I'll be careful." With one last smile and a blown kiss, he headed for his car. Cait stood in the doorway and watched until he was gone from sight. She sighed and grabbed the paper from her front porch, noting the black van was still there, then headed inside to get the twins out of their high chairs.

Her day had begun. Maybe not on a high note, but it was hers to design and Cait had never been one to muddle in misery. She froze as a headline grabbed her attention.

Gordon Darcy declared richest man in America.

Wow. That had happened fast. When Cait had worked for her father, he'd been climbing that wealth ladder, but still had quite a ways to go. How had he gotten to this pinnacle so quickly? She carried the paper into the kitchen and handed it to Damian. Valena wiped her soapy hands and joined them, reading over Damian's shoulder.

"How did one man get so rich so fast?" Cait asked.

"I don't know," Damian said.

"He wasn't anywhere near this level of wealth when I worked there."

Valena sat down, her hand gripping Damian's arm. "You don't think he's found a way to use someone's talents, do you? That he's somehow convinced Taegar to help him?"

"It's too coincidental not to be suspicious." Damian rubbed his jaw.

Cait set her empty coffee cup in the sink with a plunk. "I wouldn't put anything past him if it furthered his cause."

"What is his cause?"

"Money and power, power and money. That's what drives him. Nothing else. He's...ruthless."

Valena's grip on her husband's arm tightened. "If he's somehow subverted Taegar, or anyone, to help him... " Her voice trailed off as tears filled her eyes.

"We can't let him use Earth's *awen* for his nefarious plans. Cait, do you have a way to contact your father? To feel him out and see if you can get an inkling of what's going on?"

She stifled an involuntary shiver. The idea of having anything to do with her bio-father made her cringe. But there was a greater need here, and so far, she'd done little to help. All she'd done was provide a base and complicate everyone's lives with the twins' antics. "Yes. I have his cell phone number. I'll call him later, while the girls are down for their nap."

"Don't let him know you're aware Taegar's with him or you'll tip your hand."

Cait nodded. "I'll call him about the last month's salary I never got. It's as good an opening as any."

The crease in Valena's brow deepened. "Are you doing all right for money? I'd hate to think we're adding to your financial woes."

Cait laughed. "Not to worry. Turns out, I'm pretty good at saving. Plus, I get a stipend from my grandmother's estate. She cut her own son out of her will and gave his money to me. It's not much, but it covers my monthly expenses. And I'm so grateful for all you've done to help the twins. I'm just glad I can give back in this small way."

Valena got up and hugged Cait. "We're equally thankful for your presence in our lives. Yours and those precious girls."

Cait teared up again. Before she could reply, something crashed in the playroom and Willow ran in crying.

"Mama. Mama. Mama."

Cait picked up her daughter, hugging her as she nodded to her friends and headed to see what dire thing had happened now in her daughters' lives. "And so my day begins."

Later, after baths, playtime, then finally getting the girls down for naps, Cait settled into her office chair and picked up her cell. Taking a deep breath to calm herself, she dialed the number she never thought she'd call again, drumming her fingers on the desk in time with the sound of its ring in her ears.

"Never expected to see your name come up on my phone," the familiar voice said.

"Hello, father. I'm surprised you didn't delete me from your contacts."

"There was no need."

Oh, yes. This man did nothing without a purpose. Cait needed to be mindful of that.

"To what do I owe the pleasure of this call, Cait? I doubt you called just to pass the time."

Cait took a deep breath and plunged ahead. "I see you made today's paper."

"Ah, yes. That."

"It surprised me that you reached that point so quickly. Got a new plot up your sleeve?"

"Maybe it was killing all those costly ideas of yours that made the difference."

The power bill beneath Cait's free hand crumpled as she made a fist. She clamped onto the phone and gnashed her jaw. She'd had so many dreams and he'd quashed them all.

Except he hadn't. Not really. She'd found new dreams. And Tom. Too bad she couldn't tell him how leaving him behind had made her life better. He'd hate knowing he'd helped her, however inadvertently.

One deep breath, then another, and Cait got back to her original plan. The man loved to boast. He was careful about it, but if she worked this right, she could get a tidbit or something from him that might help them figure out what he was up to.

"Funny how the numbers showed those plans of mine were actually saving money. I haven't seen anything in the papers about a big contract or deal, but you've done well for yourself. Especially over the last few weeks. You employ some very smart people. Did one of them come up with some new ideas?"

"Not that it's any of your business, but the idea, as you call it, was all mine. And no one knows about it, and no one can touch it. Touch me. I'm invincible now."

Cait suspected Damian was right.

"You've got mods working for you?" Cait held her breath as she played her trump card.

Gordon was quiet for several moments. When he spoke, the steel was back in his voice. "Unless you have a reason for calling me, this conversation is over."

No denial of her comment pretty much confirmed it. Cait knew she'd get nothing more from him, but she had enough. "Yes, I have a reason. I'd like my late paycheck. It was supposed to be mailed to me and hasn't arrived."

"Running out of money so soon? What's the matter, your grandmother's estate didn't last as long as you'd hoped? Well, tough. You won't get a dime from me."

"I don't want *your* money. I want mine. I earned it. You owe it to me."

"So sue me," he said.

Cait could hear his maniacal laughter as the call went dead. She set her phone down with exaggerated care on the desk, pushing it away from her, the taint of evil a metallic taste on her tongue. She straightened the crumpled power bill, flattening it out on her desk with precise movements. One thing was certain. Somehow, Gordon Darcy was using the mods, either voluntarily or involuntarily, for his ill-gotten gains. This was not good. Not good at all.

"Did you learn anything?" Damian stood in the doorway, the entire troupe of druids behind him.

"Oh, yes." She shuddered. "Our worst fears have come to pass."

"Someone with talent is helping him?"

"I'm almost certain of it."

"We need to find Taeger and get her out of Darcy's clutches," Valena said. "She must be part of this and I hate that she's embroiled in whatever plan he's cooked up." She grabbed hold of Damian. "She's an innocent and he's taking advantage of her."

"Yes," Luther said, smacking fist into palm. "Valena's right. We need to rescue Taegar."

Something was happening to Luther. Something Cait didn't understand. His eyes were wild with anger and he looked ready to explode. Cait glanced at Wyeth, noting the deep furrow of his brow. He was concerned, too.

"Do we know where he is?" Wyeth asked.

Everyone turned to Cait. "I called his cell, so I have no idea. He could be anywhere. I know his secretary. I'll call her to see if he's here in L.A. or if she knows anything."

Damian glanced at the clock. "Valena and I need to leave for another interview. Why don't we all convene here for a late dinner and we'll figure out a plan."

"I don't like waiting," Luther mumbled, staring at his hands.

Wyeth clapped him on the back and Luther jumped up in surprise, arms raised, ready for a fight.

"Whoa, bud," Wyeth said, backing up a step. "Just trying to keep you in this world, not your own. What say you and I go find a gym and work off some stress?"

"Yeah," Luther said, still not quite letting go of the emotion. "That sounds good."

Valena watched him, concern written all over her face.

"Then we have a plan." Damian stood. "We'll see you all this evening."

Within half an hour, Damian and Valena left for their interview and Wyeth and Luther found a local gym for a much-needed workout. Gwen, tired, had gone upstairs for a nap. That left Cait at loose ends, rare for her these days. She grabbed the baby monitor, pulled on a coat, and went to sit in the backyard. So much had happened in the past couple of months it was hard to process it all. It felt so surreal. She had no idea how this would end, but she needed to find a way to hold on to hope. For her, for Fallon and Willow, for Tom, and for their circle, as well as everyone else's future. It seemed like they were all skating on the edge of a very sharp knife. A slice was inevitable, and how deep it cut would define everyone's future.

Her phone pinged.

I miss you already.

The text from Tom brought a smile to her face. Maybe there was still hope.

Cait went to the coat closet. It was time to make sure her go-bag was up to date.

Just in case.

<div style="text-align:center">~~~</div>

"How do you feel when you use this *awen*, as you call it?"

Valena smiled at the woman, the host of a cable news commentary program, then turned to the camera. "A sense of well-being fills me. It's like I'm one with Earth, who sustains us."

"That sounds pretty profound."

"It is, and hard to fully explain. It's like walking on air in a world bursting with happiness and health. There's also a clarity there. A message from Earth that if we use this gift wisely, we can prosper. We can find happiness."

"That's a message I can wrap my head around," the woman said. "But I don't understand how people touched by this *awen* have such different abilities."

Damian answered her. "We don't know for certain, but we suspect it's a simple enhancement of inherent strengths. Take Valena here." He touched his wife's arm. "She's always tended toward empathy and healing. She's versed in herbal and natural remedies. Now, her ability to heal is magnified."

"Like how? Can you show me?" The woman straightened her shoulders and even Damian saw the quick grimace of pain she covered up.

Damian and Valena had decided before doing any interviews that it wouldn't help if they became a freak show. So far, they'd managed to circumvent attempts to get them to demonstrate their magic.

"I'm sorry, but showcasing gifts is not what this is about," he said as gently as possible. "It's about giving back. To Earth and to the people who inhabit it. If we use our new abilities to help Earth return to the green, lush environment it is meant to be, to replenish our natural resources, help humankind see that a simpler life means longevity, then we'll all benefit. We'll all have food to eat, clean water to drink, comfortable places to sleep. And isn't that what we should be focused on? Protecting Earth and making it habitable for future generations?"

The woman cocked her head. "I'm not sure everyone, present or future, is deserving of this nirvana you speak of."

Damian frowned. The woman's tone of voice had grown dark. What was happening?

"For instance, those who are in jail. Would you want this new world of yours to benefit them?"

"The idea is that, if we can embrace this new

evolution, help Earth to flourish so we can feed and house everyone, it helps all of us."

"Does that mean you'd expect criminals to partake in this bounty?" she repeated. "Maybe even be released from prison? What about those who've raped? Killed?" Her face had flushed. Somehow, this had turned personal.

"Nothing happens quickly or without planning. And that's not Earth's message. We'll all perish— "

"But that's what you're saying, isn't it? You want us all to live together, work together. One big happy family."

"I don't have all the answers. And I realize finding them will take time. I only have a message. That, for your survival, for mine, for everyone's, we must help Earth regenerate. This affects every single one of us."

"Well, I for one, can't subscribe to this all-or-nothing ideology of yours. I'm sorry, but some people don't deserve what your 'Earth' is offering." The bitterness in her voice was palpable.

Valena reached over to touch the woman, but she recoiled.

"Our world has become one of extremes," the news pundit said. "There's no big happy family and never will be. There's good and there's evil. You have to pick a side."

"Don't you think we're on the side of good?" As soon as he said it, Damian realized he shouldn't have asked that question. He'd let her back him into the corner, but for anyone to consider what they were trying to accomplish as detrimental to society... Well, he just couldn't let that go. He waited, holding his breath, for her answer.

"I honestly don't know."

The interview ended on that note and Damian was inordinately worried that this would provoke a wave of revulsion from an already confused society. The news pundit stood and tried to walk past them. Damian moved in front of her and again, she recoiled.

"What happened to you?" Valena asked quietly.

The woman's lips became tight lines as she glared at them, so it surprised Damian when she answered. "I was robbed. Shot in the shoulder."

The same shoulder that still bothered her.

"I'm sorry," Damian said. "I wish there were something we could do to help."

"No one can help. That's what I'm telling you. As a society, we're past the tipping point. It doesn't matter what you or Earth does. Chaos is winning this war and all we can do is hunker down and try to protect ourselves."

He shook his head, saddened by this attitude that he'd encountered so often lately. "Actually, there is something we can do."

"What's that?"

"We can hope."

"What does that accomplish? Oh!" The woman froze as Valena placed a hand on her shoulder. "What are you doing? I feel warm."

"I cannot remove the memory from your mind and heart, but I can ease your pain. It's better already, isn't it?"

"It...is." Confusion filled her face, but she didn't pull away. She stood there, internalizing, as Valena rested a hand on her wound.

"I'm sorry you had to go through that," Valena murmured. "At least this will help a little bit." She pulled her hand away.

The news pundit straightened, moving her shoulder in all directions, testing it. "It's gone. All of it. The pain is just...gone."

"Your shoulder has been made whole," Valena said. "As if you were never injured. I'm sorry I cannot fix the pain in your heart."

Tears filled the woman's eyes. "You didn't have to do that. I was pretty rough on you out there." She waved at the stage behind them.

"Maybe now you understand. We want to heal, not hurt."

"I—I understand better. I wish I could take back some of what I said."

So did Damian, but he held his counsel. This was his wife's purview. She had more tact and diplomacy in her tiny finger than he had in his whole body.

"We prefer honest evaluations. You said what you felt at the time." Valena reached to shake the woman's hand. "Just keep being honest. That's all we ask."

"I will. And, thank you." She touched her shoulder. "This pain has reminded me of that night so often, and of my fear. I've relived it so many times. Maybe now, I can forget."

"Don't ever forget," Damian said. "Just because we strive for a renewed Earth doesn't mean we'll convince everyone or, sadly, that it will even change attitudes. And you're right. Both good and evil exist. Though nothing will happen quickly, we have to try to fix things. All we want from people is the truth. That's all we ask. How you really feel, what you truly perceive."

After saying their goodbyes, Damian and Valena walked out of the television station aware of a jointly made decision. There would be no more televised interviews. Ever. They were done with them. Too many wanted to tear them down or sensationalize them, and the viewers seemed to relish that.

Valena leaned on Damian's arm.

"I don't like how tired you get after healing someone."

"For every action, there must be a reaction. That's the universe's law, not mine. And it's gotten better. I don't tire as I used to."

"Good." He smiled down at the woman who held his heart. "Because if anything ever happened to you, I couldn't live with myself."

They rounded the corner to where they'd parked Cait's car and stopped short as they stared at the four slashed tires, the smashed windows, and the large-lettered *devil* spray-painted on the hood.

"Who would do something like this?" Valena said through the hand that covered her mouth. Her voice was weak and she was near tears. Damian helped her sit down on the curb, then stalked around the car while dialing 9-1-1 on the cell. The damage was extensive. They'd smashed doors, mirrors, taillights and headlights. *Satan's spawn, devil.* The car was covered in graffiti.

"We've caused Cait so much trouble," Valena said.

Damian nodded, unable to understand this act of violence. They were trying to help. Couldn't people understand that? Why would anyone think they wanted to harm others? What possible motive could they have? Rage built within him. Hatred for those who chose to hurt instead of help. Most mods talked of peace, but others wanted war.

He pounded the word *devil,* caving the hood.

"Hands up!"

Damian turned to see an officer, gun drawn. He immediately put his hands in the air, searching for Valena. A second officer urged her to back away.

"I'm not going anywhere," Valena said. "That's my husband."

To make matters worse, a couple bystanders had their phones out and appeared to be taping the whole thing.

His anger deflated when the realization hit him. He'd just given the world more fodder to fear them, to turn deaf ears to their message that Earth needed saving.

News Alert: As tensions mount, mods are pulling together, living in groups. They say for protection, but others worry. Is a global war in the offing? If so, it may well be the most destructive war ever fought.

CHAPTER TWENTY-FOUR

"I'm sorry, Cait. Hell, I need to apologize to all of you. To the world. I just made things so much worse." Sitting at the kitchen table, Damian put his head in his hands. How could he have let his temper get away from him again? A shortened video was all over the news. Him pounded the car through the officer handcuffing him. Thankfully, they didn't arrest him. Valena had helped them understand he wasn't the car vandal. Just the reactionary.

"You didn't make it any worse that it already was. And insurance will fix the car," Cait said.

"All our hard work and I just tossed it out the window in one pissed-off moment."

Wyeth squeezed his shoulder. "Not sure I wouldn't have done the same thing if I could have, but you're right. It didn't help."

"I've undone everything we've achieved so far and made things worse than ever. Perception is nine-tenths of positivity. I've set us back so far."

"You had a right to be angry," Luther said. "The

vandalism had no purpose at all. It was just malicious."

"Oh, it had a purpose," Wyeth said. "To scare us into shutting up."

"Don't they understand what we're trying to tell them?" Luther pounded his fist into his palm. "We're trying to help them."

"And we'll continue to do so," Gwen said soothingly. "Maybe we're going about this the wrong way."

All heads turned toward her. Damian, who had run out of ideas, was especially interested. He'd put them in this situation and couldn't for the life of him find a way out of it.

"I suggest that we stop...advertising. Stop trying to get the word out through the media and contacts in D.C. That we return to our roots."

"What do you mean?"

"Well, did you see the latest commentary from the woman who just interviewed you? She downplayed Damian's actions as a simple reaction to hatred. She told the audience you were good people and that Valena had healed her shoulder. That's a complete turnaround from the show she'd done just a few hours earlier."

They all nodded.

"So why don't we go back to basics? Help people, one at a time. Let the word spread organically."

"Sounds like a good idea to me," Damian said. "We certainly can't do any worse than I did today."

Quiet descended on the room as everyone mulled over this new option. Even the twins, playing in the middle of the room, grew quiet.

"I want to go home," Valena said finally. "I miss home."

"It won't be the same. Might not even be there any longer," Damian said.

"I don't care."

"We're forgetting one very important thing," a red-faced Luther said. "Taegar. We have to rescue her."

"I agree," Gwen said. "We can't leave her in Gordon Darcy's clutches."

"No," Cait said, shuddering. "We can't."

Wyeth frowned deeply. Damian knew he worried about the darkness surrounding Luther. So did Damian. "We don't even know where she is," he said.

"You've been able to tap into a prescience before," Valena said. "Do you think you could do it again? Focus on Taegar, find out where she is?"

Damian shrugged. "I'm willing to try."

Wyeth spoke up. "That should be all you do. Sorry, Damian, but given the incident over the car today, I think you need to keep a low profile. You and Valena head back to the Black Hills. If your prescience tells you where Taegar is, then Luther, Gwen, and I will go rescue her and bring her home. And we'll all spread goodwill and healing along the way."

Damian nodded. It was the best action plan they'd come up with. And he was tired of trying to cram the truth down people's throats. Gwen was right. They needed a more active and direct approach.

"So be it." Damian turned to Cait. "You've been quiet during this discussion."

"These weren't my choices to make."

Valena, sitting beside her, grasped both of her hands. "You are as much a part of our family as anyone here. You have *every* right to be part of the discussion. And you are welcome to come back home with Damian and me." She reached down and rustled Fallon's hair. "We've grown to love these girls. Come with us."

"I don't know. I'm just not sure what to do, or what

we'll find there. I need to think about what is best, and safest, for the twins."

The boom, the crash, and the flying glass all happened simultaneously as a large rock hit the floor, barely missing Willow.

"What the hell?"

Cait and Valena each grabbed a screaming child as Luther, Damian, and Wyeth sped toward the front door. Damian got there first and threw the door open. It crashed back against the wall making everything vibrate. He didn't care. Someone had thrown that rock. He was going to find out who.

Except no one was there. They searched the entire property and raced in both directions down the street. Nothing. Whoever did this had been fast on their feet.

Damn. Damian hit a tree trunk and the whole thing shook like it was about to fall over. It didn't, thank God. He looked around, praying no one had seen that. Or worse, taped it.

"Come on," Wyeth said. "Let's go back and check on everyone."

Back at the house, both twins were on Cait's lap. She was trying to console them, to no avail. Valena had her hands on Gwen's head while Gwen held a blanket to her face. She pulled the blanket back and they all went white as sheets, Wyeth especially. He rushed to his wife.

"I'm okay. Valena's already stopped the bleeding."

"But there's blood...everywhere." Wyeth's voice shook.

"Head wounds bleed a lot," Valena said, "but it's superficial. And it's almost closed now." Her voice soothed them all.

Wyeth stood and looked at the wound, tears misting his eyes as he nodded. He squatted down and, using the edge of the blanket, tenderly wiped at some of the blood.

"You're only making it worse," Gwen said with a shaky laugh.

"It gives me something to do."

Damian helped Valena to a seat so she could rest. The twins' screams finally reduced to snuffles.

Luther stood guard by the doorway, his gaze focused on the broken window.

The rock wasn't large but it had caused a lot of damage. Cait would need a new window. The rock still lay on the floor with a piece of paper tied around it. Damian picked it up and loosened the twine. He grimaced as he read it.

"What does it say?" Wyeth asked.

He turned the note for all to see.

Get out, freaks. Leave now or else.

The room grew quiet. Only an occasional snuffle from the girls broke the silence.

Cait spoke first, her voice as shaky as Wyeth's had been. "This has gotten scary. Home no longer feels like a safe place. I need some time to think."

"I think that's wise," Damian said. "I know we'd feel better if you came with me and Valena. We can't protect you when geography gets in the way."

"I'm not sure what I'm going to do yet. To be honest, you two have become almost a central catalyst in this thing. I know you want to protect me, but are the girls and I better off not being near you?" Cait reached for Valena's hand. "I'm sorry."

"We completely understand," Valena said though tears misted in her eyes.

"I miss Tom. I'd like to talk to him before deciding."

"And I need to shower," Gwen said.

"I'll help you. You might be weak from blood loss," Wyeth said, helping her stand.

"Actually, I feel great. Thank you, Valena."

Valena, who'd taken one of the twins and was playing patty-cake with her, smiled up at Gwen, then turned to her husband. "I'll help Cait put the girls to bed."

"I think they need a treat before bedtime tonight. Let's go to the kitchen and see if we can find something." Cait tickled Willow's side, gaining a giggle from the child.

"I guess that means we men get to board up the window."

"Thank you. There's some leftover plywood under a tarp on the side of the house," Cait said.

With that, everyone went in their own direction.

~~~

After treats for the girls and snuggle time before lights out, Valena went to rest and Cait headed for her own bedroom. Slumping onto the bed, she let the tears fall. Life had changed so drastically in such a short time. She wasn't sure she was strong enough to handle everything being thrown at her. And now this? What should she do? What was the best way to protect Fallon and Willow? That was what it boiled down to. Their safety was paramount. Staying with her new family, there'd be strength to protect them. Still, there was added danger there, too.

Outside of their group, no one seemed to know about Fallon's abilities yet. If Cait took the girls and went her own way, would she be anonymous enough to not be singled out or followed, or worse? She couldn't watch Fallon every minute of every day, and Fallon used her ability at will. It wouldn't take much for someone to notice. What would happen then?

She hugged herself, going over the possibilities, unable to make a decision.

She needed advice.

She needed Tom. She'd come to rely on him so much
~~~

in such a short time, it scared her. It also filled her with a certain amount of peace. She wasn't alone.

Cait reached for her phone, but before she could call up his number, it rang.

"How did you know I wanted to talk to you?" she asked Tom.

"I didn't. It's late. I'm driving, I'm tired, and I just wanted to hear your voice. You sound like something's wrong. What's happened?"

Cait told him everything, including the tentative plans the group had made.

"I don't know what to do, Tom. I need to keep the girls out of this mess. I need to keep them safe."

"Agreed." He took a deep breath. "I'm turning around."

"You can't drive another ten hours back here. You're already exhausted."

"I'll make it."

"But what about your work? They'll notice when you don't come back, won't they?"

"That's partly why I called. I heard from a friend of mine at the lab. They've taken everything, gutted my lab. My notes, research, samples, everything is gone."

"Oh, Tom, I'm so sorry." He sounded so defeated.

"It was a blow to my ego at first. All that work, just...gone. I should have copied it. Done something to hide it."

"You couldn't have known what would happen."

"That's just it. I should have. Things were getting pretty strange around there. I was always looking over my shoulder."

"I-I hate to ask, but I need to know. Will they have information on Fallon?"

"I never put her name, geographic information, age, in

the database. She's safe, at least from the government's prying eyes.

No words came to Cait. She knew what it was like to have your hard work disappear. It hurt. "I'm sorry, Tom. I know you put long hours into all that research."

"Yeah. I'm sorry, too. Listen, let Damian know what's happened, all right? I'm worried. He's the face of this whole thing. He and Valena might be next."

"I'll tell him as soon as we're done."

"Wait for me, Cait. I'm coming home."

"Oh, Tom, thank you. I miss you. And I need you. But, do me a favor. Get a hotel room and some sleep. No one will leave until you arrive, and I need you here in once piece."

He sighed. "All right. Sleep, then back to you. Hopefully by dark tomorrow night."

"I'll be waiting. I love you, Tom."

"I love you, too. Tell the girls I'll see them soon."

After their goodbyes, Cait set the phone down and a huge piece of her worry and stress fell away. She went to check on the window and tell Damian about Tom's call. After that, she planned to climb into bed and forget about everything for a while. Or try, at least.

News Alert: Well-known actor Gus Grandon has revealed that he's one of the mods.

CHAPTER TWENTY-FIVE

"Yes, I've been blessed with abilities I didn't have before Earth released its magic to help us." Gus sat back in the chair. He'd done so many television interviews, he knew how to act. But this time, his gut churned. He could help raise awareness of Earth's need for renewal, so he'd chosen to announce. He prayed it wouldn't kill his career. He wasn't ready to retire. But he needed to repay this gift somehow, and help Damian, Valena, and the rest of the circle with damage control and getting the word out. He'd chosen to interview with the same news pundit Valena had healed in the hopes she would accept his limits regarding the information he would make public.

"What abilities do you have?"

He gave her his best smile. "I'm sorry. That's not something I'm going to discuss."

She frowned, so the grin that had gotten him so many roles wasn't working as well as he'd hoped.

"What are you here for if you're not going to answer a simple question like that?"

He kept the smile on his face. "I'm here because, even

though I work to separate my private life from my public life, I've always tried to be transparent with my fans, to let them know what's going on with me as much as I'm able. But my private life must remain that way. I hope you can understand that."

She rubbed her shoulder. He'd asked her about it before the show, knowing Valena had healed her. The pain was gone, so this was a purely psychological response.

"Is your shoulder all right?"

She pulled her hand away and back to her lap. "Yes, thank you." She paused, then got the interview back on track. "I can understand what you say about your private life. However, I do believe the world has a right to know."

"I will tell you this. I'm the same person today as I was before these light streams appeared. I have the same thoughts, the same emotions, the same frustrations." He chuckled and looked directly at the camera. "Don't be shaking your heads. I have frustrations just like anyone else. But now, there is something extra within me. It's hard to describe, but I'd call it peace of mind. I feel a oneness with myself that I've never known before. Like I am whole. Because of that, I'd like to help."

"Help who?" The news pundit's smile was soft and angelic and her voice was equally so.

Gus turned back to her. "Help everyone. I want to clear up misconceptions about the *awen*. And to extend an invitation to everyone who sees this program to embrace the recent changes as well as the changes we must still make to tip Earth's healing quotient to the positive side. This is Earth's message. That there is hope for a better life, a better world, but there is also work to be done."

"Earth's message? Does, umm, Earth speak to you?" Her sharp edge returned. She was back in tough-questioner mode.

Gus chuckled. "Certainly not. It's more...my interpretation of what I feel because of the *awen*. That we have a chance to enact change and doing so will make life better for all."

God, he prayed he hadn't begun to sweat. He'd almost gone down the rabbit hole with that last statement. Thankfully, they were about out of time. The news pundit thanked him formally on air, then cordially afterward. In only a few minutes, Gus was in the back of the limo headed for home, his sanctuary.

His cell rang.

"You did good," Damian said.

"I almost botched it with that 'talking to Earth' thing."

"You did fine. Much better than I did."

"Well, I'm glad that's over. Now to see how it all falls out."

"I hope it doesn't hurt your career."

"Me, too. It was bound to come out eventually. At least by being proactive, I won't have the fallout from keeping secrets."

"Except for what your talent is."

"They don't need to know."

"The public has a funny way of figuring out what they want to know, and reaching conclusions completely different from what we'd like."

"They most certainly do," Gus said. Only time would tell now. "When are you leaving for the Black Hills?"

"Valena and I are going home tomorrow. We're taking a long, circuitous route so we can offer some hands-on proof that what's happening is a good thing. And I'll be keeping my mouth shut. Completely."

Gus chuckled. "Don't be too hard on yourself. This whole public persona thing isn't easy, even for me, and I've been at it for years."

"Still, we can't afford the kind of mistakes I've been making. I'm happy to be sidelined. And I thank you for doing what you can. Be safe."

Damian told him about the rock through Cait's window.

"You be safe, too."

Gus punched the button to end the call and sat back, wondering if anything he'd said in the interview had put his life in jeopardy. Now, he needed to prioritize safety. He sighed, letting that feeling of peace settle over him again. Even if things were getting dangerous, he was secure in the knowledge that, by being an ambassador for Earth, he was playing the most important role of his life.

~~~

After his conversation with Gus, Damian sat and stared out Cait's living room window, consumed with guilt. He'd tried so hard to convince people to change. No. That wasn't right. He'd tried to force them to change. He shook his head. He ought to know better.

The southern California sun shone brightly outside. Gwen's touch was in evidence wherever he looked. A profusion of greenery and color, unusual for this arid clime. Though it wasn't so dry any longer. Rain had been falling with almost regular precision every other night. Spreading itself around. Turning a desert into a tropical oasis. Which meant that another mod lived somewhere nearby. Gwen helped things grow, and whoever this was brought the water they needed for sustenance. The perfect combination and exactly how things should work.

All he'd done so far was to destroy any goodwill these changes had brought. Damian was lost. He didn't know what to do or how to help. He stared at his hands, knowing he needed guidance and wondering if he could commune with Earth like he had before. Damian hadn't tried since
~~~

they'd left the Black Hills. It was time.

He slipped outside and settled on the ground in the center of the rock circle Cait had built. With a silent promise to fix what he changed, he moved enough rocks so he could lay both hands on the soil beneath. Damian took a minute to settle his mind and formulate what he needed from his Earth-mentor: a direction and some hope for their future.

He cupped his hands over his face, then stretched for the sky, moving from there slowly down to reverently place his hands on the dirt.

Please, Earth. Guide me.

Damian closed his eyes, tuning into the smooth dirt, using his mind's eye to see through it, beneath it. Finally, a breath of whispered words reached him.

Do good.

"I've been trying, but all I seem to do is make things worse." *Tears streamed down Damian's face.*

Let go of anger.

"How? I haven't been able to change people's minds. They don't see."

Wellness surrounded him, a soft blanket of love. From Earth?

You and your line are the hope of our future, Damian Royan. Do good. Be. The rest will unfold as it should.

Easier said than done. Damian could do no less than try, though. He nodded. "I will do good. I will show."

Gwen was right. It was time to get back to basics. To go home.

"Thank you."

Damian lifted his hands, or tried to. Something held him fast to the soil. He couldn't get away. Another vision hit him like a freight train. *Fear. Darkness. Fury. All roared through him. He couldn't open his eyes. He felt drugged, awash in misery yet unable to help himself.*

"Help me."

"Earth?"

"No. Me. I'm lost."

"Who?"

"I can't remember who I am."

"Can you open your eyes? Let me see around you."

"It's so hard. I can't... I'll try."

A world came into focus as if through lidded eyes opening.

"Turn your head. Look around." Damian watched, trying to determine where this person was and in what circumstance. A dark room with medical equipment.

"Who are you?" he asked again.

"I don't know. Why won't you help me?"

"I can't help you unless I know where you are."

A door opened. Damian heard it like he was there in the room. The eyes closed, sinking him back into darkness, though he heard someone walk to the bedside.

"Open your eyes. I must see."

"So hard."

Slowly, the lids lifted again. Damian stared, afraid to blink. He knew he would get only one opportunity to determine who this was.

His view enlarged, followed trouser-clad legs standing beside the bed to a white shirt. A hand, holding a syringe. And finally, a familiar face. Gordon Darcy.

"No one will help me."

The syringe plunged its liquid into the I.V. tube. The eyes slid shut. Taegar's eyes. He had to be seeing from her point of view. What had Gordon done to her?

"Be strong, Taegar," Damian said as the vision faded. "We'll come for you."

His consciousness back in Cait's yard, Damian covered his face with his hands, horrified at what he'd seen. Taegar, a virtual slave to Darcy's wishes. He couldn't leave her at the man's mercy. Damian shook his head, trying to find clarity. He now knew where Taegar was. And that she was in dire straits. He could only hope she'd heard him.

He replaced the rocks and stood, brushing his hands off and heading into the house to gather everyone.

They had some difficult choices to make.

News Alert: Numerous reports speak of heavy activity at the mysterious government installation known as Area 51. Large trucks enter in the dead of night. An anonymous source says people are being held in rooms with locked doors, like cells. That the government is experimenting on mods. Quietly. Privately. Why?

CHAPTER TWENTY-SIX

"You're certain it was Taegar?" Wyeth asked.

Damian grimaced. "I was looking through her eyes. She was prone, seemingly unable to move. Do I know for certain it was her? No. But I saw Darcy clearly. Who else can the person from my vision be?"

"We have to go help her," Luther said. "We can't leave her with that monster."

At his ominous tone, Wyeth glanced at Damian. Luther's darkness was becoming more evident as the weeks passed. Damian knew the feeling. Futility. He had Valena's help, and Earth's, in his fight against despair. Luther seemed mired in negativity.

"We do, though I'm not sure how to help her," Damian said slowly.

"He'll never stop," Cait said. "I know the man as well as anyone. Even when he gets everything he wants, he will never stop."

Damian looked around the group. "This could be dangerous. It has to be a unanimous decision."

One by one, each of them agreed, Damian last. He might despair as to their chances, but they couldn't leave Taegar there.

"All right then. Any thoughts on how to accomplish this?"

Wyeth spoke up. "In your vision, Earth seemed to want you to go back to the Black Hills."

Damian nodded. "That's my interpretation."

"Mine as well," Wyeth said.

"So I think you and Valena have a different road to take. The two of you need to go home, doing what you can along the way."

"That only leaves you three to go after Taegar," Damian said.

"We're enough," Luther growled.

"Gwen should go with you, Damian."

Gwen reached for her husband's hand. "I'm going with you."

"I don't want you near that danger."

"Yet each time we're apart, nothing goes right." She cupped his cheek. "We're better together, husband."

Wyeth closed his eyes, leaning into her touch for a long moment before he agreed.

"It's settled then," Damian said. "If we can dig up some information about where Taegar's being held, you can leave tomorrow morning. Valena and I will stay for a day or two to help around here."

Cait smiled. "I'll be okay if you want to leave tomorrow, too. Tom should be here sometime after midnight."

"Gives us a little more time with those two angels of yours, Cait." Valena tapped her heart twice with her hand.

"That's an excuse."

"And one we will abide by. We're not leaving until we know there's a plan to keep you and the girls safe. Not after that rock incident."

"I'll admit, it makes me nervous."

"Then it's settled. Bhren and Roulf should be checking in soon. I'll get an update on how things are back home and let them know our plans."

"I'm going to pack." Luther stomped out of the room.

Valena, Cait, and Gwen went to get the twins from the playroom and start dinner, leaving Wyeth and Damian alone with their thoughts.

"I'm more worried than ever about Luther," Wyeth said.

"Me, too." Damian grasped Wyeth's shoulders. "You take care of yourself. All of you."

"That's the plan."

"And," Damian said, wondering if he should even voice this, "if things go south, worry about you and Gwen. Luther can take care of himself."

Wyeth glanced at the stairs Luther had just climbed. "I understand."

~~~

Before the twins woke the next morning, everyone gathered in the kitchen for an early breakfast. No one spoke. Only chewing could be heard, and they were finished too soon.

"Where's Tom?" Gwen asked as they loaded the dishwasher. "I thought he was supposed to be here by now."

"He should have been. His car broke down." Cait glanced out the window at the fall sunshine. "I haven't heard from him since just after he called for a tow truck. I hope he's all right."
~~~

"I'm sure he'd call you if there were any issues," Valena said.

"Yes," Cait said, although Valena's assurances didn't allay her worry.

Wyeth stood in the kitchen doorway. "We're ready."

Gwen nodded and followed him to the door. Cait dragged along behind them, finding it harder than she thought to say goodbye to her friends. They were family, and Gwen, Wyeth, and Luther were headed into who knew what kind of danger. Tears filled her eyes. She didn't know when, or if, they'd ever see each other again.

No. Cait swiped at her eyes. Hope was their strongest weapon and she needed to rein in her pessimism and give them a happy send-off. She smiled and joined the group on the front porch.

Damian handed Wyeth a wad of money. Wyeth thanked him and tucked it into his pack, the look between them saying more than words. Damian hugged Wyeth, then Luther, who stood stiff as a board.

"Luther... "

"What?"

"Be kind to yourself, all right?" Damian said. "And stay safe. We need you to come home to us. You're part of this family."

"Yeah, yeah. I get it. Come on, guys," he said, picking up his pack. "Let's get going."

Valena and Cait each held a twin, who'd woken up just before the leave-taking. Gwen hugged them both.

"Ugh. Your crying is going to set me off," Valena said.

Gwen smiled through her tears. "I'm going to miss you all so much. These little girls, too."

Too soon, they were in the truck with the trailer behind it. Cait, after some serious prodding of Gordon's assistant over the phone, had confirmed that Darcy most likely held Taegar at his property in Big Sur. That was where the threesome would start.

Damian came around behind Valena and Cait and hugged them both as the twins waved bye-bye. With one last wave from Gwen and Wyeth, the three got in the truck, turned a corner, and were gone. The black van, always watchful, stayed put. Apparently, its occupants didn't care about Wyeth, Gwen, and Luther. Cait glanced at the van, worried. She'd have to trust Damian's instincts that it wasn't there for her or the girls. For now.

"It's just us now," Valena said.

"I'm going to miss them so much," Cait said.

"Your house will be less crowded," added Damian.

"I've grown used to the chaos," Cait said with a laugh.

They turned to head back inside, but a honk stopped them. An SUV screeched up to the curb and a dark-haired man jumped out.

"Tom!"

Cait handed Fallon to Damian and launched herself off the porch into Tom's arms.

He broke the kiss too soon and glanced around, turning her toward the house. "Let's get inside."

What now? Cait didn't think she could take any more bad news.

Once inside, Tom took precious moments to hug both the girls and give Cait another kiss. Then he turned to Damian and Valena. "Are the others here?"

"They left moments before you arrived."

Cait could hear the worry in Damian's voice. She felt it, too. They went to the darkened front room, where Tom stared at the boarded-up window.

"Rock," Damian said.

"Cait told me." Tom hugged her. "I should have been here."

"We were well-protected."

Once they got the girls settled with toys in the middle of the floor, everyone sat, Tom next to Cait on the couch. He pulled her hand into his.

"Things are escalating," he said.

"I told them about your lab, your work."

"It's all gone. Spirited away, along with... Well, this is all second-hand, but my friend said people were being wheeled out of that secured section of the lab on stretchers and put into large trucks. People, equipment, boxes and boxes." He hung his head. "My work was somewhere in all that mess."

Cait squeezed his hand.

"Are they experimenting on people with gifts?" Valena said, wringing her hands.

Damian put his arm around her. "Who told you all this?" he asked Tom.

"I'd rather not say. The person I talked to is still there. I told him to leave, but he said he's the only one left who can get the word out. I tried to call him again, just before I got here. It went to voicemail. I hope he's all right."

"This is not good," Cait whispered.

"No, not at all."

Valena grabbed Damian's knee. "What about Gwen, Wyeth, and Luther?"

"We'll tell them tonight when they call. I told them not to turn their phone on except once a day to check in. I...had a feeling."

"Good idea," Tom said. "I won't be going back." Tom pulled the oak-tree ring from his pocket and slipped it on his finger. "They know now I'm a sympathizer, so I can't take the chance. Besides, there's nothing left to go back to." He touched Cait's cheek. "I went home and packed a bag. I'm here to stay."

Cait wilted into Tom's side, flooded with relief.

"Good," Damian said.

Valena stood. "I'm going to get us all some coffee."

"I could use some."

"What happened to your car?" Cait asked.

"It was toast. The guy who towed it had the SUV you saw sitting there for sale. Said he'd rebuilt the engine. I took it for a test drive, liked how it ran, and transferred money into his account."

"He probably charged you way too much," Cait said.

Tom shrugged. "It got me here. That's the important part. And it has a system for the girls to watch videos."

Valena set a tray down with coffee and creamer. Tom took a cup and sniffed. "This is what I needed." He sipped, sighing with pleasure and making Cait smile.

"We have some decisions to make." Tom looked at Damian and Valena. "You do, too." He rubbed his neck. "You two are the face of this whole thing. If the government is trying to control these light streams and powers, I think they'll come for you next."

"Which means we can't be here. We're putting Cait and the girls in danger," Damian said.

"They're about as close to danger as they can get right now. I kept any reference to Fallon out of my research. Logged a fake name, age, everything. But mods are being found out and sooner or later, someone's going to see Fallon do something."

Hell, no. Cait stood up. "No one. Absolutely no one, will get to my kids. They'll have to go through me," Cait said.

"And me," Tom added, giving her a gentle tug until she sat back down.

"And us," Valena said.

"I'm going to be honest here," Tom continued.

"Recent news is making it harder to be respected as a mod."

"You mean like my meltdown in that parking lot."

"Not just that. Gus going public without giving specifics, along with a slew of other events and interviews, has given the government a nervous twitch. And that's not good when their finger is on the button that could make everything go boom. Add in the fact that the public is showing more fear than acceptance and I think we've got a worldwide panic leveling up."

Damian put his head in his hands. "Neither of those are escalations we need."

Valena wrapped her arm around Damian's shoulders. "You can't single-handedly change the world's view, husband."

"I made the world's view of us worse."

"This isn't the time for guilt," Cait said. "There seems to be little we can do to stop this growing sense of distrust and suspicion except maintain awareness and help in little ways, as you mentioned last night, Damian."

He raised his head. "You're right." Turning to Tom, he told him of his and Valena's plan to head back to South Dakota tomorrow, and where the others had gone and why.

"I think those are both good plans. Try to keep a low profile, though. They'll be looking for you two, especially."

"What about you, Cait?" Damian asked. "You and the twins might not be safe here any longer."

"I've had go-bags packed for days. Figured this was coming." She took a deep breath and looked at Tom. "We're leaving. As soon as possible."

"I'm with you," Tom said, hugging Cait.

"Where will you go?" Valena said.

"I know a place, but... Do you want to know?"

Valena teared up. "It's probably better that we don't."

"All right then," Damian said. "I've been giving this some thought, about how to get out of here. Since we're being watched, I think we need to leave at night and do it in a way that allows you two and the girls to sneak off unnoticed. Valena and I were planning to leave tomorrow morning. Heading out a few hours earlier isn't a big deal, especially since there's a 10 p.m. bus heading north. There's a lot of room in that SUV. What if we load everyone up tonight and you drop Valena and me at the bus station? They'll follow us if they think you're just dropping us off, especially if you head back the way you came."

"Better yet, we'll stand in front of the house making a fuss about you leaving," Tom said, "then I'll take you to the bus station. Hopefully, the men in that car will follow. After I drop you off, I'll circle back and come through the alley so we can load car seats and supplies. Then we'll head out."

"I don't like it. That makes you targets," Cait said.

"Better us than you," Valena said.

Damian smiled. "My enhanced abilities will help keep us safe."

Valena shook her head. "You can't stop bullets, husband."

"I feel confident I can take care of the two of us," Damian said.

Cait's heart hurt. She didn't like Valena and Damian putting themselves in harm's way, though there really was no other choice. "Let's load the car seats now. One less thing to do after dark."

"Great idea. But I just got here. It'll look suspicious if I move the car so soon."

Cait stood. "You're right. How about lunch then? And a nap. You look dead on your feet."

"Maybe skip the lunch for now," Tom said, standing. "I really could use some sleep."

"Valena?" Cait said.

"I'll watch the girls."

"Thank you." Cait hugged her friend, then led Tom up the stairs and into her bedroom. He slipped off his jeans and shirt and crawled under the covers, sighing. "This feels good."

Cait kissed him. "Take a long nap. You've more than earned it."

Tom nodded, reaching up to twirl a lock of her hair around his finger. "It was worth it. There's nowhere else I want to be, except with you."

Her heart stuttered with happiness. "Sleep, love. We've got a world of time ahead of us."

His hand went limp and he closed his eyes, already so far into sleep Cait wasn't sure he'd even heard her. She ran her fingers through his hair and kissed his forehead, then eased out of the room to let him sleep.

Tom was here, and whatever the future held, they'd see it through together. For the first time in a while, hope filled her.

~~~

Cait set the eggplant parmesan on the table. Supper was a quiet affair. No one wanted to vocalize the uncertainties of their plans. And no one wanted to leave.

Valena, in particular, was teary and sad. Fallon sat on her lap, eating off her plate. Valena hugged her tight. "I'm going to miss these girls. And you, Cait."

And we might never see each other again.

Cait forced her own tears to stay put.

"We won't be taking our cell phones," Tom said. "Too easy to trace."

Damian nodded. "You've got the login for the online contact."

"Yes," Cait said, but if we don't check in, assume we're
~~~

all right. We plan to go off-grid."

Damian reached for Valena's hand, then for Tom's. One by one, they interlocked, becoming, as before, one circle, one mind. Damian said a prayer of unity and health for all of them.

Too soon, dinner was over and they stood on the front porch. Cait and Valena each held one of the girls and everyone hugged.

"I'm going to miss you, my friend," Cait said to Valena, loud enough that any hearing device would catch it.

"It's only for a week," Valena replied with a shaky laugh, following the script they'd discussed earlier. "We'll be back to help you with all those diapers before you know it."

"Good," Cait said, trying to laugh herself. "They certainly go through a lot of them."

"Come on, you two," Damian said. "It's time to go."

"I'll be back in about an hour, honey," Tom said, also loudly. "I'll stop and pick up diapers."

"Sounds good, thanks."

And that was that. Cait, holding the hands of both girls who waved at the departing car, felt her whole life change yet again. She went inside the house, closed and locked the door, and peeked carefully through a curtain. The black van was gone.

Godspeed, Damian and Valena. Cait sent a prayer skyward for their safety.

Letting the girls run circles around her to blow off some steam, Cait filled her two coolers and carried them out to the back porch, then set her purse, laptop, and car bag with videos and snacks by the back door. Tom wanted to get underway quickly, so she needed to be ready.

He was back sooner than she expected. She saw the car pull up to the back gate even though the headlights weren't on. They settled the girls into their car seats, with blankies and toys and water, then Tom loaded the coolers. Cait shoved sleeping bags and pillows on the floor beneath the girls, and blankets between their car seats. Where they were going, they'd need these things to keep them warm.

Cait went back in the house, fingering the cell phones on the counter, but leaving them. She'd left the dishes undone, figuring anyone looking through the window wouldn't think she'd gone far. Using the same logic, the lights in the kitchen and hall were on. Then, as an afterthought, she turned on the TV. With nothing left to do, she took a final look around the house she'd spent so many hours turning into a home. With a long sigh, she squared her shoulders and locked the door.

"You okay?" Tom asked as she buckled herself in.

"It's just a house," she said, reaching for his hand. "Everything important to me is right here in this car."

"That's my girl." He leaned over for a kiss. In moments, they were pulling down the alley, lights out. Cait resisted the urge to look back.

"Which way?" Tom said.

She chuckled. She'd never told him where they were going.

"North, then east."

"The freeway it is, then."

"The road to our future."

News Alert: Whatever benefit the world has seen from the advent of the light streams seems to be disappearing under the onslaught of a redoubled culling of natural resources. Conservationists are protesting, corporations claim responsibilities to their shareholders, and no one will compromise.

CHAPTER TWENTY-SEVEN

Danger.

Her mind knew the word, sensed the need for action, but her body wouldn't move, wouldn't give her the assistance she needed.

He comes.

The bad man who made everything go away. She'd been happy once. Hadn't she? She'd made flower headpieces, kneaded bread. Now she could only lay there and try to remember. Except even that took too much effort.

Do something.

The door creaked open. She moved her hand, felt the tubing beneath it. She grabbed it like a lifeline, pulling it beneath her blanket, though she didn't know why.

Footsteps. The bad man who took your memories.

Opening her eyes, she saw him. She must know him, but she couldn't remember. He never looked at her. He pulled something out of a box. A needle. A syringe filled with liquid. How long had she been there? Days? Weeks? Months?

She clutched the tube as he slid the needle in, bending, twisting, letting instinct guide her. Keeping the bad medicine from eroding her ability to think.

He left without saying a word. She didn't know how long he'd be gone. Why couldn't she think? Clutching the tube she saw it filling up with fluid above but nothing below. She didn't know what to do next.

Don't let the medicine inside you.

Over and over, she said the words. Her hand shook with the effort it took to keep her grip on the clear, thin line. It would be so easy to just let go. To let the liquid take her back to nothingness.

Do not let go.

She held on. Barely. For how long, she didn't know. Hours, maybe. Then reason infiltrated her fuzzy mind, slowly, painfully pushing the confusion aside. She wiggled the fingers on her other hand, lifted it, looked at it. It was pasty and thin. So thin. She glanced down at her sheet-draped body. There was almost nothing left of her. Muscle, sinew, everything that helped her move had been eaten away by bed-bound inactivity.

Another notch of clarity reminded her about the medicine. She reached over and yanked the tube out of her arm. Another tube, this one down her nose, got pulled next. She tried to sit up, but couldn't.

How long had she been there?

A long time.

Escape. She needed to escape. But how could she when she couldn't even sit up. She'd had friends. Where were they? They should help her. Wait. She had powers. The beautiful light had given her the gift to make things grow. She liked making things grow. Or had, until the bad man forced her to help him.

What else had the white light given her? Power. Strength? She could use that now.

Concentrating on anything was hard. So hard. But she focused, tried to find that power within her. Slowly, she levitated off the bed, so surprised she wobbled in the air. Slowly, she stood, though her feet did not touch the ground. She floated to the far wall. There were no windows.

Where was she?

She stared at the bed. A hospital bed. That's what she'd been in. A clipboard hung on the end. She thought about it and it floated to her. Pages flipped as if touched by an invisible hand, then horror filled her anew as she read how long she'd been there. So much lost time.

For weeks, she'd been held captive by the bad man, medicated until she couldn't move, couldn't think. The room looked sterile, bereft of any furnishings except for a table, a chair, and a mirror.

She floated to the mirror, appalled at what she saw. Her once-beautiful, blonde hair was stringy and brown, her face sunken, her eyes hollowed.

He'd done this to her. The bad man. He'd taken her beauty.

But who was he? She still couldn't remember. Could her magic rip the veil of confusion away completely?

She tried. Concentrated. Slowly, as if pulling off a Band-Aid, the past few weeks came back to her. With one final push of magic, all her memories flooded back.

Now, she remembered who'd drugged her. Gordon Darcy, and for the sole purpose of making himself the richest and most powerful man in the world.

She remembered her so-called friends who hadn't

come to her rescue.

She remembered who she was.

I am Taegar.

The room dimmed and Taegar found herself in a dark void of nothingness.

I am Taegar. Where am I?

The vision grew slowly from a pinhole until it surrounded her, embedding her in...camp. The camp where she'd lived. She saw herself weaving flowers. Then the light came. Taegar smiled at the wonder and joy of that moment. She reached out to herself, watching as she touched trees, caused growth.

She'd heard about vision planes, about people seeing events in their lives. Like the rune ehwaz, *this was a place of transition, of passage.*

The scene around her morphed, showing her laying on this bed, seeing someone. Not the bad man. Someone else... Damian Royan. And her friends.

Taegar smiled.

"You're certain it was Taegar?" Wyeth asked.

Damian grimaced. "I was looking through her eyes."

"We have to go help her," Luther said. "We can't leave her with that monster."

"I'm not sure we can," Damian said slowly. "She may be too far gone."

The smile disappeared from Taegar's face as his image faded. He didn't come. Damian had given up on her, decided she was too far gone to be saved. He didn't even try.

Anger filled her, such a dark, heady anger that she overflowed with energy, with strength. She lifted her arms and bolts of lightning leaped from her hands, swallowed by the darkness of the void. That was a handy talent to have. Staring at her hands, she envisioned a fireball like the ones she'd seen in fantasy movies. A round ball of golden flame filled her palm, yet didn't burn her. She threw it, watched it disappear.

The vision faded and Taegar was back in the windowless cell. What she'd heard, felt, and done stayed with her. Pointing her hand at the bed, she imagined a lightning bolt. One jagged shot incinerated her prison in a puff of smoke and a burst of flame.

Now, Taegar knew. She had powers beyond her imagining. She floated to the door and, with a hand out, threw it open, breaking the bolts that held it.

Yes, she had great power. And she knew exactly what to do with it. The bad man would die. And then she would find her so-called friends. Show one Damian Royan just how much of a lost cause she was.

The world would know her power. Soon. Very soon.

~~~

Gordon sat at his desk. The numbers that scrolled across his screen pleased him. His plan had matched his projections. Surpassed them, actually. As it should be. Buying up mines and stock had given him a corner on the precious-gem market. Then, he'd tripled—and in some cases quadrupled—the size of the gemstones. Holding back on sales had driven up the price. Now, as he slowly cashed in his stockpile, he'd rocketed to the top of the "richest people in the world" list. He'd gained endless power and wealth, all because of his brilliant plan and the magic touch of the wraith in the basement.

His lip curled back. She looked nothing like the innocent he'd seduced. The feeding tube kept her alive so her hands could fill his coffers, but weeks of lying in bed had taken its toll on her body. Once lithe and fair, she was now rail-thin and sallow. It was hard even to tell she was female. Not that he cared. He only needed the power within.

Glancing at his watch, he stood and unlocked the cupboard, pulling out a syringe and a vial of the medicine
~~~

that kept her compliant. Comatose. His to make do whatever he wanted. As he headed downstairs, he whistled his pleasure at how well things were going.

Gordon strode around the corner toward what he liked to call his dungeon and stopped short. The door to Taegar's room lay in pieces on the floor.

"What the— "

"Come in, my love," a croaky voice said from within the room.

Shit. Had the medicine worn off? If so— Fear had never paralyzed Gordon Darcy. Instead, he used it as a catalyst. This time was no different. He raced back down the hallway, away from—

"Oh, no," the voice, stronger now, wafted down the hall. "There will be no leaving. We must talk, you and I."

Against his will, his body frozen, Gordon floated back down the hall and into the room. And saw her.

No longer in bed, no longer comatose, she stood. No. He looked at her feet. More like floated, like he did. He could barely see her face. She'd taken a dark blanket from her bed and fashioned it into a hooded cloak. How, he had no idea.

"Surprised, Gordon?"

Her voice stung with deadly anger. It permeated him like a thousand needles as the force that had held him disappeared. He stood stock-still. How had she woken up? He'd monitored her so carefully and dosed her himself so there'd be no excuse. No waking up. Yet, here she was. He glanced down at her arm. No tube. Somehow, she'd pulled the tube.

The syringe and vial in his hand lifted, moved through the air to her. He saw her glare at the medicine. Suddenly, golden light emanated from her eyes, shattering both items, disintegrating them. Nothing floated to the floor except a bit of ash.

Gordon's heart froze. Not only was Taegar awake and alert, she'd tapped into powers he'd had no idea she possessed.

"What, no words for the girl you turned into your slave?"

The ominous strength in her voice almost brought Gordon to his knees. He needed to think. He could talk his way out of this. He was certain of it. Surely, she was still moldable. And he only needed to get near her to subdue her, thanks to his backup plan—the Taser in his pocket.

"We've had some good times together, darling," he said, infusing his voice with happiness. "We're a match, meant to be together."

Her eyes, somehow turned from summer blue to golden, flashed. "Is that the reason you kept me doped up all this time?"

He was barely able to suppress his shrug. "It was to keep you close until I could convince you to stay. You weren't listening to me. You wanted to leave and I need you here. With me. We're good together."

Taegar laughed, a deep, screeching sound. "Good together? Good for making you richer, you mean."

A new, debilitating tendril of fear threaded through him.

"Yes, Gordon. I know you've been using my power to make your little stones grow. You've been using me to expand your empire."

"Our empire," he said, gauging her, timing his move. "All for us, darling. All for us. I came here to remove the I.V. and show you the empire we've created. You and I. Together." He took a step toward her. Then another. A couple more and he'd be close enough.

The nearer he got, the more he could see her bobbing

up and down as if she couldn't quite control the power that kept her upright. Maybe she was weakening. Maybe the power was finite. He'd take whatever opening he could get.

"You're tired, Taegar. I can see it in your eyes, in your stooped shoulders. You need to rest and regain your strength." He took two more steps. One more and he would reach into his pocket. "Let me help you back to bed."

"Stop," she said, her voice growing louder, bouncing off the walls. "You will not come near me ever again."

Maybe he was close enough already. He reached into his pocket, only to have his hand rendered immobile before he got there. The Taser inside lifted of its own volition, floating between them, doing lazy circles in the air.

"I'm neither tired nor stupid, Gordon. Because of you, I've learned to suspect everything, even the innocent movement of a hand. Now, what is this thing you were reaching for?" It moved closer to her, swaying this way and that as she checked it out.

Gordon swallowed, struggling to think of another way to subdue Taegar. He could rush her, take her out that way. Yes, that was the only option he had left.

The Taser lashed out, its prongs digging into his shoulder, sending electrical shock waves through his body. Gordon froze, then jerked in reaction to the pain. He fell to the floor, twitching like a fish starved for water.

For the first time in his life, fear consumed him. He'd lost control.

"How does that feel, *darling*?" Taegar floated over to him.

All he had to do was reach out, grab her feet, and pull her down. He could best her in a physical contest, even with pain arcing through him. He tried, but nothing happened. His hand wouldn't move. Nothing would.

Suddenly, the air around him thickened. He was lifted and thrown against the wall with much more strength than last time when Taegar had shoved him. He remained there, feet dangling, held in place by unseen forces. Taegar's power. The door opened and a kitchen filet knife bobbed in, stopping about a foot from his face.

Terror froze Gordon Darcy better than any invisible force could. He knew he would not subdue Taegar now. He would not escape. And she had planned an agonizing revenge.

"Yes, darling." Her voice simpered with approval. "Those wide eyes of yours speak so much more truth than your words."

She flicked her bony hand and his clothes disappeared. "You're afraid."

Gordon tried to speak but no words came out.

"As you should be. You see, what you don't know is that I was abused in my younger days. Badly abused, by men who wanted to prove their ultimate power over me. I managed to escape."

Lips that stood stark in her sallow face smiled. "The men did not. I used a knife like this. Stuck one in the back, but the other one, my father... Well, let's just say that he paid dearly for his sins. Slowly."

The knife nicked the skin of Gordon's collarbone.

"As you will, darling."

The first slice of the knife ripped a thousand screams from Gordon Darcy. The pain... So intense. He couldn't stand it. Over and over the knife dipped, filleting his skin. He closed his eyes but they opened against his will, his head trained downward to watch as strips of skin were sliced from him, leaving raw, bleeding trails of misery.

"You will never get another chance to hurt me," Taegar said, slashing her hand through the air. Another knife pass, another strip of skin.

"No one will ever hurt me again."

Gordon howled, his voice finally sounding. "I'm sorry, Taegar," he said, begging for his life. "I shouldn't have done that to you. I was wrong. So wrong. Please. Forgive me."

Blood flowed freely from the wounds.

"You can have it all," he whimpered. "Everything I own. My entire kingdom."

Taegar's laughter chilled him to the bone. "I don't want it. More importantly, I don't need it. I have everything I need right here." She wiggled her bony hands.

"Now, where were we... "

~~~

Wyeth, Gwen, and Luther found Gordon Darcy's place easily enough, thanks to the information Cait gleaned from his secretary. In the middle of twenty acres of woods, it hadn't been hard to spot the mansion. There'd been a gate, but it was unmanned and the security cameras did not look operational. They'd walked right through and straight up the drive to the front door. That worried Wyeth. Gordon Darcy had seemed obsessive about his privacy. If he held Taegar here, why wasn't there protection? He'd expected guards and a state-of-the-art security system. Instead, the place was eerily quiet.

"What do we do now?" Gwen whispered.

"I don't think we want to be civil and knock." Wyeth scratched the beard he'd decided to let grow.

"Hell, no. Let's barge in," Luther said, turning the door handle, which didn't budge. Luther stepped back and brought his leg up to kick in the door just as they heard the scream.

They stood there frowning at each other.

"That didn't sound like a woman's scream," Gwen
~~~

said.

"No," Wyeth answered. "It didn't."

"I'll consider that our official invitation." Luther raised his leg again and kicked the door, which easily splintered. Inside, no one barred their way. All the blinds were closed tight and murky darkness permeated the house.

Another scream and their heads turned downward, toward the sound.

"Basement," Luther said, opening doors. The third door led them downstairs, where they burst into a room at the back and stopped short, shocked at the scene before them.

Gordon Darcy, or what was left of him, lay against the wall, though nothing they could see held him there. His body was covered in blood and raw flesh, and more blood dripped into a pool on the floor beneath him. His eyes were empty, soulless. He gave a great, gasping breath, then stopped. Never to breathe again.

"What the hell?" Luther said.

They stared at the apparition that hovered in front of Darcy. It turned slowly toward them and Gwen gasped.

Bits of stringy hair, the odor of unwashed skin, all spoke to horrible neglect. But her eyes were what drew Wyeth's attention. Furious, golden eyes. Eyes he'd never seen before. Eyes so fierce, they frightened him.

Gwen gripped his arm. "Taegar?"

"Ah, my *friends* have finally arrived."

Wyeth shuddered at the emphasis she'd put on their relationship. "Taegar, what did that man do to you?" He took a step toward her.

"Stop."

He froze, but realized it was not by choice. Some invisible force held him back.

"Do not come near me."

"Taegar, we're your friends," Gwen said. "We're here to help you."

"Yeah," Luther said. "We've come to rescue you."

"No one will ever need to rescue me again."

The force holding Wyeth lessened. Rather than provoke Taegar's wrath again, he sank to the ground.

Gwen joined him. "What happened, Taegar? What did he do to you?"

"He used me for his own purposes. I was naïve. Now, he's paid for his sins." She cocked her head. "Though I do wish I'd had just a little more time to make him suffer." Her golden eyes flashed and liquid fire shot toward the inert body. It glowed and slid from the wall to the ground. The sizzling stench of burning flesh filled the room and Gwen covered her mouth and nose with her hand. Wyeth did the same to keep the acrid smell at bay. Then, suddenly, the body was gone. It just...disappeared, leaving only a pool of blood in its wake.

"Such a weak little man."

Taegar had come into significantly more power than any of them. That much was clear. And Wyeth had no clue how to de-escalate the situation. Worse, with Darcy gone, there was nowhere for Taegar to direct her anger except at them.

Gwen stood before Wyeth could stop her. "I hate that you've been through so much pain, Taegar. Whatever he did to you, it wasn't right. And it certainly wasn't something you deserved."

Taegar didn't answer. She turned from staring at the blood to look at Gwen.

"We've missed you, sister," Gwen said. "All of us have. We've wanted you to come home. It took us this long to find you. God, I wish we'd found you sooner. Gordon Darcy was too good at subterfuge, and we didn't know where you were until just a few days ago."

"You didn't?" Taegar asked, her voice no more than a faint whisper.

Gwen's quiet calm seemed to be getting through.

"Of course not. You're family," Wyeth said, standing to place a hand on Gwen's shoulder. "That's why we came as soon as we knew where you were. To rescue you."

Taegar visibly wilted and the light in her eyes dimmed. "You're the only ones who were ever nice to me."

"Gordon Darcy did terrible things to you," Gwen said. "We're so sorry, Taegar, that we didn't stop it. That we failed."

Luther clenched and unclenched his hands. "None of it should ever have happened."

"We want to keep you safe, to bring you home, to help you heal." Gwen stood and extended her hand.

Taegar stared at her outstretched hand. "I'd like that. I'd like to go home."

"Then let's get you healthy and get out of here. We'll go back to the light, to where it's peaceful and we can be happy again."

"Where is Damian? And Valena?"

Gwen gulped. "They had to go back to our camp. There are problems."

"So they sent you instead of coming themselves."

Wyeth wasn't sure what triggered Taegar, but something Gwen said hit the wrong chord. Taegar straightened, seeming even taller. The golden glow in her eyes grew fierce once more. "There can be no more happiness, not for me. Too much has happened. Too much pain. Too many hurts. I will not tolerate it. Not anymore."

"Too many people don't accept the new order," Luther said, stepping forward.

"Yes," Taegar said, looking at him.

"We've never hurt you," Wyeth said.

"You will."

"How can you say that?" Gwen pleaded, her hands reaching out to Taegar. "We're your friends. Family."

Taegar canted her head in Wyeth's direction. "I have many new powers. Did you know that?"

He nodded.

"One of those powers is an ability to enter the *ehwaz*, the place between life and death. It shows me things. Dreams. I see futures, pasts, and truths. I see what will happen. You will attack me."

"I won't," Luther said.

"No. You won't. But you two," she pointed at Gwen and Wyeth, "and your ragtag team of do-gooders will."

Damian had a prescient ability, but Wyeth had never known him to have a clear vision of the future. "How can you know that?"

"Unlike humans, the *ehwaz* doesn't lie."

"Isn't it possible it's only showing you one of many potential truths?" Wyeth asked.

"What could happen to make us fight you?" Gwen said.

"Because I will never again let anyone dictate what I do or what happens to me. Humanity has shunned me, made me a victim." She grew taller. "I will never be a victim again. The only way to make certain that happens is to eliminate the threat."

Dread sat in Wyeth's throat like a lump of food he couldn't swallow. "What threat?"

Taegar's arm came up, her bony hand pointing. "You."

"Us?" Gwen asked, her voice no more than a whisper.

"And more. I must rid the world of light. Until darkness is all that is left."

"You want to destroy all of humanity? That's insane,"

Gwen said.

The glow increased. Taegar floated closer and it took every ounce of courage Wyeth possessed to hold his ground. He pushed Gwen behind him.

"What's insane is listening to you for one more moment," Taegar continued, her voice booming off the walls. "Be it known, there are now two circles of druids. One, your pitiful... What do you call yourselves? Oh, yes, the Guardian circle. Yes, I know about that. My circle, the Dark circle, is stronger. Because I am stronger."

Taegar extended her hand toward the pool of blood that had been Gordon Darcy. A fireball flew from her hand to the spot, incinerating all evidence of what had happened in that room.

"Luther," Taegar turned to him. "I sense your discontent. You alone understand my cause. And you may stay if you choose. You are gifted, and welcome in my Dark circle. We will not stop until all humanity bows before us, and Earth's power is ours and ours alone. For all time."

The crazed look on Luther's face scared Wyeth. They'd lost Taegar. They couldn't lose Luther, too. "Luther— "

"Stop," Luther said, his voice strong with resolve. "I haven't felt the same as the rest of you for a while now. Nothing you can say will change that."

"But Luther, you can't leave. You're part of us."

"Not anymore," he said, moving to stand beside Taegar.

She touched his shoulder and his eyes began to glow. He gasped and thrust his chest out. "She's giving me more power," he gasped. "Unimaginable magic. It's exhilarating."

When Taegar pulled her hand from Luther's shoulder, she turned to Wyeth and Gwen. "I sense fundamental goodness in you. You will never understand the headiness of this power. I offer you one respite. Leave. Now. This is neither your time nor your battle. That will come soon enough."

Still frozen in place, Wyeth searched for some way to convince Taegar and Luther of their folly until a fireball whizzed by his head and he finally accepted there was no way to change either of their minds.

As one, he and Gwen whirled and fled, past flames devouring the walls, hurrying up, then down the stairs and out of the house before Taegar changed her mind. They didn't stop running until they were at the gate. Turning for one last look at the house, they saw flames consuming it.

"Taegar! Luther!" Gwen screamed, making ready to go back.

Wyeth held her tight as she struggled against him.

"We have to help them, Wyeth. No matter what."

"We can't help them anymore," Wyeth said.

Tears streamed down Gwen's face as they watched the mansion burn. With hearts heavy and filled with fear and confusion, they turned and walked away from their family-turned-enemy. Wyeth kept his arm tight around Gwen's shoulder, needing the contact as much as she did. Knowing that they had to tell Damian and Bhren what had happened, they shared an unspoken decision as they walked down the road, shoulders bowed.

It was time to go home.

News Alert: Many people are asking how is it that, with all this abundance of food and water, the poorest countries are still starving? Why is the food not getting to them? Why has their water not been purified enough to drink?

CHAPTER TWENTY-EIGHT

"I like this place." Tom wandered around the log home's living room. "I like it a lot."

"Good, because we may be here for some time," Cait said.

Tom nodded. "Are you sure no one can tie you to this place?"

"I am tied to it, but it's a long and hard-to-follow thread. Grandmother had a lover for many years. No one knew, and this was the hideaway where they would meet." Cait ran her hand over the afghan throw laying over the back of the couch. "Her marriage was one of convenience but true love lived here."

"And you know about this place how?"

"Her lover's names was Sinclair. His daughter reached out to me after he passed. She said he wanted both families to share this cabin. I've had a set of keys ever since. Sinclair's daughter passed away a few years ago. As far as I know, I'm now the only one who knows about this place."

"Sounds pretty hidden to me."

Cait nodded. "It might become our prison."

Tom pulled her into his arms. "We need to hide for a while. To protect the girls. It won't be forever." He kissed her. "And, in the meantime, we'll make a home here. You, me, Fallon, and Willow."

Cait hugged him tight. The ache and worry in her heart eased, but not completely. "It feels like the world is working its way to some sort of confrontation. If we're stuck here in hiding, how will we know what's happening?"

"We'll have to resupply. We can check current affairs then. We passed a few towns on our way here. We'll limit what we do together or as a family and visit different towns so no one remembers us."

Cait sighed. "Hopefully."

~~~

Exhausted from several days of travel and delays resulting in too many failed attempts at sleep, Damian and Valena stumbled off the bus with a zombie-like gait, pulling their coats tight against the December chill of South Dakota. Neither of them cared if they ever set foot on mass transportation again.

Inside the darkened terminal, all but empty in the middle of the night, they slumped to a bench to figure out their next step.

"It's a long walk to the lake," Valena said.

Damian heard the weariness in her voice. It thrummed through his own body, too. "We've done it before."

"And we can do it again, I know. But not without some sleep."

He still had the cell phone with him, so he looked up motels. "There's a place to stay about three blocks from here. It's probably not the best."

"I don't care, as long as it's cockroach free. We both
~~~

need to sleep in a bed."

"Okay, then. Let's go."

The hotel was better than either of them expected. The sheets and towels were clean, the carpets, while threadbare, were unstained, and not a single bed bug or cockroach could be found. Valena didn't bother to shower, crawling into bed as soon as she shed her clothes and falling deeply asleep.

Damian sighed, letting go of the anxiety umbrella he'd been stuck beneath for what seemed like years. He took a shower, then sat in the lotus position to meditate and clear the negativity that had risen to the surface of his mind. By this time tomorrow night, they'd be home. He needed the peace of their lake. He needed to commune with the light again, to fuel the positivity within him and find peace. Then, they could try again, renew their efforts to help humanity understand. Only this time, their actions would be more personal, and come in smaller increments, like that family on the train all those weeks ago.

This time, he wouldn't lose his temper.

This time, he'd do it right.

He turned on the laptop and sent a quick message to Bhren, then climbed quietly into bed and turned out the light. Before long, he'd drifted into the same deep sleep as his wife.

<center>~~~</center>

Damian woke to sunlight streaming through thin curtains. He squinted, trying to remember where he was, his arm snaking over to the other half of the bed only to find Valena wasn't there. Damian lay quiet for a moment, listening. The shower was running.

He smiled, thinking how nice it would be to join her, to have an idyllic morning. It had been so long since they'd slowed down and taken time to be with each other. But the shower stopped, so he'd missed his opportunity. Besides, they needed to head out, and soon.

"Good morning, husband," Valena said, entering the room wearing only a towel.

Damian wondered again if he could convince her to tarry for a while.

Valena's eyes sparkled and she laughed to see his lustful looks. She cupped his cheek with one hand. "As much as I would love to spend the morning in bed, we have a long walk ahead of us."

"Yes, we do." He sighed. "But I say we at least fortify ourselves before we head out. There's a diner across the street where we can have breakfast."

"And a small grocery next to it where we can pick up what food we can carry. Who knows what it will be like once we get home."

At breakfast, Damian booted up the laptop to see if Bhren had left a message in the forum. What he read tore the warmth of the morning from him.

Everything has changed. We're not in camp. Meet us at the monument.

"What does Bhren say?"

"Not much. Just that he and Roulf are not in camp and to meet him at Rushmore."

"Then things have deteriorated."

Damian grimaced. "I'm afraid so."

Done with their breakfast and anxious to be on their way, they quickly loaded up with supplies and headed southwest through town on foot. Rapid City looked no different than any other time they'd been here, save for a darkening sky. Yet this morning they noticed an oppression they'd missed last night in their exhaustion. It was as if the city lay under a blanket, trying to hide from something.

A scraggly man on a street corner shouted in cadence

with the sign he bounced. "The end is coming. The end is near."

As businesses gave way to residential homes, the yards and streets were eerily devoid of people.

"Look," Valena said. "At the windows."

House after house, the curtains were drawn on every window as if the occupants didn't want to call attention to themselves once darkness fell. Roofs showed no signs of steam from heat vents or fireplaces. There were autos on the street, but they were few and far between.

"Either people aren't home, or they're hiding. All of them."

He thought back to the streets they traversed in the business district. "The businesses seemed like usual but come to think of it, there were very few people about."

Valena shook her head. "Do they know something we don't know?"

"I'm not sure. At this point, all we can do is head on and hope we can figure all this out."

"And help in some way."

"Agreed."

They walked in silence, both deep in their worries. Before long, they left the city behind. More trees cropped up as nature reasserted itself. Damian breathed deeply as they entered the Black Hills National Forest. It felt good to be back. His contentment dissipated as the stench of burning wood and diesel filled his nostrils. The urban smells got stronger the closer they got to the monument.

After a quick, quiet lunch, they continued their hike. As much as they wanted to go home, they bypassed the lake and headed straight for the monument, arriving just as dusk settled over the area, adding another layer of chill. While they found it hard to pass by their home—they longed to be back—the changes they saw as they walked made it difficult to believe their home was even there. The road had been widened and gates added. And fencing. Buildings had replaced trees in many places. How could that happen this fast? So much of nature destroyed. Now, a wasteland surrounded them. They could see the light stream, still strong and bright, shining off in the distance, but it wasn't a good idea to go there until they spoke to Bhren.

They circumnavigated a road-block and made their way to the Mount Rushmore overlook, hugging the columns that led to the view. The faces carved into the rock were lit for night viewing as if nothing had changed. Damian and Valena stood near the wall staring at them.

"How can a species with such artistry inside them be so unwilling to accept change?"

"I guess," Damian said, looking at Lincoln's hypnotic eyes, "that's the burden of free will. We can choose to listen or not."

"But why? Earth has given them something helpful. Why do they turn their backs?"

"I don't think we'd be able to answer that question if we had a lifetime to discuss it," a voice said from behind them.

"Bhren!" Valena threw her arms around their friend. Damian waited patiently behind her for his turn.

"We've been away too long. It's good to see you again." He hugged his brother druid tight.

Roulf stepped out from behind Bhren. After Valena hugged Roulf, Damian clapped him on the shoulder. "I'm glad you stayed and kept this old man company," he said, motioning to Bhren.

"Somebody had to keep him hidden."

Damian raised an eyebrow.

"Roulf's ability to hide in plain sight is definitely Earth-enhanced," Bhren said.

"I remember that. Nice talent to have."

Roulf grinned. "It's come in handy a time or two."

"A lot has happened since you left," Bhren said.

"Tell us, please."

"Let's move somewhere else to chat." Bhren glanced around, then raised his voice a bit. "I'm heading to the encampment that's been set up outside the new perimeters. Just wanted a last look at the monument. What a wonderful surprise to see you two. Walk with me?"

Valena and Damian frowned at Bhren, but played along. Together, they walked away from the presidents of Mt. Rushmore, away from the home where they desperately wanted to return, away from the light they needed to be near. Roulf followed along behind. Damian could see him concentrating. Was he masking their direction of travel?

Once they were deep in the forest that hadn't yet been destroyed, Bhren looked at Roulf.

"They couldn't follow us if they wanted to," the little man said.

Bhren nodded. "Come. I've set up camp a mile or so from here. Hopefully, it's outside the containment area and beyond their patrols."

"We saw the fencing as we walked in," Damian said.

Bhren nodded. "They kicked out everyone who was not a government employee with security clearance. Everyone. All of us. Gentle people were manhandled off the site. I had to sneak back in at night to get as much of our camping gear as I could. It wasn't easy. After the first three nights, the fence went up. Two nights later, they found the hole I dug to get under the fence and collect our things. After that, guards were posted along the perimeter."

"But this isn't something the government can claim as theirs. This is for everyone. For all the world. Don't they understand that?"

"No," Bhren said, his voice angry. "They don't."

"We have to stop them. Force them to leave." A familiar anger reared up within Damian.

Valena took his hand. "If we react with anger, we're no better than them."

"Yes, but—"

"She's right," Bhren said. "We have to be careful, or we'll do more damage than good."

"Like I did in L.A.?" That he had single-handedly contributed to humanity's fear of their powers was still a bitter pill to swallow.

"Maybe, but there were other factors, other mods fueling that fire." The disappointment in Bhren's voice was clear.

Damian wanted to hit something. Needed to hit something.

"It's okay, Damian," Valena said. "This would have happened sooner or later. You just hurried it along a bit. Let it go. It's not your fault that the world is so close-minded."

"It may not be, but we need more time to show the goodness in our powers."

"A lot of mods are out there doing just that. And we'll try again as well. But first, I don't think Bhren is finished telling us his tale."

"I'm not. The last time I snuck inside the perimeter, I got close enough to the magic stream to see what they were doing."

"And that was?"

"I can't be certain, but they had several giant fuel cells there. Like batteries. I think they are trying to capture and harness the power."

"No! They can't. How can they?"

It surprised Damian when Bhren laughed. "That's the thing. I don't think they can. I watched them try to connect with the magic stream three different ways. By electrical cord, by energy collection device, and finally, by human hand."

"What happened?"

"In all three cases, the same thing happened to them as happened to Gordon Darcy. Some force field sent everything flying."

Now, it was Damian's turn to laugh. *Good for you, Earth.*

"So, they haven't been able to harness the *awen*. Do they understand it any better?" Valena asked.

"I don't think so."

"Still, we need to find a way to make them back off. To let nature take its course."

Bhren stopped and looked around briefly, then reset the direction they were walking. "I don't think we can stop them. I doubt the government will ever come around to our way of thinking."

"I have to agree with that," Damian said. "Neither of our visits to Washington were productive. At all."

They walked into a small clearing where Bhren had set up two tents. There was no fire pit or any amenities.

"It's primitive, but comfortable."

Valena hugged him again. "It's perfect."

"I've set up a makeshift privy to the north since our winds tend to prevail from the southwest. And I got your tent and mat out."

"We've got our sleeping bags with us, so we're set."

"I suggest we get some sleep, then try to formulate a plan in the morning."

"I like that idea." Valena sounded worn out. Again. All the travel and activity seemed to be tiring her more than before. Damian didn't like that, and he'd have to try to convince her to stop healing people until she renewed her own energy. She must have helped twenty people along their route here. This wasn't good for her.

"Have you been eating all right? I don't see a fire pit."

"Raw vegetables, mostly. We haven't wanted to bring attention to ourselves by lighting a fire or cooking."

Full dark had almost descended but Valena squatted down to rummage through her pack. She pulled out a box of granola bars. "It's not much."

"It's better than berries and raw wild potatoes. I thank you." Bhren took one and handed the box to Roulf. Then, each man headed for their tent.

Damian and Valena prepared quickly for sleep. Inside their tent, snug in sleeping bags, they embraced each other tightly.

"Things seem to be getting worse," Damian said.

"Yes."

"I think that tomorrow, I should seek out a vision again. See if Earth can offer me some guidance."

Valena sighed. "I don't like it when you do that. It seems to sap your energy."

"Just like healing saps yours, yet you do a lot of that."

"Touché, husband. All right, but at least make sure Bhren and I are there in case anything goes wrong. Nothing's been turning out the way it should lately."

"Agreed." Damian cuddled her in tighter to his side. "For now, though, a much-needed sleep."

"Mmm-mmm."

His wife drifted off fast. She knew he would keep her safe from harm. And he would. Damian lay there well into the night, running scenarios, trying to find a way to get people to understand that the world was at a tipping point. It wasn't about some people having powers and others not having them. This was about survival. Earth, animal, human... All would be consumed if things didn't turn for the better, and soon.

Though he tortured his poor brain until the early hours of the morning, he couldn't see a solution. He finally drifted into a troubled sleep.

News Alert: The forests of southern California are on fire! Widespread flames tint the land orange.

CHAPTER TWENTY-NINE

Darkness cloaked Taegar in anonymity as she made her way across the night-shaded lands. She'd left the taint of Gordon Darcy behind her, letting the flames from his house spread like the fire burning in her soul.

There were plans to make, and help to enlist. The power grew within her, as though she were drawing it directly from Earth, but she could not be in multiple places at the same time. Yet. She'd seen, in the *ehwaz*, what must be done. To survive, to thrive, and never be ill-treated again, she must bind the magic to herself for all time. She would control it and be the most powerful druid ever. By the time she'd finished, no one would be able to touch her powers. Not even Damian Royan, who didn't know yet that he had the same untapped powers within him.

Only two things stood in her way. Control of the light streams, for which she would need an army since there were three of them, and the ancient chant of binding. To her knowledge, the only person who'd studied druidism in depth was Damian, the father-figure who'd deserted her when she'd needed him most. If he learned what he could do... She'd need to be careful taking him on. She'd need help.

Come to me, Taegar whispered, calling the like-minded. *Immense power will be yours.*

Luther, unable to mind-speak like she could, had volunteered to go in search of kindred souls to help their quest. He understood the importance of this plan, the greater good that would be served. Their greater good.

The air warmed as she got closer to Mojave. This is where they would gather. This is where she would imbue those who joined her with more power, just as she had with Luther. They would not know that power would be finite. No one would have what she had. No one.

And if they did not bow to her supremacy, they would know her wrath.

Damian Royan would yield to her. All of humankind would.

Or they would die.

~~~

After a meager breakfast of late autumn berries and granola bars, Damian settled in a meditative position on the ground, with Bhren and Valena nearby and Roulf standing guard against intrusion.

"I don't know how this will go, or what I will see. I've never done this with others around, so I don't even know if I will be able to speak during the vision. But I do retain what I see, so we can talk afterward."

Bhren nodded. Valena leaned down to kiss him. "Be safe."

"Always," he said, touching her cheek.

He closed his eyes and reached for handfuls of dirt. The change hit him with immediate ferocity.

Fire. Everything burning. So much fire, it seared his lungs.

Damian looked around, tried to determine where he was.
~~~

Nothing looked familiar. Even if he'd known this place, nothing recognizable remained. All he saw were cement foundations and the burned-out hulks of vehicles.

"Where is this? Why am I here?"

"This is the ehwaz. *And you are here because I summoned you."*

The voice, familiar, yet also gravely changed, surprised Damian. "Taegar?"

"Yes."

"Where are you? Are you with Wyeth, Gwen, and Luther? Show yourself."

She moved into view, standing amid flames that did not burn her. Damian took a step back when he saw her. She stood a head taller than him and wore a cloak of darkest black. He could barely see her face, but what he did see, and clearly, were the golden eyes that glared at him from beneath the hood.

"What happened to you?"

"I have found my true destiny."

Damian didn't understand. What was she talking about? "Are you coming home?"

"Oh, yes. I am coming."

"Good. We can sort all this out then."

"I am coming," she said again, "but not to sort anything out."

"What do you mean?"

"I am coming to have my vengeance. You and the rest of your kind will never be able to hurt me again."

"We never hurt you. We're your family."

"At one time, you were. Now, you are my enemy."

"Why, Taegar? What did that asshole Darcy do to you to make you like this?"

"He showed me the true nature of humanity. He showed me that there is no one trustworthy."

"Come home. You can trust us. Let us help you."

"Trust? What was my trust worth when you could not even come

to rescue me yourself? You sent your minions, and even they arrived too late."

"We planned your rescue as soon as we found out where you were. Darcy was very good at covering his tracks."

She laughed, a low, dark, diabolical sound that shivered down Damian's spine.

Taegar cocked her head. "If you want me to trust you, you must prove yourself. Give me the chant of binding."

"Binding?" Damian was confused. He vaguely remembered something like that, but he couldn't recall the specifics. "Why do you need that?"

"That is not your concern. It is, however, the method by which you can prove your trustworthiness. Give me the words."

Her voice had turned melodic, hauntingly hypnotic. If Damian had known the words, he might well have uttered them, he was that taken by her speech. He shook his head, trying to dispel the cobwebs that blurred his mind. How was she doing this? Had her powers grown, expanded this much?

"I can't," he said.

"Give. Me. The. Words." Her voice grew more insistent. More enticing.

"No," Damian ground out. Even if he could, he wouldn't.

"If you do not tell me what I want to know, I will destroy you. I will destroy anyone who tries to stop me, anyone with the power to cause me pain. Anyone with the ability to become as strong as I am. I will destroy you and all humankind."

She'd gone mad, and Damian knew he'd never be able to convince her to come home, nor that they were still her friends. No argument would change Taegar's mind. He bent his head, overwhelmed by sorrow. Such sweetness lost to a darkness he could not understand.

He raised his head. "Where are Wyeth, Gwen, and Luther? Are they with you?"

"Wyeth and Gwen ran from me. That is the last mercy I will

show. And their respite will be short-lived. They are headed for you. As am I."

Fear lodged in the pit of Damian's stomach. "Where's Luther?"

Something moved through the fire and stood beside Taegar. Another hooded person.

"Luther is with me."

The person pulled their hood back and Damian gasped. "Luther?"

"Hello, Damian."

"What happened to you?"

"I have finally seen the light." He shrugged. "Or the darkness, for what it is. The darkness is a thing of beauty and the only way to get the attention of those who think they can control us. Destruction is all they notice. I recognize that now. You should, too. It will make things so much easier. Come. Join our circle."

"I don't understand," Damian said, feeling the anger building within him.

"Yes," Taegar said. "Let that anger out, feed it with how others have hurt you. Have hurt Valena. Embrace the darkness."

"And join the Dark circle of druids," Luther intoned.

Several cloaked figures surrounded them, all standing in fire, all untouched by flame. Damian almost cried out in despair. How could these people accept this blackness in their hearts? Didn't they see that the only master they were serving was death?

"I will never follow darkness," he said, his voice hollow even to his own ears. So much loss. So many turned. When would it end?

"So be it," Taegar said. "Know this. We are coming. For you and for all who will not bow to our dominance. This," she raised her hand, "is just a taste of what we can do. I am all-powerful. I am Taegar. I am the isa, that which provides clarity to the world and bends it to my righteous will. I am thurisaz, creator of chaos, and tiwaz, ruler of all. I am the Dark circle."

Fire shot from her hand. Damian threw up his hands, barely dodging the flame.

Dropping flat to the soil he held tight, Damian yanked himself from the vision, all but paralyzed by fear. He stared at the ground until Valena touched his shoulder. When he looked up, the concern on her face mirrored his own.

"Your hands," she cried.

Damian looked down, saw the angry red burn marks slashing his skin.

Valena reached for his blistered appendages, but he pulled them away. "Later. We need to talk first."

"No, husband. Heal, then talk. There is no other way."

Her gentle insistence got through to him. He knew that tone of voice. She wouldn't back down. Damian held out his hands for her ministrations, chafing at the time it took, but grateful for the easing of his pain. When she'd finished, he took a long draught from the water Bhren handed him.

"We've spent all this time worrying about the government, but the government is no longer the real threat," Damian said. "Things are much worse than we ever thought they could be. It's Taegar. She has somehow tapped a great well of Earth's power. More than I've ever seen, and she can do things I've never imagined. Beguile others with her voice, stand uninjured in fire, and who knows what else. And... " Damian hung his head. "She's turned to darkness. I think she's gone mad. She considers the Guardian druids, as well as all humanity, to be her enemies."

Valena gasped, her hand covering her throat.

"It gets worse. Luther is with her. He's embraced this new Taegar. Others have as well. They plan to annihilate anyone who stands between them and the power."

"Isn't there something we can do?" Valena asked. "Maybe I could join you in the vision, reason with her, with Luther. Oh! What about Wyeth and Gwen?"

"They're not with Taegar."

"Thank goodness."

Damian cupped his wife's cheek with his now-healed hand, wiping her tears. "I know you want to save Luther, Taegar, and the others. That's your mission in life, to save people. But it's too late, my love. She's been consumed by the fire of hatred. So have Luther and the others who joined her. I don't see any argument that will bring them back to the light."

"This was our worst-case scenario," Bhren said. "That some of those gifted with powers would be consumed by malignant greed."

Damian stood, brushing his hands on his legs as Valena, Bhren, and Roulf watched him in silent worry.

"Many people feel the same as Taegar. That desire for control has been there all this time. We— I ignored the signs." He straightened weary shoulders. "If the world thought the arrival of the light streams heralded an unwanted change, they are about to see what their pessimism spawned. And we will be hard-pressed to protect them. For that is, ultimately, what we must do. We are now the only barrier that stands between goodness and evil. This is a war, one that could very well end in annihilation."

"We have some planning to do, and I need to talk to Major Swanton." Damian looked at Bhren, raising his eyebrow.

"Yes. He's still in charge."

"Good. He takes us seriously, which gives us one less hurdle." Damian reached for his pack, stuffing anything that would fit inside it.

Valena took the pack from him. "You pack like a slob. Let me do this. Take a moment to calm yourself and consider what you want to say."

Damian kissed her, relinquishing the pack. "As always,

you are right, my love."

She hugged him tight with one arm. "And you will find the words to convince the major."

Damian hoped she was right. With every cell in his body, every drop of blood that flowed through him, he prayed the end was not as near as he feared.

DISSENSION

EARTH

Why do they not take my goodness? I have given them everything I have. Do they not know that? Now, my lands are being destroyed, burned by those who want to claim my magic for their own.

And I am powerless to stop them. Oh, woe on the world.

I tried. But they would not listen.

I am so tired.

Now, I can only wait to die.

News Alert: Reports are coming in of a strange quiet settling over the world, a reaction to the palpable and growing tension in the air. Worry is abundant and there are rumors of a growing group of mods in the Mojave Desert. For what purpose, we can only wait to see.

CHAPTER THIRTY

"You have to let us in," Damian said, pounding the table in the small security room where they'd been kept waiting for over two hours, then spent another hour trying to argue their way into the glade with the light stream. They had little enough time to prepare. This delay could spell disaster.

"I don't have to do anything except what I'm ordered to do by my superiors," Major Swanton said. "And they say no one goes in."

Damian had tried everything he could think of to convince Swanton. The man remained unruffled and would not change his mind. It would damn near take an act of Congress for him to let Damian, Valena, Bhren, and Roulf into what the government now termed "the Bravo site." Data proved that the first light eruption hadn't happened near Mt. Rushmore. The primary site was the cave about one hundred miles north. The Alpha site. The site to the west, in Wyoming, was now Charlie site. They could try one of those, but Damian knew they'd have no better luck. Plus, Taegar was heading for Bravo.

So what did he have left in his arsenal to change the man's mind? If he could see what Damian had seen...

Could he?

Was there a way to bring Swanton into his vision? To let him see what Damian had seen? When Valena healed Luther, Damian had helped her with a hand on her shoulder. A simple touch had allowed him to give her enough power to finish.

Was it that simple?

"What if I can prove to you that your worst nightmare is about to come true?"

Swanton grimaced. "Look, I know you have extraordinary talents. Hell, I've witnessed them." He gestured to Valena. "But there's nothing you can say or do that will convince me to go against orders."

"Oh, you shouldn't have said that, major." Damian rose and moved his chair beside Swanton. "I'd like to try something, though there's no guarantee it will work. From our discussions, you know that I sometimes have visions."

Like everyone else who heard this, the skepticism was visible on Swanton's face, even though they'd talked about it.

"Just humor me," Damian said. "I'm going to go into the vision state. I'd like you to place your hand on my arm. I'm going to try to show you what I've seen."

Damian headed outside and rolled up his sleeve, then waited for the major to make his decision. When Swanton settled his hand on Damian's bare arm, Damian bit back a smile at the small victory. Now he had to make this work.

He closed his eyes, relaxing, finding his center. When he felt calm, he reached out for the ground and the vision. For Taegar. For the *ehwaz*.

The change was immediate and devastating.

Fire. Burning a swath across the lands, spreading out. Just like Damian had seen before. Only this time, he saw with more clarity, in more detail. He stood beside Major Swanton and both men could only watch as the vision unfolded.

Mods all over the world, all cloaked in darkness and surrounded by fire, raged against humanity. Villages razed to the ground in Africa, the Appalachian hills alive with the ochre glow of devastating fires. In South America, rivers boiled over. In the Pacific Northwest, mountains exploded with volcanic heat.

Everywhere, the devastation was total.

Everywhere, humanity floundered and died.

"There is no stopping me, Damian Royan."

The voice at the edge of his vision turned him. Taegar stood there, an army behind her.

"I am coming."

"You are coming to South Dakota?"

She cocked her hooded head in assent.

"This is your home, Taegar."

"I have no home. Not anymore."

"Why are you doing this?" Damian asked, though he'd heard the answer before.

Taegar's golden eyes brightened. "You know why. I will destroy you. All humanity will fall before me, and once the magic is bound to me for all time, I will live forever."

Bound to her? Everything clicked for Damian. She wanted the chant of binding to pull Earth's magic to her. Grateful that he couldn't recall the exact words of the chant, Damian knew there was one place she could find that information. Only his closest friends knew about the manuscript of druid ways that he'd been writing. All the chants, all the prayers he knew. They also knew where he'd hidden that book.

Damian buried the thought in case Taegar had any mind-reading ability. He tried one more time to reason with her. "We mean you no harm, Taegar. Humanity does not want to hurt you."

She laughed, a maniacal, sharp laughter that sent shivers down Damian's back. He felt the major's hand leave his arm, felt the man shrink away from the vision of Taegar and disappear.

"Give me the chant, Damian, or I will come for the book."

She knew. Damn it. She knew.

"I will destroy that book before I turn it over to you."

"Then behold your future, Damian Royan," Taegar said, waving her hand.

The vision changed. The world moved, like the twirl of a globe, stopping at the familiar faces carved into Mt. Rushmore. Faces blackened by the fire surrounding them. Then, the glade came into view. Upon that turf, Taegar stood, regal and powerful. Damian himself stood at the opposite end. They battled. Fireball after fireball fired at each other.

"You cannot best me," Taegar said.

Damian could feel the life force oozing out of him as he fought Taegar. The closer she got to the light stream, the more powerful she became. He was lifted into the air and tossed like a toothpick, hitting the ground with a grunt and a world of pain.

All around him, Guardian druids battled. Many had already fallen, including...

"Valena!" Damian crawled to her side, cradling her broken body to his. "No, no, no," he moaned, tears streaming down his face.

But before he reached her, he was whisked away to another light stream. Bhren, Gus, and others tried to keep the Dark druids from encroaching. They were quickly overrun. Blood. So much blood. Bhren went down. And Gus, their newest Guardian.

Tears streamed down Damian's face as the third light stream wavered in front of him, the same death visiting Wyeth, Gwen, and those who'd sworn to keep the light safe.

This can't be. We can't lose this battle or Earth and all of humanity will be destroyed.

Back. Please. Get me out of here. As soon as Damian thought it, he was in the glade.

Taegar stood in front of the light stream, intoning ancient words. Words he hadn't given her, but somehow she'd found. Words of binding. The sky lit up as the two other streams bent, joining, all three becoming one. Engulfing Taegar in light that turned from white to gold.

Taegar stepped out of the brightness, arms spread. Everything shone golden, from the hood of her cape to the brilliance of her eyes, to the bottom of her feet.

"I am Taegar. I am the Dark circle." She stared at Damian. "All will bend to my will or die."

She pushed out with her arms and the ground shook. Green grass took on a sickly hue, shriveling and turning brown. All around him, decay set in, destroying everything.

"I will win, Damian Royan. And you will die."

Fire burst from her hands, coming straight for Damian. He jumped back, toppling onto the ground.

"Are you all right?" Valena asked, touching his shoulders, his arms, worry creasing her brow.

They're all there. Valena, Bhren, Roulf, all there with him. All the people he'd seen...die. Damian took deep gulping breaths, pulling Valena hard into his chest. "You're alive. Thank God, you're alive." He whispered the words and he went around the room, hugging them all. Including Swanton, who slumped against a railing in shock.

Even hugs didn't calm Damian, though. He pulled his shirt away from his neck, clutching at his skin, unable to breathe. He needed air. He doubled over, clutching a gut roiling with possibilities. He'd seen the future.

No. Not the future. Only a possibility. Only a chance. They had time. There had to still be time. He stared at the ground as it hit him. Had he thrown fire at Taegar? Could he have the same powers she'd grown into? And, if he had them, could others?

They needed to make plans. Damian stood. His fellow druids surrounded him. The major gaped at him.

"You saw?" Damian asked Swanton.

The man nodded, a pasty-gray tint to his tanned skin and his knuckles white where he clutched the railing. He'd seen the possibilities, but not the ending Damian had seen.

"You'll let us into the glade?"

Swanton's nostrils flared, but he nodded again.

"Okay. More of us will be coming. Roulf, put the word out. We need any kindred spirit with talent. Earth's magic needs protecting, and thanks to Taegar, I have some ideas on how to do that. Have any mods head to the light streams. We'll need people at each of them. As many as possible."

"I'll need a ride out of here," Roulf said. "Major?"

Swanton waved to the man standing beside the building. "Take him wherever he needs to go."

Damian took the water Valena handed him and gulped it down. "We need to make plans to defend the light here and at the other two sites. Those, at least, are inside caves. Here, we could be attacked from all sides."

Swanton led the way back inside, this time to the conference room. He closed the door behind the druids and turned to Damian.

"How can I help?"

~~~

Damian leaned back in his chair, stretching to ease muscles sore from being hunched over a table all night. He looked around the now-empty room. There were no windows, but it had to be close to dawn. After hours of haggling and grappling with possibilities, they had a working plan to defend the light stream here in the Black Hills. Major Swanton's request to his superiors for assistance had been met with derision and disbelief. Was
~~~

there no one who would accept the truth without proof? Had faith succumbed to this world of instantaneous information? All the major had managed to extract was a promise that the nearest military bases would stand ready to aid if anything happened.

Rubbing at the headache that wouldn't go away, Damian knew the truth. They would be too far away. Not that it would matter in a war of magic.

Work with the mods who'd responded to their plea for help had already begun. Just about all of them could throw or push some sort of fire or lightning. Offensive abilities that none of them, including him, had known about or recognized until he'd met Taegar in the *ehwaz*. Was this a new Earth talent? Had they been gifted with more to defend Earth? There was no time to sort that out.

After much thought and discussion, they'd formulated plans for all three light streams.

The vision, fire scorching everything around him, Valena—snapshots of horror seared Damian's mind. Only he knew the truth and the burden weighed heavily on his heart. If any part of the vision came to be, none of their plans would work. Nothing they were doing to prepare would make any difference. He couldn't get the vision out of his mind. Taegar would win against non-mod forces. Only magic would stop her, and even that might not be enough. She'd spouted ancient words he'd studied for years. Words he now remembered. Words of binding.

That could not happen.

Damian walked outside, breathing deeply, needing the solace he got from open spaces. He noticed more tents. At first, just a few, but as he drew closer to the glade, tents stood side by side in long rows. People were everywhere, and not just military.

"The word is out," Bhren said, coming up beside him.

"Roulf is back. He did an interview and it went viral. They've all come to help."

"All with talents? Able to defend?"

"So far."

Overwhelmed with relief, Damian hung his head for a moment. Then together, he and Bhren walked into the glade, stopping close to the light stream. A wellspring of emotion rose in Damian as he gazed at Earth's majestic promise.

"We'll beat her, Damian."

He shook his head, reaching his hands out in supplication to the light. Not touching, feeling no warmth, just praying for some hope to ease the plight of humankind.

"Everything's going according to plan," Bhren said. "Wyeth and Gwen are here. Wyeth says there are crowds of mods at the other two light streams, ready to defend them on behalf of Earth and all humanity. He and Gwen are ready to head out to one of them, to spearhead the effort there.

"They will fail. We will fa— " Damian's hands dropped to his side. His voice caught, despair cutting the word in two, as if he thought to utter it would make it a certainty.

Bhren settled a hand on Damian's shoulder. "There was more to the vision than you told us, wasn't there?"

Damian nodded. "I saw Taegar's victory." He grabbed Bhren by the shoulders, shaking him for a moment. "Everything we do will be futile. She wins, Bhren. She wins and binds Earth's magic to her darkness."

A minute passed. Two. Three. Bhren drew himself up to his full height. "We can't let that happen."

"No. We can't. Yet I can't see how to prevent it."

"We need a new plan, a plan B."

Damian stared at the light for a long time. Something

about the vision... Taegar... Ancient words... Ancient bindings...

A thought, born of desperation, grew in his mind. Yet, to put this plan into action meant doing the unconscionable. "I have an idea," he said slowly.

"What?"

"We defend, but not here, beside the light. Not by any of the light streams. We must hold the line away from here, try to stop Taegar before she reaches the light. If it looks like she, or her people, will break through, we pull back. Just a few of us."

"You mean, abandon the fight?"

Damian turned to Bhren, let him see the tears forming. "Yes."

"Without us, everyone will surely perish. Why would we leave? What could possibly justify leaving everyone who risked their lives to help us behind to fight to the death?"

"The ancient rite of suppression."

Bhren stared at the light. "You want to suppress Earth's magic?"

Damian nodded. "To protect it."

"For who?"

"For someone stronger than Taegar."

"That's a lot to place on one person. Someone who may not even be born yet."

"I know." The weight bore heavily on him.

"Can this actually be done?"

"In theory."

"And it could well undo any chance for Earth to survive humankind's stupidity and overuse."

"I don't see any other way."

"You're the one who studied all those ancient texts."

Damian waited while Bhren weighed the pros and cons. His friend walked to the edge of the glade and back again with the measured pace of a man headed for the death chamber. He opened his mouth, then closed it. After an internal battle that Damian understood too well, Bhren nodded.

"If we can't defeat Taegar, this may be the only way," Bhren said. "Should we tell anyone?"

"I'm not sure it's a good idea to tell them we think they'll fail and that we have a backup plan. We should only tell those who need to know." Damian raced to the spot he'd buried his manuscript and dug it up. He brushed dirt off the leather cover as he formulated the rest of the plan.

For this to work, they'd need a talisman. Something they could infuse with the key to reversing the suppression rite. Something that could be used at each site. So pieces... Runes. Damian had a set in his bag. Each set of runes held twenty-four symbols carved on separate mottled brown stones. "We'll need eight druids," he told Bhren. "All with some sort of talent, at each site."

"Pulling even that many away from the front lines could well undo any chance for Earth to survive the onslaught," Bhren said. He settled a hand on Damian's shoulder. "I'll find you your druids. I guess that means we've got our backup plan."

"Now all we have to do is pray that it works." Damian leaned on the metal handrail that ran along the walkway where he stood. Layers of guilt, regret, fear, anguish, and desperation bowed his shoulders, pulling him down. He sank to the ground, clinging to the handrail like a lifeline, pressing his cheek against the cold metal. There was so little he could do. Except pray. And he'd been doing that nonstop ever since he'd seen Valena, lying there, the breath gone from her.

News Alert: A band calling themselves the Dark druids are scorching paths of ruination in all directions from southern California, but the largest swath seems to be bearing down on South Dakota. Nothing can withstand their onslaught and waves of destruction are rolling across the land.

CHAPTER THIRTY-ONE

Damian stood on the promontory in the growing light wondering how many times he'd come here, staring at the lake, trying to work through some problem. Today was no different, except this problem had no good solution. Taegar and her Dark druids grew closer with every blink of his eye, leaving nothing but death in their wake.

They'd hashed out two plans—two different ways to stop her. One of them had to work. The part he hated, though, was that for Plan B to have a chance, he'd have to leave during the imminent failure of Plan A, abandoning all those who risked their lives to save, well, everything and everyone.

Damian raked his hands through his unfettered hair. Even this serene view couldn't calm him. Maybe that was all right. Maybe he needed to be frustrated. Desperate. Angry. Ready to fight. As a pacifist, this was something he'd never done before.

He'd found, in entering the *ehwaz*, that he could reach out to Wyeth, to Bhren. The other battlefronts were as ready as they were here at the Bravo site.

Earth's magic would help their defense, but was it enough? Taegar knew her abilities better than he did. She'd had more time to practice, and practice she had, based on the news reports.

The Guardian druids had added to their arsenal. Swanton's men preferred to use guns, but this battle would be fought hand to hand.. Because of Damian's vision, they'd put the word out for other types of weapons. Knives, swords, whatever could be found.

He grabbed the hilt of the sword he now wore at his side. It was a strange feeling, wearing a weapon. Without much practice, he'd learned to wield it fairly well, for which he was grateful.

Still, would it be enough? Would *he* be enough?

The sound of someone climbing the precipice brought him around. Valena, with her own rapier dangling from her side and a battle knife tucked into her belt. He helped her over the top and together, they watched the sun rise over the lake. A fish jumped, causing ripples that barely disturbed the calm surface. A hawk cried, but when Damian searched the skies, he couldn't find it.

"It's hard to believe a battle is about to be fought here," Valena said, hugging Damian tight.

Everything would change based on today. The world would be forever different, and only a few hundred mods stood between the light and the darkness.

"Are Bhren and Wyeth ready?"

"As ready as we are." They would defend a line several miles south of Origin Cave, the Alpha site, holding the area and keeping the Dark druids from advancing. Roulf, Wyeth, and Gwen had traveled to Wyoming to make a stand before the caves there.

Damian and Valena would lead the druids that remained here.

"Major Swanton won't leave?"

Damian shook his head. He'd talked to the man until he'd gone hoarse trying to convince him that bullets did nothing against magic.

"My orders are to protect this place. I'm not going anywhere, and neither are my men," Swanton had said.

"I can't fight Taegar and protect Swanton and his men at the same time," Damian said, walking away from Valena, pacing back to her, then away again.

"He knows what he's getting into, Damian. He's a man of conviction, a man who follows orders, and I don't think he expects you to worry about him or his men."

"He said as much."

Valena came up behind him and turned him to her. "We will fight with everything we have, husband. Long and hard and 'til our last breath. That is all we can control, all we can do. This day will unfold as it will."

Damian wrapped her in his arms, kissing away the furrow between her brows that belied her calm words. "You are right, as always." He tucked her head under his chin, loving the feel of her snuggled against him. Why had all this happened? Why couldn't they just be together? Be at peace. The vision, never far from his thoughts, had become his nightmare and his motivation. He couldn't lose Valena. Damian was more scared than he'd ever been, and he needed to center himself, to focus on the coming battle.

"Are you sure I can't talk you into leaving, going somewhere safe?"

"Everyone will need my help today," Valena said. "Besides, if we do not win the day, there will be no safe place."

He couldn't argue with that. "At least stay toward the back."

"I will face this by your side. And you will not worry about me. I can take care of myself."

Not against this. Damian hugged his wife tight, trying to block the image from his vision. Together, they watched the day awaken, hesitant to leave, to begin their fateful day.

"It's time," Damian finally said. "We'd better join up with everyone."

~~~

Several hundred soldiers waited at the predetermined place, a line the enemy had to cross to get to the light stream. It wasn't enough. Drones had given them glimpses of the coming hoard before their cameras cut out.

Major Swanton stood in front of his captains, giving final orders.

Damian nodded toward the major, saw his struggle to maintain an outward calm. Inside, acid and fear probably churned in his stomach as it did in Damian's. Walking past Swanton to the hundred or so mods that stood in front, shifting their feet, their blanched faces filled with unease, Damian had no idea what to say to them.

"Is it true that a wall of fire precedes the Dark druids as they travel?" asked one young mod.

"That's what we've heard." Damian wiped the sweat from his forehead. Already the temperature around them was warmer than it should be for December. Taegar's swath of destruction had caused enough damage to affect regional temperatures.

"How do we meet that?"

Damian tied his hair back with a band and squared his shoulders. "Head on. You've all been practicing shielding?" Another trick they'd only recently learned.

Most nodded.
~~~

"That will get you through the fire. After that, use your offensive magic, along with whatever weapons you've chosen. Remember, you have the same talents as they do. We *can* do this."

Skepticism rolled through the group, but if they wanted to survive, everyone must believe it.

"You can do this," he said again, reaching for Valena's hand. "Earth gave you these talents. Earth recognized your stout heart and gave you what you need to succeed."

Valena reached out to the person next to her, taking his hand. Damian did the same. The ripple of hope, showcased by conjoined hands, spread through the group, bolstering them. He felt each one of them join. Felt their magic. Let it encourage his own heart. Many of the soldiers surrounded them, placing hands on shoulders, joining the prayer.

Damian bowed his head and, as everyone followed suit, he offered up a prayer of gratitude and hope. Afterward, the mods lined up in front of the soldiers, who formed up ranks behind them. Off in the distance, they could hear the crackle of trees succumbing to fire, and they could see the orange haze of a forest giving way to great heat.

Damian kissed Valena one more time, then drew his sword and faced forward, his free hand tight around hers.

They were ready.

CHAPTER THIRTY-TWO

The wall of orange fire came toward them at a dizzying speed. As planned, they held off using their shields until the last possible moment. The heat was unbearable. Damian's hands blistered from the intensity. He strode out in front of everyone, throwing up his shield, using it to push the first wave of druids back. The others joined him, creating a wall to hold off the worst of the enemy's weapons.

Still, they came. Wave upon overwhelming wave of dark-robed mods, throwing flames, fireballs, lightning strikes, everything they could imagine. Sweat rolled off Damian's face as he struggled to maintain the protective barrier and calm his racing heart.

The Guardian druids held their shields steady, using them to reflect the Dark druids' weapons back upon themselves. One of the enemy's robes caught fire, quickly consuming his screams. Another one sizzled from a lightning strike that hit the shield and bounced back on him. He fell to the ground, dead.

An unexpected benefit from their newly learned shielding abilities, this gave Damian hope. With no time to think, he added strength to his shield and began his own reflected barrage. Fire flew from his extended hands, slid through the shield to scorch the attackers. Screams rent the air, and the stink of burning flesh overwhelmed everything. Damian glanced behind him to see Valena helping an injured soldier, one hand covering her nose.

Fire whizzed by Damian and he felt the burn in his arm. His shirt was on fire. He slapped it out.

Keep your head in the game. She can take care of herself.

Firing bolt after bolt, Damian advanced through the attackers, searching for Taegar. He had to leave the others to the mods behind him. His part in this battle was to take down Taegar. The golden eyes from his vision beckoned him, yet he saw her nowhere. Finally, realizing that this magical fight might need to happen elsewhere, Damian reached down and plunged his hand into the dirt in his hand, unmindful of its high temperature.

"Where are you, Taegar?"

The battle around him disappeared. Nothing but darkness surrounded him.

"I wondered when you'd find me."

He whirled around. Taegar, in her cloak of ebony that made the golden fire of her eyes even more pronounced, floated toward him.

"Where did the battle go?" he asked, though he knew the answer.

"The battle happens on another plane. It is not meant for this place."

"For the dream plane?"

"Yes. For the *ehwaz*. Though you should understand by now that this is no place of dreams. What happens here has real-life consequences. The battle rages around us, but its outcome will be decided here, between you and me."

"I am not the enemy, Taegar."

"You are all the enemy."

"And you are doing this because of Gordon Darcy?"

She laughed, a maniacal sound that echoed and reverberated through Damian's head. "He was nothing but the impetus, the one who helped me find my true self."

"You are not this person. You were happy, before. With us. Weren't you?"

She cocked her head and precious time passed before she spoke. "I was happy."

"Then be happy again. End this. We'll help you find the Taegar we knew and loved. We'll help you come back home."

"There is no home left that will welcome me," she whispered.

When she pulled the hood from her head, Damian gasped. The Taegar they'd known had disappeared. Nothing remained but a skeletal face and eyes of fire. How could this have happened so fast? Tears touched his cheek at the loss of someone so young, so beautiful. At that moment, he knew it was too late. The darkness had claimed her.

"The horror on your face validates me. The power is consuming me. I am evolving into something more, something bigger and better. Something you cannot best. No one will ever be able to hurt me again."

Damian tried one last time. "Please, Taegar. We can help you."

"No." Her voice, bolder now, swirled around Damian, making his head hurt. "Give me the chant of binding."

"No."

"I can pull it from you, force you to my will."

Another new talent? It didn't matter. He would die before he gave her those words. Damian chose to remain silent.

Fire flared around her. "If you will not give me the words, then I will find them another way. I know you wrote them down, Damian. I will find your tome. It is time to end this."

He barely threw up his shield in time to stop the blast of raw power that emanated from her. A steady stream of fire. Now two streams, becoming a wall, pushing at his shield, pushing him back.

He tried to reflect her attack, but each attempt caused his shield to dip in strength. He could do nothing but withstand the barrage, though it weakened him. He felt his power draining, and knew, on some basic level, that this was one more battle he could not win. Taegar's strength had grown beyond his abilities.

Only one course of action remained to him. Pulling at his reserves, Damian clouded his shield, blinding her to his actions. Then, he dropped the dirt in his hand and left the *ehwaz*.

The battle raged around him. Fire was everywhere. Charred bodies littered the ground. He couldn't even tell if they were friend or foe.

Damian raced through the skirmishes, searching for Valena. There! On the edge of the battle. She fought a Dark druid with only her knife.

Racing toward her, Damian threw his sword at her attacker, skewering him. He tottered to the ground as Damian yanked his sword out, grabbed Valena, and ran. Away from the battle, guilt consuming him, though there was no time to give in to it.

At the rear of the battle, six druids waited as he'd asked them to.

"Come. We haven't much time."

They raced to the glade where the light stream stood strong. Forming a circle around the light, Damian began the ancient chant. Words of concealment, words of trust and hope in the future. Over and over again, they chanted the words. The light flickered. Damian reached into his pocket and pulled out the rune, one of the twenty-four he'd ensured were passed out to each druid involved. The same ritual would happen at the other light-streams. Just as they'd planned.

He pricked his finger and let his blood drip onto the rune. Valena did the same. One by one, they each imbued their rune with power through their blood. They continued the chant as the light flickered again, then dimmed. The healing power Earth had gifted to humankind for the survival of all dimmed further then disappeared completely. Sent back into the ground from whence it had come, until the day when someone came along who could match Taegar's strength.

All that remained was to complete the second part of the plan. To give hope to the future. Together, they intoned the words, creating the final prophecy that would lock the magic away until one with powers greater than the Dark druid found the key.

Shattered by darkness the magic vanished.
It lays in wait for one who's banished.
Hidden power will blossom anew.
Only by passing the darkness through.

The runic key ignites the fire
That coupled with the conduit's power
Must send the magic to the white height
Defeating darkness, restoring light.

The chant fell off. Damian's arms shook with the effort it had taken to suppress the magic. Several druids sank to the ground. Damian gathered their runes into a small bag, then hung the bag around his neck and tucked it under his tunic.

"The fire draws near," one of the druids said, standing. They all turned and saw the orange growing, coming closer. That could only mean one thing. The battle had been lost and Taegar was coming for the light. And for him, because he knew the chant of binding.

Tears streamed down Valena's face and his own cheeks were just as wet.

"You have to go," the druid closest to him said. "You have to safeguard the talisman, and you cannot be here when Taegar arrives or she will have what she needs and all this death will have no purpose."

Damian clutched the bag around his neck, torn. So many lives. How could he leave and let more fall before Taegar's wrath? "We have to help."

"Not here, you don't. This is not your journey."

Valena's tears intensified.

"What's your name?" Damian asked the man.

"Thor, believe it or not. What I wouldn't give for some of his power right now."

Damian grabbed Thor by both shoulders, pulling him in for a tight hug. When he released him, there were tears in the man's eyes.

"Good luck."

"You'll need it more than I will." Thor turned to the wall of heat and fire heading their way, already refocused on the coming battle. "Now please, make this count. Go."

Damian grabbed the pack waiting for him, his precious writings inside, and reached for Valena's hand. "Let's make their deaths mean something."

Valena nodded and swiped at her tears. Together, they raced from the glade, from Mt. Rushmore, from every brave person who stayed and fought. Guilt tore at Damian's heart, yet still, they ran. With each passing mile, that guilt was replaced by a hard-won pledge.

"One way or the other, we will make their sacrifice count."

CHAPTER THIRTY-THREE

Taegar stared at the empty space where Damian had stood moments ago, awash with fury. He'd disappeared. Left when she'd been so close to getting the binding chant and destroying the one person with the potential to match her powers, though he didn't know it. He was close, though. He'd almost figured out what she needed, and everything hinged upon his death.

Where had he gone? What would pull him away from this battle? The only thing more important was—

No!

The *ehwaz* disappeared and the real world surrounded Taegar. Bodies, burned beyond recognition, lay everywhere. The battle continued, destruction that should feed her soul, but she couldn't think about that right now. She had to get to the light stream. Damian would be there. Had he beaten her to it? Found a way to bind the light? Could he steal it from her?

Taegar raced through the battle that raged around her, throwing out a blast here and there to push back the hordes. She had to get to the light. It was the only way she'd ever truly be safe.

When she arrived, the glade was empty.

And dark. The light was gone.

No, no, no, no. This can't be. Everything had been planned out. Everything should have gone according to that plan. She was the strongest druid. The one with more power than anyone, including Damian Royan. How could he have thwarted her like this? Somehow, he'd discerned her plans well before this day.

In her ire, Taegar threw bolt after bolt of fire at the trees surrounding her, until nothing was left of the glade but a charred reminder of her failure. Even that wasn't enough. Taegar screamed, her voice shuddering out in waves of anger and frustration. Everything around her stilled. Even the battle paused, unsure what this noise meant.

Slowly, inexorably, reason reasserted itself and Taegar could think again. Somehow, Damian had made the light disappear. That didn't mean he'd bound it to himself. Taegar's head came up. Had it disappeared from everywhere?

She closed her eyes, settled her breathing, and entered the *ehwaz* again.

"Luther," she called. "Come to me."

Long moments passed before he appeared before her. His clothes were singed, his skin burned and darkened by fire, but the light in his eyes blazed brightly.

"Is the light still there? In the cave?"

"We just broke through to it. We had our toughest battle right there at the entrance."

"I don't care about your battle. Is the light stream still

there?"

"No." He spoke the single word like a student who'd just failed the ultimate test. "At least, not like I expected. There's nothing but a weak light emanating from the ground."

Taeger's anger freshened. How could Damian have gotten there so quickly?

"Did you see either Royan there?"

Luther shook his head.

"One task. Take the cave. That's all you had to do."

"The resistance was stronger than expected." He watched her, wary now, though with that hint of conceit that said he knew she wouldn't do anything to him.

He was wrong. What she gave, she could rescind. Taegar's hand shot out and she curled her fingers. Light shot from Luther, returning to her, from whence it came. She continued to draw the magic out until finally, there was nothing left to draw. She'd not only taken back her own, but his, too. Taegar dropped her hand and Luther, or the skeletal remains of him, crumbled to the floor.

Taegar no longer cared. Somehow, someway, Damian had managed to kill two of the light streams. But there was still one chance left. She tried to reach out to the Dark druids at the last light stream, but no one answered her summons. Why?

Outside of the *ehwaz*, the battle had reached the glade and raged on. An empty battle now. There was nothing more that could be done here. She let her anger loose, throwing her hands out. Fire flew in all directions, ending the conflict as both sides succumbed to death.

Without a single backward glance, Taegar headed for Wyoming and the only light stream left.

Her last hope.

CHAPTER THIRTY-FOUR

Despite their complete exhaustion, Damian and Valena pushed themselves hard to get to the place the Guardian druids had chosen to meet up, praying the entire time that Bhren and Roulf would show up with their part of the talisman.

They barely spoke. To do so meant giving voice to the changes around them. They kept to the woods, though the towns they skirted provided evidence of the chaos that this day's battles had wrought. Destroyed power grids had brought humanity back to their most basic of needs: food, water, shelter. Nothing else mattered anymore.

The woods they traversed were devoid of life and muted beyond anything Damian had ever experienced. Birds did not warn of the passage of humans beneath them. Neither rabbit nor squirrel crunched leaves in their travels. It was as if the world had gone into hiding, and that did not bode well for anyone's survival.

The battles were done, the war to control Earth's magic concluded, with no winner.

After two days of hard travel, they reached the meeting spot, the first ones to arrive. Damian had pushed them both to get here, and exhaustion showed in Valena's hollow eyes. Exhaustion and a life-draining sadness. She sank to the ground, staring at nothing.

Damian put a blanket around her shoulders, then set up their tent. As the day's light waned, he started a fire, hoping that if any Dark druids remained, they were far away. Valena needed warmth. So did he. Even more, they needed the comfort of a fire not set for destruction. After a meager dinner from the leftovers they'd packed before the battle, Damian and Valena held each other tight as they stared into the fire.

"So many... " Valena whispered. "All lost."

"We were outmatched from the onset."

Silent tears wet her cheeks as they sat there, mourning those who'd fought so valiantly, who'd given their lives so humankind could survive. If there was anyone left to survive.

Later, in their tent, Damian held Valena in his arms as she cried herself into a fitful sleep. He lay awake, listening for any signs of danger. None came, and morning arrived as quietly as the night.

They searched for vegetables and greens, adding the last of their leftover meat to water then mixing everything to create a stew. As the day progressed, Damian napped while Valena kept watch. Waking without feeling any more refreshed, Damian ranged through the area around their camp, making sure no danger lurked. It wasn't necessary. Nothing lurked anywhere. It was as if everything had gone into hibernation.

He and Valena could use a good rest. A long sleep. An

idea began to root around in his head, but he decided to wait for the others before giving it voice.

They were just settling down to supper when the quiet sound of someone walking perked Damian's ears. He stood, pulling his sword, ready to defend his wife with his life if need be. When Bhren slipped from the darkness into their camp, relief flooded Damian. He raced over and hugged his friend. "I'm so glad you made it. It's good to see you."

Valena joined them and the three of them stood there in a silent embrace, letting the misery of the last few days wash through them, no longer alone in their grief.

"We've got stew," Valena said.

"I appreciate it. I haven't eaten since I left Origin Cave." Bhren reached into his pack, pulling out a bowl and spoon.

Damian waited until they'd eaten to ask questions to which he already knew the answers. "Origin Cave?"

Bhren stared off into the distance. "The battle did not go well."

"Nor did ours."

"We did what we had to do, but the price was high. I— " His voice broke, uncharacteristically. "I am the only survivor. We suppressed the light stream, though not completely. A trickle remains."

"The same trickle remains in Wyoming," a voice behind them said.

"Roulf!" Damian jumped up, hugging the little man. "Your stealth abilities are insane. We didn't know you were there until you were on top of us."

After he returned everyone's hugs, Roulf sat down.

"Wyeth and Gwen?"

Roulf shook his head and Damian's heart bled for their friends. Never to see their smiling faces again. So much loss. He could only pray that it had been worth it.

Valena handed Roulf a bowl of stew. "Many thanks for the stew," he said, "I'm glad you didn't hear me coming. My stealth abilities are not what they were. I feel stifled. Have any of you tried to use your Earth magic?"

"No," Damian said. "The battle took so much of our energy we've been focused on replenishing it. We've avoided using it."

Roulf pulled up his sleeve to show a bloody burn there. "Got this as I was leaving Wyoming. One of those Dark druids almost caught me."

Valena placed her hand on the burn, closing her eyes to focus. After much longer than Damian expected, she sat back. The burn, while not as red, was still there and still caused Roulf quite a bit of pain, Damian imagined.

"I can't heal like I could," Valena said.

Damian tried to call a fireball. Only a small flame fizzled in his palm. "We've lost our magic?"

"I think," Bhren said, "our powers have been suppressed, just as the light stream was."

Damian paced back and forth. "We hadn't considered that this might happen. How will we mount a renewed war against Taegar and her circle if we have no powers?"

"Are we sure she survived?" Roulf asked.

"She was stronger than any of us."

"Is she still? If our powers are diminished, hers probably are too," said Bhren, always the voice of reason.

That gave Damian hope, though he didn't know what to do with it. "Should we search her out, try to deal with her by non-magical means?"

Bhren shook his head. "I think we've done what we can. I'm tired, Damian. We all are."

The others raised their tired voices to validate Bhren's statement.

"That means we continue with our original plan and leave this battle for another day. Another person—someone strong enough to take on Taegar." Damian sat down beside Valena, defeated. He hadn't been able to save to world. Instead, he'd made things ten times worse, it seemed.

Valena rested her head on his shoulder. "Someone will take up the torch we've passed. We've done all we can. It's not your fault that things are how they are, husband."

His mind knew the truth in her statement, but his heart couldn't quite catch up.

"What do we do now, while we wait for someone to come who has the power to take on Taegar?" Bhren asked.

"I've been thinking about that," Damian said, warming to the subject change. "We need to protect the talisman. That's the most important thing now. And Tom thought we'd all been gifted with longer lives."

"Yes, but what kind of shape will we be in to help the prophesied one when that person comes along? We could be ancient by then."

"Hopefully not, but I remember something I read once, about a druid's sleep." He told them what little he knew, how they could meditate to enter a deep slumber that slowed down breathing, heart rate, and the aging process.

"We could all use some sleep," Damian said, putting an arm around his wife's shoulders.

"That we could," Roulf said. "Though, for me, I think I will find some isolated place and create my own stronghold. Maybe then I'll sleep. For a while."

"Valena and I know a place we can go, a place where no one can find us."

"Including Taegar?"

"Hopefully, though there's no guarantee."

"All right," Bhren said, "but I choose to not sleep. At

least, not for long. I'll remain awake to keep an eye on the world and watch for signs of new trouble."

"When I battled Taegar, it was in the *ehwaz*. Maybe, if you see trouble brewing, you can reach out to me through that realm. It might be enough to wake me so we can help."

Bhren nodded. "It's better than my knowing where you are. If something happens and I am captured... "

Damian tapped his friend's knee. "I'll be praying none of us end up in Taegar's hands until we have the energy to deal with her." He drew a deep breath and exhaled slowly. "So be it. We'll leave at first light."

He pulled the rune bag from around his neck, opened it and spilled the runes into his hand. Bhren reached into his pocket and added his runes to Damian's. Roulf did the same.

"Twenty-four runes complete the talisman. The light stream will no longer fuel Taegar's powers and the prophecy is set. Now, the only thing left to do is wait for the one who will fulfill what we've created."

"God help us if that person never comes along," Roulf said.

"Earth help us, too," Valena said.

One by one, they joined hands and prayed silently for the future of Earth and humankind. Then, Bhren and Roulf set out bedrolls as Damian and Valena headed to their tent for the night.

In the morning, their goodbyes were as muted as the world around them.

"Take care, my old friend," Damian said, hugging Bhren tight. "And you, Roulf."

"I'll travel with Bhren for a while, then break off to find my own way."

Damian smiled, glad they'd have a little more time together. After everyone said their goodbyes, he and Valena walked out of camp, knowing they might well never see their friends again.

~~~

After seven days, Damian and Valena reached the underground caves they'd explored as newlyweds. No one was around, so they camped outside that night, with no tent.

"The stars are so beautiful. I think this is my favorite place in the whole world," Valena said, laying on her bedroll.

Damian reached for her hand, remembering their honeymoon. "We spent hours that first night here, just watching the stars."

"Well, we didn't *just* watch stars."

He chuckled. "No, we didn't. Being here with you, then and now, this place feels as sacred to me as our home did."

Valena took a deep breath and exhaled. "The air is pure here still. I wonder for how long."

"Let's leave the darkness behind for tonight. It's just us. Here. Basking in the majesty of the universe."

"I couldn't agree more." Valena turned into Damian and he put his arm around her, though neither of them slept, content to be together and watch the stars cut across the sky.

Both were up early and sat holding hands, watching the red fire of the sun's entrance into the day. Would they ever see this again, Damian wondered? He didn't know the answer, but resolutely packed up their things and prepared to go underground. It took several hours to reach the spot they'd found all those years ago. The caves were a maze, difficult to navigate. Though they couldn't see them, there must have been air vents somewhere because the air did not seem stagnant. Water dripped from the wall of the
~~~

small cavern they'd reached, its peaceful cadence matching their mood.

Damian laid out their bedrolls side by side, then stashed their packs behind a nearby rock.

"Are you sure this will work?" Valena asked, sitting down.

"No," he answered honestly. "But it's worth a try."

She reached for his hand, turning it over and tracing his lifeline with her finger. "I wish we could have all these years together, to grow old, to— "

"To raise a family," Damian finished, cupping her cheek. "I believe very strongly that will be part of our future. We will have our family. Now is not quite the time."

Tears filled Valena's eyes. Tears of hope for a future that did not involve constant struggle. She nodded, laying down.

Damian lay beside her, the runes safe in a bag around his neck, chanting the words he'd read so long ago. Breathing ever more deeply, ever more slowly, together they gave themselves over to the druids' sleep.

CHAPTER THIRTY-FIVE

Taegar passed through Casper, Wyoming unnoticed, keeping to the shadows. While the post-war anarchy fueled her dark desires, people fought in the streets over things no longer important to her. Her focus was on the caves south of this city. Caves that held the last of Earth's magic.

To get this far, the drain on her energy had been enormous. She could feel it fading away, slowly replaced by the fear that she'd lose everything.

That could not happen.

She pushed herself, and, with supreme effort, made it to the last of the light. Outside the cave, she barely registered the burned and decomposing bodies that littered the ground. They were not important. Only the light mattered.

Stepping inside, she welcomed the dimness after the sun's brightness. Darkness was her only friend now. She drank in the atmosphere devoid of most light. She turned and saw the reason for the cave's darkness.

The light stream she'd expended so much energy to reach was nothing more than a trickle.

Taegar's scream filled the cavern, reverberating outward for miles. How did they suppress the magic here as well? No. Not they. Only one person could have managed this.

One person had thwarted her plans for total dominion. And that person would pay.

Damian Royan.

Taegar entered the *ehwaz*, using it to search for her prey. He had powers, so she should be able to sense them. She expanded her awareness, dug into the nooks and crannies of Earth through the *ehwaz*.

Nothing. Not one single thread led to Damian or his wife. Where had they gone? How could they hide from her?

Returning to reality, Taegar slumped against the wall, her energy almost depleted. She needed sleep. To rest and recoup her energies so she could renew her search for the man who had become her mortal enemy.

Taegar used a little of her remaining power to send out a missive to any with dark intentions. *Find Damian Royan. Bring him to me.*

Then, she crawled deep into the cave system. Setting a shield to keep herself hidden, she lay down on the rock floor.

To sleep. Just for a while.

And when she woke, she would find Damian Royan, and she would show him the consequences of thwarting her, just as she'd shown Gordon Darcy.

Yes, she would show him. Soon. Very soon.

EPILOGUE

Cait stood beside the SUV after the strapping the girls into their car seats. She stared back at the cabin that had been their home for months. It surprised her, how emotional she felt about leaving.

"This place has been good to us, hasn't it?" Tom said, putting his arm over her shoulders.

"It has. I'm... I'm sad to leave."

"Me, too, but we don't have much choice."

No, they didn't. The cupboards were just about empty. Weeks had passed since news of the battles had reached them. Tom's forays into nearby towns had painted the world in dire streaks of dread. Now, the towns were empty. Garbage littered the streets, windows were broken out, some places burned to nothing but rubble.

Food was nowhere to be found, and no game either, in the dead of winter. They'd about used up their stores. Feeding four mouths, even if two of them were small, wasn't going to be easy.

Tom was right. They had no choice.

"I wonder if we'll ever get back here."

"If we could find a way to stock up on food, I'd come back in a heartbeat." He kissed the top of Cait's head, pulling her in tight. "I've loved this time with you, with the girls."

"I have, as well."

She gazed up at the sky, wondering what they'd find out there. From the rumors they'd heard early on, the cities had become hollowed-out shells. Power grids had failed and technology with them. Political structures crumbled next. It was impossible to lead when there was no one left to guide. Cities had emptied as people searched for land to grow food, to meet the basic needs of life.

Cait turned toward the road they would soon drive down. "Do you think we'll be safe?"

"I can't promise that. From what I've seen, it's not good. But we're as ready as we'll ever be. And we'll starve if we stay here."

They'd spent these months honing their firearm and weapons skills, even fencing with a couple of old rapiers they'd found in the attic. They had ample, though primitive, weapons with them. If they weren't caught off guard, they should be able to defend themselves.

Cait chewed her lower lip. Were they ready for whatever lay ahead? She leaned back against Tom's solid chest and stared again down the road. Tom waited patiently, giving her time, always considerate of her emotions, her needs. He was such a wonderful man. Somehow, with danger and chaos spinning all around them, they'd found each other. She'd found her soul-mate.

And she could face whatever lay ahead of them with Tom at her side.

Cait stepped away. With one last glance at the cabin that had been their home for close to a year, Cait opened the car door. "I'm ready."

Tom climbed in his side and started the engine. They had a full tank of gas, plus two more five-gallon cans tied to the back of the SUV. The rear was crammed with what remained of their food, both garden-grown and foraged, plus some clothes and cooking utensils. Their bedding was stuffed beneath the girls' feet. A tent lay snuggly strapped on top.

Tom headed down the bumpy, old logging road. Cait resisted the urge to glance out the window for one last look at the cabin. They were ready. To live. To thrive.

To survive.

The End.

Thank you for reading **Awakening.** If you'd like to read about Rianthe Royan, daughter of Damian and Valena, her story begins with **Survival**, book one of the **Earth Legacy** series. If you enjoyed this book, please consider leaving a review wherever you prefer, and know that it would be greatly appreciated.

For new release information and news about Laurie Ryan, please join her newsletter. More information is available on her website at **www.laurieryanauthor.com**.

AUTHOR'S NOTE

After I wrote the Earth Legacy series, I wasn't ready to leave this world, and I knew I had to show how Earth had become such a desolate world.

Writing this story wasn't easy. I like happy-ever-afters, so taking our contemporary world to a post-apocalyptic state went against that, though I tried to leave a thread of hope at the end. That thread comes to fruition in the Earth Legacy series.

I strove to pay homage to druid beliefs in this story because of their unfailing love and respect for nature. While most of the terms in this story are runic, I chose *awen*, a druid term, to represent Earth's magic. It translates as something like flowing spirit or inspiration and felt completely right for this series.

I believe we are near a tipping point with climate change and my fervent prayer is that we can ensure the continued existence of future generations. This story, this series, comes out of that belief.

Many thanks to Libby for making my writing shine. To Bethany for a cover that totally fits the story. And to my critique partners, Lavada Dee and Faye Avalon, for their unfailing ability to ferret out the issues with my stories.

As well, much respect to Marie Tuhart, who keeps me writing.

Last, but not least, thank you, readers. You make it all worthwhile!

Laurie Ryan

BOOKLIST

Contemporary romance stories by Laurie Ryan

Fantasy by Laurie Ryan

Survival
Enlightenment
Birthright

Romance by Laurie Ryan

Tropical Persuasions Series

Stolen Treasures
Pirate's Promise
Dare To Love

Standalone
Northern Lights
Healing Love
(also part of the Holiday Magic anthology)
Lost and Found

Women's Fiction by Laurie Ryan
Show Me

ABOUT THE AUTHOR

Laurie Ryan writes contemporary romance and fantasy. Growing up a devoted reader, Laurie Ryan immersed herself in the diverse works of authors like Tolkien and Woodiwiss. She is passionate about every aspect of a book: beginning, middle, and end. She can't arrive to a movie five minutes late, has never been able to read the end of a book before the beginning, and is a strong believer in reading the book before seeing the movie.

Laurie lives in the beautiful Pacific Northwest, in the shadow of Mt. Rainier and a short drive to beach-walking next to the Pacific Ocean, with her handsome, he-can-fix-anything husband.

www.laurieryanauthor.com

A PEEK AT SURVIVAL

(Book One of the Earth Legacy Series)

PROLOGUE

100 Years AGMW (After the Great Magic War)

Wind whistled through the many holes in the weather-worn walls of the small, thatched-roof hut where they'd found shelter for the night. Rianth Royan's father knelt on one knee and splayed his hand flat on the dirt floor. With his long, blond hair untethered and a crazed expression in his eye, he had the look of a wild man, made worse by the fact that he hadn't bathed in days. None of them had. They'd been too busy running.

"They're coming."

The small fire, lit for warmth and to dispel the night's darkness, did not keep Rianth from shivering at the fear she heard in her father's voice. It also did not disguise the changes in him. Damian Royan's shoulders held no sign of the regal bearing she'd known. The man who'd been her rock of strength for all of her ten years looked beaten. That alone terrified Rianth, compounded by a pounding in her head that beat out the wind's screech. The sonorous vibrations grew in intensity. Sounds she couldn't hear swelled to crushing levels. Something or someone drew closer and closer. Doom would visit them this night. She knew it in her soul, felt it, like her racing heart.

Her father stood, taking the small bag he'd always worn from around his neck and settling it around Rianth's. His hands, heavier somehow, clutched her shoulders. "It's up to you now. I'll hold them off as long as I can."

"Hold who off? I don't understand, Father." Her voice, not more than a whisper, shook. How had they gone from peaceful wanderers to a family being hunted by some unknown enemy?

Unknown to her, at least.

"There's no time to explain." He glanced at eight-year-old Uja, who gripped their mother's hand while she writhed on the floor. "Get you and your brother to safety. I know you can do this. You have the power within you."

"What about you? And Mother and the babe?"

Valena Royan screamed, and both Rianth and her father knelt at her side. In the final stages of childbirth, she contorted in obvious pain. Father leaned in to kiss her mother's temple, then whispered unfamiliar words. Her mother's brow soothed and she loosened her grip on Uja's hand.

Boom! The building shook under the shock wave. Another explosion quickly followed. Damian stood, pulling Rianth up with him.

"Your mother cannot travel. And it may be too late for the babe already. Help as long as you can. But when I tell you to go, do not hesitate. Grab Uja and run. As fast and as hard as you can. Head east. Find the village of New Hope. Find Bhren. He will help you."

"No. I don't want to run. Not without you. I can help you. We can fight together." Rianth pulled the wooden sword from her belt, the one she'd made so her father would teach her to fight. "We can beat them," she said, bravado barely concealing the tremor in her voice.

Her father smoothed her hair with his hand and kissed her forehead. "I'm sorry, my dear. You are too young for this war. Besides, you must save yourself and your brother now. That is your fight."

She dipped her head to keep her father from seeing the tears. He tipped her head up to wipe her cheek with his thumb, breaking her heart with the tender gesture.

"You are the hope of the future, daughter. Do not be afraid to find your destiny." With a last glance at his family, Damian drew his sword and disappeared through the rough-hewn door.

Tears streamed down Rianth's face, sorrow struggling against fear, both overpowering her.

"Daughter—" Her mother's weak voice drew her attention.

Rianth dropped back to her side. "What do I do?"

"Hold the babe as he's birthed. Cut the cord that has nurtured him all these months. Wrap him in my cloak." She gasped. "Feed him goat's milk."

"No. You'll feed him. You'll be here."

"No, daughter. My strength is gone. I will soon pass from this life. And you must run." Her mother's weakened voice held a finality that Rianth did not want to accept. She clutched Uja's and Rianth's hands. "I love you both dearly. And this little one, too." She bit her lip as her entire body tightened. "It's time. Push on my belly, Son. We must finish this now, before all is lost."

Rianth supported the babe's head, her vision blurry as the increasing clash of swords and the escalating booms from outside pulsed through her bones.

Now.

Father? How could she hear him? He was outside, yet it seemed his words filled her mind.

Run.

Yes. She knew her father's voice, even if unspoken. But her mother needed her.

One more push and the babe birthed. Her mother had been right. It was a boy. Rianth sliced the cord with her knife, wrapped the unusually quiet babe in her mother's cloak, and stood.

Run, now. Her father's urgent voice roared through Rianth's head.

"She's not breathing," Uja cried.

Panic consumed Rianth as she turned one way, then back. She couldn't do this. It was too much.

You can. You must. Go. Run. Now. Save—

His frantic words were barely a whisper in her mind now, and infused with emotion. Then, a roar of pain made her shrink back. Uja jumped up and stared at the door. He'd heard it too.

Tears obliterated Rianth's view of her still mother and an emptiness she'd never known before made the agony in her heart hurt even more. She edged to the window, pulled back a piece of the cloth covering it, and almost cried out. Her father lay on the ground, his sword still in his slack hand. Tall, ethereal shapes, barely discernible in the darkness, surrounded him. One stood near, his sword red with blood. Another, taller than the others, leaned over her father.

"I have found you at last. You cannot run from me this time." Even though the shadow did not speak to Rianth, the voice—throaty and low—entranced her, beguiling her to come closer. A calmness settled over her and she reached for the door's handle.

"Ri," Uja whispered. "What are you doing?"

Rianth turned to her brother, saw her mother's body on the floor, the babe in her own arms staring up at her. *What am I doing? What is happening?* She gasped, trying to will the strange enthrallment to leave her, the spell broken by a sharp shake of her head.

"Where is it?" the tall one said. For the first time, Rianth heard the jagged edge of intense anger. "Where is the talisman?" A bony hand grasped Damian by his tunic, yanking him off the ground.

"You will—" Damian gasped. "Never—find—"

His body began to glow, as if heating up. Brighter and brighter he burned, until it hurt for Rianth to watch. When the light dimmed, nothing remained of her father except dust settling to the ground.

The voice that had enthralled her let out a soul-curdling scream of frustration and hatred. So much hatred it hit Rianth like hot coals from a fire, burning hot and forcing her back. She brought her free hand up in an attempt to ward off the wave of emotion. Turning away, she almost cried out when her mother's body started to glow with the same heat as her father's just had. In moments, only the ashes of a life snuffed too soon lingered.

Rianth swiped at her tears with one hand and stared at the babe in her arms. It was up to her now to keep her brothers safe. She glanced outside, saw the shrouded shadows moving toward the hut. Saw golden eyes no longer defined by skin that chilled her to the bone. She knew she must leave with her brothers now, before the fate of her parents befell them.

Stifling the terror of what she'd witnessed and the crushing grief that pulsed in her heart, Rianth held tight to her new baby brother, grabbed Uja's hand, slipped out the back of the hut, and ran.

~~~

Cloaked in robes the color of night, the men walked in a solemn, unwavering line. The cave, large and round, was lit by an eerie glow that emanated from a central, circular stone altar and smelled dank and rotten. Shadows hugged the walls, shrouded figures that swayed to and fro with an unnatural fluidity. The novices approached the altar, forming a semi-circle around it.
~~~

No fear emanated from any of the candidates, only the eager focus of the enthralled. Taegar, taller than any person or shadow in the grotto, drank their fervor in, her power swelling as their devotion poured into her. Her euphoria was only temporary. She knew that only the *awen*, Earth's magic, could sustain her for the eternity she coveted. Soon, she would have everything she needed. Soon she would be the most powerful druid and magician of all time.

Soon all would bend to her will.

Damian and the rest of his weak circle thought she hadn't known about the talisman and its ability to bind the right person to the *awen* forever. She'd waited all these desolate years for it to resurface. Taegar's bony hands clenched into fists with a subtle crunch. She'd had it within her grasp when she'd caught Damian Royan. Yet the means to harness total control over Earth's power had once again slipped through her fingers.

Damian had surprised her by not having the talisman. He'd hidden himself well since the war, using the druid's sleep as a shield. She'd sensed his awakening several years ago, though attempts to find him had frustrated her at every turn. She knew nothing about his life to aid in her search. Only a tip from one of her disciples sent out in search of him had led her to the empty-handed Damian.

Inside the nearby hut where she'd finally found her old nemesis, Taegar had found only ash. Damian had not been alone, though. A scent wafted in the air, a tinge of fear. Someone else had been there. Someone who may very well hold the key Taegar must control.

Earth's magic imbued light, emanating from the center of the altar, had become tinted with the orange of anger. Taegar slowed her breathing, calmed herself and reached out with her mind. The light dimmed, fighting her until she suppressed its will, forcing the *awen* to blaze with the purity of white that fed the darkness in her soul. She moved forward to the altar and reached into the glowing light, the direct contact permeating her with its potency. She consumed it and the fire consumed her in return.

Taegar raised her head, showing all the golden power in her eyes. One by one, she directed her gaze to the men in front of her. Light shot from her into each of their souls, infusing them with a limited magic. In debt to her by the endowment, they would do anything she asked of them. Little did they know their power was both finite and infinitesimal.

Only she must have unlimited power. For that to happen, she must find the talisman and bond with Earth's magic. Then, all would be hers. Forever.

Taegar gripped the altar. The time had come to send more of her soldiers out in search. As the light dimmed, she gave each acolyte a silent directive, then watched as they filed out of the cave, knowing they would do her bidding or die in the attempt.

Only when they all left did she slump over, giving in to the weakness that ravaged her each time she tapped into Earth's *awen*. It worsened with each use and now she couldn't even leave this cavern, which held the only stream of magic she'd found. She must find the talisman or she'd be remanded to the druid's sleep by necessity, not choice. That must not happen. She had to find it. She would find it.

Soon…

To keep up with Laurie Ryan news, please join her newsletter. More information can be found at **www.laurieryanauthor.com.**